The

APPETITES
of GIRLS

The
APPETITES
of GIRLS

PAMELA MOSES

AMY EINHORN BOOKS
Published by G. P. Putnam's Sons
a member of Penguin Group (USA)
New York

AMY EINHORN BOOKS
Published by G. P. Putnam's Sons
Publishers Since 1838
Published by the Penguin Group
Penguin Group (USA) LLC
375 Hudson Street
New York, New York 10014

USA · Canada · UK · Ireland · Australia
New Zealand · India · South Africa · China

penguin.com
A Penguin Random House Company

Library of Congress Cataloging-in-Publication Data

Moses, Pamela.
The appetites of girls : a novel / Pamela Moses.
p.   cm.
ISBN 978-0-399-15842-1
1. Female friendship—Fiction.   I. Title.
PS3613.O7793A67   2014   2013037701
813'.6—dc23

Printed in the United States of America
1   3   5   7   9   10   8   6   4   2

BOOK DESIGN BY AMANDA DEWEY

For my mother and for my father
With all of my love and gratitude

Part

ONE

FOR OLD TIME'S SAKE

· 2003 ·

This, above all else, binds the four of us together: standing side by side, each struggled to believe the best in herself, hearing amid the dark doubts in her mind the whisper of triumph.

Long before we grew in strength, we began life in separate corners. In my first moments, I made only small whimpers, my family tells me. Then my face turned red as beet soup, my fists tight as knots, and I cried with a roar that seemed beyond my tiny lungs. Opal was born into the arms of midwives in a country house outside of Paris. Her mother reclined on feather pillows and sipped lemon water until it was time. Francesca claims she bellowed her first day morning through night until the nurses relented, freeing her from her swaddling blanket. And Setsu's life opened just as her mother's closed, her cries lasting longest of all.

Far we have come since those beginnings, and long the journeys to victory over doubt. But always, in us, were stirrings of possibilities, and we would find the will to hold fast to these hopes.

. . .

In the eleven years since graduation, Francesca and I have phoned each other regularly, as we have with Setsu and with Opal, a pledge we made long ago and kept. But in the spinning hum of our grown-up lives, our visits became sporadic, and not since our final college year have all four of us been together in one place. This past spring, though, just days after Francesca had come into Manhattan, meeting me for lunch and a stroll through the American wing of the Met, she called, insisting the baby I was carrying deserved a celebration. Besides, what better excuse could the four of us have to reunite? For old time's sake, she said. Wouldn't it be fun?

"Oh, no, Fran, you don't need to. Thank you, really . . ." I had fumbled for the appropriate words to decline her unexpected offer. In part because it is not in the Jewish tradition, a baby shower had never crossed my mind.

"*B'sha'ah Tova*—in good time," my aunts and sisters and mother had said when they learned that I was expecting. *One's hopes should not rise too high before the hour comes. Congratulations may bring bad luck,* they worried. My grandmothers and great-grandmothers would not have so much as knitted a bootee before a baby's arrival. "Why tempt bad spirits?" Nana Leah had cautioned with an old wives' superstition.

But shouldn't I have known Fran would persist? "Ruth, you are bringing a daughter into the world. How can you refuse her some festivity?"

There was a time she could talk me into many things because I lacked the courage to trust my own mind. Now, though, with the sudden possibility of reuniting with my suitemates, I realized I missed not just each of them separately, but all of us together as a group. Our weaknesses differed, but our journeys to overcome them were shared. We learned from one another's struggles, and learned, too, we were not alone in struggling. In our day-to-day living together and the friendships formed in those years, we gained strength to fight for our deepest yearnings. And now as I take this new step toward motherhood, it seems fitting that we four come together again.

So here we sit at this table beneath the tulip tree: Francesca, Setsu, Opal, and I. Our spoons dip into shallow dishes of chilled soup as the tree's high branches cast soft, swaying shadows across our faces and arms and the plates of luncheon food before us. Years ago we could not have dreamed we would ever be this picture of contentment. But no storms rage forever, not even those that whirl within us. Yes, each of us was stronger than she knew. Even I.

Fran has thought through every detail. Her garden table is set with linen place mats and napkins, at its center a crystal vase thick with daffodils. At the table ends stand two pitchers of iced mint tea, their handles wound with ivy and tiny white flower buds as intricate as snowflakes. And beside each plate, someone has placed a pair of cellophane-wrapped baby shoes made entirely of pink sugar.

This is the first time any of us has seen Francesca's new Connecticut home, and when I arrived, ringing the bell to the right of her paneled front door, I heard her calling to someone—"Got it! *Got* it!"—and then the familiar pounding of her running feet.

"God, it's great to have you here," she said, kissing me, walking me through the house, hanging my spring jacket in her hall closet. As we pass the kitchen, I glimpse the food to be served—dishes I had seen in magazines—crustless sandwiches rolled like pinwheels, bowls of pastel soup with scrolling loops of cream at their edges, salads of nearly transparent green leaves no larger than rose petals. A trim woman in a starched white blouse stands to the left of the double sink, slicing raw vegetables—Lucienne, Francesca introduces her.

"This is really so beautiful, Fran—everything. And so generous—"

"Oh, goodness. You're welcome." She shrugs off my words, never comfortable with sentiment. "Let's talk about you. You look *wonderful*. How are you feeling? Are you getting any sleep?" It was the one trial of her own pregnancies, she remembers. How for hours in her bed, with eyes wide open, her mind would whir.

"Sleeping, yes, but I've never had such vivid dreams," I tell her.

As we speak, a dream of the four of us from the night before returns to me: we are racing along the shore, kicking up the foaming water. And how young we are. Only girls, but then in a twinkling we are women, with our shadows stretching far, out into the ocean.

Then we are interrupted by the arrival of Opal, followed soon by Setsu. "I can't believe you're here," Fran says. "You both look terrific. And doesn't *Ruth* look terrific?"

But Setsu and Opal are already embracing me, asking me exactly how many more weeks, exclaiming that I'm radiant.

In the kitchen, Fran mixes mimosas, pouring them into tall flutes. "Occasional drinks in the third trimester are permissible, aren't they?" She winks at me.

"Just not the way you make them."

She laughs, surprised by my retort but approving of it, and fills a separate flute without champagne.

Lucienne arranges the bowls of soup on a tray, and we follow her, carrying our glasses across the lawn, settling around the table. And now as our spoons clink against Francesca's china bowls, we begin to chat, at first taking turns, speaking of work, of families, of things we've heard of other college friends. But before long, we are talking together and at once, the way we used to do. A rhythm suddenly familiar as chords from well-loved but, for a time, forgotten music.

Setsu surprises us. While sorting through some files at home, she has unearthed some photos from our college days.

"Oh, look at us. Is that freshman year?" Opal asks.

"Yes, it must be finals week. We look *exhausted*. Remember how we studied until morning and Fran kept us all awake with chocolate-covered coffee beans?" Setsu smiles at Fran.

"That's right! And, Ruth, you collapsed on your books right on the floor!" Fran recalls.

We laugh and agree it feels both a lifetime ago and just like yesterday.

As we put aside the photographs, and as I look from Setsu to Opal to Fran, I see their clothes are more tailored than they once were, their hair more stylishly cut, the angles of their faces more defined. But in other ways, how little they have changed. Setsu's long fingers still fold beneath her chin as she speaks, pressing to her mouth now and then when she has finished. Francesca's voice pierces with the same old boldness. And as the soup begins to disappear, how well I recall Setsu's tiny meals—mouse portions, I thought them—that gave her rope-thin arms. Opal's insistence on measuring, analyzing every morsel before it passed her lips, scrutinizing each bite before she swallowed. Francesca with her penchant for frosted cakes, her French baguettes and Brie from the gourmet store in town. Much of those years has faded and blurred, but these and other things I still see clearly. And I cringe at what they surely, maybe especially, remember of me.

As the soup slides along my tongue, I gaze at each of the women and think of the hindering roots that had found soil in our earliest experiences of life. Entangled with a thousand secrets and unshared stories, and thickening as we grew, becoming, after a time, almost as hard to cut away as our own limbs.

But these struggles are part of what it means to be human—struggles with our own natures, often undeclared, as if unnoticed by those who know us, even by ourselves. Yet such battles must be waged and won if we are to grow, if we mean to claim what is truest within.

SWIMMING LESSONS

(My Story)

· *1983* ·

On the third Saturday of May, exactly one month after my thirteenth birthday, I was to become a bat mitzvah. Already seated in the temple, waiting for me to recite my Torah portion, were my eight aunts and uncles and my eleven cousins. The Kramers had come all the way from Farmingdale, the Martins from Staten Island. Neighbors from our building had shown up as well—the Schafers, the Rosenbergs, the Kleins from across the hall. Mama, Poppy, Sarah, and Valerie had spread across the first pew, Mama in the center in her new navy Anne Klein suit and her best patent leather purse with the gold horseshoe-shaped clasp.

Though the temple was only a six-block walk from where we lived in Riverdale, north of Manhattan, we had, at Mama's insistence, been dressed and squeezed into our building's narrow elevator two hours before the service began. "I want to be sure of securing the front row, the one closest to the bima," Mama had informed us. She'd been standing before the bathroom mirror, spraying her hair—which had been styled just the day before at the salon—filling the apartment with the sweet scent I associated with Saturday mornings and all significant occasions. Even for weekly services, Mama made certain we were fifteen minutes early so she could turn and wave to friends as they arrived. But this day, of course, was of far greater importance. "It's only once you become a bat mitzvah, hmm, Ruthie?" Mama licked her thumb to flatten a strand of hair that had loosened from my rhinestone barrette. "Poppy and I want to be just an arm's length away when you stand to read."

During the service, Jessica Neier and Harold Green would also be called to the Torah, and, of the three of us, I would read last. As Harold recited his passage, I gazed at my new chocolate-brown shoes with their almost-grown-up heels, which Mama had bought at Saks Fifth Avenue especially for this occasion. Most items for my wardrobe, and those for my younger sisters, she purchased at a bargain basement in Brooklyn, scrutinizing labels and buttons and seams until she was satisfied that, despite the discounted prices, she had found top-quality clothes. But at the beginning of the month, Mama had taken Sarah and Valerie and me by bus to midtown Manhattan, to the girls' department at Saks. At the back of the store, a carpeted elevator chimed softly when we reached our floor. And there, on orderly racks, hung dresses and gowns like those I had seen in the fashion magazines Mama bought now and then. Gowns overlaid with lace, silk ones with sashes and pleats or with shoulder straps as fine as shining strings. Dresses like those my sisters and I noticed on girls our age during our occasional trips to the Upper East Side, their hair tied back with ruffled ribbons, on their way to parties, we guessed, or expensive restaurants. In my bedroom closet at home, between my plaid wraparound skirt and my gray flannel one, hung the outfit I had always assumed I would wear: a charcoal suit, wool with four black buttons down the front of the jacket and a slight scallop along the skirt's hem—a purchase from the last High Holy Days that still fit and seemed appropriately solemn. But the Saks dress Mama chose was a deep rose taffeta with a velvet collar and a large bow, and she paid more for it and for the blue crêpe dresses for Sarah and Valerie than I could remember her spending on any previous shopping excursion.

I proudly ran my hands over my lap, feeling the smooth taffeta, prettier than the beige wool of Jessica Neier's. As she was called to read, I repeated again and again in my mind the trickiest phrases from my portion.

Every Wednesday for months, in one of the third-floor classrooms of the temple, I had studied with Cantor Rothman the Hebrew syllables, the pronunciation and meaning of each word, as well as the musical symbols indicating pitch.

"She's making fine progress, Mrs. Leiser," the cantor had said to Mama when she arrived on her way home from work to fetch me. "She seems to have an ear for the Hebrew language." And he had winked at me, folding his thick arms over the mound of his stomach.

"Thank you, Cantor." Mama had shaken his hand. "That's reassuring." But she had sniffed in a way I knew meant she was not yet convinced. Cantor Rothman had a reputation for praising even the least capable students. Mama had heard this from mothers of older children in our neighborhood when I had first begun attending Hebrew school some years before. And she had been privy to what the cantor had not, had listened as I'd practiced at home, had heard how the words sometimes stuck in my throat even with Poppy's occasional help and with the practice tapes Cantor Rothman had given me.

How many, many sounds there were to memorize, how much for my ear and tongue to learn. So Mama had begun to study the tapes as well, until she knew every line better than I, believing that she, too, could be of assistance. When she was young, not many years after arriving in this country, Mama had planned to be a school principal, or even a professor at a university. A goal she certainly could have achieved, she liked to tell us, having maintained for years in a row her position at the top of her class, even though most others had been here since birth.

I had heard snippets of what her life had been from the late-night chitchat of Mama and my aunts, after my sisters and cousins and I had been excused from Friday Shabbat dinners. After the reciting of the Kiddush and the completion of the meal, after our plates had been carried out to the kitchen and when our parents thought our ears were buzzing only with our own child-games. Talk of when Mama's and Poppy's families had made their way to America from Poland. Poppy's family coming first, years before Poppy was even born, Mama's coming later while Mama, Aunt Helena, Aunt Bernice, and Uncle Jacob were children. Of how turns of fortune had saved Mama's family from the fate that had blotted out so many of our people, turns that, in the end, had allowed them to make the voyage here: of their escape to Vilna, of a Japanese diplomat there who had issued them visas, of the safe haven they had eventually been granted in the Jewish ghetto of Shanghai for the duration of the Second World War. And then talk of how both Mama's and Poppy's families had eventually settled in Washington Heights, and then, some years later, here in Riverdale, just north of hustling, bustling Manhattan, where the streets had more trees and the apartments were a bit roomier. Of how the families had hoped for what others already enjoyed—wages that increased, prospects that widened. How grateful they all were to be here. Still, now and then, I heard Mama and my aunts allow that if only Papa Marvin had started a business of his own as some others had . . . For those with the foresight to follow certain paths, opportunities never seemed to run out.

"Always, always we should remember our blessings," Mama would say. But she never explained why she'd changed her mind about becoming a professor or heading a school, why she had opened her shop,

Broadway Paperie, where she sold gift cards and personalized stationery and all styles of writing implements, instead. I'd gathered it had something to do with the printing plant where Papa Marvin worked closing down while Mama was in college, with his taking up woodcarving and oil painting to pass the time "because no one was hiring middle-aged men who operated the old presses" (as I remembered him recounting), and with Mama leaving college and returning home to take a secretarial job. "Just a matter of circumstances," was all she would ever reply if we asked, as if to mean, "It all worked out in the end." But I saw how carefully she read through any mailings from Barnard, the college she had attended for just two years, scrutinizing the alumnae notes, the descriptions of added courses and publications by faculty, making me wonder if there were things she regretted. And if these were the same regrets that made her complain about the hours Poppy dedicated to his journals—the anecdotes of our family that he wrote with pencil in green cardboard-bound notebooks, even typing up a few and submitting them to *Riverbank Press*, a small literary magazine he'd heard about through a coworker. Recently, now that I was older, he would allow me to read over his stories as he worked, explaining why he'd chosen this word and not that, how he'd elaborated for the sake of humor and artistic merit, even asking if I had suggestions. Poppy had bought ten copies each of the issues that included his pieces. "See that, girls! Your Poppy is famous!" he'd joked, showing off his name—Aaron A. Leiser—in black print, listed between Kyle Jessup and Alice Novak on the back cover.

"How many people even read the magazine?" Mama had wanted to know.

"Not many. But that doesn't lessen the glory, does it?" Poppy had laughed.

"Our family's private affairs for the amusement of a few strangers?" she'd asked. (Poppy's second entry was about our trip to Philadelphia the previous summer when we had lost Sarah in the crowd on line to see the Liberty Bell.) But I could tell it was not embarrassment that made her press two knuckles beneath her chin and look at Poppy as if there were things she wished she could change.

I hope you girls know how important it is to use time wisely," Mama taught us. "If we're not careful, it pulls away from us like so much thread unwinding from a spool." She started a new routine. At the dining table each evening, after the supper crumbs had been wiped from the floral tablecloth, she directed me to close the sketch pad I now liked to draw in every night, illustrations meant to accompany Poppy's stories. There were other things we needed to attend to, she said.

"I may not be fluent in Hebrew, Ruthie, but I'd like to think I have something of value to offer anyway." And so she rehearsed my Torah passage with me, prompting me each time I hesitated over a word, whispering the correct Hebrew enunciation until I was able to read from beginning to end with near perfection.

That winter, we had received a printed invitation to my cousin Gregory's bar mitzvah. For the past three years, Poppy's older brother, Uncle Leonid, and Aunt Nadia, Gregory, Isaac, and Jack had lived in Scarsdale in a two-story house with four bedrooms. I remembered how Mama's eyes had widened just slightly the first time Aunt Nadia had shown us their backyard with more than ample space for the swimming pool she mentioned they were considering. Mama's sisters lived in apartments the size of ours, and ones we could walk to, and Poppy's younger brother, Uncle Josef, and Aunt Malina were also nearby, on the bottom floor of a two-family town house on Delafield Avenue. But after Leonid and Nadia's move to Westchester—following short on the heels of Leonid's promotion to supervisor of the Rockland Textile Company—we rarely saw them for Friday Shabbat dinners or casual Sunday afternoon visits. And they and my cousins seemed different now. Gregory and Isaac and Jack wore leather shoes instead of sneakers, even to play outside. And our old routine of

Blind Man's Bluff and Chutes and Ladders seemed to bore them compared with the games they could now play on the brand-new Atari computer in their family room.

Aunt Nadia had begun to dress in frilly skirts made of some stretchy material, strutting proudly in them, though I thought they made the cheeks of her bottom look like two flat couch pillows. She ordered garments from a catalog Mama had browsed through once. "You could buy plane tickets to Europe for the cost of one of those! Or even a small auto!" Poppy had joked, glancing over Mama's shoulder at the featured outfits. "I know. Ridiculous, aren't they?" Mama said, but I'd seen how she turned through the pages a second and then a third time, pausing to study a photo of a black sequined dress like the one Aunt Nadia had worn for Uncle Leonid's recent birthday celebration. But what surprised Mama more than Nadia's new shopping habits was the full-time housekeeper she had hired to cook and clean five days a week—a woman who now practically *lived* with them. Though we did not keep kosher as Nana Leah and Papa Marvin had, or Nana Esther and Papa Elias, Mama still prepared the foods of our people's heritage, traditions Nadia's Jamaican housekeeper, Adelaide, surely was not following. "You'd think Adelaide was family, for God's sake," I'd heard Mama mutter once to Poppy after we learned that, on evenings when Adelaide worked late, she was offered the spare bedroom to sleep in. A bedroom that, in the opinion of Mama and her sisters, should have been set aside for Nadia's father to live in rather than the home for the aged two towns away. I knew in the old country—though it was before Mama was born—her grandparents had lived always in the house with Nana Leah and Papa Marvin, and with Uncle Jacob and Aunt Bernice and Aunt Helena when they were very young. And though I'd complained to Poppy and Mama about having to relinquish my room—sleeping on a cot between Sarah and Valerie's beds for those months before Nana Leah passed away—I knew none of us would have considered any alternative.

. . .

As we had driven up the Hutchinson River Parkway to the temple in Scarsdale where Gregory's ceremony would take place, Mama had folded down the car's visor and checked her reflection in its rectangular mirror. She'd adjusted the pearl choker at her neck so that the largest pearls were centered. The last time we had visited, Aunt Nadia had worn a double strand of pearls, hanging nearly to her navel.

"Do you think Gregory feels nervous?" Sarah asked.

"I suppose he might," Mama replied, though I knew Aunt Nadia had employed a high-priced Hebrew tutor to coach Gregory for his reading. And in the temple, with his prayer shawl draping his shoulders and his gold-embroidered yarmulke, as ornate as Poppy's or Uncle Leonid's, Gregory looked almost a man. Then as he chanted words from the Torah, his voice rocked—high-low, high-low—like the rabbi's. Only once did he stumble over the difficult phrases. When he finished, I looked up at Mama seated beside me to see if she was impressed. But she gave only a small nod, then, bending her head to mine, tucking my hair behind my ear, whispered, "You will be even better." And for the remainder of the service, I sat still as the stone walls of the temple, silent with wonder for what Mama thought I would do.

When my turn finally came and Rabbi Levi called me to the podium, I smiled at him as my new heels thumped against the wooden floor. I recited the first several lines, using my finger to trace each symbol as Cantor Rothman had taught me. And I raised my voice, remembering his direction to speak so that those in the pews at the back of the temple could hear. But midway through, something caught in my throat, a feathery tickle. And by the time I coughed it away, my finger had slipped from its place. Suddenly, the Hebrew figures—which had, just a moment before, stretched across the page in clear, logical rows—scattered into a haphazard jumble of dashes and squiggles, making the soles of my feet go damp in my stockings. When I looked out across the congregation, I saw Harold Green's mother and Jessica Neier's and a hundred other waiting faces. Two women in silk neck scarves, seated in the pew behind my family, murmured to each other behind their programs. In panic, I fixed my eyes on Mama. There were creases of worry between her eyes, hollows above her jaw I had never seen before, making the thudding in my chest quicken. Then, to my relief, she leaned forward, closer to me still, and began to chant, so softly that only I could hear.

So I followed Mama's voice, singing together with her. One phrase and another with Mama as my guide. Then finding my place once more, I mumbled and stuttered through the remainder of my Torah portion until I reached the final, shameful "Amen."

All of the family and friends who had come to watch me paraded back to our apartment when the service ended. In a steady stream, still huffing from their walk from the temple, they poured through our door, squeezing themselves onto the sofa and the wing chairs and around the scratched baby grand. In expectation of the celebration, Mama had laid the dining table with a feast of food. Earlier that week, she had bought beeswax candles for the silver candleholders and pink tulips for our Waterford vase. She had placed three small cakes of lily-of-the-valley-scented hand soap in the china dish in the bathroom and draped the best lacy hand towels over the rack beside the sink. *"Shayna Maideleh!"* Aunt Bernice and Aunt Helena embraced me, pinching my cheeks. Sarah and Valerie were passing trays of salmon and capers on toast, moving with small sideways steps to weave through the crowd, the white bows Mama had clipped in their hair that morning still perfectly placed. Sarah would not become a bat mitzvah for another year, Valerie for another three, but from the way their lips pressed as they concentrated on the platters in their hands, I knew they were no longer looking forward to these occasions. When they reached me in the corner beyond the couch, the least conspicuous spot I could find, they both smiled and whispered "Congratulations." But they attempted the word so halfheartedly, I could feel a flush spread along my neck.

Mama was offering around a platter of her chicken meatballs. That morning I had helped her stick them with toothpicks, dotting each with a leaf of parsley.

"Well, there you are, Ruthie. Mazel tov! Mazel tov!" Mrs. Rosenberg and Mrs. Kramer kissed me, then Mama. "This is a big day, yes? Very exciting!" The front of Mrs. Rosenberg's dark hair puffed in a cresting wave, just as she had styled it the year before for her daughter Amanda's thirteenth birthday. She accepted two meatballs and a cocktail napkin from Mama's hands then blotted just the corners of her mouth, leaving her lipstick untouched. I had no doubt I would be the pitied subject of their conversation for the entire afternoon. So, slipping past forearms, chests, elbows, and plates of food, I escaped into the kitchen.

On the windowsill beside the cupboard stood the brightly colored bat mitzvah cards that had arrived in advance. When they had come in the mail, I had arranged them against the window, liking to reread their bold-lettered messages each time I entered the kitchen: *Congratulations, Bat Mitzvah! We Celebrate You on This Day!* they announced. Mama, holding her now-empty platter, pushed open the kitchen's swinging door. The small gold hoops with diamond studs, which had once belonged to Nana Leah, quivered in her ears as she began to spoon liver mousse into a pastry bag, piping it onto crackers, her jaw shifting to one side as she worked.

"Don't you want to join your party, Ruthie?" Mama wiped her fingers on a dish towel. "Everyone is here for your sake."

"No." I shook my head, sinking into one of the chairs at the kitchen table, resting my heels on its metal rung.

"They'll begin to wonder what happened to you, hmm? Are you going to hide in here all afternoon like a chipmunk in a hole?" Mama laughed as she placed a hand on my head, but I could tell she had been worrying. A smudge of plum lipstick stained the white of her front teeth, evidence, I knew, that she had been chewing her bottom lip over my morning failure.

"Please don't make me go back out, Mama. I can't, I can't!"

Mama shrugged her shoulders. "Don't gnaw, Ruthie." She tugged my thumb from the corner of my mouth, lifting my hand for me to see the cuticle—shredded and raw once more despite the attention she had given my fingers the night before with warm water and lotion.

"Did you notice at Gregory's bar mitzvah"—Mama opened the oven door, allowing a rush of hot air into the room, a quick change of subject to distract me from my misery—"Nadia hired caterers to make and serve *all* the food. She never had to lift so much as a pinkie."

"Yes. The meatballs were dry and the liver canapés flavorless." I knew this was what Mama wished to hear, affirmations that even professional caterers couldn't top her dishes. She never said it, but now and then Mama hinted at what we all knew: that of the entire extended family, she was the finest cook. Neither of her two sisters nor any of the sisters-in-law could match her in the kitchen.

"I don't think Nadia's caterers actually used butter in their liver mousse. I added chopped walnuts this time. A definite improvement, I think. Did you try it?"

"No, Mama." I cupped my chin in my fists. "I don't think I can eat."

"No? At your own bat mitzvah! Perhaps it's better not to dwell on it, hmm, Pea? What's done is done." Drying her hands, Mama pulled a chair next to mine.

"But I don't understand how I lost my place." I began to pick at the thick sash wrapping my middle. "The others didn't make mistakes. I was the only one!"

The hair at Mama's temples had begun to dampen slightly from the heat of the kitchen. "It was not so bad, Ruthie. You made it to the end, didn't you? Really, it could have been worse."

But from the way she frowned as she began to stroke my cheek, I thought she was trying to convince herself as much as me. "What's the good in comparing yourself with someone else, hmm? We are all different. No two children are the same. When your sisters were babies, they plumped like dumplings. Just breathing seemed to make them fatten up. But you were small from the beginning. You always required a bit more care—"

"Yes, Mama."

"So we are all unique from the start, each with our own special needs. And with a little help, a bit of attention, everything evens out." As if to prove her point, the corners of her mouth curving into a half-smile, Mama patted the bulge of my stomach below my ribs.

"Try to eat something, Ruthie. It will make you feel better."

Standing up, Mama reopened the oven, spearing with a knife three crispy potato pancakes and dropping them onto a dish. She scooped dollops of applesauce over them, then drew her chair closer until our knees bumped. It had been hours since breakfast, and I began to section off a chunk of the shredded potato with the side of my fork. One bite and then another and another. Until the warm pancake filled me, stuffing down the worries of the day.

⁓

The summer after my bat mitzvah was much like every summer. Always, in the months of July and August, many of the children in our neighborhood disappeared on extended vacations or to sleepaway camps. But long trips were a luxury our family couldn't afford, and in Mama's opinion, sleepaway camps were ill-supervised and of little benefit. So my sisters and I attended the morning summer school program at our temple, singing Hebrew songs, making dolls of papier-mâché, learning the stories of our people's history. Then, in the afternoons, since this was the season business slowed, Mama would leave Ruby, the college student she had recently hired, to manage Broadway Paperie, and she would devote the remainder of the day to all she had planned for us: a full schedule of activities that she believed would keep our minds active. *We* would not squander our time between the end of one school year and the beginning of the next, as so many of our friends did. From us she knew that Ellen Reid and her sister, when they were not at theater camp, spent day after day stretched on the roof deck of their apartment building for the sole purpose of deepening their tans. And that Jenny Frankel, until her family left for Lake George, was allowed to bring a TV into her bedroom and watch from morning till night. "Someone should tell them that by September their brains will turn to gelatin!" Mama liked to joke.

Once, when Mama and Poppy attended a funeral in Trenton for one of Poppy's former coworkers, my sisters and I spent the entire day and evening with Jenny. When Mama came to get us after dark, we had fallen asleep on Jenny's pink shag carpet, our unfinished glasses of 7UP, our shared plate of Doritos beside us. Later, walking home in the warm nighttime air to West 256th Street, the glow of the building lights and of the street lamps on the avenues seemed almost a continuation of the fantasy hours of *Charlie's Angels* and *Gilligan's Island* and *The Love Boat* we had just spent at Jenny's house, a dream so complete and prolonged it had seemed it might last forever. Could we ever watch TV the way Jenny did? we pleaded, our feet tripping along the sidewalk in our buckled sandals. Not every day, but just sometimes? Once a week, maybe? Until summer ended? But Mama answered the way we supposed she would: Just because Jenny was permitted, did that make it a good idea? If Jenny leaped from the George Washington Bridge top, would we follow her in that foolishness, too?

Still, for weeks, before rolling from bed in the mornings, I would imagine I was Mary Ann or Ginger from *Gilligan's Island*, lovely in my swimsuit with endless days in the tropics. Sometimes, with the pad and paper I kept on my night table, I would draw elaborate scenes of the grass hut where Mary Ann lived or write poems about the sea or the groves of palm trees along the sand. But, as we expected, our TV restrictions were never altered—*Wild Kingdom* on Sunday evenings, because it was educational, and one hour of our choosing on Saturday mornings. And the next time Mama needed to be away for a day, she brought us to Aunt Bernice's, where we played hangman and tic-tac-toe and dominoes with Aunt Bernice and Uncle Mickey until she returned.

How much effort Mama gave to making sure our summer was not wasted, drawing up a calendar of projects she believed would put us at an advantage when school resumed in the fall. She bought a jigsaw puzzle of continental Europe, a second of the Americas. From the public library, she borrowed children's history books on ancient Rome and the early explorers and on the Silk Road in China, listening as we read them aloud over bowls of her pea soup and plates of egg salad, correcting when we mispronounced a word. On Friday afternoons, she gave directions from recipes for the evening's Shabbat—to fill tablespoons with flour, quarter cups with broth, and so on—so that we would learn our measurements. She invented a scavenger hunt math game, hiding clues around the apartment that could be found only by solving arithmetic problems. Though my sisters were younger, they made fewer errors than I. I knew my multiplication tables and fractions, of course, but sometimes my thoughts drifted to outdoor sounds—the squeals of the Pomerantz children down on the sidewalk, the thump-thump of their ball against the side of the building, the rattling wheels of the Italian-ice cart in the neighborhood—leaving my sisters to win the majority of the games. To make up for this, Mama insisted some days on helping me. "We'll work as a team, Ruthie," she would say, guiding me toward correct answers if I began to go astray, embarrassing me far more than did losing to my sisters. And as the summer days crawled by, I thought of Jenny Frankel, now on Lake George, and of Ellen Reid and her sister off with their grandparents in the Berkshires until Labor Day.

But though I could never tell Mama, I did love one day of the week: Sunday. The day Mama shopped for our weekly groceries, then scrubbed the corners of the apartment that she complained Inez, our Wednesday morning cleaning woman, had overlooked. Sundays were the days Poppy would drive Sarah and Valerie and me to Long Beach for the afternoon. He would roll down the windows of our old Chevrolet wagon and fiddle with the radio dial until he found the station with the least static.

"You're all going in today, right, girls?" he would say, checking us in the rearview mirror. "No chickens in this car!"

"No chickens, Poppy!" we would laugh. And once we'd made this promise, he reminded us, there'd be no turning back. No matter how the surf stung our feet with cold as we stood at the water's edge or how our arms and legs bristled with goose bumps. The rule was we had to submerge ourselves shoulder deep. Then, if we were brave enough to stay in longer, he would teach us to swim—freestyle, breaststroke, even the backstroke. For the first few weeks, I had watched for half the afternoon, dry above my ankles, as my sisters splashed about with Poppy beyond the breakers, daring to plunge in with them only after much coaxing. But, eventually, I gained courage and allowed Poppy to show me how easily my body could float on the surface if I relaxed, how quickly I could propel myself by pulling at the water with long strokes and fluttering my feet.

"What a little tadpole you are, Ruthie! A natural swimmer!" Poppy would tug at my streaming wet hair. And then how reluctant I was to leave, staying in long after Sarah and Valerie, despite the numbness in my hands, feeling I could swim forever, past the umbrellas far, far down the shoreline.

On the way home, my hair still hanging in damp strands, leaning my head against the blue vinyl seat, I would dream of swimming all the way to the horizon and back, swift as the wriggling fish below, free as the clouds overhead. If traffic returning to the city was slow, Poppy would stop with us at the Friendly's off the highway for cheeseburgers and milk-shakes, calling Mama from the restaurant pay phone to say we would be home later than planned. On these evenings, there was no time for Mama's math games or reading. And I heard her at night, through my bedroom wall, protest that after so many hours at the seashore—and maybe it was also the junky food we had been eating—we were completely spent. Even the following day when she worked with us, she said, we were often unfocused, as if we'd been overbaked in the sun! Certainly there were other things Poppy could take us to do. How about a visit to the Metropolitan Museum or a walk through the gardens of Fort Tryon Park? Did it have to be the beach every time?

"But the girls love it," I was relieved to hear Poppy reply.

So Mama changed her market day to Mondays after work. She found time for her housework in the evenings once Sarah, Valerie, and I had gone to bed. And she began to accompany us to the beach, packing a picnic basket full of food she claimed would nourish us properly, and learning games for the car since we would not get to them that night. She would sit in a folding chair in her white beach cover with red trim, her wide-brimmed hat tied beneath her chin with a red ribbon. Always she brought the Sunday *Times* crossword, which she later liked to tell her sisters she had finished in its entirety (though I thought, on more than one occasion, I had caught her checking the answers in the following week's paper, then filling in the spaces she had missed).

"Don't you want to come in, Judith? It's warm once you get used to it!" Poppy would call to Mama, running up from the water onto the first ridge of dry sand. He looked handsome, I thought, in his black bathing trunks, his hair slicked from the wet. But Mama, who had admitted to us once she'd never learned to swim well, would tuck her feet under her chair—her legs, from lack of sun, much paler than the rest of ours—and wave her hand in a way that meant, "No, go ahead without me."

Though one morning, after many requests, Poppy did convince her. She waded in with small steps, raising her elbows as she slowly reached waist-deep water, then waiting for a long break in the waves before edging out farther.

"Come to where we are, Ma!" my sisters and I cried from where we swam with Poppy. But as she stretched out her arms to paddle, her chin up, her neck stiff, a wave broke over her. And as soon as her head was above water once more, she quickly retreated to the shore, coughing into her hands.

"Come on, Judith! Give it one more try! We'll go together," Poppy offered as Mama made her way back to our belongings.

But she only shook her head and resettled in her chair with her crossword. She did not even notice Sarah and Valerie, some time later, tossing back their hair with their eyes closed, puckering their mouths like the man and woman embracing near us in the water. It was Poppy who eventually declared, "That's enough, girls," shielding his eyes from the sun to look at Mama as my sisters and I giggled bubbles into the salty water.

Mama stayed put until precisely noon, when she signaled us to come towel off and break for lunch. Then she pulled from her basket liverwurst on chewy rye. Or some Sundays, tuna salad with chunks of pickle, even deviled eggs with paprika sprinkled on top, setting it all at the center of our checked beach blanket for us to sit around. Now and then she would turn to glance over her shoulder at groups gathered nearby, families with hot dogs and pretzels from the concession stands, teenage girls drinking diet sodas, nibbling from small packets of chips. And as she sniffed then looked back to us, munching our sandwiches and eggs, I knew what she was thinking—that our meal was far superior. But this seemed the only part of the day she enjoyed, and, guiltily, I would sometimes wish she had not come. I knew it was because Poppy sensed Mama's impatience that he shortened our afternoons, the parking lot still packed with cars when we drove off. The radio remained silent now on the ride home as Mama read aloud a book of Aesop's Fables from the library. And so I would pretend drowsiness, closing my eyes until Mama believed I was asleep so that I could imagine I was still bobbing on the surface of the waves, drifting with the rhythm of the vast ocean.

⁓

Summer days seemed to pass more slowly than those of other seasons, but the summer I was thirteen seemed to disappear before its time. The Tuesday following Labor Day weekend, school began again. But this fall I would not be returning to the public school in our district. Since the previous autumn, I knew, Mama and Poppy had argued over where to enroll me for my eighth-grade year, their voices sometimes waking me hours after I had gone to bed. Poppy was eventually expecting a raise from the factory where he worked as a mechanical engineer, and partial scholarships, Mama had recently learned from our neighbor Babbie Schafer, were available for qualified students at her son's private school. If they could find the money for the remaining tuition, shouldn't I be given every advantage? Mama demanded. But Poppy thought our local public school was challenging enough. It was good enough for Bernice's and Helena's children, after all, and for the children of so many friends. Besides, even with a scholarship, he was sure the cost would still be in the thousands. That kind of money wasn't falling out of his pockets. This sounded like one of Poppy's jokes, but I heard no laughing. I wished Mama would forget the whole notion. But she was insistent. Maybe the raise would come faster if Poppy spent less time on his journals, which earned us *nothing*, and more time in the office. She'd heard what Babbie's son was learning, only a grade ahead of me. "Have you considered the opportunities this could mean, Aaron?" Mama's words grew louder, covering Poppy's. I remembered the Passover some years before when I had walked into the kitchen and found Mama and Nana Leah quarreling over things from the past. "That's not *so*, Mother! It *would* have made a difference if I had finished all four years! How many choices do you think there are without a degree?" I had never seen Mama short-tempered with Nana before. As soon as they were aware of my presence, their conversation ended. But for days afterward, I wondered what Nana had said before I'd entered and about the things Mama would have changed. And from something unwavering in her voice as she argued with Poppy, I knew she would make sure things went differently for me.

Then, some weeks later, I heard Poppy announce to her that an increase in his salary had finally come. And so he agreed that I should apply; and if I was accepted, since they now had the means, I would be given the finest possible education. Then, hopefully, the following year, they could plan to send Sarah, too.

In addition to my usual summer lessons, Mama, during that July and August, drilled me on the rules of grammar and composition. "Extra preparation for your new school can't hurt, can it? I imagine some new things will be asked of you now." For my practice work she brought me, from her shop, a red marbleized fountain pen she knew I had always admired, one of the pens fancy enough to be kept in the locked case to the right of the front window rather than in the rows of plastic bins above the loose writing paper.

Along my walk to school on the first day, I felt for the pen Mama had given me—easily accessible in the pocket of my windbreaker. I headed past the shops of Mosholu Avenue, turning onto Fieldston Road, to the Fieldston section of Riverdale with all of its large homes of stone or brick or stucco, grander than Leonid and Nadia's house in Scarsdale, a world just minutes from our apartment but one that I'd rarely entered.

That first Monday I had six courses to attend. The school had mailed me a copy of my weekly schedule, and on its grid of squares Mama had color-coded each subject—yellow for history, blue for math, red for English, and so on—making it simpler for me to keep track of where I needed to go. The campus of my new school was more expansive than I'd remembered from my visit the previous winter, with its scattering of structures, its lawns far wider than even those of the homes I'd passed on the way. (My old school had only a single building with an asphalt play area in the back.) Here the high-ceilinged hallways seemed to swallow sound, the voices of the students seeming more subdued as they moved from room to room—the boys in fitted jeans or khakis, sockless loafers, the girls in ankle boots and designer sweaters. Though many were Jewish—I knew from talk in the neighborhood—I saw not a single yarmulke, not one below-the-knee skirt like the several Orthodox girls in my old school wore. Was this something Mama had noticed, too, when we visited earlier in the year? I vowed that the next morning I would wake early, allowing plenty of extra time to dress more stylishly.

By only the second week, I was assigned an eight-page English essay comparing the characters of Edward Rochester and St. John in *Jane Eyre*, the dense novel we had been required to read over the summer. Casually my classmates folded the essay instructions into their notebooks, none of them seeming alarmed by having to complete a paper of this length within just ten days.

For several evenings after dinner, at the corner living room desk, I studied the book, scribbling pages of notes then erasing much of what I'd written, a pile of crumpled papers forming at my feet. Each time I tossed a balled sheet to the floor, I thought I could see Mama glance up from her reading. Since the start of the school year, I'd noticed, rather than spending her evenings at the kitchen table with order forms for holiday cards or sealing wax or decorative stamps for her shop, she had taken to sitting in the upholstered chair not far from where I worked.

"Can I get you anything from the kitchen, Pea?" Standing up, she would give my shoulder a squeeze. She smiled, but I saw, before I answered, that she scanned what she could of my scrawled paragraphs, and that, for a moment, her bottom lip drew inward, as if she were pinching back some remark.

I would shrug. "Yes, okay. Are there any more of those oatmeal cookies?" Then, as soon as Mama walked away, I would read again the sentences I had just written, wondering if they flowed in a logical manner.

As the deadline for the paper drew closer, I spent longer and longer evening hours poring over the chapters of the book, but the more I tried to organize my thoughts, the less sure I was of them. This was nothing like helping Poppy with his stories, which seemed alive and whole before we ever put them on paper, like songs already playing in our heads that needed only their notes recorded and embellished.

"How is it coming?" Mama would ask.

"Making progress!" I would say cheerfully. I did not tell her that as I worked I found myself drawing absentminded doodles of Jane Eyre and Edward Rochester around the margins of my pages, or that I was not certain my paragraphs contrasting St. John's morality with Rochester's expressed all I meant to say.

"Yes? Oh, good, good." But she squinted at the growing mound of papers beneath my chair and the untouched plate of cookies. And I thought I heard the small snap of her tongue when I raised my fingers from my lap, revealing the newly bloodied skin around my nails.

Then, four nights before my essay was due, I saw that Mama, in her chair, her feet propped on the ottoman, was carefully inspecting the pages of a new book. Its cover was hidden by her hands, but when she rose to fill the kitchen kettle with water, I peeked at its title—*Jane Eyre*, by Charlotte Brontë! A silver Doyle & Co sticker was adhered to its spine, a brand-new copy from the bookshop next door to Mama's store.

Before I could return to my seat, Mama emerged from the kitchen sipping a mug of tea. "Oh!" She waved an arm toward the book and laughed, as if she'd almost forgotten what she was reading, her cheeks pink as carnations. "You don't mind if I read the story, too, do you? And this way, if you have any questions—"

"I don't think I'm allowed to accept any help on this assignment. Anyway, I can do it on my own." I yanked at the neck of my wool sweater, which had begun to itch, and hoped I sounded confident as I tried to recall the long list of essay rules my English teacher, Miss Fielding, had written across her blackboard in yellow chalk.

Mama flicked her hand and smiled, as if to say she understood perfectly, but for some time I could hear, over my shoulder, the scratch of her pencil as she underlined passages, and, now and then, to my annoyance, when I turned around, I caught her turning down the corner of a page.

The following day in English class, while Miss Fielding led a discussion about the meaning of symbols in our novel, I studied my fellow students. How rested and calm they looked, and I imagined that none of them was keeping my late hours. But when, later in the period, Miss Fielding checked over what each of us had written so far, she complimented my understanding of St. John's values versus Rochester's and of Rochester's development throughout the novel. "You are off to a good start," she said. "Now rethink how you will pull your argument together in the closing sections so that you do not stray from your topic."

At home that final afternoon before the essay would be turned in, Sarah and Valerie were in their room, their door closed, singing along with the *Cats* cassette playing on their shared stereo. (Now that I was in eighth grade, Mama believed we were old enough to look after ourselves for the short hour between our return from school and hers from work.) I spread my papers once more across the living room desk and considered how to rework the last two pages of my essay. Despite the music thumping from my sisters' room, I dashed off three revised concluding paragraphs, my thoughts tumbling out almost more quickly than I could record them.

"Hello, girls!" Mama called when she entered, hanging her fall trench coat in the hall closet, shaking off her buckled heels. She walked to where I was working, kissing the top of my head. "Almost finished?" she asked offhandedly, as if the question were no more than a politeness. But from where she stood behind my chair, I knew she was hoping for a glance at what I had composed.

"Yes, just about! Until today I thought maybe I'd made a mess of it, but Miss Fielding said she liked much of what I've written, and I think I've almost fixed the parts that were wrong."

"Oh, so fast?" Mama smiled, but her voice was low, as if the words were thick in her throat.

"I know—the ideas just flew out of me!" I grinned and twirled my pen between my fingers.

"Good, very good. Now that you're close to finishing, perhaps I should take a quick peek at what you have so far—"

"What, Ma?"

"Just as a simple proofread, a second pair of eyes. Only to catch things you may have missed or to give a simple suggestion here or there. Especially if only yesterday you still had concerns. . . . It can't hurt, can it? I'm sure it's perfectly acceptable."

As Mama searched for a pen in the desk drawer and pulled over one of the dining chairs, setting it beside mine, I was not entirely certain Miss Fielding would say it was *perfectly* acceptable; but suddenly fearing I could not possibly have sorted out my points so quickly, I nodded my agreement.

Mama read through the paper once and then a second time, and as she did, she found many things to question—things I had not yet considered, things that had not caught Miss Fielding's eye. But Miss Fielding had given only minutes to my paper, and Mama hunched over my essay with me until long after midnight, until my eyes stung with fatigue. And gradually I saw that what had seemed so ordered earlier in the day had only been a tangled muddle. And I resented Miss Fielding for having made me believe I'd had only simple revisions left.

"What if you said this instead? Just an idea."

"Oh, yes, Ma. Yes, that's good." Always her new phrase seemed better than what I had written. Change after change after change, until, by the time our final draft was done, I could no longer remember what the essay had once been.

I received an A— on the assignment Mama had helped with. *Well executed*, Miss Fielding wrote on the final page, *though I am surprised you abandoned the original plan for your paper.*

"A-minus, Ma," I said later that day, and showed her the mark. But I did not mention Miss Fielding's comment on the essay or that I wondered what my grade might otherwise have been.

⁓

The next September, as Mama had hoped, another small increase in Poppy's salary allowed them to enroll Sarah in private school as well. "Your turn will come, too." Mama had stroked Valerie's hand the first morning before Sarah and I set off together as Valerie sniffled over her boiled eggs. I liked having Sarah's company as we trod along Fieldston Road to school each morning and back each afternoon. I now looked forward to the walk, which had seemed lonely the year before—to the earthy smell of the leaf piles along the curbs of the landscaped yards, to the game Sarah and I sometimes played, imagining scandalous secrets of the inhabitants of the most stately homes. In the evenings, of course, with our many assignments, all games ended. And we toiled over our work as Mama remained close.

But during the third week of the semester, I brought home a slip of paper—a notice to all high school parents of the options for participation in some extracurricular activity. I could choose a club—drama, chess, or debate—or a sport—track, volleyball, or swimming. All activities met after school, the clubs two times a week, the sports teams five. The slip was to be signed, it said, by a parent or guardian.

As Mama scanned the paper, she adjusted the reading glasses on the bridge of her nose, pushing them close to her eyes, then pulling them forward, as if she could not find just the right position. "Do you really think it's wise, Ruth, to take hours away from the time you need for schoolwork? And you're in high school now—your assignments will only become more challenging."

"But the activities don't last the entire year, Ma. Besides, I've been keeping up with all of my quizzes and papers."

I saw the pen Mama held in her hand. Already I knew which box I wanted her to check. The previous year, the windows of my homeroom had overlooked the school's glass-walled pool, and at the end of the afternoon, as I packed my books, I had often caught glimpses of the swim team members stretching on the pool deck in their racing suits, diving gracefully into the water, skimming the surface like sailfish.

As I'd walked home that day, I had imagined myself gliding beside them and wondered if I could remember all of the swimming techniques Poppy had taught me. When I told Mama what I was hoping for, she nodded but looked past me, out the kitchen window, as if something there annoyed her. Over the weekend, we had driven to Scarsdale to visit Nadia and Leonid. Gregory had just joined his school's Model United Nations Club. "They investigate *all* kinds of international affairs," Nadia had told Mama. "Gregory was the ambassador from France in their last debate." She showed Mama all of the materials Gregory had studied to prepare for his role and then the award he had received for Best Delegate. Mama had looked impressed. "It's too bad your school doesn't offer Model United Nations, isn't it?" Mama had turned to me.

But now she said, "Five practices a week, Ruthie. What about the chess club? It's far less time-consuming. And did I ever tell you Uncle Jacob and I used to play chess for hours together in the Shanghai ghetto? Jacob made us a set out of bits of wood. And then when we came to this country, our Papa bought us a real set with all the proper directions. I still remember lots of tricks. I could teach you—"

But when I begged and begged, Mama finally agreed, as long as I promised that if my grades suffered in any way, I would quit.

The first swim practice was scheduled for the following Monday. In my blue bathing suit with orange piping and wrapped in the beach towel Mama had packed in my bag that morning, I followed the other team members along the corridor of the gym and down the cold tile stairs that led to the pool. The towel was meant to cover me when I was not in the water, but no one else, I noticed as we settled ourselves on the bleachers, bothered with such modesty. So before taking my seat, I quickly pulled at my towel, rolling it into a loose ball on my lap.

Coach Hadley, as I heard the older team members call him, stood facing us, his back to the room's windowed wall. In the late-day sun, his gray hair, thick as steel wool, shone almost silver. With his fists plunged into the pockets of his satiny red jacket, a gleaming whistle dangling from his neck, he announced that we were forty-one strong this year, twenty-two boys and nineteen girls, an encouraging number in his estimation. He was particularly pleased, he said, indicating those of us new to the team, with the addition of nine freshmen.

Our practice, he explained, would begin with a simple warm-up. He would time us in heats of four to check our individual speeds. He reminded us to avoid splashing as we kicked, to pull at the water with deep strokes, to breathe only when necessary. Before my turn to race, I silently recited these directions, trying to recall simultaneously all of the pointers Poppy had given me in summers past.

By the time I finished the two required pool lengths, my chest pounded as if it would explode, but, much to my delight, I discovered that my time, though far from the fastest on the team, was better than many.

"Not bad, not bad," Coach Hadley pronounced. I needed to learn proper flip turns, I needed to correct the alignment of my elbows, I needed a rubber swim cap to eliminate drag, but he could see that I had potential. He patted my shoulder, the same sign of camaraderie I had seen him give some of the returning team members earlier in the practice. I nodded to show my eagerness to comply, biting the sides of my cheeks to keep from grinning.

When I returned home that evening, Mama was already home from work, quizzing Sarah on the capitals of the fifty states for her upcoming geography test. She waved a hand at me, but did not look up from Sarah's book. "It's nearly dark outside. You must be worn out."

"Only a little." Then as Mama left Sarah's side to spread the floral cloth on the dining table, folding five paper napkins into neat rectangles, setting out knives and forks and glasses of water, I described all that Coach Hadley had taught us that day. Mama nodded but said nothing so that I wondered if the topic held no interest for her. But the following evening, she told me she had a surprise. In the sporting goods store near Broadway Paperie, she had come across two magazines with articles on swimming. Managing to browse through them during her lunch hour, she had been impressed by the nuggets of information they contained, the descriptions of physical techniques as well as mental exercises that would most certainly be to my benefit. "See. Take a look, Ruthie." She opened to a two-page diagram in one of the magazines. "Physiologists have studied how our bodies move best through water, secrets most swimmers don't know. This is the newest research." Over the next several days, I found these materials opened on the dining table when I arrived home, Mama's reading glasses resting on one of the glossy pages to mark her place. As I washed my hands at the kitchen sink or unpacked texts and folders from my schoolbag, she would read aloud tips. But Coach Hadley had already critiqued our every move. He had shown us how to visualize our performance before we entered the water, how to dive from the starting blocks for maximum speed, how to angle our fingers and point our feet, how to roll our necks gently as we breathed, conserving motion. And for many afternoons after the cool-down, he had drilled me on my turns until I could tuck my body into a tight coil, propelling myself from the wall like an arrow.

"Yes, Mama. I know! These are things we practice every week!" And I would rotate my arms like a windmill to show off my new expertise.

"Oh, well then—" Mama shrugged, and the sports magazines were stacked with her other reading material on the kitchen shelf underneath the telephone. But now and then, when I mentioned some new skill I had learned in swim practice, she turned to glance at the magazines, as if she still believed they held information of greater value.

. . .

On the first day of the swim season, Coach Hadley had advised us about our diets—heavy meals could slow our systems; we were to think about eating for speed. For some time I had noticed how carefully my classmates, the girls especially, chose the foods they ate. I overheard them in the cafeteria comparing calories, sharing recipes for meals low in fat as they picked at half sandwiches, salads with cottage cheese, diced fruit. But until our coach's warning, it had never crossed my mind that there was anything to be done about the plumpness around my thighs or the thickness of my middle. "You should be proud to have a healthy phy-sique, Ruthie," Mama had always told me. "No one's frame is meant to be skin and bones like so many girls I see these days." In temple or riding the bus, she would nudge me, jutting her chin disapprovingly toward women whose waists were as small as children's. "They look as sickly as refugees!" Even Ruby, her new employee, had dropped ten pounds since summer, drinking only strawberry diet shakes for breakfast and lunch. "But now she tells me she is struggling to keep up with her classes," Mama said. And the other day Mama had caught her incorrectly filling out an order for a wedding announcement—embossed instead of engraved. "Well, what did she think would happen from existing on fruit-flavored sugar substi-tutes! How can she possibly think straight?"

But after swim practice, in the girls' locker room, as I blotted my hair with a towel, I began to sneak peeks at my teammates—at their stomachs flat as stone slabs, at the perfect slope of their breasts, at their arms and legs as lean as the classical Greek figures we sketched in art class. To me, they didn't look bony, but beautifully muscled, feminine and strong. If I followed our coach's guidelines, would my body slice through the water more quickly? Could I, too, be womanly and sleek? And I stared down at the protrusion below my waist, the lumpiness of my hips.

That evening, Mama, to my dismay, served a supper richer than usual—potato-lentil soup, buttered noodles, veal roast smothered with fat mushrooms, glazed challah rolls. My mouth watered as she placed dishes of the steaming food on the dining table. But I was determined not to weaken. I requested only a single ladleful of soup, rather than the usual two or three. I handed the basket of rolls to Poppy without taking one. Later, when the platters of veal and noodles were passed around the table for seconds, I shook my head, "No, thank you."

"Is something the matter, Ruthie? An upset stomach?"

"No, Ma. No, I feel fine!" But there was a good reason, I explained, for my modest portions, and I recited the suggestions Coach Hadley had given.

There was a pause in the scraping of Mama's fork and knife. "It seems your coach has appointed himself the authority on all kinds of matters, hasn't he?"

But Papa laughed before there was time to answer Mama's question. "Sarah, Valerie, did you know your sister was turning into such a dedicated athlete!" And he stroked one hand with the other as he did whenever he was pleased, causing my face to warm with pride.

Sticking to my new diet regimen took more effort than I had anticipated. I craved Mama's breakfasts—salmon scrambled eggs, buttermilk pancakes, oatmeal with brown sugar. And dinners of turkey with gravy, stuffed cabbage, kasha with onions. How easily I would have given in, but after some weeks, I thought I noticed what seemed almost a miracle—a slightly smaller bulge to my stomach, a bit less flesh around my upper legs. Was I merely wishing it? No! When I stood sideways before the full-length mirror on my closet door, I was quite sure I could make out a change. Along my route to school, I began to check my reflection in the windows of the nail salons, the coffee shops, Ganiaris's fruit market. If I squinted my eyes, I could make my translucent self almost slender, curving only where I longed for curves. I thought of Cole Freeman, our swim team captain, who reminded me of handsome Luke Skywalker from my cousin Gregory's *Star Wars* cards, and wondered if Cole would ever notice me the way I had noticed him. "Ooh . . . how do I look?" Sarah teased if she caught me, one hand grabbing her hip, the other cupped behind her head, sashaying down the block until I broke down in laughter.

After a time, I thought I discerned another difference, as well. It seemed I was somehow lighter in the water now, that I felt a quicker energy in our practice drills. So I found the discipline to leave my meals unfinished. To fill myself instead, later, with yogurt and sliced bananas. During a Shabbat dinner at Aunt Bernice's, as I whispered with my cousin Eva about the R-rated movie she had just watched while on a sleepover with a friend, Mama pressed her lips in annoyance at what remained on my plate. At home that night, she warned me not to believe all of Coach Hadley's advice. "You know you can't possibly give proper attention to your homework without solid food in your stomach. Your coach should tell you no one ever got anywhere by starving herself!"

But I laughed and kissed her cheek to show her how wrong she was. "I'm not starving myself, Ma! See, I've never been stronger!" And I rolled up my shirtsleeve, revealing the newly defined muscle along my shoulder.

Several weeks into the season, our team was scheduled for its third meet, but the first in which I would be participating. For days, I thought of little else. At night, I lay awake in bed, listening to street noises, my mind rushing like the cars that rattled past outside my window, imagining how my opponents might leave me behind in a wake of bubbles.

We were driven to Brooklyn, to our rival school, in two yellow vans, and as we drew close, the trembling I had felt in my stomach since that morning worsened.

"Jitters are very normal for a first race," reassured Celia, a senior team member whose voice turned to music whenever she spoke to any of the boys on the team. Now she let the words drop flatly. "Nerves can even work in your favor, Ruth." But I was not sure I believed her, and as I was called to my event and curled at the edge of my starting block, I was certain I could see my knees shaking.

But there must have been truth to what she said, or perhaps it was my new eating regime. Never before had I swum so quickly; my arms and legs churned like motors through the water. And at the end of the race, I was presented a third-place medal hanging from a long red, white, and blue ribbon. During the bus ride back to Riverdale, I cradled the medal in my palm, tracing with my thumb the tiny figure of a swimmer etched into the surface. I closed my eyes as our van hummed along Flatbush Avenue and over the Brooklyn Bridge. This was the feeling of winning!

Once at our building, I sprinted up the four flights of stairs, too impatient to wait for the crotchety-slow elevator. By the time I reached our apartment, I was panting so that I could hardly speak.

"Look, Ma! Look!" I dashed into her bedroom, where she was returning to its hanger the silk blouse she had worn to work that day, carefully re-buttoning its pearl buttons. Gasping, I dangled the medal before her.

"What is it, Ruth?"

"Third place. Third out of six, Ma. I had to beat three other swimmers to earn it!"

"Oh?" Mama turned back to her blouse for a moment, fastening the final button. The skin beneath her eyes looked tired; this was holiday season, her busiest time at Broadway Paperie, and the one I knew she most disliked. "Congratulations," she said, but in a way that made me wish I had explained it differently. A medal was a medal. I had won a point for my team. Maybe if she had been there she would have understood— all of the swimmers were fast, none of them easy to outdo.

Then, soon, I had new reasons for excitement—another third-place medal, and a tie for fourth at an invitational meet where five teams competed. In my bedroom, I hung my second award with the first where they were visible to anyone who entered, from the latch of my window beside the stained-glass flower I had made in art class. Some evenings I draped one around my neck like a necklace, feeling the sway of it below my collar.

Other members of my team were still faster than I, but Coach Hadley began to compliment my progress, and each afternoon I burst through our door to announce to Mama, Sarah, and Valerie the strides I had made in practice that day. I predicted the medals I thought I could win in future competitions, then repeated these boasts for Poppy as soon as I heard his footsteps at the entry.

So full was my head with dreams that I swallowed the food on my plate each dinner almost without tasting. How easy it was to turn down seconds now, and more often than not, my first servings went unfinished. I began to refuse anything in heavy sauce. I peeled the thick skin from Mama's spiced chicken legs, cut my pot roast into strips, avoiding every marbled streak of fat.

"What passes the lips resides on the hips!" This was the rhyme other girls in my class sang as they assembled their lunches of sliced pita and unsalted rice cakes and raw vegetables, and I repeated it now for my family as they stared at what lay untouched on my plate.

Poppy would laugh and rap the top of my head with his knuckles. "Dieting like the fashion models, heh!"

"We're fashion models, too!" Sarah and Valerie would giggle, thrusting their shoulders back in an exaggerated manner, cutting their food into tiny mouse bites.

But the more Poppy and my sisters joked, the quieter Mama grew. For three nights in a row, she said little throughout supper. Silently, she stacked our dishes and carried them into the kitchen, shrugging off the work as if it were nothing when we offered to help. Even her plate washing seemed quieter than usual, only the light scratching of knives on platters, the gentle splash of water. One evening when I followed her into the kitchen for a glass of water, I found her poking with a fork at a plate on the counter.

"Did you eat anything at all tonight, Ruth?" Mama pointed to the bits of lamb chop I had discarded, the remaining pile of barley.

"Yes! Yes, of course I ate! But I'm on the diet of champions—lean, lean, lean!"

Mama pushed the food across my plate. "Do you know you left your geography text and notebook here this morning? I discovered them after you left for school. Last week I found your French homework loose on your dresser.

"Ruthie—" Mama smiled at the medal around my neck in a way that made me feel suddenly silly for having worn it. "If this diet is so effective, don't you think you would see, well, other results?" And though she said no more, I knew what she meant. But I would get other medals—seconds and even firsts! I had only been improving! And as Mama reached a hand to brush my cheek, I quickly ducked my head and began pulling at a thread hanging from my shirt cuff, afraid the tears I felt choking my throat would spill out at the first stroke of her fingers.

In January, the culminating event of our swim season was scheduled to take place, the final championships in which every team in our league would be competing. This was the final push, Coach Hadley said, the time for us to show what we were truly made of. He assigned me to swim the one-hundred-meter backstroke, a race I had swum before, but in this meet I would have many more than my usual number of competitors.

For days preceding the competition, my stomach clenched with a nervous excitement I couldn't seem to quell, even with the deep-breathing exercises Coach Hadley had taught us. And in the mornings, I found I could swallow no more than teaspoon-sized bites of oatmeal or boiled egg. Coach Hadley extended our weekday practices an extra twenty minutes, and, for three Saturdays in a row, we were required to attend morning practices, as well. Then, several days before the competition, Mama did something she hadn't done before.

"I have boots to drop after work at the shoe repair just two blocks from your school. So maybe while I'm in the neighborhood, I'll stop by your practice. You wouldn't mind, would you?"

"No, Ma." I shrugged my shoulders, but I couldn't help hoping she would change her mind or somehow forget. Other parents occasionally arrived at the very end of practice to pick up sons and daughters, but none of them ever stayed for any length of time as Mama seemed to want to do.

"Is that someone's mother?" "Whose mother is that?" My teammates turned their heads as we filed onto the pool deck for our warm-up. Mama was seated at the center of the top bleacher between two lavender plastic shopping bags, her camel coat belted tightly. When she spotted me, she curled her finger in a tiny wave. I responded with the same small gesture, wondering how many on my team had noticed.

As Cole Freeman led us through our usual series of stretches, I could see Mama from the corner of my eye. So once we dove into the pool to begin our drills, I attempted to concentrate only on Coach Hadley's directions, but I could not help stealing quick glimpses upward toward the bleachers. Then "One hundred back!" Coach called, signaling the practice for my championship race. "Leiser, take lane four," he directed. A center lane meant he expected my time to be one of the best! Gillian was in the water to my left. I had outswum her earlier in the week. Mandy Robb was to my right, but she was not normally a backstroker. I will *win*, I thought as I pulled myself close to the starting block, high out of the water. With Mama here, too—I will *win*.

Out I flung, far, far, arching and back, kicking under the water, two beats and then breaking the surface. I could not see the others, only the spray from my arms and legs, but I thought—yes?—perhaps I was leading. I knew what to do—ignore everything but my own fluttering feet.

But, for the briefest moment, toward the end of the first lap, my eyes wandered to Mama where she sat, her shoulders forward—watching. I needed to regain my focus, but before I could turn to find my place in the pool, I felt a sudden *crack-crack* in my arm and then my head. Pain fired from my elbow to my fingertips and down my neck. How had I missed the string of flags that hung over the pool marking the approach to the wall! Blinking water from my eyes, clinging to the side with my uninjured arm, I shook my head to stop the room from reeling. Within moments, Coach Hadley and most of my teammates had reached me. They offered their arms to lift me from the pool and walked me to one of the benches behind the diving board.

"Excuse me! Allow me through, please! I'm her *mother*!" Mama was struggling through the crowd to get to me, her coat streaked with patches of wet from the dripping bathing suits and limbs she had pushed past.

"Looks like nothing's broken. Just a couple of bad bumps," Coach Hadley told her. "She may have some tenderness for a while, but she'll mend."

"Thank you." Mama nodded but without turning to him, so I knew she had dismissed his words, that this was something she would determine for herself.

Instead of walking, Mama, using the school's pay phone, called for a taxi, a splurge she and Poppy made only on occasion. She ordered the driver to go slowly, reprimanded him when he failed to avoid two potholes.

At home that night, Mama applied ice packs to my bruises and a heating pad to my neck to counteract the cold. When Sarah and Valerie approached with questions about my injury, she directed them to the kitchen. "Turn on the water for rice, will you, girls? What your sister needs more than anything is rest and a decent meal." And so I knew what Mama implied: that I should have listened, that all along she had known better. That if I'd only been feeding myself properly, I might not have done something so careless.

. . .

At the beginning of the swim season, Coach Hadley had taught us what he called "visualization techniques." We could use them to picture ourselves swimming with greater endurance, increased speed. If we employed them often enough, he claimed, they would enhance our performance. So over the next two days, while I rested at home, I tried to envision my energy returning, my body free of aching. I imagined myself finishing my race in record time. But on the second evening, the Thursday before the final swim competition, Mama knocked on my door. She held a paper in her hand. My French quiz on passive verbs. I must have left it on the living room desk, the red C+ visible through the back side of the sheet.

"It was just one quiz, Ma! My other grades have been fine!"

"One thing leads to another, though, doesn't it? And besides, even if you hadn't been injured, how much do you think you should be giving up for this? It's a sport, Ruthie. It's not your future. Especially if you're not—"

"Not what, Ma?"

"Find things you will succeed in, Ruth. Give your time to those. Doesn't that make the most sense?"

But what could she mean? I had won medals, and I was getting better. I *knew* I was. Then, for some reason, I thought of the gold spelling bee trophy on the shelf beside Sarah's bed. And I remembered the two certificates Mama still kept in her top bureau drawer: *Judith Feldman: First Place Entry, Science Fair* and *Judith Feldman: Junior Math Contest Winner.* Third out of six. It wasn't winning, was it? It was only the middle.

"But, Mama, on the day you came to see me, that day I was first, wasn't I?"

Mama slid her tongue slowly along her front teeth as though thinking how to answer. And then she shook her head. Silently at first, and then the word smacked out like the slap of a hand: "No." No! She had come to watch me and I hadn't been leading, hadn't even finished the race.

. . .

O n the Saturday of the league championships, Mama, dressed for services in her tweed skirt and olive chiffon blouse, offered me a mug of tea. "Are you coming?" she asked.

"No, not today, Mama. Everything still aches." Ached too much for going to temple. Or for studying my Cahier d'Exercices for the next week's French test. Too much for cheering on my teammates at the championship meet. Too much for racing one hundred meters of backstroke.

———

Swim season ended. The remainder of my freshman year seemed to drag toward summer. And then suddenly it was September again. Now we were sophomores, and was I imagining this, or had the other girls in my grade returned from the vacation even slimmer than they had been the year before? Some were taking exercise dance classes in the afternoons at the studio on Broadway, and toted to school their leotards and leg warmers in canvas bags slung over their shoulders. And there was excitement over the announcement that aerobics would be added to this semester's after-school offerings. *Thin Is In!* proclaimed the slick covers of the magazines my classmates read in the hallways and cafeteria during free periods.

Mama, I knew, would never agree to aerobics classes; she thought them frivolous, a ridiculous excuse for women to parade around in skintight clothes. So, instead, with a little leftover bat mitzvah money, I bought from the bookstore near school a paperback entitled *The Ultimate You*, full of step-by-step color photos of callisthenic exercises. If I followed the techniques provided, it promised, my body would quickly transform until it resembled those of the girls in all of the pictures. So, night after night, in the secrecy of my bedroom, I twisted and lifted and lunged until my muscles cramped.

But the pounds that had crept back over the summer did not melt away. And when I was sent home once again with a notice giving my choices for extracurricular activities, Mama checked the box marked *Chess Club* on my slip as well as on Sarah's.

"You did say you wanted to try chess instead this year, right, Pea?" Mama leaned over the chair where I was working to brush hair from my brow, and as she bent close, I could smell the sweet orange tang of her perfume.

Coach Hadley had asked if he could count on my returning to the team, but I knew the answer. "Yes, Ma," I nodded.

Mama signed our permission slips and tucked them into our back-packs. "I'm glad you'll both be playing, girls. You can practice together. It's a wonderful game! Some of the finest minds in the world are chess players. Let me see if I can find my old set. And maybe I still have that book of pointers—all the tricks I used to use when Uncle Jacob and I played together!"

As Mama rummaged through the closets, Sarah and I smoothed wrinkles from the kitchen tablecloth, creating a flat surface on which to play. And when Mama unfolded the checkered board on the table and placed the pieces, one by one, on the black and ivory squares, explaining their various roles—the pawns and rooks, knights and bishops, king and queen—I nodded to prove I was interested, hoping the disappointment I felt, heavy as wet sand, did not show on my face.

For days before the first club meeting, Mama taught us the many rules of the game. Then, once the season began, she devoted time in the evenings, after our homework was done, to giving us what she termed "Special Tips and Hints."

"This move Uncle Jacob and I used to call The Double Hit. Next week maybe I'll show you The Diagonal Knockdown!"

But I seemed to have no memory for Mama's strategies. When she whispered suggestions in my ear, minutes later I would forget them.

I extended my nighttime routine of toning exercises by ten minutes, but there was no change to the roundness of my waist and thighs, the old softness of my upper arms. So I began to wear loose sweaters over my collared shirts. In school I made multiple trips to the girls' room, re-adjusting my skirts to cover my knees. I took consolation in the fact that the weather was getting colder. Soon everyone would be bundled in padded jackets and turtlenecks. Who would even notice my bulkier clothes? But word began to circulate that in the spring the miniskirt would be return-ing. Even the other girls on the chess team—far from the school's most daring dressers—began to talk of buying these leg-baring hemlines.

Perhaps the spring would be a good time to start a new diet. And this time I would stick with it. This time I would see something through to completion. Mama often said diets doomed people to failure. They were designed by advertisers to keep people hungering for things that would never satisfy. When she and Aunt Helena and Aunt Bernice were young women, just before Aunt Helena's wedding and when they all still lived at home, a saleslady had knocked on their door hawking carbonated drinks for suppressing appetite. Despite Mama's warnings, Aunt Helena had bought two box loads. And what was the result? On the day of her wed-ding Helena had felt too sick to dance and looked pale as flour.

But that was long ago, Mama! I wanted to tell her. *On* my *new diet I will be fine!* Because maybe Mama was wrong about me. After all, she couldn't be right about everything.

So maybe in the spring—yes, the spring!—my new diet would begin.

SEXY GIRL

(Opal's Story)

· *1982* ·

At the Passionflower, the bar-restaurant of our hotel, the men out-numbered the women. Especially after nine o'clock, when most of the married couples had disappeared to their rooms and the young lovers down the beach, strolling barefoot through the lapping water. Then Mother would smile at the men straddling whalebone bar stools who winked and raised glasses in her direction. We knew all of the regulars—the black island natives as well as the transplants from Europe and America, some with sun-parched wives or girlfriends, most bachelors.

At the hotel, there were few children my age (I was eleven), and those I met stayed only a week or two, on holiday with their parents. During the day, they vanished on boating excursions or hikes through the botanical gardens.

"Make the best of it, Opal," Mother said when I complained. "As soon as school resumes, you'll be surrounded by a hundred boys and girls.

Promise, promise." And what freedom I had here. What child wouldn't envy my carefree hours in the sand or floating on the turquoise sea? she asked. Didn't I like swinging in the hammock in the courtyard palm grove, breathing the frangipani, watching the tropic birds soar overhead?

Yes, I nodded.

Wasn't this much prettier than faded blue town houses, the only view from our San Francisco apartment?

"Yes, much prettier."

We were on a small island in the West Indies, and Mother's plan was to stay for a year, possibly two. "Working as a realtor in Pacific Heights loses its charm after a time," she'd explained, stroking her legs distractedly as she flipped through travel brochures during the months before we left. "Life should offer some excitement. Don't you think?" Through the travel agent, she had heard about the White Heron Hotel with its attached surfside restaurant and bar. As hostess of the restaurant, Mother would be entitled to a three-room suite for a nominal fee. In May, she had found renters for our apartment, and after my school year ended, we would go. When I returned to classes in September, it would be at St. Agnes, one of the island's two elementary schools.

Our first afternoon in the Caribbean, Mother had dumped, from suitcases onto the cotton spread of her bed, an array of colorful outfits I had never seen her wear—boldly printed skirts, bright sundresses, sandals with ribbon-thin straps. In the filmy mirror of our small shared bathroom, she'd shaken the ends of her orange-gold hair, which had waved in the damp heat as soon as we'd stepped from the plane. Wet strands had clung to her neck.

"Oh, it's a slice of heaven!" she'd said, stripping to her pink lace bra, leaning against the window frame to gaze at the ocean. "Isn't it paradise?"

During the day, Mother's responsibilities were few. The lunch crowd was always light—some of the elderly hotel guests, a few islanders breaking for Hairoun beers. She was rarely required to do more than meet briefly with Ezra Dupree, the White Heron's manager, to go over the details of the evening's menu and seating plan. The busyness of our routine in San Francisco soon seemed a foggy dream. We spent most of the morning and afternoon hours reading in the shaded yard or sprawled across our fringed towels on the hotel beach, snacking on fried plantains and salted peanuts, sipping lemon sodas. Within a week or two, Mother's skin darkened from cream-white to nut-brown. As we stretched in the sun, she lathered her arms and legs with milky oil from a green bottle to prevent peeling. Men on the beach twisted their necks, and I suspected, despite their tinted glasses, what their eyes followed.

At one of the boutiques in town, Mother bought a batik bikini with yellow tropical fish and a matching one for me. Though I yanked and fussed with the ties of the suit, the material bagged and puckered at my hips and across the flat of my chest. Pretending to study the other bathers on the beach, I sneaked peeks at the fullness of Mother's bikini top and the way she bent one leg into a vee, crossing it toward the other.

Mother could bask on the sand for hours, but the heat stung my paler skin, and I ran to the water every few minutes, pinching my nose and plunking beneath the surface. When cruise ships anchored at the mouth of the port, sending small boats of passengers ashore, I had company as I swam—packs of Germans or English or French. Sometimes the foreign boys glanced at me, and then I would paddle out to the raft, climb the ladder, and dive into the sea, pointing my toes "gracefully as a swan," as Mother had taught me. But always, by the time I reemerged, they were no longer watching.

Between four and five o'clock each day, we shook the sand from our beach towels, gathered our empty soda bottles and sunscreen, and returned to our suite. From my bedroom, which was separated from Mother's by a peach-painted sitting area, I listened to the pattering of water as she showered. On my bed, flat on my back, I pulled down the edge of my bathing suit and examined the disappointing progression of my tan. If I splashed in the waves less and sunbathed more, as Mother did, maybe I would see more impressive results.

When I heard the creak of the shower handle and Mother's feet padding from the bath, I stepped in, rinsed grains of sand from my scalp and ears, scrubbed my stomach and arms and legs with the round, honey-scented cake of soap placed in our soap dish each afternoon. I dawdled in the water until the skin of my palms began to shrivel. Then, wrapped in two towels, I watched Mother from the wicker armchair in her room as she continued to dress. Before slipping on her clothes, still in her pastel underwear, she emptied the contents of her vinyl makeup bag onto the bureau. On the balls of her feet, leaning toward the bureau's unframed mirror, she massaged her cheeks with blush and dabbed her eyelids with a silvery shadow, making the green flecks of her irises dazzle.

"Opal, have you seen my lipstick anywhere?" she would ask, rummaging through the tubes and compacts on the dresser for her favorite bronze shade, which seemed to disappear now and then to unexpected places. If I found it for her, she would blow me a kiss. "Thank you, dearheart, thank you. Nothing is dowdier than a woman with no lipstick."

I watched as she parted her lips to apply the color, then mustered my courage. "Can you put a little on me?"

Usually she relented, dotting my bottom lip with a pale coat. As I inspected my reflection in the mirror, I wished for another coat of lipstick and plumper lips like hers.

"Ooh, la, la! So grown up," she would say, laughing over her shoulder as she fastened gold starfish earrings to her ears. "Try not to drive the boys *too* crazy!"

And I would steal a second glance at the mirror, wondering what it was about my expression or the makeup on my mouth that amused her.

Mother, it seemed, knew many things about men, secrets of how they thought and what they liked. In California, after the divorce, she had dated frequently. One blond man had lasted for two months—Cyrus, who reminded me of a fairer version of the photo of my father, which Mother kept among the many snapshots in her travel album. And in these first weeks on the island, I began to notice, everywhere we went, men asked her name, told her jokes, stroked their fingers along her arms. Sometimes I saw other women staring in our direction, and I would toss my shoulders proudly, smiling at the attention.

D inner at the Passionflower began at six, and it was Mother's job to seat the guests and check their meals, and to make sure the customers at the bar received a steady flow of drinks. For the first two hours or so she floated from table to table beneath the restaurant's palm frond awning, pausing to chat with the diners at one table before gliding on to the next. So there was little for me to do. Most nights I asked Atneil, the bartender, for a ginger soda with ice. "Thank you so much, Atneil," I would coo, imitating Mother's soft voice, forcing myself to draw nearer despite the ragged scar on his neck, which gave me gooseflesh, and offering him my hand as she did now and then. From the cooks in the kitchen, local island women, I ordered curried chicken or lamb stew or fried conch fritters, depending on my mood. If they were not too busy, they let me watch as they cleaned redeye fish or gutted chicken cavities, wiping scales and blood across their apron fronts and singing songs about the island, about whalers out to sea and the heartbreak of poor Josiah Moody, abandoned by his cheating wife. When I joined in singing the parts I'd learned, they chuckled. "Funny child! Don't you have better things to do than watch a bunch of biddies work!" I shrugged and then shook my head, which only made them chuckle more. "Will you sing the one about the fisherman's daughter?" I would ask. Usually they gave in, sometimes sharing with me the hunks of papaya or toasted coconut they munched from bowls. Then when they tired of singing, I carried my plate to the bamboo love seat against the wall of the hotel. I took tiny swallows of soda and poked at my conch or chunks of lamb, trying to make my supper last, passing the time until the dinner crowd thinned and I could rejoin Mother.

When the families and couples began to disperse, Mother chose a table at the open end of the floor, closest to the sand, and faced the shore, inhaling the salt of the ocean.

"Surprise me!" she would say, throwing her hands in the air, when one of the kitchen staff asked what she wished to eat. Holding a fresh glass of ginger soda, I would slide into a chair beside her.

"Goodness, Opal, you scared me! I forgot you were still downstairs!" Her loud words confused me because I could not tell if she was annoyed or merely teasing.

"Where did you think I went?"

"Oh, I don't know. Off with one of the hunky British boys!" She laughed, and I tried to laugh in her same careless manner, not wanting her to think how childishly, impatiently I'd waited for the end of her shift.

Then within a minute or two, it seemed, a man approached, looming over our table. Sometimes he was an acquaintance, a resident of the island who frequented the bar, but more often a stranger, a guest of the hotel or the skipper of a boat in the harbor. He had not yet eaten, he would say. Would my mother mind some company? He swirled a glass of pale brown liquid and handed her the cocktail stuck with slender straws. He was from France, he said, or Italy, New York, California, Brazil. As he sniffed, I could see into the dark nostrils of his carved rock of a nose. And Mother would smile, nodding at the wicker chair across from us, sipping at the straws in her drink. She waited until his dinner arrived before beginning her own. "Sharing a meal with a man is a gesture of intimacy," I remembered her telling me once, and I'd wondered if she and my father had eaten together in this way; though I knew he'd been a part of her life only briefly, a season of just a few months while she'd lived in Europe.

In a man's presence, Mother ate differently from when we were alone. At home, in San Francisco, she had made chicken cutlets or ordered mu shu pork and Chinese noodles from the Shanghai Palace down the street. And at our kitchen counter, we had piled the food onto our plates, scooping forkfuls almost without tasting as Carly Simon played on the stereo. Now she savored every bite, cutting delicately into kingfish or spiced shrimp.

"This is *divine*," she would say, arching her neck so that I could see each swallow. And I noticed the man always watched, too.

"Try a bite of mine," he would offer, and they would both stretch across the table, turning their shoulders from me so that she could reach his fork. Afterward, they might share a dessert—a slice of coconut pie, a bowl of orangey mango sherbet. In slow rhythm, their spoons dipped into the dish, and the man would regale Mother with stories. She would tilt her head to one side and lick at the corners of her mouth. "Do you know how beautiful you are?" the man would tell her, and they would begin to joke about things I struggled to understand.

"You don't mind if I take your mama out for a sail under the stars?" a Portuguese banker with a mustache that coiled at the ends like periwinkle shells asked me one evening. "I promise to have her back by daylight!" Mother giggled into her glass.

"Oh, I *love* to sail," I said, speaking rapidly, as they did, crossing my arms on the table in my most sophisticated manner. But to my dismay, this only made them laugh harder. The man rattled the ice in his drink and gazed at Mother. "That's not quite what I had in mind."

"Oh, to be eleven and innocent again." Mother let out an exaggerated sigh, and she and the man smiled as they tapped their glass rims together, making a dull clink.

I began to pull at a stray thread in the hem of my shorts, sensing that my ignorance was the subject of their toast, hoping the blood I felt rising to my cheeks wasn't visible in the dimness.

Some nights Mother sent me up the stairs to bed alone, telling me to go to sleep—she would follow soon. But though I listened for her key in the door for what seemed long hours, she rarely returned before I drifted off. And the next morning, when she breezed into my room, smelling faintly of seawater and cologne, I wondered what excitement I had missed.

How enticing this adult world was, full of whispered jokes and mysterious secrets. And often, in my nighttime dreams, I imagined I, too, was a part of it, that I had learned the grown-up ways of speaking and acting that allowed my inclusion.

So I began with the bottled peanuts we kept in our room, experimenting in the mornings before Mother awoke, nibbling with my mouth closed, shutting my eyes dreamily as I chewed. I tried purring softly in enjoyment the way she did. When the local boys with fishing rods slung over their shoulders passed our beach towel, I lay on my side, a hand on my hip, like the ladies on the covers of magazines Mother read, and practiced eating plantain chips in my new alluring fashion.

"Do I look older than eleven?" I asked Mother.

She shaded her eyes with her hand and squinted at me. "Oh, infinitely. Easily twelve or thirteen." But a flickering in her smile as she turned again to her latest paperback made me determined to try harder.

On Saturdays, we visited the market in the center of town. For these excursions, Mother laid two or three sundresses on her bed, holding them against her one at a time before choosing. She donned her large-brimmed straw beach hat and round, black sunglasses. Before the mirror, she arranged the hat at various perches until she found the prettiest angle. Then we strolled along the road by the water, following the path lined with palm trees to avoid the swelter of the midday sun.

"'Oh, the fisherman's daughter, she cry, she CRY . . .'" I sang out the words I'd learned from the White Heron's cooks.

"Is this performance for the benefit of the whole island?" Mother joked when my voice swelled.

At rickety stands under the tree branches, local women sat beading coral bracelets. "Lovely ladies! Something pretty for your wrists? Just five U.S. dollars for such lovely ladies." I waved as we passed, wishing I had a pair of heeled sandals like Mother's that clicked on the pavement.

Some Saturdays we browsed through the boutiques. My favorite was called Lusanne's by the Sea. It was where my mother had bought her straw hat and two sleeveless blouses with frills adorning the chest. Everything in the shop flashed with bright colors—purple shell pendants that hung in the windows, gauzy skirts printed with birds or giant flowers, beach wraps that stirred on their hangers in the breeze from the open door. One morning the boutique bustled with tourists from a Norwegian cruise ship. Pale women fondled the trinkets and garments. In the doorway leaned three boys who looked close to my age. They were laughing with open mouths, taunting each other, pointing to some of the women and teenage girls in bikinis who sauntered up from the beach. I smiled at the tallest boy and gave a quick flutter of my eyelids. But he didn't seem to notice, and I suddenly longed to be wearing something other than my baggy shorts and flat shoes. At the back of Lusanne's was a small selection of sandals, all with cloth straps and thick, angled heels like Mother's. I slipped my feet into one of the sample pairs and studied my reflection in the full-length dressing mirror, then strode across the room toward the boys, swinging my hips from side to side with each step.

"Sexy girl," hissed one of the boys in his Nordic accent, bobbing his chin at me. His eyes trailed from my waist to my feet, and I sucked at my cheeks to keep from grinning.

To my delight, Mother agreed to buy me the shoes as well as a checkered halter top with gathered pleats in front, which gave me, for the first time, the illusion of a tiny bust. That evening, I allowed extra time in readying myself for dinner, adjusting my halter top until its folds fell in the most flattering places, winding the straps of my sandals high above my ankles. When Mother disappeared into the bathroom, lathering her legs with scented lotion, I asked if I could try applying her lipstick on my own.

"Ooh, quite the little lady tonight, aren't we?" she said, but though I waited, she added nothing further, only shook the contents of her lotion bottle.

So I fished through her cosmetic bag until I found the tube, then, with careful strokes, coated my top and bottom lips with a thicker layer than I had worn before.

Downstairs, while Mother attended to the dinner guests, I leaned against one of the wooden pillars dividing the dining area from the bar. A family with two boys my age or slightly older sat at a table to my right. I spun the ice in my ginger soda, checking my halter top now and then to make certain the pleats had not shifted. With each lull in the family's conversation, I gently kicked one of my sandaled feet into the air, flexing my calf, the bare skin of my neck and shoulders prickling as I imagined their eyes on me. But it was one of the men at the bar who noticed me first, a Carib Indian whom I had seen at the Passionflower once or twice before.

"Enjoying your drink, missy?" He cocked his head to one side, staring, so that I felt he absorbed every bit of me from the silver barrette in my hair to the wedge heels of my new shoes. Like other Carib Indians on the island, he had high cheekbones, dark eyes, and such a smooth, brown complexion that it was impossible to tell his age.

I nodded and sipped from the thin straw in my soda, trying to remember Mother's dainty way of swallowing.

"What do you have there? A Coca-Cola with rum?" He motioned with two fingers for me to take a step closer.

I smiled as I did so, pleased with his assumption. "No, just a soda," I said, as though it were simply my choice for this particular evening.

He grinned so that I could see the pink crescents of his gums and lifted his Hairoun beer to his lips. "Do you have a name, miss?"

"Opal," I told him, lowering my voice to a half-whisper as my mother did when introducing herself to men.

"Ah, a pretty name for a pretty girl." His mouth glistened wet from his beer. I flushed from the flattery, not knowing what to say.

He told me that his name was Donavan and asked what he could buy me from the bar, pointing to my nearly empty glass.

"Another soda, please," I said, swinging my leg so that the overhead lantern light caught my sandals.

As he handed me the glass, his fingers grazed mine for an instant, just as I had watched men do who offered drinks to Mother.

That night, under the cool of my sheets, I silently recited Donavan's compliments. He liked my shirt, he'd said, the way it didn't quite meet my shorts. He liked the strand of coral beads around my neck, which, he'd declared between swallows of beer, looked very grown-up. For hours I watched the wind twisting my curtains and the honey-yellow moon gleaming through my open shutters, wakeful with eager thoughts.

The following week, I convinced Mother to buy me a second halter top and a fitted red miniskirt with a calla lily painted on the pocket. And I began while dressing to take scraps of toilet tissue from the bathroom and fold them into two wads. These I arranged under the cotton of my blouse so that two small mounds protruded. I was learning the right clothes to wear, the way to stand with my hip askew and smile in order to draw attention. I was discovering the womanly manner of chattering nonchalantly that invited approving, winking eyes.

No longer did I eat my suppers in solitude on the bamboo love seat in the corner, finding that if I lingered near the bar, pointing my toes, glancing every so often at the crowd, it was only a matter of time before Donavan or one of his friends approached me with a soda and soft phrases that seemed to seep through my skin. "Looking so lovely in your skirt tonight, missy." "Such a nice smile you have, miss. Sweet like sugar."

One evening after Mother finished her shift, I announced to her the many attentions I had received that night, tossing my wrists as I spoke as though these were things to which I had grown quite accustomed.

"Oh, Opal," she said, sweeping her fingers through her hair so that it fanned behind her neck. And she shook her head, her lips curling as though I had made some silly mistake. "Lord *knows* how many drinks those men have had!"

No! No! She didn't understand how their eyes had glittered as they talked to me, how their voices had crooned with meaning. But before I could tell her, Mother was joined by some visitor from a neighboring table. Within minutes they were deep in conversation, their shoulders brushing, no longer aware of my presence.

Midway through the summer, a group of twelve Americans arrived at the White Heron. They would stay for five weeks, we learned, in the guest bungalows at the far end of the courtyard. Among the twelve were two middle-aged couples, a family with three small children—white as the guinea fowl in Ezra Dupree's coop, two young women who wore matching hair scarves, and a graying, olive-skinned man who reminded me of Cary Grant, the old movie actor. Raymond Mordue, we soon discovered, was his name.

"*He's* handsome, isn't he," Mother said, spotting him across the restaurant patio as we descended for dinner.

"Oh, yes," I agreed, repeating her enthusiastic tone. "Very handsome."

She shook her head with amusement as if she hadn't really expected me to respond. "A little old for you, my pet, don't you think?" she laughed.

I smiled as broadly as I could in case she should suspect the lump tightening in my throat. Then I watched as she glided off to seat the first table of guests, the diaphanous rose of her skirt fluttering behind.

Late into the third evening of his stay, after dining with his friends,

Raymond Mordue meandered toward the dimly lit table where I had joined Mother, and asked if he might pull up a chair. He wore a thick cologne that tickled my nostrils, like the scented incense coils that burned in some of the local shops. He had just returned from traveling through all of Asia and much of Africa, he said, having recently retired from his job in advertising. He traced his tanned fingers over the tabletop as he spoke, outlining a map of his route. In the autumn, he would be joining a friend's wine import business, but a few decadent weeks in the Caribbean seemed a perfect conclusion to his time off. Unlike the other men whose company Mother had accepted, Raymond addressed his every word to *both* of us. As he told of safaris in Kenya, mountain hikes through Tibet, he gazed into my eyes as well as Mother's, was pleased, I thought, with my interest as much as hers. I nodded as he talked and propped my hands on the table edge, displaying the iridescent pink with which I'd polished my nails earlier in the day. Every few moments I peered at Mother, wondering if she recognized the way I was being included.

Soon Raymond began to join us not only for drinks but for meals. In the afternoons, too, he would find us on the beach and, removing his terrycloth shirt, stretch in his swim trunks alongside our towels. Always he arrived bearing some special food that he had purchased from one of the vendors in town—papaya juice, lime-colored breadfruits, guava jam, pumpkin bread.

"One should always experience new tastes, don't you think?" he said in his smooth voice that seemed to match the hush of the waves.

"I couldn't agree more." Mother smiled, then bit into soursop ice cream or a custard apple, allowing shining rivulets of juice to trickle down her chin, giggling and licking her lips as Raymond dotted below her mouth with the corner of his shirt.

At our luncheon table, Raymond would tell us to close our eyes, then would present unusual dishes he had ordered from roadside stands or convinced the kitchen staff to prepare—salt fish fritters, curried figs, broiled eel.

"I'll try some, too," I said, watching as Raymond lifted forkfuls of eel for Mother to swallow.

She shook her head so that the shell earrings in her ears jingled. "Trust me, Opal, you wouldn't like it. Wait a few years. In the meantime, finish your soup." Then turning to Raymond, she laughed. "Quite precocious, if you know what I mean."

I crossed my legs as elegantly as I could, my heart throbbing, hoping my voice wouldn't choke. "Yes, I *would* like it. I eat all *kinds* of things!"

Mother only shrugged her shoulders, and Raymond did not look up from his plate. But a moment later, when she excused herself to the ladies' room, Raymond, to my delight, scooped a bit of the fish onto his fork and leaned toward me.

"Oh, thank you," I said, trying to use my most careless tone, as though being fed by men were an ordinary occurrence for me. I straightened in my chair to make the profile of my padded bustline more prominent.

"Do you like it?" I could tell that Raymond watched me carefully as I chewed, awaiting my reaction.

"Delicious," I nodded, though I had not truly tasted the food; I could concentrate on nothing other than Raymond's outstretched fingers patting my knee, just as I'd seen him sometimes cup the roundness of my mother's shoulder. And as perspiration threaded down the center of my back, I tried to memorize the position of his hand, proof of my sophistication.

There were other occasions, also, I believed, that confirmed Raymond's appreciation of me, verified my initiation into adulthood. Once, while Mother was napping, I caught him standing ankle-deep in surf, gazing at me as I swam in the water, his sunglasses pulled low on his nose. So I glided with my longest strokes through the rippling waves, careful not to smack the surface like the young children splashing near me. When I emerged onto the sand, Raymond strolled toward me, my towel draped over his arm.

"What a natural swimmer you are," he said, grinning as he folded the towel around my shoulders. "As pretty as a little mermaid."

And not long after this he showed his fondness, too, through a ritual he began of hiding treasures for me in his breast pocket. Whenever Mother disappeared to order a drink or have a word with the hotel manager, he would rub the front of his shirt so that I could hear some secret thing inside snap or crinkle. Then he would bend forward, pulling at the edge of his pocket for me to reach in. There I would find a cellophane bag of sugared pecans, sweet-smelling tamarind candies wrapped in foil, a heart-shaped molasses cookie. "Just for you, Opal," he would pronounce as I reached into the cotton material to retrieve my gift. After savoring my treats, I would smooth the bits of ribbon or shiny paper in which they had been packaged and lay them in the straw dish on my bedside table, creating a growing display. Just as Mother kept on her bureau top an amber-colored bottle of perfume from Raymond and two pearly white stones he had found for her on the beach, I had my own evidences of his favor.

But as days passed, I began to notice that, when the three of us were together, they had less time for me. Always Mother insisted on sitting with her arm linked through his, her hair bouncing against his shoulder, murmuring phrases so that I could take no part in their conversations. She began to disappear with him—leaving me behind—to take oceanside walks to the cove around the bend, or beyond the cluster of manchineel trees down the beach to view the evening stars. From the hotel porch I could see their shadowy silhouettes—Raymond's head bowed toward Mother's, one hand slipping along her side and hip as, with the other, he fed her the sliced pineapple or orange he had brought with them. "Be good, Opal," Mother always said before they left, as though I were no more than a baby. And I would fiddle with the ties of my sandals, pretending preoccupation, squeezing my jaw until it ached, determined not to shed a single tear.

I was certain, however, that it was not Raymond's choice to neglect me. Several times he turned to wink at me over his shoulder as they left.

And one night, before the two of them wandered off to his bungalow, he lingered behind for a moment, pausing to kiss his fingertip and press it to my cheek. So it was Mother, I decided, who sought their solitude, wanting for herself every minute of his time.

One afternoon, as we waited for Raymond to join us on the sand, Mother rolled on her side to show off the curve of her hip and announced that she and Raymond would be chartering a sailboat at the end of the week to explore one of the neighboring islands, an all-day excursion.

"Raymond thought it would be nice if he and I spent the day alone together. Can you find a way to amuse yourself, Opal? Why don't you introduce yourself to some of the local children?"

I crossed one knee over the other, too angry to respond, jiggling my foot in my heeled sandals, which I now wore even on the beach. Never before had Raymond dismissed me like this, intentionally excluding me from their grown-up plans. But I *knew* why. *She* was making him forget about me. With her constant sighings in his ear, her exclamations over each meal they shared, the new dress she flaunted that bared her back. I tried to count the days since Raymond's last gift to me—a chunk of fresh coconut in a chocolate shell; it had been many. If I could only speak with him—just for a few moments—talk to him without Mother's interference. Then he would recall the pleasure he had found in my company, as well. And Mother would be amazed by how quickly he would change his mind, asking me—please, please—to join their trip.

M ost evenings Raymond, I knew, did not appear at dinner until close to eight o'clock, two hours after Mother's hosting duties began. According to her, he liked to relax in his bungalow before eating, reading a book in his canvas chair beside the window or listening to classical music on his portable cassette player. This, it seemed, would be my only opportunity, and I resolved to use it. So, one night, I paid even more than the usual attentions to my face, my hair, my outfit, sneaking dabs of Mother's silver shadow for my eyelids, fussing with the seams of my halter top and shorts until I was satisfied. And as soon as Mother waved a kiss and rushed out the door, I reached for the amber bottle on her bureau, spraying a fine mist over my neck and shoulders.

It was beginning to grow dark. The kerosene lanterns along the courtyard path had been lit, and insects flitted in a gray-white halo above each one. Raymond's cabin was the last one on the left, and as I drew closer, I thought I could hear strains of music through the open windows. My hands began to shake, but I told myself this was foolishness. Didn't I look stylish and grown-up? Hadn't I practiced what I was going to say?

And when I reached his front step, I saw how silly my nervousness was. How happy Raymond was to see me, he said, ushering me in through the screen door, clearing a stack of books from a wood-framed sofa for me to sit down. He turned a knob on his cassette player, lowering the sound of pulsing stringed instruments. What a welcome surprise! Would I like some pineapple juice and tonic? He brought me the glass and then, leaning his hip against the bookshelf across from me, listened intently as I spoke. No, oh, no, he said when I had finished. Where did I get the idea he no longer enjoyed my companionship? Of course, it was true, my mother was quite beautiful; he would not deny her charms. But, no, never once had he thought of me as a baby. If I wished, later we could discuss my inclusion in the boating trip. "Would you like that, Opal?" he said, suddenly putting his drink aside and striding toward me. He was whispering, whispering as he moved, then whispering through my hair, "Opal, Opal. Opal is not a baby but an exquisite young woman." My heart thudded with the unexpected compliment, the words humming through my mind. But to my shame, the shaking started again as Raymond looped a strand of my hair around his forefinger, his face so close to my neck— just as I'd seen him bend against Mother's—that I could feel the moisture of his breath, I could hear the *shhh* of his every exhale.

"Just as lovely as your mother," Raymond said. "May I show you that

I like spending time with you, too? How about a bite to eat? May I feed you something, something that your mother enjoys? Would you like something exotic, Opal? Hmm?"

I nodded to show my willingness and opened my mouth as he reached into a bowl and dropped what seemed to be dark berries on my tongue, tangy and ripe. I tried to smile as I thought Mother would. I pressed my hands together so that he would not see the trembling. *An exquisite young woman.* I was *an exquisite young woman.* I would not act like a little girl. And a young woman, I told myself as Raymond bent closer, would only laugh when a man's mouth kissed her cheeks or her forehead or her chin. She would not flinch if his fingers hovered over her lips. She would not start if his hands slid below her ribs. But though I reminded myself of these things, the shaking only grew worse, spreading to my thighs, my knees, my chest. Would the shivering make Raymond stop? Soon, soon it would make him stop, was all I could think as he peeked beneath the elastic of my halter top, as his hands squeezed me until I went numb. But he did not stop. He would not stop, he said, because I had shown him I was not a little child. Didn't I want to know the things men did with women? he asked as he dangled a bit of dried fruit for me to taste.

But the things I learned as the hardness of him sawed back and forth, back and forth inside me made me quake so that it seemed I could hear my bones rattle. They rattled and rattled while he taught me, until I thought something in me would shatter.

⁓

The group of twelve Americans, including Raymond, was scheduled to leave on a Saturday in the final week of August. Eight days away. Hot, breezeless days that I thought would stretch forever. The night I'd returned from Raymond's bungalow I had drawn closed the linen curtains in my bedroom, folding their ruffled ends under the screen. But now and then, in the following days, the material would fly open without warning, revealing an unexpected glimpse of Raymond's cabin, triggering another bout of shaking I could do nothing to quell.

I spent those next mornings and afternoons curled over books in the quietest nook of the White Heron's reading room—complaining to Mother of heatstroke—trying to ignore the way my hands stiffened against the volume in my lap with each male voice that echoed up from the beach, each heavy set of footsteps that crossed the patio outside. For eight nights I ate early suppers, hidden in the empty pantry off the staff kitchen, disappearing to bed before Raymond's arrival at dinner. And no longer did I request the fritters, curried stews, tropical fruits, and other adventurous dishes I had favored in the past. Suddenly I could tolerate only the blandest foods—dry toast, vegetable broth, boiled chicken. At breakfast, I watched as Mother slathered banana muffins with the passion fruit jam Raymond had recommended. Each time her spoon scooped into the sticky jar, I felt my stomach turn. When she returned to our suite late at night, I caught whiffs of the dinner odors that emanated from her clothes. Spices and briny seafood smells, smells that made me think of Raymond, smells that made me choke.

On the morning of Raymond's departure, I lay in bed watching the shifting patterns of sunlight and shadow on my slatted ceiling. I did not stir until the commotion of banging doors and dragged luggage ceased and the rumble of the van that would take the American group to the airport died, fading into silence down the dirt road that led across the island.

Moments later Mother peered into my room. Behind her left ear she had tucked a wide-petaled frangipani. I saw that she was holding an enormous matching bouquet.

"From Raymond," she said in explanation, lifting the bouquet so that it touched the tip of her nose. "Oh, and he left something for you, too." She pulled from her sundress pocket a sheer plastic bag filled with shiny foil-wrapped discs. Holding the bag by its cherry red bow, she placed it on my dresser. "Looks like little bonbons. La dee da. Getting fancy gifts from men now." And, laughing, she lightly stroked the flower over her ear.

"I don't want them!" I said. "I don't want them. You take them!"

This only made her laugh again. "Opal, don't be silly. Men won't want to give you presents if you toss them away frivolously. I guess"—she smiled, tapping me on the head with her thick bouquet—"there is much you still have left to learn."

She continued to speak, but I stopped my hands to my ears and squeezed shut my eyes. Wishing, wishing to block out the things I had yet to know.

PARTIES IN THE PENTHOUSE

(Francesca's Story)

· *1984* ·

Peering over the banister at the top of the stairs, I could see the feet of the arriving guests. Black, glossy men's shoes, blue and slate and pin-striped trouser cuffs. Pointed toes and women's heels poking from beneath silky skirts.

Christopher, my younger brother, was already downstairs, his feet rocking excitedly in his penny loafers. In a moment or two, my parents would discover my absence and scold me for failing to greet their entering guests. When Mother and Father had parties, Christopher and I were instructed to make an appearance, to introduce ourselves to their friends, and, as Mother put it, "to engage in polite conversation." But I so detested the outfit Mother had chosen for me this night that I had decided to take a stand. When she'd slid the dress from its plastic Bergdorf bag earlier that evening, I had crossed one arm over the other. "I won't wear it!"

"What's gotten into you, Francesca?" Mother traced fingers over her hair, which had been puffed and coiled at the salon that afternoon. "It's a lovely dress. Besides, it's the style for girls your age this season." She made a small kissing sound and patted the side of my cheek.

"Why can't I wear my purple jacket and skirt? What's wrong with my purple suit?"

"Please, Franny!" And then Mother rushed from my room, the skirts of her stiff red gown rustling. One of the caterers had called to her from downstairs, a question about a tray of sliced fruit.

Once zippered into the dress, I had squinted at my reflection in the gilt-framed mirror above my bureau. The gown had a gathering of pleats at the waist that accentuated the thickness of my middle. When I turned sideways, an ugly excess of stomach protruded. And the material was an odd grayish taupe. Somehow it made the pale brown of my hair duller; it emphasized the freckles that sprinkled my nose and chest.

It is because of the new apartment, I thought, yanking at the slippery folds that clung to my hips. Just three months before, we had moved from a ninth-floor apartment in our building on Park Avenue—my home for the first fourteen and a half years of my life—to the penthouse. The move upstairs, during the third week of January, had followed Father's promotion at Scully & Freed. "What great fortune! You've worked hard for this, Spencer!" Mother exclaimed when Father first gave the news. She had toasted him that evening at dinner with a fancy bottle of wine, pouring quarter-glasses for Christopher and me as well, including us in the celebration. Later, after Christopher and I had brushed our teeth and changed into pajamas, she had squeezed us tightly, rumpling our hair as though we were still tiny children. "We're not babies, Mother!" I'd said, but she'd only smiled, her eyes flickering with expectancy, wide, wide-awake, the way I thought I recalled her eyes had looked when I was much younger. So I'd wondered if some better life awaited us now. A life happy enough to swallow up trouble, the things I still remembered from the year I was eight, when I had caught Mother returning from certain late-night parties before Father. Then her bedroom had been just across the hall from mine, and I'd seen her, slipping in, turning on her light, watched through her half-open door as she'd studied herself in her vanity for long minutes before unhooking her dress or pulling earrings from her ears. She was so pretty, prettier than the mothers of any of my friends, so I could not understand what she saw that made the edges of her mouth sag with sourness or made her strip the pins from her hair, scattering them on the vanity top, not caring that a few fell to the floor.

Later she had smoked a cigarette in the bathroom down the hall—a smell I recognized at that time from visits to my uncle Theo's but never from her. She had once complained the odor disgusted her, but now, just like that, she seemed to want different things. In the mornings, she no longer shared breakfast with Christopher and me, but sipped only coffee, lighting a cigarette before pouring milk over our bowls of Life or Captain Crunch. She bought pants I knew would not have fit her months before and spent longer minutes in the bathroom fussing over her makeup before walking Christopher and me to school.

And things began to vex her, things I knew once hadn't: the way Christopher regularly spilled lunch down his shirt and pants at school or woke during the night calling for water. Or that I had dressed with my ballet leotard tag-side out for the Mother-Daughter recital. She'd snapped only a single photo while other mothers' cameras clicked noisily. "What a treat," she said when it was over, but she seemed to have no intention of lingering as she had the year before, wanting me to pose for a final picture in the hall near the dressing room, telling me she was very proud, helping me loosen the tight bun at the back of my head, then combing out my hair with her fingers.

I did not like her new habit, when Father tried to joke with her, of replying only with matters of business—the bill that was due to her ladies' club in midtown, the dinner plans they had for the following weekend. Or her way of turning to the nearest chore—refilling the hall candy dish with mints, plucking dead petals from the potted azalea—if Christopher or I added jokes of our own.

"Don't *placate* me," I'd heard her hiss to Father as he placed his hand on the small of her back, crossing Ninetieth Street on our way to church one Sunday. Afterward, she had wanted to skip lunch at our favorite neighborhood restaurant. I guessed Mother's dissatisfactions had something to do with Anne-Marie Werther—the Werthers, friends my parents had seen almost weekly for cocktails at our house or theirs, or at parties with mutual acquaintances. Because, with no warning, we stopped seeing them. The only communication now between Mother and Anne-Marie seemed to be occasional notes or postcards from vacations. And when Christopher and I received an invitation to Trevor Werther's tenth birthday—a swimming party at The River Club—Mother called to say, regrettably, we'd made previous plans, though I knew this was a fat fib.

"But I *want* to go, Mother!" I said as she returned the phone to the receiver.

"We have a full schedule this week, Franny," was all she answered, her face flushing in a way I knew she was thinking her own thoughts, as she seemed *always* to be doing now. She had hardly heard my words at all as she popped open a bottle of Perrier from the fridge and blew smoke straight up over our heads, tapping and tapping over her little blue glass tray long after her ashes had dropped off.

When I was eleven or so, a card arrived from the Werther family, a brief greeting from their recent trip to Florence, inside a Polaroid shot of the four of them, Mrs. Werther in a fancy wide-brimmed hat. "Oh!" Mother said when she opened it, her voice so sharp I thought she'd nicked her finger on the edge of the envelope. After a moment, I saw that her hand holding the card was uninjured, still I could not stop thinking of how, the week before, I'd seen Father move the letter opener, from its usual spot where Mother kept mail, to the desk in his study; and this seemed suddenly a selfishness beyond explanation.

"You're much prettier than Mrs. Werther, Mother!" I told her.

But Mother did not smile gratefully or lift her hand to pet my hair as I expected she would, only tucked the card back into the pile of mail to be sorted later, making a small cough of a laugh. "What a funny thing to say, Franny." She glanced at the reflection of us both in the front hall mirror—she in the denim pants worn only around the house because she said they made her hips look wide, I in my sundress with the navy and red stripes, the one Mother had tried for months to convince me to give to Goodwill because it stretched too tightly across my middle now. And she squinted in a way that made me wish I had never given the compliment.

But things would change in the penthouse. Mother loved it so much there would be no time for short tempers, for old worries. She loved the ten-foot ceilings with their dentil moldings, the spacious bedrooms on the second floor, I heard her tell Father when we walked through the apartment as a family for the first time. And the paneling in the library and—Oh!—the French doors to the terrace, which wrapped the apartment on three sides. So I began to count the days until the renovations would be finished. It had not occurred to me that, with this formal home, Mother would find only more to preoccupy her, more things she wanted just so. For my bedroom, across from Christopher's, at the far end of the upstairs hall, Mother had purchased sage-colored damask drapes to match the heavy fabric of my dust ruffle, and thickly stuffed pillows for my bed. When I asked if I could paint the borders at the base of the walls, as I had in my previous room, with a pattern of butterflies and rainbows, she forbade me. "It would be such a shame to mar your beautiful moldings, Franny!" And she claimed the clay animals and pinch pots I had made in school over the years and liked to display across my bureau must have disappeared in the move, but I had other suspicions.

"I liked it better in our old house," I told Christopher as we worked on a one-thousand-piece jigsaw puzzle on his carpeted floor. And he nodded agreeably but, to my irritation, glanced over his shoulder at his brand-new bed and tall windows and the bookcases holding his model cars and lead soldiers. Only ten years old, he had agreed without complaint when told he could no longer leave his Lincoln Log or Tinkertoy constructions around the room for days on end nor sprawl on his bed in the daytime for fear the duvet cover would crease. "You're just too young to be angry about how properly we have to keep *everything!*" I told him.

And now, even my own appearance, it seemed, required improvement. These were the injustices I stewed over from the stairwell as louder and louder fragments of conversation from Mother and Father's party, peals of laughter floated up to me. Above the voices, I could hear Father addressing his guests by name, ushering them out of the foyer and into the living room. The swirl of Mother's red skirts crossed the hall—once, twice, three times—as she moved from friend to friend. If she looked up, she would see my legs through the banister rails. *What are you doing, Francesca? It's half past seven! I expected you downstairs thirty minutes ago.*

No. No, I refuse to go unless I can wear something else! I envisioned the flames that would flash across Mother's cheeks at the strength of my tone. *Then* she would understand how unhappy she had made me. *Then* she would apologize, stroking my hair with both hands as she used to do when I was little. *I'm sorry, Francesca, truly, I am sorry.* The imagined words brought a scratchy lump to my throat.

A combination of smells I couldn't name began to emanate from the kitchen. The trim black pant cuffs and patent leather shoes of caterers whisked back and forth. I wondered if they were serving any of the miniature fried egg rolls that I loved. Usually these were passed with a sweet, plum-colored dipping sauce that made the roof of my mouth tingle.

The front hall began to clear; everyone had wandered into other rooms of the apartment. A man with a raspy voice was telling jokes. I could hear the clink of ice in glasses as women laughed. Two caterers returned to the hall and paused at the table near the entry before scurrying back to the kitchen. Creeping down a few steps, I could see that, surrounding a vase exploding with white roses, they had set silver trays of food on the marble tabletop. One tray held wedges of cheese and clusters of purple grapes, another strips of chicken on wooden skewers.

There were plates full of meat pastries and heart-shaped potato fritters and crackers topped with a pink spread. Then, at the end of the table, I spotted a lazy Susan piled with the egg rolls I'd hoped for. If I dashed down the stairs and quickly ran up again, I could escape being noticed.

A stack of powder-blue linen napkins lay on the table. With quick fingers, I grabbed a handful of the rolls, a few pastries, cubes of yellow and orange cheese. I dropped them into a napkin and darted back upstairs. The crispy rolls were still warm from the oven. As I chewed, they filled my mouth with steam. It was eight o'clock. I had missed the first hour of my parents' party. Incredible that my absence had gone unnoticed for this long. Ha! I covered my mouth with both hands, afraid I would giggle out loud. The hallway was still empty; I might as well run downstairs for another fried roll. Plucking a fresh napkin, I added to my bundle two potato fritters the width of my palm. At the head of the stairs, I spread the napkin across my knees and pushed a hole in one of the fritters, sticking my tongue into the center, licking at the salty softness inside. Between the shreds of potato hid melted drops of butter. When I had hollowed out the middle, I popped the remainder into my mouth, swallowing it down in a single bite. After the second fritter my stomach began to bubble noisily with air. I eyed the egg roll still in my napkin. Its greasy shell had left a spattering of stains on the blue linen. I folded the napkin in quarters over the roll to save for later.

Mother and Father's friends seemed almost to be shouting now, and I wondered how they could hear one another. If I were downstairs, I thought, some guest would be questioning me about school—my favorite class, whether or not I was studying a language, what sport I most enjoyed. I would be introduced to one of my parents' chatty acquaintances and then another. I unfurled my napkin and sniffed the roll, then rewrapped it. It was already ten minutes to nine. No one had crossed the hallway for some time.

"*Franny?*" My heart pounding, I rose to my feet. Was it Mother calling to me from downstairs, angrily, having realized my absence? Or had it been another name? Another woman's voice? It was so difficult to tell among the chaos of words. Then: *"Dan-ny?"* I heard it again, not my name at all. I squeezed the napkin wrapping the roll into a wad and shifted in my seat on the steps. The hard wood had begun to numb my backside, and I wanted to stretch my legs. If I tiptoed quietly along the stairs and poked my head into the living room for just an instant, who would catch me? Just a quick peek at the dresses and suits, the plates of food.

There were even more guests than I had imagined. How was it possible my parents knew so many people? And they seemed to know one another, too, weaving from living room to library to terrace to greet one another, the men clapping shoulders, the women kissing cheeks. There were even a few children, some close to my age. I recognized two boys from Christopher's school and a girl who had been in my art class years before. One girl wore a dress similar to mine in pastel yellow. Her arms, her waist, her hips were as slender as flower stems. She was nibbling a tiny cookie, running a finger around her mouth every so often to check for crumbs. Father was at the far end of the living room, only the back of him visible in his navy jacket. Christopher was beside him, one fist thrust into his pants pocket as Father's was. Father patted the elbow of the man on his right, and Christopher offered his hand, too, for an introduction. The room seemed a blur of sequined blouses and shimmering skirts, jeweled wrists and drink glasses, so it was hard to focus, hard to concentrate on any one person in the crowd.

Eventually I spotted Mother among a circle of women, a champagne flute in her right hand, a small plate in her left. Even from a distance, I could see her cheeks glowed pink. The red hem of her gown fluttered above her feet as she laughed with the women around her. Then she turned and began searching the room. I followed her gaze as it swept over each band of guests, each face. And it was not impatience or irritation I saw in her eyes but concentration. Or was it concern? Oh! I would permit her to find me where I stood. *No.* No, I would rush to her! But then I saw her eyes fix on Father instead. He was stepping over to Mrs. Mitchell, whose hair was loose for a change and whose black gown had a long slit along her right leg. So it was *he* Mother had been checking for, and she did not look away until one of the caterers moved to the center of the room with a tray of stuffed pastries. Then Mother seemed suddenly to remember something, and setting her dish on the coffee table, began to thread through the guests. Smiling, the burgundy of her lipstick glittering against her teeth, she waved to the caterer, and he followed her through the crowd, balancing his silver moon of a tray high in the air.

When they returned to the group of women, the caterer, with a bow of his chin, gently lowered the tray. Fingers reached for napkins and pastries. Mother handed an hors d'oeuvre to a woman in a sheer sleeveless blouse—the mother of the girl in yellow, I decided, since the girl seemed always to be standing behind her, blotting her lips carefully, taking cautious sips from a clear plastic glass. Then Mother leaned toward the girl, speaking something near her. When the girl nodded, Mother motioned to the caterer and gracefully lifted a pastry from his tray, then placed it into the girl's open palm. They stood so close their blond heads nearly touched. The girl's hair brushed Mother's shoulder as she smiled with tiny, closed lips, her narrow nose twitching slightly. Instead of chewing the pastry in one gulp, she took miniature bites at its edges, licking it now and then to prevent the filling from dripping. I watched her until every bit of the pastry had disappeared.

In the hall, the marble table was still piled with appetizers. I crammed my napkin with as many fritters and cheese squares and crackers as it would hold. Then I climbed the stairs with clattering footsteps, not caring who heard me.

Seated cross-legged on the handwoven Indian carpet Mother had recently purchased for my room, I devoured one hors d'oeuvre after another. Within minutes, a dusting of crumbs littered the new rug, but I made no attempt to brush them away, only gobbled bite after bite until the first heave of nausea hit. Then, when the last morsel had been swallowed, I threw myself onto my bed unwashed, having tossed my dress to the floor, letting it lie in a crumpled puddle.

In the first days of September, before my ninth-grade year and Christopher's fifth, the streets of New York flooded again with zigzagging cars and jostling pedestrians as they did at the close of every summer. We, too, had just returned from two months away at the house we rented in Montauk for every July and August.

"It's invigorating, isn't it?" Mother said one glaringly blue morning as we stood on the terrace watching the bustling people below. "The city rushing with life—surging once more with energy." She sipped from the polka-dotted mug of coffee in her moisturized hand and tucked a stray wisp of hair behind her ear. She'd lightened it a shade, I thought, more streaks of yellow.

"You must be excited for the first year of high school."

I shrugged my shoulders. "I guess it won't be much different from last year."

I squinted through the trees of Central Park to see if I could make out the flat gray oval of the reservoir.

"If you want to invite any friends to the recital tomorrow night, you are welcome to. Everyone must be back from vacation by now."

I shrugged again. I had only two girlfriends, really—Sharon Frasier and Emily McKenzie. Sharon was expected home for dinner every night, and I was temporarily avoiding Emily—she'd responded to none of the letters I had mailed her at summer camp. "I'd rather not." Besides, I couldn't imagine any reason they would want to sit in our living room for two solid hours of harp music, even if the harpist *was* "heaven inspired," as Mother had exclaimed after seeing her perform the previous spring.

"Are you sure? Larissa Balliet is so gifted. I bet your friends would enjoy her. I think it'll be fun!" Mother leaned her hip against the terrace rail. The breeze lifted the hair from her neck. Then, glancing at her watch, she said, "I suppose I should make a few phone calls. Breakfast is

on the table. Just don't touch any of the wrapped appetizers in the refrigerator, love. They are to be saved for tomorrow evening."

The afternoon before the recital, white-painted rental chairs with gold
cushions arrived and were arranged in rows facing the living room fire-
place. Mother adjusted their fabric ties and placed the programs she'd had
printed on each seat. She set bowls of pink rosebuds on the two living room
coffee tables and a vase of white tulips and lilies and peonies in the foyer.

"The house looks nice," I said. It had suddenly occurred to me that
possibly the Dempseys had been invited, and if so, might bring their son
Jamie. "The East Coast Hottie," Sharon and Emily called him because Emily had kissed him once at a wedding reception in Amagansett and told us
his lips made her feel she would slide to the ground and melt into a puddle.
Behind her back, Sharon and I agreed she was exaggerating, but this did
not stop me from thinking of Jamie Dempsey when I watched movie love
scenes, or imagining what it might be like to kiss him in the pouring rain.

"Are the Dempseys coming?" I asked Mother as nonchalantly as I could.
"Or the Hanovers?" I added, just so that she would not grow suspicious.

"Dempseys—no. Hanovers—yes."

"Oh," I said, as though the answer made no difference to me, and
stood watching Mother for a minute. Her flowers really did look beautiful, her arrangements always prettier than those from the florist. And I
considered telling her so.

"Is there something else you need, Fran? I've a *million* things left to
do," Mother sighed.

"Not a thing." And I would not say a word about her flowers.

It had been hours since lunch. From the fridge door, I poured myself
a glass of Pepsi. On the refrigerator shelves were rows of finished hors
d'oeuvres in protective plastic. One metal tray held puffed orange wafers
that looked to be made with cheddar, the appetizers I had been forbidden
to eat. But who would miss one from the corner? I took a gulp of soda
then fished a single wafer from under the cling wrap. It had a spicy flavor

that I liked, and I snatched another. Then a third. A fourth, and then one more, until a gaping hole formed in the center of the tray, too large to hide.

Several minutes before her guests were expected, Mother rapped on my bedroom door. "There's something I'd like to discuss with you later this evening, Francesca." She spoke quickly, breathlessly. Through the closed door I could smell the sugary, petal scent of her perfume.

"What is it?" But she was already gone. I could hear her heels thumping on the carpet. So she would wait until after the recital for her reprimand. Perhaps she thought the delay would give me time to regret my actions.

After the final chord from Larissa Balliet's harp, after the last guest had left, I sat in bed waiting, my bed lamp switched on, my copy of *To Kill a Mockingbird* propped open on the blankets I had pulled to my chest. I had finished the first two chapters and begun the third. Down the hall I could hear water running in my parents' bathroom, the murmur of their voices, the clicking on and off of lights, and footsteps fading down the corridor. Then . . . nothing. Quiet. Only the faint rhythm of car tires whistling on the avenue below. During the hubbub of the recital, had my misdeeds been forgotten? Ha! I folded down the corner of my page to mark my place and set the book on my night table, then switched off my bedside lamp. Ha! Ha! But I turned in my tangled blanket for what seemed like hours before finally dropping off to sleep.

Every morning Mother directed Carmen, our housekeeper, to set a blue lacquered plate of croissants or brioche rolls on the breakfast-room table. This was more civilized than the bowls of cereal Christopher and I used to gulp down at breakfast, I heard her tell Carmen. After sipping her coffee and extinguishing her cigarette, Mother sometimes picked at a pastry, but always, I slathered my rolls or croissants with strawberry jam, finishing them entirely, then washed them down with a glass of orange juice. But by early fall, I noticed I felt unsatisfied even before I'd walked the nine blocks to school. So I began to visit the cafeteria before my first class for a cream cheese bagel and a carton of fruit punch.

In the afternoons, by the time I returned home, another wave of ravenous hunger overtook me. While Mother was busy upstairs with her late-day regimen of toning exercises, I combed the cabinets and refrigerator. From leftovers, I created elaborate snacks—cold slices of quiche, steamed dumplings, pecan cookies—eating these with my right hand, my left holding open whichever volume I was currently reading of the solve-your-own mystery series I'd discovered at the local bookstore.

I had always been plumpish around the midsection, but after some time, I could not deny a growing change in my body. I studied the swelling in the full-length mirror on my bathroom door as I undressed each morning and night. But it was not really a worrisome gain. Just a slight lumpiness at the tops of my thighs, a minor spreading above my hips. This was part of maturing, anyway, according to Mrs. Donald, the health teacher at my all-girls school, who brought charts and diagrams with embarrassingly accurate renditions of female forms into our classroom to indicate how our figures would thicken and curve. She, herself, had mentioned, during her talk on menstruation (which had made us all roll our eyes at our neighbors and fidget in our desk chairs), the increased appetite we might experience. Besides, I had noticed proudly, along with the expanding of my legs and middle, two small mounds were taking shape, conspicuous enough that Mother had returned with three lacy training bras from the misses department.

One morning after gym class, Sharon recited the regulations of a new diet, her latest among a slew of weight-loss experiments from teen magazines. Though, as far as I knew, she was as fickle with these as she was with her exercise routines—running, jump-roping in place, a toning video with Jane Fonda.

"This one's all-citrus," she said, wiping perspiration beads from her brow with the sleeve of her gray sweatshirt. "Maybe we could do it together." She twisted to inspect her backside, which had been disproportionately large for her body since third grade, making a firm balloon in her gym shorts, in the tunics we had worn in lower school, and now in our navy skirts. "Talk about irony," I'd said to her once, watching her fuss with the pleats of her uniform. "They give us these to make us identical, but the same outfit on forty-four girls only exaggerates our differences! Ha!" But Sharon had only given a final tug to her waistband, and, looking insulted, accused me of being disagreeable. Now she opened her locker and studied the poster she'd taped inside of Farrah Fawcett in a red swimsuit, breasts thrust forward, winged hair tossed back—this the image of womanly perfection personified, Kenneth, her older brother, had told her—the photo serving as a constant reminder, she'd once explained, of her ultimate, ultimate goal.

"How can you keep that poster?" I asked her for the hundredth time. "It's for hormonal teenage boys! And about your citrus plan—I am *not* interested in fad diets."

Sharon shrugged her shoulders. "It works," she said. "I saw a program about it on TV." She seemed to be examining my middle as I shimmied out of my sweatpants and into my school skirt. To my annoyance, I had to inhale deeply before the buttons would fasten.

"Grapefruits are a diuretic," she informed me as we carried our books to math class. "You can lose ten pounds in a week!"

"Who wants to live on grapefruits?" I stuck out my tongue in disgust, my stomach muscles beginning to ache from trying to suck them flat.

At the end of November, our school began preparations for the holiday concert, given each year before the winter break.

"You don't have to go," I had told Mother when the invitation arrived in the mail in its square, pine-tree-green envelope lined with red. "You won't even be able to hear me. I don't have a solo, and I stand at the far end of the stage."

Mother was in black spandex pants and a thin T-shirt, her hairline dark from dampness. Recently, she had purchased a treadmill and a stationary bicycle, which she kept in the spare bedroom. "Need to keep things tightened up, you know!" she'd laughed to me, patting her rear when the equipment had been delivered. Now, though, she was sorting through newly received holiday cards, some of which included photographs—families seated in front of Christmas trees or standing atop snow-covered mountains in sleek skiwear. I knew from the way she chewed the side of her cheek she was measuring, comparing.

"Oh, don't be silly, Franny. I'm looking forward to it. Your father, too. See. It's already in my calendar." And uncapping a pen, she scribbled a note in the datebook on her desk.

For weeks, our chorus director, Mr. Slattery, drilled into us the rhythms of "Adeste Fideles," "O Little Town of Bethlehem," and "I Had a Little Dreidel." He taught us to overenunciate every syllable so that the audience would catch each word. Again and again, we practiced processing on and off the stage, bowing for applause, singing with our chests up, our shoulders down, our arms majestically still at our sides.

On the night of the concert we were instructed to wear our pleated blue skirts, white collared blouses tucked neatly at the waist, and dark dress shoes.

Some hours before we were to leave, I had been surprised to hear Mother twice remind Christopher to finish his homework quickly. "We wouldn't want to be late for your sister's important performance, would we?" she'd asked. And something in my throat had jumped. *Important performance*, as if this were an event as significant as Larissa Balliet's recital at our home earlier in the year.

I had carefully smoothed the buttoned front of the new oxford that hung in my closet. Neatly I arranged my shirttails beneath my skirt until every line and pucker disappeared, then checked my reflection in my bathroom mirror. It was only in profile that the bulge of my stomach was visible. Head-on, I thought, the skirt pleats covered my roundness quite nicely. With slow strokes I brushed my hair to straighten every snarl, clipping it in place with my favorite star-shaped tortoiseshell barrettes.

My parents, with Christopher, had chosen a row near the front of the auditorium. I could just see them through the side entry to the stage, where I waited with my grade. Mother folded a camel cape with a fur-trimmed hood across her lap, then pulled at the tips of her gloves, one finger at a time. She had changed into a brown tailored suit, a dressier outfit than she'd been wearing earlier; her nails gleamed glossy pink from a visit to the salon. Father hung his arm over the back of Christopher's seat. Christopher was chattering to Father, his knees jiggling the way they did when he was excited. Every now and then Father would nod and pat Christopher's shoulder, his eyes blinking heavily behind his glasses. Mother was sitting beside Mr. and Mrs. Preston, whom I had seen at several of my parents' gatherings; their daughter Audrey was a tenth-grader. Until the music began, during the hubbub of murmured conversations and families settling into seats, Mother and Mrs. Preston leaned forward, lifting their red programs to cover their mouths as they spoke. But as soon as the lights dimmed and the first few piano chords of "The Little Drummer Boy" sounded, Mother straightened and smiled, her brows rising as she skimmed the line of girls then settled on me. Mr. Slattery's hands began to jab at the air, demanding our attention, but I was sure I could still feel Mother watching. By the time we reached "Deck the Halls," I was aware of the heat of my cheeks. Could my parents actually distinguish my voice from among the others? With precision, as we'd been taught, I uttered the syllables, imagining they were chimes ringing from my lips. Yes, my voice soared like a silver flute, trilling through the auditorium!

We strolled home along Park Avenue, past the trees adorned with twinkling white lights, my parents in front with elbows linked, Christopher and I a step behind. And I hummed the melodies still in my ears. I hummed in our lobby and in the elevator and in the kitchen as I cut a slice of pound cake from a silver tin on the counter. So I didn't hear Mother enter my bedroom after me or set her purse at the foot of my bed. I had the cake on a dinner plate, and I had begun pulling chunks from its edges with my fingers, popping them into my mouth.

"Francesca—" Mother said, startling me. She paused, stroking the back of one hand with the fingertips of the other, her two gold bracelets jingling on her wrists. When I was young enough to be read bedtime stories and kissed before sleep, Mother would press her forehead to mine before extinguishing the light. And as she hesitated now, I thought she might do the same, or stretch her arms to embrace me; she seemed to be finding just the perfect phrase to express her pride in my performance.

But instead, "You've eaten a full dinner," she said. "Are you really hungry still?"

What did she mean! I swallowed the cake in my mouth then broke off another piece, a bite so large this time it filled my cheeks. After the concert, I had glimpsed Mother greeting Mrs. Preston's daughter. I had seen the way she smiled at Audrey in her fitted blouse, snug around her narrow arms, her tiny ribs, and little plum-sized breasts. *Are you hungry still?* Now I could feel Mother's eyes, not on my face, but on the tight band where my skirt cut my shirt. Was that why she had watched me closely as I sang? Well, if so, what did I care? Not a *bit*. Not for one instant!

I chewed the egg-colored piece of cake and shoved in another, finishing every morsel, ignoring the crumbs that showered from my mouth and fingers to the floor. Then, as though I'd heard not a word, without so much as a glance in Mother's direction, I strutted to the bathroom and banged shut the door. Then listened in silence until I heard the clip of footsteps exiting my room.

. . .

In the following weeks, Mother stocked the kitchen with baskets of apples and ripe bananas, and the refrigerator with plastic bowls of cubed melon. But I ignored these foods. In her presence, I groped behind the diet sodas on the pantry shelf for a root beer bottle, pouring it into a tall glass, adding fat dollops of ice cream. I returned from school with bags of popcorn or squares of walnut fudge from the deli along my route. At the kitchen table, licking salt or sticky sugar from my fingers, I peered at Mother from the corner of my eyes as she gabbed on the telephone; I watched to see if her hands faltered as she jotted notes in her datebook or ran her silver-handled file across the tips of her nails.

In the meantime, Sharon had discovered another diet, low in wheat. To my surprise, she had followed it for several weeks.

"It's simple," she told me. "I just avoid bread and pasta." At lunch, she ate only the innards of her sandwich, leaving the outer roll on her lunch tray. If I was still hungry, I took her remainders onto my own plate, munching the crusts.

"I don't mind sharing," she would say as I tore at the bread, "but you're making a big mistake. Once in your system, wheat transforms instantly to fat."

I was not sure I believed her, but Sharon claimed she had dropped five pounds. I noticed that she began to scroll the top of her uniform skirt to reveal her thighs as some of the other girls did, despite our school rule forbidding it. Before sports class, she tied a knot in her gym shirt, drawing it tightly across her hips like twig-limbed Carlene Bradley and Sloane Fenton.

"You think *that's* going to make them like you?" I asked, pointing to her silly shirt the first time she wore it.

"Don't be such a grump, Francesca," was all she said, dabbing iridescent lip gloss from a pink pot onto her bottom lip and smiling smugly as if she thought I was jealous.

But I did not envy Sharon! It made little difference to me that my stomach had begun to hang over the elastic of my panties and that there was a sagging around my upper legs I hadn't seen before. From morning to night, I ate whatever tempted me. During my parents' parties, each time Mother or Father turned in my direction, I gobbled a fried dumpling or plucked a handful of marzipan from a caterer's platter, pretending insatiable hunger even when I felt full.

But no further criticism came. When Mother replaced my navy school skirts with three of a larger size, I awaited some comment. I prepared my defiant response. The skirts had been laid on my bed, cleanly pressed, still blanketed in gauzy tissue. But when I arrived downstairs the next morning in one of the roomier uniforms, Mother betrayed no frustration. And I began to notice, too, that she now ignored the heaping snack plates I carted to my room. Was this some new tactic? Was she too consumed of late with other things to pay attention? Under my covers at night, I pondered these matters, plotting for hours in the darkness as I blinked at the black ceiling.

Some evenings later, my parents attended a cocktail party downtown hosted by one of Father's business associates.

"We'd much rather stay home with you," Father said to Christopher and me as they were preparing to go. "The party should be a real bore." But from the way he laughed as he brushed at the sleeves of his overcoat on his way out the door and twirled the bottle of wine in his hand, I knew he planned to enjoy himself. Mother had ordered marinated lamb and roasted tomatoes and had left two plates for Christopher and me in the kitchen. As always, Christopher poured himself a glass of milk and took his plate from the counter, heading to the television upstairs, where he would sit hunched on the floor, his dinner dish in his lap. With the prongs of my fork, I poked at my lamb, then opened the refrigerator and scanned the shelves. Hunks of cheese in foil, leftover pâté, a tureen of clear soup flecked with scallions, which seemed to have been set aside for future company. These choices were not especially appealing, and I opened the cupboards for something more tempting. There, on the first shelf, I found a bag of cream-filled cookies and a tin of crumb cake. Surprisingly, Mother had made no attempt to keep these sweets from view. I tore open the cookie bag but seemed suddenly to have lost my appetite. Instead, I took a few bites of lamb and nibbled one of the roasted tomatoes, then returned to my room to finish the latest solve-your-own mystery I had brought home from the bookstore.

"Mid-April would be a good time for the party, don't you think?" Mother asked Father one brisk Sunday as we meandered around the boating lake of Central Park at Father's suggestion—a rare weekend afternoon when we were all at home. She squinted at four mallards paddling across the water. "We have the space for it, after all. Wouldn't it be a nice gesture?"

The party under discussion was to celebrate the recent engagement of my cousin Michelle, the daughter of Mother's older sister, Binny. Michelle lived in Massachusetts and we saw her each family holiday. My most vivid memory of her was from a New Year's party some years before—making constant trips to the hall mirror to reapply her makeup and fuss with the pleats of her velvet suit in order to flatter the deep vee of her cleavage. I had met her fiancé, Stanton, only once, at a dinner at a French restaurant in midtown where he had tried to clutch Michelle's hand during the entire meal. "It's obvious she's no prude," I had once overheard Father laugh to Mother. But Mother had only sniffed and called his comment "tasteless." For this reason, I had spent much of the evening imagining Michelle and Stanton in bed, shrouded only loosely by a single sheet, their naked bodies tangled, an image from the cover of a romance novel I had once discovered in the top drawer of Mother's night table.

After a flurry of phone calls between Mother and Binny and Michelle, it was decided that the party would be held at our apartment on the second Saturday of April.

"Give some consideration to what you would like to wear for the occasion," Mother said as I gathered my books for school. But how unlike her not to have already selected some outfit for me. So perhaps she had given up. Would she no longer fret over my appearance? So. I should have known! For days now I had eaten smaller portions at meals, but she had not even *noticed*.

These were the matters I chewed over later that week when I spotted the display window of Grace's Teen Boutique. In the small shop on Madison, which I passed every day to and from school, a floor-length apricot dress with beautiful satiny skirts shimmered behind the front glass. The sleeveless dress had silver strands for straps studded with delicate crystal beads. The store's wigged mannequin wore matching apricot shoes with dainty bows, like ballet slippers. As people bustled by me on the sidewalk, I shifted my schoolbag from one shoulder to the other. A woman and her red-haired daughter had entered the shop. They were gesturing to one of the saleswomen and pointed to the apricot dress. The saleswoman disappeared through some curtains at the rear of the store, and the red-haired girl bounced on her toes, her hair swinging against her shoulder blades. She said something to her mother, and the mother lifted a hand to her daughter's head, stroking behind the girl's ear, sifting the red hair through her parted fingers.

I leaned forward, closer, closer, until my forehead met the cool of the window. It was *this* dress I would wear for Michelle's party. Yes, I had to have it. As the guests arrived, I would descend the staircase, my slippers peeping from beneath the sway of my apricot hem. Head aloft, I would walk as though unaware of the eyes raised to me. And I would not deign to glance in Mother's direction, at her mouth gaping in shock.

For days I savored this image until I had fixed every detail—the pearl choker I had received as a Christmas present at my neck, my amethyst ring on the middle finger of my right hand. But in these daydreams, my body was transformed, too—my limbs narrow, my waist, even my face thinned, my cheeks hollowed. I pictured Mother's eyes, hazy with regret, stricken with guilt for having underestimated me.

As Mother arranged terra-cotta pots of geraniums and jonquils on our terrace one afternoon, I announced there was an apricot dress I wanted to buy for the engagement party.

"Apricot sounds lovely," she said, tamping down the soil beds with gloved fingers. She handed me a check so I could pick up the gown myself. "I will phone the shop and tell them to expect you. You don't mind, do you, Fran? I'm just swamped with errands for the party."

Each morning after brushing my teeth, I checked the waistband of my school skirt. I wondered if I could now more easily slide my fingers between my stomach and the woolen fabric. Using a measuring tape I had discovered in the hall linen closet, I recorded the circumference of my thighs, my hips, my waist, imagining how someday, when the numbers changed, Mother would make surprised apologies.

"Do I look any thinner?" I asked Sharon in the school cafeteria as we trudged with our lunch trays to a corner table.

She frowned, studying me from shoulders to knees, fiddling with the new charm bracelet Robeson, a boy she'd now had five dates with, had bought her as a birthday gift. "I'm not sure. It's possible. Maybe I need to see from a different angle."

"Never *mind!*" I should have known better than to ask. Sharon had been annoyingly superior ever since Robeson's first phone call.

Mother's check I kept safely folded in my wallet. I was determined to wait until a day or two before the party to purchase the dress; I wanted the smallest possible size.

⌒

During the week before the party, Mother bought a carved bronze lion doorstop for the front hall, an enormous cut-crystal bowl for the dining room sideboard, and an intricately patterned gold picture frame to display a photograph of Michelle and Stanton with their hands entwined. She repeatedly scanned the radio dial for weather reports. Rain or a cold front would mean keeping the doors to the balconies closed and placing coatracks in the vestibule. But Saturday morning was clear and unseasonably warm.

"It's really a *perfect* day," Mother said, rushing with several bags to the kitchen. She had just returned from a salon appointment and smelled faintly of mousse, her hair formed in an elaborate knot woven with slender ribbons. A florist was already at work in the foyer, draping garlands of lilies from the banister. Hours before, caterers had marched in with food for the occasion, stacking trays and bowls in the refrigerator and on every available kitchen counter. The servers would arrive later to arrange the buffet tables and hors d'oeuvre platters.

My new gown lay in a protective garment bag across the foot of my bed, the apricot slippers on the floor below it. Though I'd discovered in the fitting room of Grace's Teen Boutique that I hadn't reduced a single size (let alone the two I'd hoped for), my disappointment dissipated after modeling the dress before my bedroom mirror. In the glow of my dresser lamp, the material glimmered with opalescent flecks, the beaded straps sparkled on my shoulders. The guests were expected at four, two hours away. But I chose not to wait. I fastened my pearl choker at my neck, scrubbed my face three times, brushed my hair with vigorous strokes until it shone. I dabbed L'Air du Temps perfume behind my ears, uncapping for the first time the sample vial Mother had given me after a shopping excursion. And with makeup I remembered Sharon had left at my house some time ago, I coated my lips with gloss, swept a bit of greenish shadow across my eyelids, until I imagined that even Jamie Dempsey, who was home from boarding school and joining his parents for the occasion, might possibly notice me, until everything was as I had envisioned.

Downstairs there seemed to be a lull in the frenzy of preparations. The kitchen, in fact, had been entirely abandoned, and I entered to survey the display of food. What I found across the counters, in the cupboards, and on the pantry table far surpassed any presentation I had before seen. There were sculpted salads, carved vegetables, pastries imprinted with curling leaf designs. There were cookies as sheer as parchment paper and glass dishes filled with caviar. Then, on a corner counter in the pantry, I discovered the cake. It seemed almost to have been molded of frosted glass rather than anything edible. It consisted of two circular tiers iced in pale yellow. A necklace of white dots, like gemstones, ringed the base of each tier. But it was the top of the cake that was most stunning—a profusion of pastel sugar flowers, like a bridal bouquet—roses, tulips, lavender forget-me-nots, each with delicate petals and deceivingly real. I was inspecting the cake and a bowl of diamond-shaped chocolates beside it, when I heard Mother's footsteps. So I straightened, adjusting my shoulder straps, and strolled toward the table of vegetables, conscious of the rustling of my skirt and the tautness of the zipper against my back.

"Oh, Francesca!" Mother said. She was wearing an embroidered silk robe tied tightly at the waist, having not yet changed for the party.

I gave a distracted toss of my hair. It will take her a moment to search for the right words, I thought, and despite my resolve of steadiness, my heart began to pound.

"Franny, you haven't touched any of the food, have you? The caterers spent hours on all of it, I'm sure." Then, her hand flying to her chin, she asked, "Did you just hear the doorbell, or was it my imagination?" And without another word, without so much as a second glimpse at me, she padded toward the dining room, her silk robe billowing behind.

So she'd noticed nothing! Really, it was almost funny. Ha! Ha! Ridiculous to have thought she would! One of the straps of my dress slipped from my shoulder, but I did not bother to fix it. For several minutes I paced the kitchen, unable to think of anything to do. A sharp pang of hunger jabbed below my ribs. I'd seen cold cuts for sandwiches in the refrigerator, but I knew these would not satisfy. Neither would the pistachios in glass canisters above the oven. I returned to the pantry. Who would notice one less chocolate? Or two?—the bowl was enormous. Even if I scooped a handful, no one, not even Mother, would perceive the difference. The chocolates were more bitter than I anticipated. As I let them dissolve in my mouth, I could smell the lemony sweetness of the engagement cake and another scent, as well, something delectably pungent like vanilla—was it the icing or the filling or something emanating from the decorative flowers on top? I leaned over to sniff it, the tip of my nose almost touching the rim. My mouth watered. And suddenly, before I knew it, I had flicked at a bit of frosting with my tongue. Such a delicious mixture of citrus and cream. I inspected the new flaw in the icing—nothing too large, nothing the caterers could not cover. But I was hungrier now and began to study the flowers on the surface. There were so many—if I broke off a single rose, who would be the wiser? I would take a small bud from the edge, but the large one in the center looked more tempting, with full reddish-pink petals.

The flowers flaked off easily, flimsily attached, almost as easily as the top layer of icing peeled away, revealing the moist cake inside. And I gorged myself until the cake was a caved-in yellow shell, until a deep hollow formed in a tureen of pâté, until holes speckled two quiches and the sculpted salads where I had plucked the tidbits I found appealing.

Something dark and sticky had trickled down the front of my dress. When I dabbed at the stain, it began to smear. It was three o'clock. My parents' guests would be arriving in one hour; the caterers would return any moment. I could hear Mother in the hall giving last-minute directions to the florist: "Could we try raising the wreath on the door one half-inch? Yes, that's better, I think. Just lovely . . ." In a minute she would retire to her bedroom to change, then descend to the kitchen to oversee the work. It would take only an instant, a gasp from one of the servers, and she would discover the destruction. Ha! If not for the ache of my stomach, I would have laughed aloud. Pulling at the stiff midriff of my gown where it constricted my waist, I climbed the stairs, kicked off my apricot slippers, and waited.

TORU

(Setsu's Story)

· 1974 ·

My first violin was a sixteenth-size, just the right length for my four-year-old arms. When my mother handed it to me, showing me how to lean my chin into the cupped chinrest and tuck the smooth wooden neck between my parted thumb and forefinger, my father snapped pictures.

"You know, Setsu, your birth parents were both musicians," my mother said, helping me to curl my fingers onto the thinnest string spanning the fingerboard.

Yes, I nodded silently. Mentions of my Japanese birth parents always made me shy. Perhaps it was the solemn tone in which my mother spoke of them, pausing between her words now and then to pat my shoulder or the back of my hand as if she were expecting some reaction. But what it was I could not quite figure out, and, certain I had not produced the appropriate response, I only bowed my head politely.

My Japanese mother had died the day I was born, in a hospital near

Osaka, my father disappearing soon after. This was all I had been told of my birth parents, all my adoptive parents seemed to know. Only this and the fact that they had been musical—my birth mother, a violinist; my birth father, a cellist. "What a wonderful heritage you have, Setsu," my mother would sometimes say to me. "*Two* musical parents. A double blessing." Then she would tell me the story of how she and my father had gone to Japan and chosen me from among all the little boys and girls at the Osaka Blessed Children's Orphanage.

"When we first spotted you in your crib, you were lying on your back, your thin little arms raised as though bowing a fiddle." My mother would raise her own arms in imitation. As lovers of music themselves, they had read this as a sign. "And just days after we brought you home, here to Bethesda, Maryland, not long after your third birthday, we noticed each time we played Vivaldi or one of Beethoven's symphonies on the phonograph, you put your toys aside to listen."

I would stare down at my hands and my wrists and my elbows, inspecting with some amazement these parts of me that had been responsible for my good fortune.

It was for this reason, I understood, that I was now being given a violin of my own.

"It's yours to keep," explained my father. "Don't be bashful. We want you to have it." In Japan, after all, many children were given their first instruments as early as three, even two, he said. He invited me to lift the lid of its case, helping me to unbuckle the silver clasps on either side of the black handle. "Do you like it?"

I could only nod, yes, thank you, as I reached inside with a single finger to press the pretty green velvet lining on which the violin rested. I was afraid to touch the instrument itself, so shiny was its polished wood, so perfect the swirl of its scrolled tip. But my mother showed me that it was safe to pick it up as long as I lifted it gently, and that the bow, too, was not difficult to hold and could make such lovely sounds when moved a certain way across the strings.

Every day she taught me something new—down bow and up bow, how to play B, C, or D on the A-string, how to make a note last, how to make it stop short. But she knew only certain things, she said. There was much more that I could learn. So on Saturday mornings she and my father began to drive me to Georgetown to a brick town house with black window boxes on either side of its gray door. This was where Mrs. Dubois lived and where she gave lessons, my parents told me, to many, many boys and girls.

Mrs. Dubois had short curly white hair and wore dresses printed with flowers. At the beginning of each lesson, she offered me chocolate nut candies wrapped in silver paper from a porcelain tray. "You're such a tiny thing. Here, take a handful. They'll help to fatten you up," she would smile. Not wanting to seem rude, I would pick only one and nibble it slowly or place it in my pocket for later.

For many Saturdays, we worked on simple scales and a series of arpeggios. Once I had mastered these, Mrs. Dubois presented me with my own white-and-black-covered music book and began to teach me some of the beautiful melodies inside. "Edelweiss," a lullaby by Brahms, "May Song," Bach's "Minuet in G." How I loved the soaring high notes of the minuet and the soft, surging notes of the lullaby.

"You can practice these at home, Setsu," she said. "And soon you will see that the bow will become steadier in your hand, every note sweeter."

So each evening before supper, while my mother worked in the kitchen and my father flipped through newspapers in the living room armchair, I closed my bedroom door to avoid disturbing them and played the new pieces I had learned. The notes vibrated through my fingers as I held them to the strings, making my hand tingle. Some nights I imagined my whole body humming the melodies, a swaying and swelling in my chest and in my throat that moved out and out along my limbs until I reached the final measures of a piece. The concluding notes that seemed so sad, fading until no music remained. I almost hated to play them and sometimes drew the bow in slow, slow strokes to make them last. Other times, I rushed through as quickly as my fingers would fly, hoping I had time to start once more at the piece's happy beginning before dinner.

I visited Mrs. Dubois through the winter and spring, and in the summer, too, when she would laugh and say that even the violins were too hot and wished to stay hidden in the cool of their cases. Her chocolate nut candies oozed through their foil wrappers so that, after I took one, I had to carefully lick the stickiness from each of my fingers. But as soon as Mrs. Dubois opened my music book, propping it on the metal stand beside her piano, and seated herself at the piano bench, winking that we could begin, I forgot all about the perspiration trickling down the back of my neck and the itchy heat of my legs under my cotton jumper.

Sometimes, at the conclusion of a lesson, Mrs. Dubois would usher my parents onto her sunporch, where they would sit on her wide sofa with its lace doily arm covers. From the music room, where I had been given a glass of apple juice and a picture book to browse through, I could see Mrs. Dubois pouring iced tea from a pitcher. Then she and my parents would murmur in hushed tones, and though I could not catch their words, I was quite certain that I was the subject of their discussion. And the thought that such a long conversation could be about me alone made my face flush as I sipped from my juice glass.

On the return trip home from my lesson, I was often lulled to sleep by the steady motion of the car, my father driving with shoulders rounded as he peered over the wheel, never speeding or screeching like many of the cars that passed us. But one afternoon, as I sat in the back, clutching my violin case so that it would not slide from my lap, my head beginning to nod drowsily, my mother turned to face me. Blotches of red shone from the center of her cheeks, making me think of the little crimson tomatoes I had seen her bring home from the grocery store and pop in her mouth like sweets. She brushed at the blond bangs that covered her forehead and reached across the seat to give my hand a pat.

"Setsu! We have some good news!" She smiled at my father, then bit her lower lip, leaving traces of lipstick like filmy pink feathers on her teeth. I began to lift a finger to my own teeth to show her what she'd done, but she seemed not to understand, so I curled my finger under my thumb instead.

"What do you think Mrs. Dubois told us today? Can you guess? She said you have *unmistakable, true talent.* Those were her exact words! She believes you are gifted, Setsu. She thinks you may be good enough some-day to play with a fine orchestra or perhaps even to become a professional soloist. This is something she suggests to only a few of her students, to only the best!" My mother inhaled quickly, making a tiny squeak. "Aren't you proud?"

I tucked my chin to my neck in a small nod, unable to speak. The things my mother said seemed too big to hold on to. Never could I re-member having seen my parents so excited, and this made my stomach flutter as if I had swallowed a hundred bubbles.

That evening my mother announced that we must have a small cele-bration. "A special dinner for you, Setsu. What is your very favorite? What would you like to have?"

I glanced around the kitchen at the fruit basket on the counter, the avocados ripening on the windowsill, feeling there must be some par-ticular meal she hoped I would pick.

"Anything you want, dear. Anything at all," my mother said after a time. She placed an arm around my neck, her touch soft as snow. "What about spaghetti with meatballs? That's something all children like, isn't it? Is that your favorite? And I could toast a loaf of garlic bread to go with it."

"Yes, please. Spaghetti with meatballs," I nodded, thankful that a solution had been given.

And as we sat at the table, I tried to wind the noodles carefully, care-fully onto my fork, afraid that in my new happiness, in my rush of excite-ment, I would seem ungrateful and gobble my food too quickly.

Over the next few years, I saw Mrs. Dubois not only on Saturdays but once each week after school, as well. She gave me new music books with pieces by Schubert and Mozart and Bach, pieces so beautiful they sometimes made me hold my breath. They were as beautiful as the melodies my parents played on their phonograph, as wonderful as anything I could have imagined. Mrs. Dubois taught me to use vibrato so that my notes would shimmer and sing. She showed me how to slide my hand up the fingerboard toward the bridge for higher and higher pitches. I learned when to use the taut tip of my bow and when the bottom, and the way to pluck the violin's strings for pizzicato.

At home, when I practiced, my parents now often chose to put aside their reading. "No need to close your door, Setsu," my father would call from the living room. "We like to listen. And why wouldn't we, with a budding Isaac Stern under our very own roof!"

So I would rifle through sheets of music searching for the études and sonatas I thought they would most enjoy. Every so often I would hear my mother gasp, "That was lovely, Setsu. Really splendid!" My throat throbbing with pride, I would mark the selection, a reminder to play it for them again. "Setsu's playing comes from the soul," I had heard Mrs. Dubois tell my parents. And I felt as if something special had been born inside—not that I had made it happen—the way young ladies in my book of fairy tales had been born with kind hearts and rose-pink cheeks.

Then, in the autumn of the year I turned ten, my parents began to have soft conversations that stopped when I entered the living room. If I woke in the dark of night for a glass of water, I could hear rapid whisperings through the crack of their bedroom door. And one afternoon in November, my mother explained that there was something they wished to discuss with me. She smoothed a wrinkle from her tweed pants, then patted the plush seat cushion of the living room couch, motioning for me to sit down.

"What would you think, Setsu, if we said we wanted to bring home a brother or sister for you? Someone to keep you company. Someone you could play with."

My father pressed my mother's hand in his. "A boy or girl from Japan, just like you. Do you want to be a sister, Setsu?"

This news was so unexpected I could only clasp my hands to my chest and nod.

"Would you like that, Setsu?" my father repeated, leaning forward, stretching the buttonholes of his wool cardigan sweater.

"Oh, yes. Yes, thank you," I managed to murmur, afraid they would take my silence as a sign of displeasure.

I spent the next days trying to imagine the new boy or girl who would soon live in our house. I wondered if he or she would have black hair like mine. Hair as straight as leaves of paper, and dark eyes instead of blue like pale water. In the mornings as I stood before the mirror of my closet door, tucking my blouse into the waist of my skirt, I imagined how the two of us would walk with matching footsteps up the paved path to Chilton Elementary like other pairs of siblings in my school. And how in the afternoons we would wait for our parents side by side on the benches near the school's entry, where people who passed could look and see that we belonged together.

Then, one week before Christmas, my parents announced they had found a boy they wished to adopt. He was older, twelve years of age, and he was right here in America. His name was Toru, and he, too, was a gifted violinist. Until he was seven he had lived in Japan. "Think how much you will have in common, Setsu! Imagine how much you and your big brother will have to talk about!"

To bring Toru home, my parents would not have to take a long airplane trip as they had done for me; they had only to drive to southern New Jersey, to the home of Toru's uncle's closest friend. From my parents' nighttime discussions and evening telephone calls during the ensuing days and weeks, I gathered tiny bits of information about my new brother, reviewing each item again and again in my mind so that I would not forget it. Five years before, his mother and father had died in a terrible car crash, and he had left Japan to live with his uncle in California. His uncle knew many musicians and had paid for Toru's violin lessons, overseeing his daily practices. But when Toru was almost eleven, his uncle had been given a new job in Australia, embarking on a life that could not include Toru. And so Toru had been sent to live with his uncle's friend on the East Coast until he could be properly adopted. In bed at night, before I fell asleep, I thought about all of the places Toru had lived and wondered if his many goodbyes had made him sad. I wondered if he was lonely and if he had ever wished for a sister with whom to spend his time.

In preparation for Toru's arrival, my parents converted the library into a boy's bedroom with navy curtains and a poster bed with a matching navy quilt. Over the bureau they hung an enormous framed poster of Mozart, Toru's favorite composer.

"We should try to make Toru feel as welcome as possible," my mother said when I watched from the doorway as she folded boys' shirts and pants into the bureau drawers. "You understand, don't you, Setsu? We have to expect that it may take him some time to feel comfortable."

"Yes." I nodded solemnly, eager to show my readiness to help. Then I remembered the leaden Mozart figurine on my bedroom wall shelf. I had bought it with my birthday money the year before. After dusting its tiny painted red shoes with my fingertip, I carried it to Toru's bedside table, carefully choosing a spot where he could easily see it.

My parents left early on a Sunday morning to pick up Toru, leaving me at home with our next-door neighbor, Mrs. Biddleman. While Mrs. Biddleman's knitting needles moved through skeins of yarn, I hovered at the windows flanking the front door, where I could view the driveway and my parents' returning car.

Despite my mother's concerns, from the moment he walked in with his canvas duffel bag and his violin case, Toru seemed not to feel the least bit out of place. When my parents introduced us, he marched directly to the far end of the hall where I stood, stopping just inches from me.

"This is your sister, Toru. She is a violinist, also. A very accomplished one, like you," my mother said, making me blink with embarrassment.

Toru's teeth flashed in a flickering smile. "They told me all about you in the car. I heard you are adopted, too?" Then before I could answer, he shrugged his shoulders and, whistling, turned down the hall where my father had explained he could find his room.

That evening, long after I'd climbed into bed, through my bedroom wall, I could hear Toru arranging and rearranging his possessions—the zipping and unzipping of his duffel bag, the creak of opening and closing drawers, and once or twice a dull scraping sound, as if something very heavy were being dragged across the floor. Later that night when I passed his door, waking to use the bathroom, I saw that he had repositioned the room's desk and chair and shifted his bed several feet to the left. On his nightstand he had placed a thick stack of music books and a chrome-sided digital clock, so that I could not be sure he had noticed the Mozart figurine.

O ur house with Toru in it soon seemed alive with noise. His heels smacked the floors as he dashed from room to room. And when he spoke, his voice seemed to echo through the air even after his words had ceased.

"Toru, you have the most marvelous self-assurance!" my mother said to him after he had been with us for a few days. She clapped her hands beneath her chin, her eyes widening. "We're glad to see how easily you are making the transition to your new home."

Though he was not fat, we soon learned that Toru had an enormous appetite, and my mother began to buy far greater quantities of food. She would return from the market with bag after bag of cheeses and spreads and bulky packets of deli meat for Toru to snack on. At dinner he surprised us by taking second, sometimes even third, helpings of roast beef or green squash or applesauce, flicking impatiently at the wisps of dark hair that frequently fell across his brow.

"What a healthy eater you are!" my parents would exclaim.

"Mmm, mmm." He would nod with laughing eyes, his mouth too full to speak.

I could not remember ever having met anyone as bold as Toru. During our meals, I could not take my eyes from him—from the brave way in which he asked for the things he desired, without a single stutter or blush of shyness—so that often I would neglect to finish the food on my own plate. Then I would find myself longing for another chicken wing or spoonful of potatoes, but only after it was too late, the table already half-cleared, my mother packing leftovers in plastic containers.

When the dishes had been rinsed, my parents retired to the living room with their papers and books, and Toru disappeared into his room. Through his door, which he left partially ajar, I could see him seated cross-legged on his bed, sifting through sheets of music or making notes to himself with a black marker and lined yellow pad. After some hesitation, I would cough softly, hoping he would hear me in the hallway and invite me in. Already I had planned the questions I would ask him if he ever did, imagined the things we could talk about. One night, as I watched, he shuffled through a pile of photographs, sorting them into small mounds on the quilt of his bed. And, overcome by curiosity, I forgot myself and tiptoed so close to the entry of his room that my nose poked through the door frame.

"Pictures of Japan," Toru said suddenly, making me start; I was unaware that he had noticed my presence. Quickly he waved his hand over the piles before him, gesturing, I assumed, his permission for me to take a look.

"Oh!" I gasped, glimpsing a photograph of a jagged mountain, its pointed crest glistening with snow, and another picture of a very young boy standing on a wooden bridge, behind him a shallow waterfall streaming between moss-covered stones. "Oh, so beautiful!"

"My parents' house," Toru said, tapping the snapshot of the boy on the bridge. "Gardens like this don't exist in America, only in Japan."

"I was born in Japan, too. I lived there for three years," I said, embarking on one of the conversations I had long envisioned we would have and had often rehearsed in my mind. "Just like you."

"Hmm?" Toru said, still studying the photographs. "Where?"

"The Osaka Blessed Children's Orphanage."

"Oh. Then you have probably never seen the Temple Gardens in Kyoto or been to Shinjuku in Tokyo?"

"No."

"At the orphanage did you eat ebi tempura or okonomiyaki with squid?"

"I don't think so," I said, trying to guess the meaning of these words and to recall more than my few fuzzy recollections of the children's home.

"I guess an orphanage is different." Toru shrugged, then continued to sort through his photographs.

For some time I watched him in silence. But he did not offer to show me any more pictures, and though I thought and thought, I could find no way to reintroduce the conversation that had ended so soon.

After a few weeks, once my parents felt Toru had grown accustomed to his new routine, they asked if he would like to resume his music lessons. "Setsu has a very good teacher," they said. "She has agreed to take you on, as well. You could have joint lessons twice a week if Setsu doesn't mind."

"Oh, no, I don't mind," I said, smiling at Toru so that he could see my willingness to share.

He pushed back his shoulders then nodded his consent. And in my gladness that Toru wished to spend this time with me, I pressed my hands to my mouth to hide my broad smile.

.   .   .

Toru carried to our first shared visit with Mrs. Dubois an armload of his own music books. After we had completed our scales and arpeggios, he asked if he might play for her the piece he had been working on most recently. Before starting, Toru plucked his strings to be sure they were in tune. He rubbed his bow with the rosin he kept in a bottom square pocket of his violin case, then, shaking the hair from his forehead, he signaled to Mrs. Dubois to begin the opening measures on the piano. Notes burst from his instrument the moment his bow met the strings, reminding me of the firecrackers I had once heard on the Fourth of July. As he played, he rocked on his feet; he dipped his violin forward and back. His sound grew louder and louder, until it seemed to shoot to the far walls and as high as the ceiling.

"Well done! Well done!" Mrs. Dubois said when he had finished. "You have talent, just like your sister." Toru silently swatted the hair from his brow as if he were waiting for her to continue. "There is much strength in your playing!"

"That is what my last teacher told me," he said, but he turned to me as he answered her, his mouth curving into a funny expression I could not understand.

It was not long before Mrs. Dubois invited my parents in for conferences about Toru, just as she had held for me. She confirmed what my parents had been told by Toru's uncle. Toru, too, Mrs. Dubois hoped, might have a future as a soloist or with a significant orchestra. With consistent practice there was every reason to think we would both enjoy such successes.

One Saturday, as we descended Mrs. Dubois's front steps, my mother grabbed Toru's wrist with one hand and mine with the other. "Who could have imagined *two* such talents in one house! In one family! Isn't it a thrill!"

My cheeks rushed with warmth. Being praised with Toru was even nicer than being praised alone, and I turned to him. But his eyes were fixed on the pavement before him, and he did not glance back.

I n the afternoons, when Toru and I returned from our lessons, my parents asked us to demonstrate what we had learned. Bashfully I would hesitate, but Toru would flip open his violin case and play passages from the pieces Mrs. Dubois had taught us.

"Wonderful! Wonderful!" With every one of our parents' compliments Toru's bowing arm seemed to weave in larger and larger arcs, his notes building to crescendos. And each time, he played more passages than the time before, giving my parents more to be proud of.

As soon as he finished, my parents would insist, "Now it's your turn, Setsu." So, blushing, asking what they wished to hear, I would lift my own instrument, resting it beneath my chin. But always, after my first few measures, I noticed that Toru snapped his violin back into its case. Then, tucking it under his arm, he would tread with clacking footsteps down the hall toward his room. So while my parents clapped their approval, I could not help wondering if there was something I was doing wrong, whether there was something in the way I played that my brother did not like.

So after supper when Toru practiced in his bedroom and I in mine, I would pause, listening to the strains of music coming through his wall, trying to discern the ways in which our sounds differed. Then I would continue where I'd left off, playing concertos and lullabies and waltzes as beautifully as I knew how, hoping that I had merely imagined his displeasure.

"How well you played tonight, Toru," I told him if I passed him later emerging from the bathroom after washing his face for bed. "Just like a professional on the radio!"

Toru's lips curled into a half-smile, and he would thrust his hands into the pockets of his dark green bathrobe. "Oh? My uncle used to tell me it .was in my genes." He lifted his arms questioningly. "Ha! Who knows?" Then, with no mention of the pieces I had played, he plodded back to his room, his slippers slapping the tiles.

But, with my own ears, I could not hear what my playing lacked. So when we had returned from our lesson one afternoon, I approached Toru. He was reclining on his bed, his head propped against a pillow, taking notes once again with his yellow pad and marker. Softly I tapped on his door.

"Toru, I'm sorry to interrupt. It's only a quick question I have. Would you mind, please . . . Could I ask your advice?"

Toru made another note on his yellow pad, then shrugged. "I don't think my method is something I can teach. I've been told the way I play was born inside me."

"Oh," I whispered, tucking my chin to my neck with disappointment.

Toru cleared his throat, then blew his nose loudly into a handkerchief. "But if you really want, I guess I could try."

"Yes, please. Oh, yes, please."

So each day I would watch Toru and then try my very best to copy his techniques, attempting to make my fingers flit, my bowing arm slice as his did.

"How was that, Toru? What did you think?"

But Toru would only squint, observing me from across the room, one arm folded over the other. "Hmm. Well, maybe you have made a little improvement. As soon as I see more, I promise to let you know."

Every afternoon and evening I practiced the things Toru had shown me, hour after hour, sometimes stopping only when my mother called me for dinner. As I took my seat, I would glance at Toru, knowing he'd heard the pieces I'd played. I studied his face for hints of his opinions. But Toru seemed to see nothing but the dishes before him, especially now that my mother had enrolled in a new cooking class and began to make meals from her two new Japanese cookbooks—chunks of fish covered with sticky rice, dumplings filled with shrimp, deep bowls of soup with shredded egg floating on the surface, and long noodles as sheer as glass.

"Toru is more fond of these recipes," my mother explained as I helped her to set plates and napkins on the table and, at Toru's place, a pair of bamboo chopsticks, which he insisted made his food taste better. "Do you mind?"

"Oh, no." I shook my head, worried she would stop making the things Toru liked most and that I would somehow be responsible.

Presented with his favorite meals, Toru's hunger seemed to grow even greater. He heaped his plate with tangy beef and strips of pork in brown sauce. He finished large mounds of white rice in the wink of an eye. Every few days he remembered another dish he especially liked—tuna with wasabi, ginger chicken, vegetables fried in thick batter. It was not long before his shirts began to stretch across the middle and his ankles to protrude below the cuffs of his pants. Since moving into our house, Toru had grown two inches.

"Good for you, Toru!" my father said. "What a healthy boy you are!" And he took him to the city to purchase a new wardrobe of larger clothes.

When they returned, laden with shopping bags, my father teased, "And what about you, Setsu? Are you sure you're getting enough to eat?" He laughed, patting my head. "Such a string bean! Isn't she a wisp of a thing!" he said, turning to Toru. "Maybe your sister should take lessons from you!"

I smiled to join in the joke, but as soon as my father and Toru walked away, I stretched my arms out before me, inspecting the skinniness of my wrists, the knobbiness of my elbows, wondering if the thinness of my limbs was partially to blame for the flaws in my playing.

When I asked Toru about this, he arched his brows and turned out his palms. "Your body won't change just because you want it to, will it?"

"Maybe it would help if I ate more. What do you think? If I ate big portions like you?"

But Toru only frowned. "Who can tell?"

So at supper I began to pile larger and larger spoonfuls onto my plate. But only now and then did I have the chance to finish them. For after Toru had scraped up the last grains of rice, the remaining shreds of beef from their serving bowls, he claimed his stomach still growled with hunger. And eyeing the food on my plate, he would say, "Setsu, can you really finish *all* that?"

"No. No, I can't. The rest is yours, Toru." And I would pass him my plate.

In the early spring, Mrs. Dubois announced to Toru and me that she wished us to perform in an upcoming recital. It would take place in a small concert hall not far from the capitol building and was an event that musicians and teachers from the finest music schools often attended. This was a significant opportunity, she explained, her voice grave and low, but she had no doubt we had the ability necessary to participate. All that was needed, over the next eight weeks, was to practice the piece she had selected for us to perform until it was perfected—"Sarabande and Allegretto" by Corelli; she wished it to be played as a duet. "We will devote your lessons to it," she said. "And, of course, you will work on it daily at home."

"Sarabande and Allegretto"—I had heard the piece before, its more rapid section reminding me of bird wings fluttering.

"Oh, Toru, what do you think!" I said, turning to him to see if he shared my excitement. But he was busy adjusting the tuning pegs of his instrument.

That evening Toru and I set our music stands side by side in his bedroom and began to practice the Corelli together as we had been instructed. But after only a few measures, Toru stopped suddenly, vigorously shaking his head.

"What is it, Toru?"

"Something doesn't sound right. One of us is off."

So we began once more, and I listened as carefully as I could, trying to hear what was bothering Toru. But again he flicked his bow from his strings in irritation, and his fingers tightened around the neck of his violin.

Late into the evening we rehearsed the piece but never completed more than the first page. Again and again Toru would stop, insisting we were making no improvements. Then, studying me through half-squeezed eyelids, he bit his lip as though there were something he wished to say.

"Am I doing something wrong, Toru? Tell me and I will try to fix it."

After a long pause, he said, "We do not bow with the same staccato— I use more, you use less. And here and here," he said, pointing to two places in the music, "our tempos are different—yours is slower than mine. How can we play for an audience with such different sounds?"

But the more I tried to blend my sound with Toru's, the more errors I seemed to make. And each day, Toru stamped his foot with a new complaint—C-sharps that didn't match, an overuse of vibrato in the final notes, insufficient crescendos. Soon my head began to buzz with these corrections so that I struggled just to hear my own playing.

As the recital drew nearer, Toru complained that we were making no advancements; in fact, he thought, things were only getting worse. To soothe his frustrations, he fed his growing appetite. In the afternoons, before our practice, he polished off entire boxes of seaweed crackers, which my mother kept on a special kitchen shelf just for him. At night, after finishing his own dinner, he eyed what I had not yet eaten on my plate.

So I found that I left more and more meals with a stomach unsettled from hunger. Some nights when Toru and I played together, I felt almost too dizzy to stand, and all that I had been trying to learn grew more muddled in my mind. Even things I had long known seemed to be slipping from my grasp. One evening, as Toru fidgeted and huffed more frequently than usual listening to me play, two thin tears rolled down my cheeks. And setting my violin in its case, I covered my eyes with my hands.

"I'm sorry, I'm sorry. Tell me what to do, Toru!"

For a long time Toru uttered not a single word. Then, scratching beneath his nose with his fingertip, he said, "Maybe what I told you the first time was right. I guess the way I play is not something I can teach." Then slowly stroking beneath his chin as if a new thought had occurred to him, he said, "The Corelli is not normally played as a duet, you know."

"But what do you mean? The recital is less than two weeks away. How can we perform anything else?"

Toru only crossed one arm over the other and shrugged his shoulders. But I knew what he wanted me to do.

When I told Mrs. Dubois I wished to withdraw from the recital, she pursed her lips. "This comes as quite a disappointment, Setsu. Perhaps you will reconsider."

For an instant my chest pounded with new hope, and I glanced at Toru, who stood several steps away sorting sheets of music. But I could tell by the way he arched his neck, slowly turning through the pages, that he listened to our words. And I shook my head, brushing away the fleeting thought. "No," I told her, despite her repeated urgings. "No, I am quite sure."

For some time, I awaited my parents' attempts to dissuade me from the decision I'd made, for their insistence that I had given up too readily. So I even had my explanation prepared and repeated it silently in bed before dropping off to sleep. But the protest I had braced myself for never came. And I wondered, for just a moment, if a year earlier it might have. A year earlier, before . . . But I did not finish the question because surely, surely this could not be true.

My mother told Toru, for the night of the recital, he could choose any dinner he liked. "Whatever your heart desires," she said, fanning her cookbooks across the kitchen counter.

After some consideration, Toru selected three elaborate dishes: rice balls with salted salmon, egg custard, and vinegar-steamed shrimp. My mother began early in the morning, dicing assorted vegetables, peeling shrimp, rolling rice in seaweed. She worked until she called us to the table that evening. Toru was the first to sit down. He was dressed in a brand-new suit and an orange silk tie, which my parents had bought especially for the occasion. His hair was brushed neatly off his forehead. Earlier that evening, after he'd finished rehearsing, I had seen him at his bedroom wall mirror carefully combing every strand, slicking it with gel. And I had dabbed at the ends of my own hair, unable to stop myself from imagining things that would not come true.

"You look very handsome tonight, Toru," I told him as he adjusted the knotted gold cuff links at his wrists, then piled one rice ball after another onto his plate.

"Thank you, Setsu." His face was beaming. His eyes, his teeth, even his skin seemed to shine.

"If you want, I will show you the rest of my pictures from Japan," he said between noisy swallows. "I have more than fifty, and you can hold them, too."

"Oh, yes," I said softly, surprised by Toru's sudden generosity.

"But maybe we will wait until tomorrow. Tonight when we return from the recital, *you* may be rested, but *I* will be exhausted." He smiled at me with his biggest smile. "What do you think, little sister?"

I nodded, unable to speak. Despite Toru's kindness, my throat swelled with tears.

With a tap of his wooden chopsticks, Toru scooped up the last remaining morsel on his dish. Then, from the corner of my eye, I saw that he gazed at my plate, at the mound of egg custard I had not yet touched.

"Such a large portion you have tonight, Setsu. Do you plan to finish it all?"

"No, Toru. It's yours," I said. And I took only one last swallow. It was a small sacrifice; it was only fair, I told myself as I watched Toru gobble the last of the custard. For I believed that his hunger was much greater than mine.

Part

TWO

THE WORK OF A WOMAN

(My Story)

· *Freshman Year* ·

I n college you make friends who last a lifetime," my cousin Gregory
had told his brothers, my sisters, and me last winter, having returned
home with a full semester under his belt.

"Always showing off," Sarah had whispered to Valerie and me later.
"Now even his friendships are better than ours."

Yes, so ridiculous. But as my new college suitemates and I formed a
circle on the cinnamon-brown carpet of our common room on our first
afternoon together, I could not help thinking of Gregory's claim, wondering if it could possibly be true. His roommate, Eli, had visited him in
Westchester for part of the winter break. With straighter hair and a nar-
rower mouth, Eli could almost have been Gregory's twin. Even their
voices sounded the same when they spoke of family or joked about their
professors or recent parties they'd attended. But how much would I find I
shared with Setsu, Opal, and Francesca, the three girls I was now sitting
with?

Earlier in the afternoon, our head counselor, Nora, had stopped by with an assignment: a questionnaire for us to answer in order to learn as much as possible about one another.

"Are we being graded on this?" Francesca had laughed.

Nora looked like some of the other older-looking girls I'd seen on campus, with her jeans worn through around her tanned knees and her plaid shirt cut large enough for my uncle Leonid.

"Oh, I'm kidding. *Kidding*." Francesca had joked with Nora as if she, too, had been attending the school for years rather than mere hours. "We'll answer every question faithfully, won't we?" And she had looked around at the rest of us with amusement.

Now Francesca balanced the two sheets of paper on her left knee. At the center of our circle, she had dropped a box of mini–blueberry muffins in paper wrappers, a large silver bag of chive potato chips, and a clear plastic baggy filled with candies. She had remembered she had munchies left over from her drive up—a drive she must have made on her own, I was gathering, having heard her mention to Opal the car she was beginning to regret having brought with her now that she realized the distance from our dorm to the off-campus garage.

"Might as well have something to snack on while we spill our guts, right?" Francesca laughed again, this time a bark of a laugh that seemed, somehow, not to match the prettiness of her face.

It occurred to me that Opal, whom I'd heard make two phone calls to Logan Airport—checking on a bag that had disappeared somewhere along her journey from California—must also have traveled here on her own, a choice I knew Mama and Poppy would have considered out of the question for me. With her wire hoop earrings, her fluttery white skirt, the measured evenness of her voice, Opal could have been one of the girls from my high school who'd hardly noticed me.

After helping me unpack, Mama and Poppy had been reluctant to leave before meeting my new suitemates. But the truth was I couldn't help being glad none of my suitemates had appeared until later in the day, glad they had not been around to see the attention Mama had given to the arranging of my room, or to hear her cautioning reminders about walking through the campus alone at night.

I reached for a muffin and a handful of chips, then realizing I was, so far, the only one to have done so, nibbled them slowly, as if I weren't very interested in them after all.

"So, should we get started?" Francesca scanned the first sheet of the questionnaire. I felt some relief as she helped herself to two mini-muffins. I was relieved, too, she would not try to talk us out of the first responsibility the school had given us.

"Yes, I think they mean for us to complete it today, don't you?" It seemed that Setsu, like me, was anxious to follow the rules. She was a beautiful Japanese girl with a voice as soft as air and reminded me of a sylph from a fairy tale, with her graceful, tiny figure and curtain of dark hair hanging to her waist.

Fran smiled, obviously still amused. "Well, the first questions are hardly probing ones: 'What is your middle name? Where were you born?' Who wants to go first?" None of us said a word. Fran plowed ahead. "No one? Okay, I don't mind." She swallowed a mouthful of muffin, large enough for me to see the bulge of it move down her throat. "Lane and New York City." She had kicked off her leather sandals, tossing them carelessly—though they looked expensive—toward the corner of the room. She wore only a black elastic band in her hair and no jewelry, but I knew the price of her sleeveless peasant blouse, one my friend Jenny had saved several allowances to buy from a tiny boutique in the Village where, she bragged, Madonna sometimes shopped.

"Am I next?" Opal leaned back, supporting her weight with her palms. "Hélène. And I was born in San Diego, but I hope we won't be asked every place we've lived. I'm not sure I'd remember them all." She laughed just briefly, though it seemed to be at some ironic thought of her own rather than with us. This would be her first time living in the Northeast though, she admitted, as if it were the only place left on earth where she had not stayed.

I wondered suddenly what my family was now doing in the apartment that had been my only home until today. And then I wondered how different this day, this night would feel if I'd had as many homes as Opal. Maybe this was as casual a change for her as dozens she'd made before. I thought she might go on about her travels, but she said nothing more, and not once, I noticed, did she move forward for a handful of Francesca's snacks. Nor did Setsu for many minutes, until eventually two tapered fingers dipped cautiously into the open candy bag and, even then, selected nothing more than a single caramel.

After we'd gone around our circle, Fran glanced down at the questionnaire again: "'Share your favorite passage from literature.'"

Setsu recited a poem by Emily Dickinson. Then Francesca read a page from a book she had recently bought, written by the older sister of one of her friends. "*Beneath the Waves*. It's totally obscure, but it has this great main character, a female deep-sea diver. Anyway, maybe not my *all-time* favorite passage, but it's my favorite today."

Opal was next and selected a section of Faulkner's *The Sound and the Fury*, which I had never read, though both Fran and Setsu seemed to know the book well. As Opal recited from memory an impressively long passage, I racked my brain for something as interesting as what my suitemates had shared. But what choice did I have but the lines from *Jane Eyre* I still remembered from having studied the novel my eighth-grade year, the only literary passage I knew by heart?

It seemed ages after I recited the lines until anyone spoke, and then, "That was lovely," Setsu said, though she seemed sweet enough to give a compliment regardless of what I'd selected.

Fran continued: "'What is your favorite pastime?'"

"Maybe going to the opera," Setsu offered.

Fran's was a tie between skiing and seeing U2 in concert, Opal's a walk on the beach before sunset.

"Going to the movies, I guess——" This wasn't true, but it was the first thought that came to my mind and seemed an answer others might give.

Francesca flicked the questionnaire in her lap, making a dent at the center of the paper. What could she have found so objectionable about my reply? But she was not listening, rather reading from the sheet. "'Who has most inspired you and why? What is your best quality?' Boring! Boring! Right?" She grinned conspiratorially, revealing beautifully even, white teeth.

"I don't think we're meant to skip any, do you?" Setsu asked, but Fran ignored her, continuing to scan the paper.

"Here we go. This is better: 'Describe something you did as a result of peer pressure.' It's a start anyway. Your turn, Setsu."

Setsu's cheeks blossomed pink, and her eyes blinked like small, flickering bulbs. "Okay, give me just a minute——"

"Good Lord, Setsu. We're not going to bite." Francesca popped another mini-muffin into her mouth.

"We don't have to go in order, do we?" Opal said.

Setsu smiled gratefully.

Opal pulled at her hoop earrings, stretching the lobes of her ears. "I never stayed in one place long enough to have many friends. Except maybe Delilah—Delinquent Delilah, I always thought of her. I think she played hooky at least once a week! She was the daughter of my mother's boyfriend at the time. We met when I was thirteen. She was a year older. She didn't pressure me into much. But she *introduced* me to certain things." Opal tucked her hands under her thighs.

"You mean——?" I was thinking the question but had not meant to ask it aloud. To my embarrassment, Francesca rolled her eyes at me and laughed.

"Sometimes Delilah would take out her secret stash—cola bottles half-filled with vodka, rum, gin, sambuca, which she had siphoned off, a bit at a time, from her father's liquor cabinet and kept hidden in a dresser drawer beneath her bathing suits and training bras. She would turn off the lights and we would stare up at her mobile of glow-in-the-dark planets and sip from the soda bottles until we were too dizzy and nauseous to move." Opal squeezed closed her eyes for a moment. "That I didn't mind, but she had a bunch of pervy magazines she'd stolen from her cousin. She knew I couldn't stand to look through them. Still, somehow it seemed I ended up at Delilah's house almost every day."

"Maybe you liked the magazines more than you thought!" Francesca looked around at the rest of us to see if we were as amused as she.

I giggled, but Opal only sniffed, her upper lip tensing momentarily, as if she were about to make some retort then decided against it. Setsu smiled and rolled a thin link bracelet with a heart charm up and down her wrist. I stared down at my khaki shorts. For some moments, no one spoke.

Opal's story made me think of the afternoon in Mr. Gupta's variety store just off the route I took home from school. And I almost told it. How I had needed pipe cleaners for my U.S. history project. How Mr. Gupta had been seated on a stool behind the counter and waved when I entered, then bent over his newspaper, humming with the lively Indian music playing on a small radio behind him. As I searched for the wire cleaners, I came upon every kind of oddity jammed on the shelves, and in the quiet of the back aisles, a host of things I'd never seen up close: a box of contraceptive sponges, a book called *A Woman's Guide to Good Sex* with directions inside, and magazines perhaps like those Opal had mentioned— some of women thrusting their breasts, others of men gripping the bulges between their legs. But what would my new suitemates say if I told them how I had ripped some of the photos from the magazines? Pictures of things I'd known little about but others must have. How I had stuffed them inside my pocket and run, bumping into a rack of greeting cards, bruising my forehead!

"So, that's it? Setsu? Ruth? Nothing? You must all be a bunch of *saints*," Francesca said. "God, I think I smoked, drank, and slept my way through high school!" She was kidding, mostly, she said, but she turned to me as if she knew the New York I'd grown up in might as well have been a thousand miles from her Manhattan.

"It's what colleges do, isn't it? Match us to roommates with experiences different from our own?" Francesca pulled a box of Parliament cigarettes from the pocket of her white denim jeans, removed one, dangling it between two fingers, and snorted as if this amused her, how dissimilar our lives must have been. As she blew a ring of smoke, I wondered if she was right. Maybe my cousin Gregory had been lucky or exaggerating about his new close friends.

Francesca, with friends from the coed school her parents had transferred her to her sophomore year to "broaden her horizons," had spent every Friday and Saturday night at bars that never checked IDs. By seventeen, she knew twenty different vodka drinks and had begun dating a twenty-three-year-old, a Wall Street trader, whose downtown apartment she sometimes stayed in until close to dawn, slipping home into her own bed just a couple of hours before her family woke.

I imagined her with her grown-up boyfriend. I wondered what they'd done in private, wondered if it was like what I had caught unexpectedly at night from my bedroom window—the young couple in the apartment across the way who occasionally neglected to draw their shades.

I no longer remember the other questions from our assignment, but there was still plenty of early-evening light by the time we finished, and someone—maybe Setsu—suggested we head outside and have a photo taken of the four of us to commemorate our first day together as roommates. We agreed on a spot just in front of the university's entry gates as the most appropriate place, a symbol of all that awaited us. Francesca stopped a boy in a faded NASA T-shirt, with narrow shoulders and arms half the width of mine, and asked him to do the honors. In the picture, Francesca is standing between Opal and me, one wrist draped coolly over each of our shoulders. Opal's face is turned slightly toward Francesca's, a flattering angle as someone accustomed to being photographed might instinctively ease into. Setsu is on my left, her fingers folded together, her hands cupped like a neat basket, one delicate ankle crossed in front of the other. I recall, at the time, feeling I was the only one who had not found a comfortable stance. Later, Fran made copies of the snapshot for each of us, and when I look at it now, I still see my awkwardness: the way my right shoulder bends slightly under Francesca's hand, the way my arm crosses in front of me in an attempt to block my midsection from the camera's lens but draws attention to it instead.

Returning to our dorm, we talked of other things that night. Of why we'd chosen Brown, of Setsu's older brother—a musician, of Francesca's younger brother, and of my sisters. We talked of two Caribbean islands where Opal and Fran had both spent time and of the trip Francesca's family had taken to South America over the summer, one she declared a total disaster but which made my family's occasional vacations to the Catskills seem too mundane to mention.

And I learned that Francesca was not the only one who'd had boyfriends. Opal had dated a boy for a summer in Mexico. He was sweet and never pressured her and drove her everywhere on the back of his Vespa. And Setsu told of her senior-year boyfriend from her calculus class whom, she admitted, she'd never found terribly attractive. Still, she had stayed with him to quiet the friends who had started to call her Snow White, never telling them she and the calculus student did little more than hold hands and share dry kisses in the park near her home.

I tried to summon up some anecdote to contribute to this conversation, but my few encounters with boys had been fumbling embarrassments. My first kiss—only my sisters knew—had been with my step-second-cousin, Harold Panter, who had convinced me during a game of Spin the Bottle that, since he was not Benny's son through blood, we were doing nothing wrong. Second Base I had visited only once, on the night of the prom with Charlie Schoenfeld, who smelled of vegetables and perspiration. At the after-dance party at Elena Richardson's home in Fieldston, couples had disappeared into shadowy dark corners. I'd known what they were doing, and not wanting to be the only one who wasn't, I hadn't stopped Charlie when his hands traveled to the back of my dress where my bra was hooked, or when he'd buried his face in my chest. And that was it—the extent of my interludes. But in college people changed, didn't they? They grew up. And as the hours passed, as my new suitemates stretched across the carpet, their voices rising and falling, lapping over one another's like waves, I imagined a time when I might have such stories of my own.

⁓

For years Mama had wanted Columbia for me, the only Ivy I could attend and still live at home, or possibly Princeton, not much more than an hour's drive away. She knew my private school's reputation for placing students in the most competitive colleges—it was one of the reasons she and Poppy had sent me, after all—and under Mama's careful watch, I had been making A's in almost all of my classes. "They'd be lucky to have her," Mama informed Mr. Radnor, my college adviser, as if she weren't sure he recognized my qualifications. Her accent had all but disappeared long before I was born, but hints of it returned now and then; and as we sat in Mr. Radnor's office under his framed diplomas from Stanford and Harvard, it flared. I wanted to sink into the folds of my wool turtleneck as Mr. Radnor explained that even students who were first or second in their classes—his polite way of reminding there were others *more* qualified than I—could not count on placing into their top two choices. There should be at least six schools on my list and not all of them Ivies. Mama leaned forward in her chair, and for a moment I thought she might argue. But she said nothing, only twisted a button on the cuff of her blouse. So she agreed to adding Yale and Brown (both relatively close to home) and three schools Mr. Radnor referred to as "much safer bets."

"I don't believe this full list is *really* necessary," she said to me later, after we'd been ushered out of Mr. Radnor's office, but I saw that she had chewed her bottom lip until only traces of lipstick remained.

When some months later we brought my applications to the post office, paying extra for proof of receipt to the clerk in his collared uniform, Mama closed her eyes briefly, and I knew she was casting a prayer to heaven for the "top schools." "They'll take you," she said, as though pronouncing the words made it more likely to happen. "Let's hope," I said. Over the past two years, I had agreed to the SAT courses, to Tuesday afternoon math tutoring with Mrs. Lieberman, and then to the Thursday sessions with her as well for "general homework help," to the hours spent with Mama carefully wording my college essays. Mrs. Lieberman's study system had seemed to do the trick: for the last four semesters I had made honors. Before each test or assigned paper, I would repeat to myself what Mrs. Lieberman always reminded: that I knew the material, just needed to trust myself. And with this, I rarely froze up as I had in years earlier. Still, an Ivy seemed too much to believe for, and I had never told Mama I was afraid she was only wasting wishes.

Princeton and Yale arrived first—both no's. Then Columbia—a wait list. Mama searched the letters again and again, as if there must have been a mix-up. "Maybe I should call their admissions departments, just to check?"

So the next afternoon when the white envelope arrived from Brown University, Mama pulled it from my hands before I could unseal it. A large envelope, we both knew, was a good sign; still, a single page would mean bad news. She lifted it to the light by the living room window, trying to determine what was inside, shifting its position; but the sunlight could not penetrate its heavy paper.

"Just open it, Ma!"

But she was already tearing the envelope's edge, peering in at its contents. "Oh, Ruth!" Mama kissed my mouth, wet flecks of mascara speckling her cheeks. "I knew it! Oh, I knew it!"

I took the envelope from her, yanking out the folder inside, wanting to see it with my own eyes. In the top drawer of my desk lay the Brown University brochure I had taken from Mr. Radnor's office, inside photographs of Brown's thick-boughed elms with leaves dappled by New

England sun, its wrought-iron fences and velvety deep lawns where pensive-looking students curled over the books propped on their knees.

That night Mama phoned Aunt Bernice and Aunt Helena, and then Aunt Nadia in Scarsdale. "Guess where your niece is headed in the fall!" Most of my cousins were still in grammar or high school, but Gregory attended Kenyon—though we all knew he'd hoped for Harvard—and Larry was finishing his final year at SUNY Binghamton. The week before, Bernice had called to announce Larry would be graduating Phi Beta Kappa, but Mama knew Ivy League trumped honors from a state school. And Brown, which had once been low on her list because of its greater distance, had become, within the last hours, her very favorite. She winked at me from where she sat at one of the kitchen chairs, still chatting.

At temple, when the Neiers and the Colemans came to give their congratulations, Mama eased around in her seat, sliding one leg over the other, cool and smooth as cream, as if she had known all along this was how things would turn out. But when they returned to their pews, she squeezed my hand hard.

We drove north—Poppy, Mama, and I—in the blue wagon we'd owned for as long as I could remember, with crates and canvas bags and wicker baskets stuffed with my belongings. How strange it seemed not to have Sarah and Valerie in the backseat on either side of me. I tried not to think about how, as I'd left, I'd seen Sarah bury her head in Valerie's neck, heard the soft snuffle of tears they couldn't quite hold back.

"How are you feeling, Ruth? Excited?" Mama pushed her sunglasses to the top of her head, twisting in her seat to face me as we finally approached the Providence exit and Poppy signaled our turn off Interstate 95. She smiled, but her cheeks stiffened as they did when she was preparing for a photograph. From my window, I could now see two church steeples and a tall, modern building I thought I remembered, from my visit the previous year, belonged to the college campus. Providence was small, I knew, in comparison to cities like New York, but from here the structures seemed so spread apart. I tucked a finger through the braided pink and yellow string bracelet Sarah and Valerie had tied around my wrist that morning. "A friendship bracelet," they'd whispered, having already fastened matching ones to their own wrists. "Always even more than sisters."

Most freshmen were assigned double rooms, but I would be sharing one of the few suites on Brown's campus with three other girls. "It's here, Aaron! Don't miss it. On the corner of Charlesfield and Benefit," Mama announced, reading from the orientation packet that the admissions office had sent weeks before. She directed Poppy to a street behind the brick dorms where we could park.

By the campus map included with the orientation information, we found the entrance to Keeney Quadrangle, where a swarm of laughing students crowded before the building entries, calling to one another with teasing voices, jostling past us as we crossed the green. Mama lifted her eyebrows and her shoulders at once as she turned to me, as if to say, "Won't this be fun!" But she reached for my hand as she used to do crossing a street with me when I was little, as if she were afraid we might lose each other in the throng.

Inside Jameson House, most doors were closed, soft music and the thud-thud of hammering behind a few, others quiet where residents had not yet arrived or had already unloaded their bags and headed off to explore new things. The door to my suite was ajar though, and inside, we found it empty save three matching leather suitcases, each the size of a small hill! with the initials *F.L.C.* in shining brass. They filled the central living area with a sharp, flowery scent I recognized from the samples Mama sometimes tested at Whitman's cosmetic counter but never bought. Near the entrance to the closest room sat what must have been Francesca's fourth suitcase. Mama inspected the three unclaimed rooms, then stepped into the one just past Francesca's.

"I think this is the best of what's left," she said, pointing to its window with a view of the grassy quad and a small tree. "We'll make it nice." She fingered the strand of coral beads at her neck, but I saw how the edges of her mouth sagged at first sight of the sparse walls, the narrow metal-legged bed and curtainless window. She and Poppy would stay until I was completely unpacked, she insisted. "You'll want to make a place for everything, won't you, Pea?"

I was certain my suitemates' parents would not be making such arrangements for them, but since Mama, more quickly than I, seemed able to make sensible order of my belongings, I watched as she folded my underwear into dresser drawers, stacked books on shelves, set a ceramic-framed photo of my sisters on the faux-wood desk.

After the last of my clothes and linens and toiletries had been unpacked, my posters taped to the walls above my bed, a spare set of keys made for my room "just in case," Mama and Poppy had walked the campus with me, remembering the buildings from our tour the previous fall: Faunce House, John Carter Brown Library, Wilson Hall, the Sharpe Refectory, where I would eat most of my meals. On Wriston Quad, we passed the fraternity houses, one with a spray-painted sheet draped from a third-floor window announcing a party later in the week.

"You coming?" two boys in shorts and flip-flops and blue baseball caps called from the patio beneath the banner. But I knew they didn't mean me, sandwiched between my mother and father like a child. Even on my own, I had never been the one boys phoned late at night or followed down the sidewalk, asking my name.

"Who's that?" Mama asked, as if I could possibly know. She frowned, then checked over her shoulder, scanning the patios of the other fraternity houses as if to be ready in case someone else should call out.

Later, after Mama and Poppy had kissed me for the final time, Mama holding my face in her hands once more before climbing back into the car, I returned to my room. There I retouched little of what Mama had organized earlier, only hiding away the pink ballerina music box and stuffed mother and baby koala bears, which she'd brought from home and left embarrassingly in plain view. Which was worse—the fact that she had packed these girlhood toys or that, before tucking them behind my sweaters on a closet shelf, I'd hugged the bears to me and cried into their gray matted fur?

On my desk chair, Mama had placed a white paper bag with the remainder of the lunch she had prepared for our car ride—corned beef and mustard on rye bread—just like what she had made for Sarah and Valerie and me time and time again. Flopping onto the bed, I unfolded the sandwich's protective wax paper. It was already six o'clock. My admissions packet informed me that, in the Sharpe Refectory, an orientation dinner was being held for all first-year students at six-thirty. But, still, I bit a corner from the sandwich Mama had made, the bread softening on my tongue as I chewed. My last taste of home.

~

By the end of my first week of college, a care package arrived from Mama—fancy assorted nuts, dried cherries, her own homemade shortbread cookies. I had hesitated before cutting open the package, knowing that as soon as the familiar smells escaped, the loneliness I had pushed from my mind all week would return with a throbbing rush. How disorienting everything seemed when the yeasty, sugary scents from home mingled with the must of my dorm room carpet and the slightly acrid odor of its cinderblock walls. How odd to see Mama's shortbread in Tupperware on my dormitory bed, beside my Brown University notebooks, instead of in the yellow earthenware jar on the kitchen counter, and I felt somehow I was in the wrong place.

I wondered if such anxiety ever plagued Opal or Setsu or Fran. But they all appeared perfectly adjusted as they strode in and out of our suite, their canvas bags slung carelessly over their backs. At night, I stuffed a towel into the crack beneath my bedroom door, afraid my suitemates might hear my sniffles of homesickness. I had lied our first evening together, claiming I'd spent part of the last summer on an Outward Bound trip with high school friends, not wanting to be the only one away from home for the first time. (Opal had traveled everywhere and had passed the month before school began at a youth art program in San Diego. Francesca's parents had sent her on teen tours throughout Europe, and Setsu had spent her Augusts at camps.) I could never let them know that, when I closed my eyes at night, I pretended I was in the bedroom beside Mama and Poppy's, with the rosebud wallpaper and faded pink curtains—this the only way I could drift into sleep.

At Mama's insistence, I had enrolled in Survey of European History and a political science course entitled American Constitutional Law—courses she declared would give me a solid foundation for a host of more advanced classes in the future. Then, just days later, I had met with my student adviser, Dean Salkin, in her office among its countless stacks of books. The far section of the floor seemed a haphazard arrangement of paperbacks and faded, fabric-bound books and new hardcovers with glossy jackets; but in the area nearer the entrance, there seemed an order to the spacing of the stacks, like columns from some ancient temple ruins.

"Perhaps I should employ this as an intelligence test for my students," Dean Salkin had joked, running a hand through the fringed ends of her cropped, gray-blond hair, as I'd carefully wended my way through the maze of books to a leather chair across from hers. After a long discussion involving many questions about my interests, I had added Psychology 10 and Beginning Fiction Writing, which, she'd advised, would round out my course load nicely.

"Fiction writing? That was the dean's suggestion?" Mama was surprised.

"I think she's been teaching for a while, Ma. You could practically circle the campus with the books she's collected!"

Still, wasn't it the dean's job to help me make the most of my opportunity? Storytelling seemed something I could do during free time. Did I know how saturated the world was with authors whose names would never be heard? Too many to count. She hoped for the following term I would consider some economics or even engineering classes, subjects more practical, subjects that opened doors.

How's my scholar?" Mama would ask when she called each Sunday and Wednesday evening. "Great, Ma." I didn't say that I sometimes wished I still had Mrs. Lieberman's assistance, that the pep talks I tried to give myself now seemed far less effective. Or that almost daily my hand cramped as I scribbled down as many of my professors' words as I could catch, but when I pored over my notes later, hunched with a bag of Starburst candies at my dorm room desk, occasional portions of what I'd written made little sense at all. I never told that when I'd asked Opal and Setsu, who took European History with me, to review a rough draft of my paper on humanism, they had found two sections they thought needed strengthening.

I spent a week on the humanism essay—"Humanism and the Art of Leonardo da Vinci"—but received only a "Pass." *Next time use fewer quotations. Rely more on your own arguments*, Professor Stone had scrawled in black ink across my cover sheet.

"A 'Pass'? What does that mean?" Mama asked. "Are any other marks given?" I thought I could hear the click-click-click of her nails against the Formica kitchen counter.

"I don't know, Ma," I said, though this wasn't true. I had seen the large A on Opal's essay. And later, after Opal was asleep, I had read through what she'd written, her paper having been left on the low, rectangular table of our common room beside some sketches for her art class.

Sartrean thought asserts that "Existentialism is Humanism," her first line read, a reference I was not sure I entirely understood.

Then before I reached the end of her essay, I felt what came when I least wanted it to: that unsettled sensation in my stomach that always turned to bottomless hunger. Mama's second care package was stashed under my bed, out of sight to decrease temptation. Her friend Arlene, she'd heard, sent only junky chips and candy bars to Albert at Bates. But Mama packed stuffed dates, rosemary crackers, an expensive cinnamon swirl loaf from Zimmerman's Gourmet wrapped in fancy royal blue tissue. *How many of your classmates get* this *from home!* she'd printed on the attached Broadway Paperie card cut in the shape of a heart—the closest resemblance to a love note I ever seemed to receive! I had noticed that my new jeans had begun to strain at the waist and across the seat. And that a few red pimples had sprung up at the sides of my nose—from too many fatty foods, I was sure. Still, I couldn't help myself. And reaching behind the suitcases and extra shampoo bottles and my L.L. Bean duck boots, I pulled out the box Mama had sent. And I ate and ate and ate until I ached.

My suitemates and I began to spend our Saturdays together. Though we didn't plan it, it became a habit, something we came to expect without advance discussion. With no classes or meetings to attend, we passed the morning over handfuls of Raisin Bran from boxes we'd smuggled from the Sharpe Refectory, reading each other articles from the last week's *Brown Daily Herald*s or excerpts from the celebrity magazines Setsu occasionally picked up, finding the ones that most amused us. Later, we walked down the hill and across the river to the few downtown shops or, if it was warm, sought out a sunny section of the Green.

Then, eventually, for lunch, we made our way to the Refectory—or "Ratty," as we soon learned students had nicknamed it. My roommates, I noticed, seemed unfazed by the sports teams who moved through the cafeteria as a single, solid force, their hair still wet from post-practice showers, or by the fraternity brothers or the older girls in their worn-in Brown sweatshirts who seemed to own the center of the room. Once we had found a table, Opal and Setsu constructed dainty, colorful mounds of lettuce and peppers and sliced cucumber from the salad bar, arranging their dressings on the sides of their trays in coffee cups as so many other girls did, ignoring the more filling choices I piled onto my own plate.

Soon the scale in our hall bathroom reported what I already feared—unless it was off by several pounds, I wondered, scrubbing my face at the row of scratched sinks. It wasn't a fancy doctor's scale, after all, just the cheap, unreliable kind you might find at a drugstore. Besides, the square of plastic covering the numbered dial was chipped, so goodness knew how old the thing was. As I mulled over these points, I spied Opal in the mirror. She stepped from the shower, her hair long dripping ropes, a large striped towel in her hands; and before she'd wrapped it tightly around, I glanced at the perfection of her. She glided to the sink beside mine, arranging her soap, a washcloth, toothbrush, and an assortment of tubes and bottles on the narrow shelf below the mirror, attending even to this with a flawlessness that made me wish I hadn't made such a scattered mess of my own items, and that I wore something other than my old terrycloth robe, which stopped bluntly at my knees, always, somehow, making my calves appear thicker.

"It's never the same as showering at home, is it?" Opal smiled, squeezing toothpaste onto her brush. She filled a small paper cup with water, then opened a white bottle and shook a brown capsule into her hand. "Vitamins," she said, tapping the bottle after she'd swallowed the capsule. "A multi. You want one?"

"Okay. What's it for?" I hadn't had vitamins since I was a girl, but the thought that they might be part of Opal's beauty ritual made them seem suddenly exotic.

"Oh, general health, I guess. They have a little of everything. The label on their container even claims they curb appetite." Opal turned on the faucet and ran her toothbrush under the water. For a moment, her eyes met mine in the mirror, and I knew what she hinted at. Though I was usually careful to conceal my binges—brushing up every crumb before emerging from my room, spraying the air, to mask any scent, with the Bonne Bell perfume Sarah and Valerie had bought for my birthday two years before—she had caught me once, the door to my room having opened without my knowing. And she had seen everything.

With my hand towel, I blotted the last spots of dampness on my neck and forehead, glad for this brief excuse to hide my face. "Sometimes my mother sends enormous care packages. There's probably enough in each one to sustain the entire dorm for a week! So—it makes it difficult. You've probably never had to think about *your* weight."

Opal laughed and slowly combed fingers through her wet hair, checking her reflection—her narrow nose, the sweep of her cheekbones, her green-green eyes—as if she might possibly spot some blemish. "I can only imagine what my mother's idea of a care package would be. Probably nothing legal for eighteen-year-olds! But to answer your question, I guess I'm just very careful, that's all," she said, as if it were nothing more than a choice. Did she think I *wanted* to eat as I did.

"You should come shopping with me tomorrow. I discovered this great health store off Wickenden Street, near the river. It's amazing what you can find there."

Opal used her walks to Wickenden as part of her exercise routine, wearing running sneakers and white spandex pants. As we crossed the campus, two older-looking boys in crew jackets turned, their eyes on Opal's waist, her hips, her arms as she raised them to adjust the long-toothed clip in her hair. She hadn't even caught them staring, but I saw in their faces a wanting no one had ever focused on me. Even other girls—a group of blondes with frosted lipstick—the California girls, everyone called them, though we knew they probably just looked it—studied Opal as they emerged from Chapin House. And I saw how their eyes contracted as if they were memorizing her—her shape and the rhythm of her walk, and how her shoulders swayed slightly, with a confidence even greater than what they exuded.

When we reached Hope Street, passing the French bistro where I'd heard couples on campus went for dates, Opal quickened her pace, her arms swinging energetically at her side. "Is this okay? I try to fit in aerobics when I can."

"Oh, sure! This is great!" I said, though by the time we could make out the Seekonk River, I was gasping like a caught fish.

Opal's route, which zigzagged along side streets to maximize the walk, took us past two Portuguese bakeries, a darkened tobacco shop, and a secondhand store displaying Mexican-printed ponchos and African masks, a sickly-sweet incense wafting from its half-opened door. We were now on a street almost empty but for a sallow-skinned man crouched near the narrow entry of Angel's Sweet Shop, who spat noisily just after we passed. I turned, looking up the hill, no longer sure of the way back.

"Don't worry. Almost there." I thought I saw the beginnings of a smile at the corners of Opal's lips. I wondered if my skittishness tickled her. Embarrassingly, I had reached for her arm like a frightened child when a group of men and women dressed in coal-dark jeans and boots rushed up behind us, only later identifying them as Brown students, residents of Machado House, one of whom Opal recognized, waving, exchanging words in Spanish.

Opal had brought a long shopping list with her to Eastern Garden. I watched as she scanned the shelves, checking off each item, then exchanged "hellos" with Lena, the pixie-nosed tennis player from our dorm who Fran declared had had implants: *Either that or she's packing tennis balls in her bra. They're way too round and perky, and no one that bony-assed has a chest that size.*

I trailed Opal through aisles of dried mushrooms and soy cheeses and turnip chips.

"May I make some suggestions?" she asked. Watercress soup cleansed the system, cranberries were a natural diuretic. And if it was weight loss I was hoping for, she said, nothing worked better than bran for breakfast and lunch, steamed veggie wraps for dinner. She had tried this, herself, and had immediately dropped three pounds.

For two weeks, I tried to follow Opal's diet. But the needle of our bathroom scale refused to budge. The bran muffins and cereals stuck in my throat, dry and rough as wood; and by each afternoon, the veggie wraps, when removed from their plastic covering, smelled of something rotting. By the end of the third day, I had polished off an entire coffee cake, a box of Golden Grahams cereal, and a bag of toffees from the convenience store on Thayer Street. I sat on my bed, my stomach bloated, knees tucked to my chest. I had promised myself that here, in college, my old weaknesses would not get the better of me. I blamed Opal for touting a diet that had made me hungrier than ever. Where did she find the discipline to stick with it? Was there some trick she hadn't shared with me? That night I dreamed I disassembled our dormitory scale—spreading its springs and nuts across the floor until I discovered how they should have been arranged all along. Then, in nothing but my size large Bloomie's panties and bra, I stepped on—Opal and Setsu, and Winnie and Kay, the two southern girls who lived across the hall, surrounding me as we waited for a number to appear.

In Providence, the cool of autumn seemed to turn cold more quickly than in New York. My roommates and I, in Fran's parents' convertible (which she was keeping in a garage near campus), drove to a pumpkin farm in Cumberland. We rode in a hay-filled wagon to the pumpkin fields and trudged up and down the planted rows, until we found an enormous though somewhat lopsided pumpkin, which we all agreed had character. Back in our suite that afternoon, we carved it with triangular eyes and a jagged grin.

"Our fifth roommate," Fran said, arranging a baseball cap on its head, inserting a cigarette in the gap between two of its crooked teeth.

In the warmth of our dorm, our jack-o'-lantern grew mold and had to be discarded after only two days. But outside the ground hardened, and patches of frost settled on the grass of the campus greens each night. I began to need my hooded parka even for the short walk to and from the library each evening. My assignments for Constitutional Law and European History had become longer and more complex, or perhaps I merely had other work I preferred to be doing. After hours on the library's fourth floor, I would come away with pages of material for my fiction class but only unfinished notes for my essay on the Italian Renaissance.

"What topic did you choose?" Opal asked one evening. She was making final edits to her own Italian Renaissance essay at the carrel behind mine, barefooted—her pink flats tucked under her chair—and seated Indian-style in black leggings that made her perfectly skinny thighs appear even thinner.

"I haven't decided which influences from classical antiquity to emphasize," I told her. "I've gotten a bit of a late start. The next couple of nights will be long ones."

"Would you like a second opinion? I'm happy to take a look," Opal offered. But it irked me the way she chewed her pen cap as she read, scribbling little notes now and then in my margins as if she were my teacher.

"Never mind!" I almost snapped, almost snatching the paper back. But I refrained. And with a recommendation or two from Opal, this time I received a B.

"B is better than a Pass, I assume?" Mama asked over the phone. "So maybe next time another improvement . . ."

"Yes, maybe next time, Ma." I had also finished another story for my writing class. I had entitled it "By the Light of Day," I told her.

"Oh?" she said, in a way that made me think, for a moment, she would ask to hear it. But she had only a question about my upcoming psychology test.

I n December, during the week before the winter break, the fraternities and social dorms on campus threw holiday parties. The high point, I learned, was Saturday night. This was when the houses along the quads decorated their patios with evergreen boughs and yards and yards of twinkling lights. Candles were placed in windows, bands hired to play jazzy renditions of holiday music. These parties were open to everyone, and according to Francesca, *everyone* attended. She and Setsu, along with Winnie and Kay, had driven Fran's car to Boston's Copley Square and purchased short Calvin Klein skirts and high boots with zippers on the sides—outfits I had never worn.

But Setsu and Fran had surprised me, knowing, I supposed, the prudish-looking contents of my own closet. "An early holiday gift," Francesca laughed, and placed a silky, pearly-gray camisole top in my hands. It was similar to tops I had seen Setsu wear, and I gasped at their unexpected generosity.

"You really didn't have to do this—"

"Just try it on." Setsu kissed my cheek, then gave my back a small push toward my room.

I gingerly slipped the camisole over my head and stood before the mirror of my closet door. I looked nothing like Setsu or Opal would. The top pulled a bit across my chest and did nothing to hide the fleshiness of my arms. But the color wasn't half bad with the dark of my hair, and I happened to have a velvet skirt I sometimes wore to dinners at Aunt Nadia's that matched it.

Opal claimed she could think of better things to do with her evening—that nothing distinguished one campus party from the next.

She was recuperating from a recent cough, her eyes slightly puffy, the skin at the corners of her mouth dry. Even her hair was messier than usual, still plaited in its nighttime braid and flattened on either side of her part. It was wrong, I knew, wanting her always to look this way. Wrong to hope Francesca and Setsu wouldn't convince her to come along. Wishing she hadn't, in the end, decided to fix her hair or highlight her cheekbones with pink blush, or root through her clothes until she'd found her jade wrap dress. I knew how I looked beside her.

The party Francesca and Setsu wanted to stop by first was at the Sigma Chi house; it was the one they had heard from Kay and Winnie was best. Snow was falling lightly, leaving a veil of flecks on the hair and overcoats of the arriving crowd gathered outside on the fraternity's front patio. They were laughing, sipping punch from plastic cups, undeterred by the white flakes melting in their drinks. Two fraternity brothers in matching Sigma Chi sweatshirts stood on the patio's low stone wall serenading all who approached with off-key versions of "Good King Wenceslas" and "Winter Wonderland." Inside, a lanky boy with deep-set hazel eyes, whom I'd noticed on line at the Registrar during the first week of school, removed our wraps for us. I saw how his thumb brushed Opal's arm, how he took more time with her coat and with Setsu's than with Francesca's or mine.

"He's probably a pledge. He won't officially be a brother until next year," explained Francesca. As roommates, we had attended a few parties in our dorm—a Halloween costume party on the floor above ours, a sixties party for which Setsu had made us tie-dyed shirts, a few impromptu all-female gatherings in Kay and Winnie's room over berry wine coolers and fat-free popcorn. But Fran had been to several more fraternity parties than the rest of us. "Let's go to the back room. That's where all the food and drinks will be."

The back room was dimly lit. A Christmas tree adorned with plaid ribbons and silver tinsel stood in the corner. At the center of the drafty room's wooden floor danced tight circles of girls in their low-backed holiday dresses, flimsier than my top despite the cold. Some were girls I recognized but had seen before only in school sweatshirts and jeans, their hair bound up in ponytails rather than curled and falling past their shoulders. Near them danced couples with foreheads touching, legs rubbing. Among them, though I would not have known her at first, transformed, shimmering in gold sequins, Nora, our head counselor, clasped her hands behind the neck of someone tall, his head bowed toward hers. We followed Francesca through the milling guests and past beer kegs to a table laid with cheese cubes and pretzel sticks and star-shaped cookies. She filled a plate for us to share then moved to the far end of the table, where we could choose from every kind of alcohol: a display of bottles like those at the weddings and birthdays, the bar and bat mitzvahs, where my cousins and I had sneaked half-glasses of Manischewitz or splashed rum into our Coca-Colas. But never so much that our parents would notice. I knew the things Mama said of the Wolmans' daughters, who shamed themselves and their family. She had forbidden me to attend high school bashes even though my friends were permitted: "I wasn't born yesterday, Ruth. I *know* what goes on at those parties. Someday you'll thank me for wanting you to be better!" But now Francesca, chuckling, handed me a glass of red punch before crossing the floor to greet her friend Jackie—"Remember, Ruth! Vodka and fruit juice—it slides down like candy!"

Nibbling the star cookies sprinkled with green sugar, Opal, Setsu, and I watched the dancers from the edge of the dance floor. After several songs, the music softened and slowed. The crowd thinned, leaving only couples, who pressed closer, their fingers intertwined. Setsu was swaying to the rhythm of "What a Wonderful World," humming lightly under her breath with Louis Armstrong's raspy voice. From the way she arched her back, one hip jutting out, I could tell she was hoping someone would invite her to dance as well.

The boy who had taken our coats when we first arrived reappeared and now stood near the doorway. He was taller, his shoulders squarer than I had at first noticed. Despite the semidarkness, I could follow the path of his eyes over the heads of the dancers, around the room. When he noticed the three of us, he smiled, but I knew for whom it was intended. And then, to my surprise, just behind him—though I'd never dreamed he'd be caught dead at this kind of thing—I spotted Gavin Rutledge, a sophomore from my Psychology 10 class. He leaned against the wall, the heel of one foot, in its hiking boot, kicking aimlessly against the other, one hand tucked in the back pocket of his jeans, the other swirling and swirling a drink, as if he were too bored even to swallow it.

Earlier that week, I had learned that for Psychology 20 the following semester Gavin would be my assigned lab partner, as Georgie Farnsworth would be transferring to another section due to a scheduling conflict. But I had noticed Gavin long before because he had sat alone at the back of the auditorium, slouching slightly in his chair, a checked scarf wound around his neck despite the warmth of the room. He had a thin face, thin nose, fidgeting legs, and a hairline that was beginning to recede ever so slightly at his temples. He wore silver wire-rimmed glasses, which he tapped occasionally with his forefinger. "A few rungs short of drop-dead handsome!" my sisters and I once would have said. In no way did he resemble the boys on campus I knew my classmates murmured about. There was nothing chiseled about his face like the pledge with the hazel eyes or like Matty Cronin, whom, I knew, Francesca, earlier in the fall, had followed around for weeks. But he stretched his arms so decisively across the empty seatbacks on either side of him and squinted with such intensity throughout Professor Wren's lecture that I could not help turning to stare.

"I think he's looking at you," Setsu hissed in my ear. "You should go talk to him." And was it my imagination, or had he lifted the cup in his hand in a greeting—not meant for Opal or for Setsu, but for me?

Setsu grabbed Opal's arm, leaving me alone with my drink and our shared plate of half-eaten cookies. Gavin's voice was liquid and low, the words pouring, though his lips seemed hardly to move. "So you're going to be my lab partner in Psych next term, right?" He tilted his chin, draining the remaining contents of his glass.

"I guess." I did not think he knew me and had never imagined he'd given a thought to having me for a partner. I hoped he couldn't tell how certain I was we had been paired, hoped he hadn't caught me watching him in class. I felt for the feather-thin edge of my camisole, which seemed to cling to me now as closely as skin.

"You'll regret it. I'm always weeks behind in the reading. You'd be far better off without me." He let out a small laugh but without curving his mouth so that I could not tell if he was joking or sincere.

For an eternity I tried to think of something clever or interesting to say. I thought he would move on, find someone else to talk to. But he stayed, drumming his fingers against the rim of his cup, keeping the rhythm of the music. Was it possible he liked this—just standing side by side in silence? Was it possible, if I dared turn to him, I might find him gazing at me as boys so often gazed at Opal?

But when I finally looked again, he was gone. So he hadn't been. Of course. And I had only been wishing—ridiculous things.

Through the open window, I saw that it was no longer snowing but that flakes still drifted from the tree branches. A few solitary flakes floated inside, one landing on my arm. As I turned my wrist to watch it melt, ice clinked in my punch glass. I had almost forgotten I was holding it, remembered taking no more than a taste or two. But when I looked down, I found it empty save for a few pink droplets running along the side. A radiant moon was visible through the white-dusted trees, a series of iridescent glowing rings surrounding it. As dazzling as in the TV romances my sisters and I used to sneak when Mama was out. Bright enough to make the night sky glisten with magic, and with the promise of bold, new things. But not yet for me.

After the winter break, my first shared lab with Gavin included an experiment on obesity in mice. Would I mind conducting it while he observed? Gavin whispered so that Professor Wren could not hear. As usual, he had neglected the previous night's reading. Several days after completing each lab, we were required to turn in a report outlining the experiment and its results in detail. I wondered if Gavin would ask that I alone take responsibility for these as well, but instead, he offered his dorm room as a workspace. "My roommate's never home. The place will be quiet, and there are two desks and two chairs." He shrugged his shoulders in a way that made me feel foolish for ever hoping the things I had during our weeks away from school, for ever imagining his thoughts might match mine.

So every two weeks, I knocked on his door, my Psychology 20 text and lab notes in hand. In Psych, the course reading was straightforward, and with adequate hours of studying for the tests given periodically, I received high marks. It soon became clear that my understanding of the subject matter was greater than Gavin's. So, often, he spent much of the time quietly watching from the chair beside mine as I, seated before his computer, perused the relevant materials, then typed out the various sections of our report. But one afternoon as I worked to phrase and re-phrase a particularly lengthy report on the nervous system, I felt a whispery touch beneath my arm, along the side of my ribs, so light I thought at first I had imagined it. But then I felt it again and this time, the distinct press of fingers, sending through me an explosion of fear and heat. For some seconds I froze, my hands motionless over the keyboard, my mind spinning with fragmented thoughts. "You distract me, Ruth. Do you know that?" Gavin murmured. I nodded, though I hadn't meant to. I was concentrating on keeping my hands from shaking, wondering if I should summon the courage for some similar declaration. But when the report was done and I stood to leave, he rose and leaned in the doorway, thumbs tucked in his woven belt, as casually as he had every time before.

That night, I lay in bed watching the yellow glow of light that shone through my window from the quad below and listened to the late-hour sounds of students returning from Funk Night at the Underground and the pubs near campus. I recognized the voices of the European girls who shared the suite down the hall and dated only older boys, and of the field hockey girls from upstairs who'd claimed boyfriends within weeks of the start of school. And as they laughed over their shared escapades, a flutter moved through my chest with the thought that I might soon have my own taste of the things they knew.

Of my suitemates, I was fondest of Setsu. She was the easiest to talk to and, lovely as she was, always full of compliments—noticing a bangle I hadn't worn before or a new hairstyle. On nights when Fran went out and after Opal was asleep, we often spent hours in her room or mine, listening to WBRU Radio, sprawled on the carpet, our feet tapping to the rhythms of Edie Brickell and Elvis Costello and the Indigo Girls. Sometimes Setsu talked of her brother, the violinist, or of the places they had visited where his youth orchestra had played. She was curious about my family, about what it had been like to grow up with so many aunts and uncles and cousins. "I think I would have liked that," she said.

"It was never lonely, but my sisters and I couldn't get away with a *thing!*" I told the story I had been too shy to relate our first night in the suite—of my afternoon in Mr. Gupta's shop.

"You did not! Did you honestly run into a rack of cards?"

The ridiculousness of what I had done seemed to strike us simultaneously, and we howled until our ribs hurt. But even as I laughed into my cupped hands, I wished I had described it differently or hadn't told it at all. I remembered how Setsu had danced at the Sigma Chi party and, modest as she was, known how to draw the attention of boys. She never would have said, but I knew the story made me seem such a baby. Maybe the next time I would tell her what had happened with Gavin just days before instead.

. . .

Before my next visit to Gavin's, at my closet door mirror, I held against me in succession my turquoise turtleneck, my red sweater, a salmon-colored one, then one with brown stripes, trying to determine which best flattered me, disguised the lumpiness around my middle, narrowed the melony roundness of my backside. Finally I chose a loose white shirt with buttons down the front. To make it look more feminine, I unbuttoned the top button, then, my pulse speeding, slipped open the second button as well, revealing a generous vee of flesh.

"That looks pretty, Ruth." Setsu was dressing, too, fastening a moonstone necklace she had bought earlier that week from a jewelry vendor at the student P.O. "Where are you headed?"

"Oh, nowhere. Just meeting my lab partner."

"Really? Well, you look great." She dabbed a finger to my cheek, showing me an eyelash that had fallen. "If you blow on it, it's good luck," she laughed, offering it.

"Thank you. I'll take what I can!" I said, watching Setsu pull the ends of her hair forward so that it draped her shoulders rather than hanging down her back. Then she wound an ivory scarf around her neck, arranging it so that it showed the moonstones beneath. As she stroked the scarf's fringed edges, I wondered if she had reasons she'd never told for making herself look lovely, and, shy as she was, if even she had done things I'd never dared.

Strains of music I'd heard before but couldn't name—something Jamaican, maybe—sounded from Gavin's room as I made my way down his hall, the bottom edge of my textbook pressing into my belly. I shifted it in my hands, afraid it would crease my shirt or, worse, leave a line of perspiration and cling in an unflattering spot. As I lifted my hand to knock, I noticed that Gavin's roommate, Victor, a bassoonist for the Brown band, had taped to the door above the plastic note board new photos of himself and three other band members performing for a recent Brown Bears hockey game. The collection of snapshots below the board remained—of Victor and friends in maroon graduation caps and gowns—these encircling a bumper sticker with *Indian Falls High School, PA* in red letters. More than midway through the year, Gavin must still have felt no inclination to add anything of his own to Victor's memorabilia.

"Hi there," Gavin said. The music was no longer audible and he held some paper in his left hand, a letter, I guessed, and seemed so engrossed that I wondered, with a small, burning twinge in my throat, if my thoughts of the past days had been nothing more than fabrications. We began our work as usual, I making notations in the margins of our assigned reading, Gavin looking on. But after some time, he drew his chair closer to mine, so close I could hear his breathing, could feel the moistness of it on the back of my neck.

"Your skin is the color of white marble," he murmured. "Has anyone told you that?"

"No." I shook my head. When I was younger, Mama, in the summertime, had slathered all of us with sunscreen to protect what she called "the Feldman and Leiser women's milky complexion." But always I had regretted the paleness of my face and limbs, that even after hours at the beach my skin darkened only slightly, bubbling with pink blisters if I was not careful. I had envied girls who wore shorts and sleeveless tops to show off their amber-gold skin. I bit my lip too hard, tasting blood, not sure whether or not to believe Gavin's compliment when his fingers clasped me again. This time they lingered longer, bit by bit inching forward, his wrist squeezing my ribs, his hand then moving upward to the back of my neck, winding through my hair. "Pretty girl," he whispered. *Shayna Maideleh*, my aunts had said, pinching my cheeks when I was younger, and I had never believed it, but I wanted to believe Gavin now. I could not stop the small wheeze that sounded from my throat but did not pull away as my mind began to fill with new desires.

This became our ritual: sometime before I left his room, before our lab report was completed, Gavin, with calloused palms that smelled of the pink liquid soap from the bathroom dispensers, would take my wrists, pulling me toward him. "I thought of you all day, Ruth," he would say as his hand slid under my sweater, under the elastic of my bra. We never kissed as I left or made any other plans to meet. Still, when I passed the Alpha Chi girls trading secrets behind the stacks of the Science Library, I smiled to myself over the things we shared. With the pocket money Poppy and Mama provided for me each month, I began to buy luxuries I had seen my suitemates tote in their wire baskets on their way to the shower— fragrant lotions that promised to keep my skin soft, lilac-scented hair conditioners, cleansers in tinted glass jars. I massaged each product into my face, my legs, my neck until they glistened and wondered if Gavin would like the smell, the feel of them, if he would notice and know it was for him I did these things. In Professor Wren's lecture hall, we still sat rows apart, but I remained conscious always that, at any moment, from his seat in the back, Gavin's eyes could be on me. And when, on occasion, his name was called to answer one of the professor's questions, my chest rose with a secret pride.

The summer before I'd left for college, Jeanie Rosenberg from 9B had stopped by with juicy gossip for Mama, her voice a low buzz: Daria Weiss had left NYU, home, every promise of a future, for some waiter who fancied himself an actor—a nobody. The Weisses were beside themselves, and now Carly, the younger daughter, had been spotted traipsing all over the city at ungodly hours with boys she had no business being with.

Yes, Mama had already heard.

"Can you *imagine?*" said Jeanie.

Mama shook her head and pressed a finger to her lips. I knew what she held in, what the whole building knew: Jeanie's own seventeen-year-old, Cecily, made midnight trips across town to meet her boyfriend while her parents slept, bribing Ferdinand, our late-night doorman, not to tell.

"Such a shame. It must be awful for all of them." Mama offered Jeanie hot tea, and as she walked to the kitchen to start the kettle, she paused, cupping her hand under my chin, as if to say to Jeanie Rosenberg that she and Poppy were the lucky ones, never worrying about such troubles with me. Then later, after Mrs. Rosenberg left, Mama repeated the story to Poppy, pronouncing each detail carefully, slowly, enjoying the triumph, I knew, of our superior family.

So I could not tell Mama about Gavin. But almost *all* girls did these things. Even shy, sweet girls. These things and more every day.

For my second-semester fiction writing class, I wrote a story about a Russian girl and her young husband who, while fleeing the pogroms in their homeland, become separated during a storm at sea. The words seemed to rise out of me like birds taking to air. Four pages became eight and then twelve.

"Lovely use of metaphor," Professor Richards praised as he returned the story to me. I saw that he had placed check marks, their long tails streaming like blue comets, beside the passages he thought best.

"My fiction teacher liked my last story," I told Mama when we next spoke. "It's a tale of romance."

"Oh?" I could hear the soft slurp of her tea.

"I could read it—"

"How tragic," she said before I reached the end. But that was all. She wondered if she'd told me of her conversation with Babbie Schafer. She'd bumped into her grocery shopping at Zimmerman's. Robert, now a sophomore at Cornell, had just begun a research project with his biology teacher in addition to his assigned classes. "Babbie says it will help with his applications to graduate schools in a couple of years. Very smart, don't you think?"

"Yes, Ma." But what I really wanted to say was that maybe if she listened to my story in its entirety—and this time more carefully—she might hear something to compliment.

. . .

Days later, before any of us had dressed for classes or breakfast, Opal raised the window behind the couch and held out a hand to check the outdoor air. "It's warm for February." She peered out. "There's Jess. God, she's out early, isn't she?"

"She must be coming back from Cory's." Setsu worked the belt of her pale blue cotton robe into a pretty bow. "She told me they've been spending every day together."

"And every night apparently, too. Ha!" Francesca laughed, pulling at the Cat Stevens T-shirt, which just covered her bottom, and poured Pepsi into her chipped china mug as she did every morning. "Well, good for her. I'm glad *someone* around here is enjoying herself." She grinned at Opal and Setsu as if they, but not I, could appreciate her joke. Only days before, I had interrupted Francesca with Winnie. They'd been standing in the entrance to Winnie and Kay's room, laughing about the medical student Winnie had been dating for a few weeks. I had seen the foil rectangle studded with plastic-coated pink tablets in Francesca's palm.

"Out! Out!" Francesca had shooed me away as soon as I'd entered the room. "We don't want to corrupt innocence!"

Winnie had laughed. "Oh, don't listen to her," she'd said with her hint of a southern accent. "Of course you can stay." But Francesca had tucked the pills back into the pocket of her French designer jeans, and the conversation had ended.

So I knew what they all thought. But they were wrong to think they had to exclude me from their secrets. And I could *prove* it.

"I guess I haven't told you, but I've sort of started seeing someone, too," I announced to my suitemates. I described my meetings with Gavin, the things between us that had now become expected.

"That's it?" Francesca plopped onto our sofa, curling her bare toes around the edge of the coffee table. She removed a black elastic from her wrist and wound it around her hair.

"Don't make fun," Setsu defended. She patted my arm with her thin hand as if to say, "There was nothing wrong with your story."

But I wished I had made it sound more mature, or told it in a more dramatic way that even Francesca could not criticize.

Some time later, for our report on consciousness, I agreed to meet Gavin in the evening rather than the afternoon. *I'll be out during the day*, he had scratched in high, angular letters on the only remaining blank corner of our memo board. *How 'bout seven instead?* When I knocked on his door, fingering the tiny amethyst pendant on a thin silver chain (which I had eventually decided earlier in the evening was the prettiest of the modest items in my jewelry box), he motioned me inside with a sweep of his arm. I noticed he had styled his hair differently: it was neatly brushed back and seemed to shine with something damp. And when he moved, a sweet cologne odor I had never smelled on him before emanated from his khaki shirt with its turned-up collar. A quiver of happiness darted through me at the thought of him standing before his mirror preparing for my arrival.

The room was dim. Victor's bassoon in its case was a black shadow against the far wall, and the collage of photos above Victor's desk and Gavin's framed print of a desert with its fork of a cactus were only dark rectangles.

"I prefer the lights low in the evening." Gavin flashed me an odd smile. "It's more mellow." He flicked a thumb toward his drawn, brown-stained window shade and the T-shirt he had draped over his desk lamp to soften the glow. "Don't you think?"

"Oh, no . . . yes . . ." I said, shaking my head or nodding—I was not sure which—distracted because Gavin, rather than pulling out chairs for us to sit in, had extracted the books from my arms and placed them on his bureau.

"Stay awhile," he breathed into my ear. And then, suddenly, his open mouth was on my neck and then my shoulders, his fingers coiling my hair. "Do you like this?"

I managed to raise and lower my chin in acquiescence, my heart drumming so furiously I could not think of words to speak. *Do it! Do it! Don't be afraid!* If others had, so could I. I could also be strong. *These* were the things couples did in solitude. But what did the girls do back? Surely, surely, I knew because I had heard it spoken of. From the girls who gossiped late at night in the second-floor lounge, and from what Opal told us she had seen during her countless travels: they ran their tongues along their lips; they sighed and moved closer. Yet I could only stand with stiffened limbs while Gavin worked at the buttons of my blouse, of his shirt, at the buckle of my belt. Then I was on his mattress, under the heaviness of him. The hair of his naked chest tickling, scratching. Earlier that day, I had dabbed rose oil between my breasts, a secret, I'd heard Francesca say, to stir men's longings. How many hours and hours ago that seemed. Now I was a pillar of stone. Numb beneath the weight of Gavin's body, cold as earth as he moved against me.

Before returning to my room, I lay without sleeping, blinking in the dark at the sheen of the posters taped to Gavin's ceiling. Fully dressed once more and wrapped in two blankets, still I could not stop shivering. Visions of Mama and Poppy, Sarah and Valerie, of Temple Beth Immanuel, of Hebrew school lessons, of family gatherings for Thanksgiving and Purim and Rosh Hashanah flashed before me. An avalanche of memories, all that my life had been until this evening. *This* was something that changed people—I knew that from magazines and books, from the rumors in the dorm. A tense pulsing choked my throat, but no tears reached my eyes. I pressed a hand to my mouth and listened to the hiss of Gavin's breathing.

⌐◦

Sixteen days later, what Mama referred to as "my pesty friend" and Aunt Bernice called "a lady's curse" had not yet arrived. I made continual, worried trips to the bathroom but, still, nothing. I knew what I needed to do. Winnie had once confided her fears to Setsu and me, and we had accompanied her to the very back aisle of McGee's Pharmacy, where all unmentionable products were kept—ointments for rashes, powders for hygiene, and the small blue and white boxes marked *Home Tests*. One line meant you were lucky; two lines meant you were not. In the farthest stall of the dormitory bathroom, I grasped the wand in one trembling hand and studied the dragging tick-tick of my watch while I waited. *Oh, God. Oh, dear, dear God. Could it be a mistake?* So I took a second test and then a third, but each time, two fuchsia lines glared through the window in the wand's plastic tip.

For the next few days, I dressed and ate and attended classes—those I remembered to attend—in a panicked haze. Whom could I talk to? Who could tell me what to do? Finding her before she left for the library one night, I swore Setsu to secrecy.

"Oh, no! Oh, Ruth! What does Gavin say?" Setsu closed the door to her room, fiddling with the dial of her radio until music played loudly so that we would not be overheard.

"I haven't told him."

"But you need to. Don't you think waiting will only make things more complicated? Gavin will be understanding, won't he?"

"Oh, I'm sure." But the truth was I could not begin to guess how Gavin would respond. For all the hours we had spent together, still Gavin and I had hardly spoken. And this I could not admit; it seemed, somehow, more humiliating than the situation itself.

Setsu took my hand in her soft fairy fingers. How I envied her as she gazed at me. I wanted to be the one with eyes tearing only with empathy, only for troubles not my own. Wanted to be able to smile sweetly because the dimpled creases between my brows were for aches I did not hold.

"Do you have real feelings for him, Ruth? Do you think you want this to last?"

"I don't know. I haven't even had a chance to think. Maybe." I understood what Setsu meant: a romance that developed into a marriage, a family, a lifetime together. But it was absurd to consider these things with someone I'd just met. And even if *I* were willing . . . But, *sometimes*, love grew with the passage of time, didn't it? And as I sat with Setsu, I allowed myself this brief dream: Gavin holding me to him after hearing the news, his voice tremulous with emotion as he bent his forehead to mine and whispered that he felt this was a blessing.

"I'm no expert, but in relationships, I've found, it's always best to talk things through." Setsu squeezed my hand with the smooth pads of her fingers. "I really believe Gavin will want, more than anything, to put your happiness first. The two of you will work this out." She pronounced these last words with such tranquillity, almost as if she were concluding a prayer, filling me with reassurance.

But later that evening, I opened my bedroom window to release the stuffy heat pumping relentlessly through my radiator and glimpsed Gavin. Was it? Oh! He was crossing the quad below, his arm around the waist of a giggling wisp of a blonde, his hand resting just below the tiny curve of her hip. And sinking to my bed, I understood the truth.

I was never certain if Setsu's revelation to Francesca and Opal was as unintended as she claimed. Perhaps she felt she needed them, or I needed them. But only a day after I had confided to her what I'd seen from my window, I found my suitemates on the sofa and two armchairs of our common room, seated still and straight as the fences enclosing our campus, awaiting my return from a late-morning class. I had never seen them so sober. What they wanted me to know, they said, making room for me among them, was that they were here for me. All of them. Whatever I chose, they would support me.

"He's a dog!" Francesca's neck was red with emotion. "You know that, don't you? This is *not* your fault."

"Francesca, please!" Setsu lifted her hand, requesting silence. "You are not helping."

Opal ran her fingers along the groove between the couch cushions. She was frowning at the wheat-colored material as if there was something about it she had just noticed and disliked. "If it's of any comfort, I had two girlfriends from Los Angeles who went through this. They chose not to continue things—" She was speaking slowly, and I was aware of how carefully she selected each word. "But they both had the best of care. And in the end, they were fine. Really fine." She pulled her legs up, crossing her ankles, and twisted the leather knot in the cowry-shell anklet she always wore. I could see she was about to go on, then decided against it. I wondered if she'd had some other friend, known some other girl for whom things had not gone so well. "If it's what you decide, I know of a clinic downtown. I pass it on my way to the women's shelter where I volunteer. I can get more information—"

"Okay," I nodded but said nothing further. My thoughts the last days had been like a mess of loose strings, disconnected, coming to nothing. I could not even allow myself to imagine what Mama would say if she knew. How could I begin to make a decision until my mind stopped floating like a shred of cloud.

"Opal, you're pushing her," Setsu said.

"I'm not pushing, I'm only sharing information!"

"She's right, Setsu." Francesca was calmer now, her arms propped on the back of her chair. "The more information she has, the better."

"I just don't want her to make a choice she could later regret." Setsu smiled despite some sadness in her voice, in her dark eyes.

"She won't make a mistake. She'll do what's right for her." Francesca rapped her box of Parliaments matter-of-factly against the edge of the coffee table. She drew out a cigarette, balancing it between her middle and forefinger, but seemed to forget to light it.

On and on my suitemates talked, words meant to strengthen me, to give me solace. My ears ached as if my head had swelled with heat—from shame, from worry, but also from a perverse sort of pride at being the focus of their intense attentions.

It was a reading assignment for my second-semester Shakespeare class—my course work now the only thing that served to distract me—that filled me with a new ambition. The assignment was a supplement to *Romeo and Juliet*, the first four acts of which our professor, Dean Draper, had already given us to read. *It is crucial to keep in mind*, the supplement advised, *how very young these lovers are—Juliet a mere thirteen, Romeo not much older.* I checked and double-checked the sentence to make certain I had not misread it. Juliet, so full of passion and strength, had, by the beginning of the third act, already defiantly wed her true love. Could she really have been a full five years younger than I? Pushing my chair from my desk, I stood with my fingers folded over my abdomen. My hands still, I imagined I could feel the pulsing of the mysterious, growing life inside me. What marvelous work my body was doing. Not the work of a mixed-up girl but the work of a woman. With the help of *no one*, I thought, gazing down at my swollen breasts, I was doing something truly significant. Something more than Opal, more than Francesca. Perhaps this was not a ruinous mistake. Perhaps this was the most important thing I'd ever attempted. So why couldn't this continue to be?

I began to eat the very healthiest of diets—grain cereals, meat trimmed of fat, fruits and low-fat yogurts from the market blocks from campus. According to a magazine I had found on a stand in the university's bookstore, these were the foods recommended for those "in the family way." *Give yourself and your little one the benefit of all the best nutrients*, the article advised. On line in the dining hall, I scrutinized my choices carefully before making selections. Then when I sat to eat my unsugared oatmeal, grapefruit, sliced apple, I pictured each nourishing, vitamin-filled bite slipping from my throat to the place in my stomach I imagined was beginning to bulge. The numbers crept slightly higher on the bathroom scale but now for a right reason. And when Mama's next package of treats arrived—she still convinced these were the only decent foods I would consume while away—I was able to resist because she was *wrong*: these were *exactly* the things I was supposed to avoid. So I found willing recipients among the other freshmen in Jameson. And when the last cheese scone or nut muffin had been handed out, pride rippled through me over my newly discovered self-control.

———

At the end of the month, I was to return home for a few days for the celebration of Passover. Mama and Poppy had sent me my train ticket in an envelope sealed with clear tape. It had been two weeks since I had taken the home test, and still I had not broken the news to my family. This weekend, I knew, would be the right time to do it. Yet the thought of pronouncing the actual words before them made the center of me seem to fall away, and I could not help wondering if waiting just a bit longer would be so terrible.

Setsu and Fran had accompanied me to the downtown train station, insisting on carrying my bags. They hadn't asked, but they must have guessed this was the weekend I would tell what I'd been hiding. "Call if you need anything while you're gone." At the gate to the train platform, Setsu's thin arms encircled my neck, her cheek to mine. "Even if you just want to talk. We will be around."

"Remember, Ruth—" Francesca's voice was low, but her jaw pivoted from side to side for a moment as if she were thinking hard. "It's *your* life. You have nothing to apologize for to *anyone*."

I wished I could bring Setsu and Fran home with me, and Opal, too. With them, somehow, it seemed it wouldn't be so difficult. But there to meet me at the New York station was my entire family, and at the sight of them, any fortitude I had felt on my ride down abandoned me. At a single glance, I was certain, they would detect some change in me. But they seemed to notice nothing. "There she is! Our Ivy League girl!" Mama and Poppy kissed me on both cheeks, and I climbed into the backseat of our wagon—my homecoming and the heaviness of my bags enough, I supposed, to merit fetching the car from the lot rather than taking the bus. I sat between Sarah and Valerie, just as we used to do as girls, my knees bumping theirs with every pothole or dip in the street.

In three days, for Passover Seder, Mama was expecting Aunt Helena and Uncle Martin, Aunt Bernice and Uncle Mickey, Uncle Leonid, Aunt Nadia, and my cousins, as well as the Kleins from 5C. She had been baking and roasting and stewing, I knew, for the better part of a week, and as soon as Poppy unlocked the door to our apartment and I stepped inside, I breathed what seemed a hundred familiar scents—fried potato and sweet onions, chicken broth for soup, cloves and cinnamon and wine for haroset.

"Smells like home, hmm, Ruthie?" Mama smiled, pulling my coat from my shoulders. But though the fragrances were the same, I noticed quickly that other things had changed: Mama's hair, for instance, was shorter than I'd ever seen it and layered in a current style, a fact she had failed to mention during any of our recent phone calls. Also, the heavy gold living room drapes had been replaced, since my visit home in December, with airier lace ones. Then there was the new material on the dining chairs, a leafy print I never could have imagined to be Mama or Poppy's taste. These were things my family took so for granted now, I realized with a twinge of irritation, that it did not occur to them I was seeing them for the first time.

Mama had set out cream of potato soup and special knishes kosher for Passover from Hoffman's deli. I had expected that, at home, Mama would insist I eat, that she would want to see me nourish myself with something other than what she called "institutional slop." But, too preoccupied, perhaps, with work for the upcoming holiday, she did not even offer the food, only left it out for anyone who wished some. So it was easy to avoid the heavy snacks I knew were not recommended in my condition. I took a few small spoonfuls of potato soup, a mere bite or two of knish. When Mama cleared my plate, I waited for her to fret over what remained, but she cleaned the dish without a word, seemingly unaware of how much I'd left behind.

What made it even easier to turn away food was the queasiness that for the past several days had been nearly unceasing. "Morning sickness," I remembered Aunt Helena whispering to Mama once as they peeled carrots together at the kitchen sink, Helena's face ash white and beaded with perspiration, her belly stretching her paisley dress. But what I had lasted into the afternoon and evening, the odor, even the mere sight of certain dishes enough to make my stomach churn. What I craved were things I thought Mama would snap her tongue at: plain crackers, bananas, soft vegetables. In her opinion, these did not constitute a meal. So at lunches and dinners, I conjured up excuses for when she would confront me, my ears rushing with heat throughout several meals as I awaited the argument I knew would follow.

But Mama appeared not to see what I discarded or to notice that, shortly after some meals, I dashed to the hallway bathroom, one hand cupped to my mouth. I discovered tricks to hide my sickness: ran water from the sink to muffle the sound of my heaving; scrubbed the toilet rim, my hands, my mouth; sprayed the air with the freshener Mama kept beneath the sink. When I reemerged, I found my family at their usual pursuits: Poppy flipping the pages of a *National Geographic* magazine; Mama with her crossword puzzle, sections of newspaper spread across the kitchen table; Sarah and Valerie giggling in their shared bedroom over some mutual friend. How many worlds of things I knew now that they could never imagine; and the thought of my new separateness sent shivers along my back and made me tense my fingers across my middle where my secret grew.

The Friday of Passover was particularly mild for early spring. Poppy opened every window in the apartment to allow in outdoor air, the damp, pollen scent mingling with the matzo balls and spinach kugel and baked chicken Mama was cooking. When our guests arrived, Mama placed on the table the silver engraved plate she used only for Passover, with the lamb bone, roasted egg, bitter herbs, and haroset spaced equally from the center. Beside this went the tray of matzos and the traditional cup of wine, which would remain untouched. Once we were seated, Poppy read and sang songs from the Haggadah. Then Mama, her brows arched in a manner I knew meant she was working to hide her pride, carried in platter after platter of steaming food, each one greeted by louder sighs of satisfaction than the one before.

The adults talked of our new president, George Bush, of Yitzhak Shamir and the recent general election in Israel, of the plane bombing over Lockerbie just months before. They talked of their work, and of the Kramers, who had not been able to join us this year. But after a time, Mama turned the conversation to the recent accomplishments of children, delighted, I knew, that with Sarah and Valerie making honor roll again and my acceptance to Brown, no one at the dinner outdid us. "Ruth took European History last semester. You should have seen her textbooks—heavy as boulders. I don't even know how she carried them! Right, Ruthie?"

"Right, Ma." I nodded my agreement. But the mounds of food, the ringing laughter, the heat from the kitchen and from so many warm bodies made my head spin and my stomach toss; and more than once before dessert, I had to push out my chair from between Cousin Joel's and Aunt Bernice's and excuse myself from the table.

Despite her many distractions, this time Mama must have noticed my absences and the pecan chocolate cake, which I usually gobbled greedily, still untouched on my plate. "Something wrong, Pea?" she asked, her eyes narrowed with concern as I helped her carry cups of tea and coffee from the kitchen.

"No, nothing, Ma," I lied, trying to smile cheerfully. But for the remainder of the meal and for hours after, as my uncles and aunts and cousins lounged on the living room couches and chairs, I sat in silence, unable to concentrate on anything but my fear of what I knew must come, the enormity of what I hid, and the strange realization that the people in the room before me could be the family of some other girl for all they knew of the truth.

That night I lay awake in my childhood bed long after I had turned off the lamp. From the kitchen I could hear the shush of running water and the clink of china and silver as Mama rinsed the last of the holiday dishes. Poppy must have dozed off in his favorite living room chair, for I could hear the whistle of his exhaling in sleep. When the phone rang, Mama answered it, her words too hushed to distinguish, but I listened to the rise and fall of her voice, a rhythm I knew as well as my own breathing. So many familiar sounds of home, they should have lulled me to sleep. But I could not stop the hum of thoughts in my head, so when Mama, with rushing footsteps, threw open the door to my room, allowing it to crack against my corner shelves, sending two wooden dolls clattering to the floor, I shot up but was already wide awake.

"What is it, Mama?" I began to call, but the words faded in my throat before I could finish them. In the haze of the hallway light, I could see that her eyes were swollen from crying, her mouth contorted in a strange expression that made me draw my knees to my chest.

"That was Bernice on the phone," she said as she walked to my bedside, standing over me. "She said she heard and saw things while she was here. Things—" Mama paused, her voice so choked I did not know if she would continue. "Things a mother should *know* about her own daughter. Things I never dreamed I would have to ask of *you*! So! So, do you have something to tell me, Ruthie!" Mama knelt at the edge of my bed, her lips curled so tightly against her gums I thought for a moment she might strike me. But instead, she buried her face in my blankets.

"Mama—" I reached for her, but the sight of her crying and her mention of the secret I had carried for these several weeks made my throat ache with sobs. I wiped at my eyes with my nightgown sleeve, but the tears came and came. After some time, Mama drew me into her arms, stroking my hair as she had done when I'd scraped or bruised myself as a child. "How many weeks?" she whispered in a tone so low I almost thought I had misunderstood.

"Four," I said, my heart hammering at the sound of the word spoken aloud for the first time. And I knew, as I'd known all along, even as the word came out, what had to be.

"Good, good." Mama was rocking me now. "Four weeks is still early." She began rocking more rapidly, as if there were something we needed to catch up to. "Tomorrow we can call a doctor for an appointment. Yes, early tomorrow. So who needs to know? I won't tell your sisters," she hissed in my ear. "Not even Poppy."

I nodded slowly but for some moments said nothing. I knew what the doctor would do. Opal had gone with two of her friends to the clinics. Yes, I knew what had to take place, but still I asked . . . "Mama . . . Mama, how old were you when I was born?"

"Ruthie, what are you saying!" She clapped hands to her ears as if shutting out my words. "Have you gone mad? Do you want to toss your whole life away? You're only a *child*!"

What I had thought to say next was that for the last few days I had had a sense, a premonition, that the tiny life inside me was a girl. But I could hear that Mama's breath was coming faster and faster until she was almost wheezing, almost gulping for air. Never before had I seen her so panicked, and my own throat began to tighten with dread over what I had done. Oh, how I had wanted to be strong, like Francesca and Setsu and Opal. But this was a thing so large, far larger than even the things they took on. And was it even strength? Or was it weakness? Which were my fears and which were Mama's? So I stuttered all the promises I could think of. "I'm sorry. I'm sorry. You're right, Mama, it was just a foolish thought. Tomorrow, yes, tomorrow we will make the appointment."

Only a few extra days off from school were required for me to have the procedure. Mama explained my lengthened stay to Sarah, Valerie, and Poppy as the result of mild stomach troubles. Early, on the day before my appointment with Dr. Sicher, Mama stepped out to see Sarah and Valerie off to school. Seconds later, the kitchen phone rang. One ring, and then a second. My heart jumping, I ran to it. But the woman on the line sounded nothing like Setsu. Nothing like any of my roommates. And why had I thought the call was for me at all? What was I hoping for anyway?

On the morning of the procedure, I was allowed to eat nothing, so the night before, once the rest of the family had retired to bed, Mama made me a special meal. "To give you strength," she said as she spooned onto my plate two poached eggs, a browned potato pancake, three salted slices of tomato. In the last days, my nausea had only increased, and the smell of the cooked eggs, the pulpy juices from the tomatoes left me with no appetite. But I saw Mama watching over her shoulder as she scrubbed dishes at the sink, waiting as each forkful hovered over my plate. So I managed somehow to swallow one bite and then another and another until only crumbs remained.

The room Dr. Sicher showed me to was frost-white. The walls, the counters, the trays of silvery instruments gleamed as if they had never been touched. Mama, instructed that she would have to remain in the waiting room, squeezed my hands. "I'll be just on the other side of this door," she whispered, smiling despite the dark lines marking her brow.

I was given a mint-green gown with ties at the waist. It left my lower legs and upper back bare, and I shivered in my sockless feet as a bony-wristed nurse scribbled notes on a pad of paper. "The doctor will be back in a few minutes, dear." She smiled, revealing discolored front teeth. "He will go over every step of the procedure with you. All right?"

But when the doctor asked if I had questions, I said I had none. I heard nothing while he gabbed about what the equipment was for, not a word of what would happen while my body went numb. If only he would stop. If he would stop talking, stop repeating and reminding, I could endure what was to follow.

When it was over, the nurse puffed my pillows and offered me ice chips from a hard plastic cup. Someone called to Mama to return to the room, and the nurse handed her a list of things I could and could not do while I recuperated. Mama nodded silently as she read the directions. I could see that the peachy powder on her cheeks was streaked from tears. When the nurse excused herself, Mama pressed her forehead to mine.

"Ruthie, Ruthie, it's all over now. You didn't want to grow up so quickly, did you? And throw away everything? You are meant for better—" Her voice thickening, she paused to kiss my cheeks and hands. "In just a few hours we can go home. I'll make veal and dumplings if you like. Your favorites."

But Mama's words seemed hardly to penetrate my ears, her kisses to dissipate before reaching me. I was aware of only one thing—a new lightness, a hollowness where my body had once been solid. From my high school biology class, I knew that at four weeks of pregnancy, a woman carried an embryo no larger than a kidney bean. Gazing at my arms and middle and thighs, I could see that my plumpness from earlier in the year had not disappeared, yet my only sensation was of shrinking, of lessening. I was weightless. So weightless that with the tiniest push, I would float away.

A MATTER OF SMALL CONSEQUENCE

(Setsu's Story)

• Sophomore Year •

From the beginning, Ruth and I had understood things in each other our suitemates never could. Not things we'd confessed, simply things we'd recognized. That first night in our suite, I had seen it in her wide-open eyes, the questioning tilt of her head, heard it in the pauses as she spoke: her self-doubting, her eagerness to please. We made no grand revelations to each other, only shared small details from our pasts, our homes. But these were enough. She had always been obedient, but once, her sophomore year of high school, Ruth said, she had cheated— checking her answers on a math exam with those of the boy at the neighboring desk. "Such a stupid thing!" she'd said. She'd known the answers; it was just that her eyes had seemed drawn to his paper. How could she explain it? When she'd been caught, she had received a "Fail" on the test. But what had been unbearable—what she would remember for as long as she lived—was the way her mother had looked at her when she first learned the truth, as if something had broken between them, as if she were seeing a girl who was not her own. Our stories differed, but we feared the same losses, knew the same longings. I told her how Toru had liked to play tricks: sprinkling my sheets with plastic spiders and centipedes that made me scream, or, for years, hiding Anabelle, my favorite doll, in the clothes hamper or washing machine. But I had never tattled, knowing, if I did, even the small moments of attention he allowed me would be withheld.

I had known Ruth would not judge me for letting the violin go without a fight. And so I had told her the whole story. How, when Toru was fifteen and I thirteen, he had quit our shared lessons with Mrs. Dubois. Through a professional pianist friend of our father's, Toru had learned of Mr. Levine's reputation for coaching the most gifted students in the Washington region. Mr. Levine was far stricter, far more demanding of his pupils than Mrs. Dubois had ever been. Not infrequently, Toru had returned from an afternoon in the city to show me his knuckles, red from having been rapped with Mr. Levine's conducting wand.

"Ohh, Toru!" I gasped. But he only smiled and swept his hand through the air as if to say these were the things a serious musician, a musician who had begun to enter competitions, had to endure.

For some time, I continued to visit Mrs. Dubois alone but soon began to wonder if her offers of juice and chocolates were a bit babying. Her repeated compliments, which had once made me glow with pride, now made my feet squirm in my penny loafers. And when she clapped her hands or embraced me at the end of a session for my "excellent, excellent progress!" my cheeks burned at her coddling. So when a few of my lessons were canceled because Toru had joined a youth orchestra and needed chauffeuring to weekly practices, I did not mind so terribly. And soon, as my school workload began to increase, I found reasons to miss even more. Honors history and science, advanced algebra—my nightly homework left me little free time, but weren't my sessions with Mrs. Dubois just for fun? So during the summer I turned fourteen, I told my parents I was too busy to keep up my music studies.

"Are you *sure*, Setsu? But music has always been so important to you."

"I guess I have changed," I said. And then I waited for their arguments.

"If the universe is kind enough to give you a gift, it is yours forever," my father had told me once, the first time I played "Silent Night" for him. But now they only said, "We can't pretend we are not disappointed, Setsu, but you have reached an age at which you should decide these things for yourself." And that was all. Nothing more.

So I tucked my violin in the back of my closet, behind my snow boots and a faded stuffed giraffe, and tried to imagine what they would have said had it been Toru instead. I thought of the afternoon the month before when Toru had been told he could not attend an additional orchestra practice because it conflicted with my scheduled lesson. "I'm sure Mr. Mann will understand," our mother had said. "And isn't there still plenty of time until the concert?"

"No! No, there isn't *plenty* of time!" Toru stared, his eyes narrowed as blades, as if he were carving this moment into memory, the details of how he'd been wronged. Then I had seen the wave of panic that moved across our mother's face before she could smile it away. And I'd heard it in the tone of our parents' whisperings late that night—"He really is so dedicated. Yes, maybe more than we realized"—their fear of Toru. Their fear of upsetting him. And I wondered if there was some part of them that was relieved by my choice.

"No more music lessons!" I planned to announce to my best friend,

Allison, on the phone that evening. But my tongue stuck dryly to the roof of my mouth, and a loneliness came over me, like the old loneliness I had felt as a child when, in bed late at night, I pretended to remember my birth mother's face, the sound of her voice, the softness of her hands. And I found I could not speak the words.

Following his senior year of high school, Toru left home in order to attend the prestigious Juilliard School in New York. I had helped him pack his bags, folding his shirts and sweaters in even piles, separating them with sheets of tissue to prevent creasing.

"Thank you, little sister. You are a gazillion times neater than I would be!" he'd said as he rifled through his music books and cartons stacked with now yellowing sonatas and concertos he had played over the years, sorting what would go with him. "I guess I've outgrown most of this, but it seems a shame to throw it all out." He dropped one of the cartons with a noisy thud. "Who knows, maybe when I am famous, it will be worth something. Right!" He laughed, tossing his head, shaking a strand of hair from his eyes. "What do you think?"

Since his acceptance to the conservatory, Toru had begun to make references to his big break, his future fame. Always his words were followed by a laugh, but his eyes flickered with excitement, glistened with visions of the successes awaiting him.

"You're welcome to what's here." Toru had tapped one of the boxes, shrugging his shoulders.

I smelled the familiar, musty scent of the sheet music. "Oh, thank you anyway, Toru," I said, hoping he could not hear in my voice the lump of longing I felt rising in my throat. "No, you keep it. Maybe someday you will want it back."

"Yes, well, I guess it's no longer of use to you, eh!" For some reason, the fact that my violin now lay in its case untouched, and had for the past two years, seemed always to tickle Toru's funny bone. Whenever the topic was raised, his eyes twinkled. This time he'd even jabbed jokingly at my ribs.

"No, no use at all," I said.

During Toru's first two years at the conservatory and my final years of high school, we saw him only when he came home for Thanksgivings and Christmases, for weeklong holidays in the spring. Over suppers, he showed us photographs of his adventures in New York—posing with friends on the observation deck of the Empire State Building, dining in Little Italy, attending a symphony at Carnegie Hall. His descriptions of the city's fast-paced days, its long, glittering nights made our Maryland town seem sleepy and unsophisticated. And he seemed to have little patience now for idle time in the suburbs; during vacations he would disappear to see performances in Washington, visit museums, join the throngs on the National Mall.

As soon as Toru returned to college, the house would be oddly quiet again, the only music coming from the recordings of Brahms lullabies and Strauss waltzes my parents played at low volumes on their stereo, soft hums in comparison to Toru's forte scales and études. And meals we finished in near silence, making only small dents, it seemed, in the enormous quantities my mother had grown accustomed to preparing.

"Just who was supposed to eat this?" I had not been able to stop myself from saying one evening as I helped my mother clear plates from the table. She had prepared rice with egg and deep-fried pork, one of Toru's favorite dishes. It was a small thing, a silly thing, but as I'd watched her fill large plastic containers with the leftovers, seemingly oblivious to the fact that there were, once again, only three of us, I had wrapped my arms around my waist in irritation.

"So what did your mother say to *that*?" Ruth had wanted to know—her voice rising as it always did whenever she was excited or indignant—when I'd told her the story. "Was she angry?"

"No, no. Maybe because her mind was too full. Too full of thoughts of Toru to understand my complaint."

"Then you should explain yourself. Tell her how you've been over-looked." We were sitting side by side on Ruth's nubby tan carpet be-tween the end of her bed and the elephant ear plant in its green plastic container that she had picked up at a street fair just the week before, two large leaves already browning. She had kicked off the fleece-lined slip-pers she usually wore with her peach plaid pajamas in the evenings. Cot-ton balls were wedged between our toes as we coated our nails with the same petal-pink polish, alternating turns dipping the brush into the enamel. "You and I share the same weakness, you know. We are too will-ing to keep our own wishes buried." Ruth leaned against the hard cool-ness of the wall, smiled at me then down at her feet, wiggling her long, thin toes—"The only part of me that doesn't need a diet!" she'd joked once.

How strange it was. Ruth's home, her family were so different from mine, but the same thoughts, the same feelings seemed to live in us. I wondered what she had been like as a very young girl, if she had once felt stronger or bolder, if she had once trusted her own hopes.

It was hard to change what had always been, but college, we agreed, seemed full of people remaking themselves. We saw examples of it every day—students trying new wardrobes, new groups of friends, new atti-tudes. Here people changed all the time. Or maybe they were discover-ing their truer selves, what they were always meant to be. Why couldn't we do this, too? So we made a declaration, a resolution I could not have shared with anyone else: no longer would we allow our own desires to go ignored.

. . .

In late December of my first college year, I returned home for the winter holiday. Toru was home from school as well. After dinner the first night, my mother filled four glasses with sparkling cider to honor our all being together once more—the same kind she had bought the previous spring to toast my acceptance to Brown. But on that occasion, Toru, at the last minute, had changed his plans for the weekend, wanting to attend a band concert with friends instead.

My father raised his glass. "Toru?" He took a sip. "Do you ever come across people with connections to Brown? I imagine, because of its fine music department, you might now and then—"

Toru had not tasted the cider. Instead, he reached for the teapot my mother had set on the table. He shook his head and shrugged, pouring a generous serving of milk into his cup. The year before, when I had first shown him my letter of admission, Toru had blinked blankly, as if I'd received nothing more significant than a grocery-store coupon or a clothing catalog. Now his mouth twitched with amusement. "Ever get a little bored on the campus of the liberated and grungy? Is there anything to do there but join rallies for inane causes? What are you all protesting these days? The conformity of bathing? The existence of men?" He laughed. But this time I did not smile agreeably at Toru's teasing. I thought of Ruth and kept my eyes on the cloud of Earl Grey seeping from my teabag.

My father went on, he and my mother ignoring, as usual, the jokes Toru made at my expense. As he talked about Brown's fine academics, its distinguished professors, its renowned collection of books, I watched Toru slurp from his cup, giving only slight nods to prove he was unimpressed. I poked and stirred the granules of sugar that had settled at the bottom of my tea, my spoon clinking angrily against the sides of my cup until my father stopped talking and I could feel three pairs of eyes on me.

My voice was almost no louder than a whisper, but I made myself heard: "Why do you insult me, Toru? Again and again!"

Toru laughed and let out a huff of annoyance, then for minutes no one spoke. My hands were quaking, hard enough that I could not replace my spoon to my saucer without it rattling. But I had done it, and when we returned to school, I would recount to Ruth this small triumph.

 ⌒

I had been the one to answer when Ruth's call came, just days after she had returned home for Passover. She would be back in about a week or so, she said. And I knew from the dried-up sound of her voice the choice she had made.

"We miss you, Ruth," I told her. "We're thinking of you all the time."

For a while she was as silent as the evening mist dampening the campus beyond my window. "Thank you."

Then her mother's voice came from some other part of her apartment—"Who is that? Are you on the phone?"—not flat like Ruth's but fluttering and sharp, a mother bird protecting her young.

"It's only Setsu, Mama."

How bent on independence Ruth had seemed when Francesca and I had seen her off at the Providence station just the week before. But to be that cared for—Ruth was lucky in ways she did not know.

 ⌒

Summer break drew closer, and as I completed final essays and exams, attended the last classes of the freshman term, and, like my suitemates, packed my books and clothes and pictures into boxes, peeled posters from the walls, I thought of the stiffness I heard in my mother's and father's voices when I called home now, a change I had noticed since my outburst over Christmas. During telephone conversations, they were careful to avoid mentions of Toru, as if fearing my reaction.

Over the three-month holiday, Toru spoke to me only when necessary. I never apologized for the accusation I had made when I had last seen him. But now when he interrupted me, I kept the peace as I always had before. Perhaps some things were more important than pride, more important than proving assertiveness. And toward the end of the break, when my parents asked if Toru could have the violin I had not played since junior high—he knew someone at the conservatory who wished to buy it—I swallowed the bitterness rising to my throat. Perhaps they meant this only as a sensible solution, a means to take something useless off my hands. Still, I felt sickened at the thought of someone else playing the instrument that had once seemed an extension of my own body. "No, I guess I'll keep it," was all I said. And, at the end of August, before I returned to Brown, for no rational reason, I brought my violin to an instrument repair shop in Georgetown, changing the old worn strings for new ones, replacing the brittle horsehair of my bow. I set the violin beside the bags that would make the return trip to school with me, knowing, once I arrived, it would do little more than take up space.

Early in our freshman year, I had thought we might eventually go our separate ways for other terms of school: Francesca to room with Winnie and Kay in one of the large off-campus rentals on Prospect Street, Opal—liking independence—to one of the singles on the Pembroke Campus. But we had made a promise that April while Ruth was away: if she returned, and if she was willing, we would stay together our sophomore year as well. Perhaps I had suggested it first, but Opal and Fran did not hesitate.

"People offer help so easily without really meaning it, don't they? But Ruth should know, *really* know, she can rely on us," Opal had said.

"Yes, not just as roommates, but as friends." This from Fran had surprised me at first, but I had begun to understand, from the many times she'd glanced at the phone in our suite during Ruth's absence as if expecting it to ring at any moment, that, though she might not admit it, she was as concerned about Ruth as any of us.

We felt Ruth needed us, though she might never ask. And we had been right, Ruth's eyes squeezing closed with relief when we made the suggestion.

"I'm surprised the four of you are sticking together," Winnie said to us just after we announced our decision. She was skipping her Scandinavian literature class, failing to finish *Miss Julie*, and had plopped herself onto our couch with her ball of tan yarn, her crochet hook dipping up and down, forming the first several rows of a scarf. She swatted at her sun-blond bangs, brushing them out of her eyes. "It's just unusual, that's all I mean. Almost *no one* is staying with the roommates they were assigned freshman year." She tilted her head, dimpling the corners of her mouth as though she meant nothing by it, but I knew Kay, at the last moment, had decided to room with Heather Kelly instead of Winnie, and that Fran had been Winnie's last hope.

"I guess we've grown on each other." Fran winked at Ruth. "Like algae, or crabgrass."

Ruth and Opal and I laughed, but Winnie only studied her looping stitches. Some weeks before, Winnie had asked if I was planning to live with Kimi Endo's group in the house on Brook Street. "No," was all I'd told her. I would not share that they had not asked me anyway. Aside from my suitemates, Kimi had been my first friend on campus, inviting me to several parties and dinners sponsored by the Japanese Cultural Society. She and several of her Japanese-American friends attended these en masse, but despite our common backgrounds, conversations did not come as easily for me with them as they did with Ruth, or even Fran and Opal. I had little to add to their jokes about un-Americanized parents or the antiquated traditions of relatives still in the East. And when I missed a few dinners because I'd made previous plans with my suitemates, Kimi's calls had grown less frequent. And she'd filled the eight spaces for her house with girls who spent all of their time with other Asians.

"I didn't realize you'd become so *close*." I heard the sizzle of Winnie's words as she stood later in the doorway with Fran. Still, I felt a little sorry for Winnie. But we would not tell her we had reasons for the choices we'd made, sensed we knew something others around us had still to learn: how easily one's life could fly into pieces. And because we had learned this, we would not abandon each other at the first spark of friction. We heard the rumors on campus: Riley and Dee, who lived down the hall, were no longer speaking, arranging their schedules around each other, together in their room only when they slept. Phoebe Locke had caught her boyfriend, Chip, with Ana Walters, Ana's shirt open, her headband and stockings tangled in Chip's bedsheets. Story after story of the way friends turned on one another, as careless as wildflowers twisting in the breeze. But real friendships did not last merely one year or two, Ruth and Fran and Opal and I agreed. We made this pact: regardless of circumstances, we would be able to count on one another. For *all* of our years here. And even beyond.

We received, through the housing lottery, what we had hoped for our sophomore year: a suite for four in one of the dorms off Hope Street, an arrangement similar to what we had been given the previous year but quieter, with only three other apartments per floor. We would do something more with our common room this time around, we decided—give it some sort of coordinated theme, rather than leave it a hodgepodge of our mismatched belongings. Francesca suggested Mediterranean touches, which we agreed to. And in her car, we drove to Swansea, Massachusetts, and bought beaded throw pillows for the sofa, a terra-cotta platter painted with bright yellow lemons for the center of the coffee table, posters of the Amalfi Coast and of a square in Naples, and a swag of blue-green material to hang from the curtain rod above the double window.

Driving back, our eyes tearing from the lowering sun and from the wind, our voices hoarse from laughing, shouting to one another above the cars and the rushing air, I felt, for a moment, how it might be to have sisters. I had not told Ruth or Opal or Fran how thankful I was for the pact we'd made, for our choosing to continue as roommates. *Setsu is a quiet girl, tentative in her relationships*, my grade school teachers had commented repeatedly on my progress reports. But they mentioned it as if it were a choice, not understanding what I craved more than anything.

We spent much of the next day decorating, trading stories of the highlights and disappointments of our summer vacations as we arranged our couches and chairs, our photos and keepsakes from home, as well as our new purchases.

"It looks *so* great!" Ruth said when we had finished, her words punching with enthusiasm. The summer had been good for her. "Time heals all wounds," she told us when we asked. Still, the way she laughed, more loudly than the rest of us at every joke, made me think she needed to prove her happiness to herself. And I noticed a difference now in her conversations with her mother. They bickered regularly over all manner of things: Ruth's neglecting to be in her room one Sunday night in time for her mother's usual eight-o'clock call, the title of a movie they had once watched together, the name of a certain shoe store in Brooklyn. And especially over Ruth's forgetting to phone home for her sister Valerie's birthday. Still Ruth did nothing to make things right. I knew what she thought: that she was finding strength. But it seemed to me she was only drifting toward loneliness. In her position, I could not begin to know what I would feel. But I did know this: never, *never* would I cut myself off from concern, from affection that was offered. Sometimes compromises had to be made to hold on to love.

⁓

It was only a few weeks after the start of sophomore year when I met James. Francesca had convinced me to accompany her to an off-campus party hosted by some theater majors she knew, mostly juniors and seniors. "Their parties are *far* more interesting than what's on campus.

You'll see," she'd said. "You grew up near a big city, so you know what I mean. Fraternity parties can be *so* juvenile, can't they?"

The house was south of College Hill, near Wickenden Street, and far enough from campus and from the shops on Thayer and Angell that I had never before had occasion to pass it. Light from a single street lamp shone on its tiny front garden where someone had arranged flat stones in the shape of a peace sign, and beyond it, a family of plaster gnomes, all in red jackets and pointed hats, the largest with a Brown University sticker adhered to its middle. "Very creative landscaping," I said.

Francesca laughed and looped her arm through mine. "Actors. Everything's very tongue-in-cheek." As further proof, she pointed to the front door, which had been propped open by a chipped plaster owl. Below the circular knocker at the center of the door, someone had written *Kiss a Thespian*. Inside, the windows were framed by long drapes, their skirts forming dark fabric pools on the floor. The walls and ceilings had been painted deep maroon like the entrance to some underworld realm. "You'll get used to it," Fran smiled. I followed her through two smoke-filled rooms to a spot near the kitchen where three kegs of beer kept a flow of people coming and going. Francesca had immediately filled plastic cups for both of us. She leaned against the wall, her free hand resting on her hip as she waited to be approached.

James was a graduate student, a teaching assistant in the political science department, he informed Francesca and me. He had eyes as solemn gray as rivers and high cheekbones and a thick mustache that covered his upper lip. He stood shoulders above the other guests, and I had to tilt my chin just to speak to him. In the haze of cigarette smoke, the whirl of animated voices, I listened as James and Francesca compared stories of a few acquaintances they had in common and of recent summer trips each had taken to Argentina. They had even stayed at the same hotel in Buenos Aires. "With that horrible, nosy manager. She looked like a female Mussolini!" Francesca laughed, leaning close enough to James that her arm brushed his. James would be drawn to Francesca, in her tweed blazer, her jeans and wide, brass-buckled belt that flattered her larger size. She exuded a confidence, a maturity that reminded me how girl-like, how thin-boned and straight I had been since the age of fifteen. She was not a reed to be easily shaken, as Ruth or I seemed to be.

When James phoned our suite three days later, my roommates and I were watching *Cheers*—our Thursday evening ritual—an episode we'd seen once before.

"Let it ring. This is a good part," Opal said.

But Ruth picked up the phone, afraid it might be someone's parents, not wanting to cause concern. "Who? Setsu? Oh, yes, she's here."

And before I knew it, I found myself stuttering a surprised acceptance to James's invitation to dinner at his home.

"Who's James?" Ruth wanted to know.

I saw Fran's blue eyes widen slightly, as if she were not sure she'd heard correctly.

"I didn't expect it, Fran," I said. "He talked with you all evening. I can call back—"

"Oh, God! Please!" She kicked at one of her leather clogs on the floor near the sofa and made a snapping noise with the gum in her mouth. "He really isn't my type anyway."

Aside from accompanying him to our senior prom, I had never had an official date with Gerald, my high school boyfriend, nor with the few boys I'd spent time with freshman year of college. Opal and I had gone out a few times with Clay and Andy—brothers in the class ahead of ours—but we had only played foosball and eaten cold pizza in the basement of their dorm. "We'd have had more fun if we'd stayed home and studied for Friday's history test!" Opal had whispered to me the last evening as we stood to leave.

So I was not used to dressing for an occasion like my dinner with James. But Opal had a wardrobe of stylish clothes, so the morning of the dinner, I found her in her room. She was stretched on her stomach across the white duvet cover on her bed, reading *Dubliners*. Her feet were up, her ankles crossed in cotton leggings that showed the long curves of her thighs.

"It's amazing, Opal. You always look so glamorous," I said, as part of my explanation for seeking her advice. I spoke quietly. Ruth's room was beside Opal's, and for some reason I did not want her to know my plans.

Opal rolled onto one elbow and blinked at the sun that was now slanting through her window and with the boredom of someone who'd heard the compliment too many times to care. I felt silly for having made the observation. "Maybe I'm interrupting you——"

"No. No, stay. I've been reading for hours anyway." She stood, squaring her pretty shoulders, running her thumb and forefinger along the narrow line of her nose.

"Always start with your hair and face," she said, seating me at her desk chair, adjusting the tilt of my head to suit her, then pulling a brush and a quilted bag of cosmetics from her top desk drawer. "Your face is like a canvas. Makeup can bring your features into focus, but the colors must work together." She poked at my brows with tiny strokes from a brown pencil, lined my eyes, coated my lashes with quick, curling motions from her mascara wand. I sensed she would rather be doing something else, but this was work she nearly could complete with her eyes closed as she tipped my chin up and then down, turned my face to one side and then the other. I tried, in the meantime, to think of some topic to pass the time. "Are you going to any of the homecoming games this weekend? I know we all missed them last year, but I thought I would at least try to make the football game this time. I think Ruth is, too. If you want to come——"

"Not really my cup of tea," she said, without looking up.

So, indicating her book, I asked if she still liked her James Joyce class, if after *Dubliners* they would be reading *Ulysses*, which I had attempted once in high school but failed to penetrate.

"You tackled it on your own? That was ambitious. Well, if you took the course, you'd understand it," she said, though I wasn't so sure.

Another lull in the conversation followed. I could think of nothing to say to interest her. I mentioned the small unframed watercolor to the left of her window. It had not been there the day before—a new addition to her mostly bare walls—the silhouette of a boy, all angular, spare lines, behind him black rocks and a slab of gray ocean. "Is that yours?"

"It's not finished," was all she said, making it clear she was no longer in the mood for chitchat. With deft fingers, she swirled creamy powder over my cheeks, dabbed gloss on my lips.

Opal approved of the dress and fitted, mandarin-collar coat I had considered but not of the flat shoes I had chosen to wear with them. "Why don't you borrow these?" She took from her closet a pair of black patent leather sling-back heels. "You can keep them if you like. I really never wear them anymore."

"Oh, thank you, Opal, but I couldn't."

"Of course you can." She moved her hand wearily over her hair, and I knew I had tried her patience.

On the phone, James had given directions to his apartment, a ten-minute walk from campus, off Benefit Street, toward downtown Providence. He was renting the first story of a dilapidated blue Victorian house with a sagging veranda. Wet leaves coated the steps, and large chinks where the wood had rotted pocked the porch's floorboards. I tiptoed to the doorbell, afraid of tripping or snapping a heel from Opal's dress shoes.

James arrived at the front door in jeans, a braided leather belt, and a cantaloupe-orange shirt, its cuffs rolled back, its top two buttons unfastened. "Did you find the place without any trouble?" When I removed my coat, he smiled at my sleeveless silk frock and heels.

"Oh, yes, the directions were perfect," I nodded, embarrassed by how ridiculously formal I now looked as I stood in his foyer, clutching the scented candle I had brought as a house gift.

James smiled, indicating my present. "Is that for me?"

"Yes, yes. Oh, I forgot——" As he took the candle from me, I could feel, to my shame, a slight sticky dampness where my palms, despite the cool weather, had left perspiration on its plastic wrapping.

"Come in," he offered. "I was just opening a bottle of Chardonnay, and I've ordered Indian food. There's a great place in town that delivers." He ushered me through a dim hallway to his kitchen. On one crowded counter lay a brown paper bag filled with takeout containers, beside it an uncorked bottle of wine. He poured a glass for me, then a slightly fuller one for himself. Through his kitchen I could see a small dining nook. James had already set the narrow table and had laid between our place mats a wreath of pinecones and autumn leaves, which I imagined he had gathered himself. He placed the candle I had brought in the center of the wreath and lit it.

In high school, though I had attended a number of my classmates' late-night parties, I had drunk only partial glasses of alcohol, tiny sips, afraid the odor on my breath would give me away when I returned home, a habit I had broken only now and then during the last year. So the tall glass of wine James poured me began to make my lips tingle before I had even finished its contents. When I answered his questions, my words sounded garbled in my ears. So I was grateful that he seemed to know much about many subjects and that I could remain fairly silent as we settled into our chairs and began our meal. He understood things that were happening in places I knew only vaguely: revolts in African regions, ethnic wars in Eastern Europe, the names of diseases that ravaged lives in faraway towns and cities. He was familiar with the cuisines of many countries and the beverages that complemented them. He knew the history of Brown and its founders, the best places nearby for hiking, kayaking, antiquing. And when he began to speak of orchestras and musical events on campus, I still did nothing more than smile and nod, worried that if I opened my mouth, something foolish would tumble out.

Though James did most of the talking, he managed to consume large portions of food, many times more than what I had eaten. "You have a bird's appetite," he laughed, pointing with his fork to my partially finished serving of lentils and spinach, the round of flatbread, the chicken curry remaining on my plate. "I guess that's how you keep your petite figure." He smiled broadly, and heat rose to my cheeks as I felt his eyes learning every inch of me.

Always my suitemates and I had spent our Saturdays together, but James began to invite me to his apartment Saturday afternoons and then evenings, and soon he began to call on weekdays, as well. More than once, when Francesca and Opal had other plans, I thought about inviting Ruth to join James and me for a walk into town or for lunch, knowing how she disliked eating in solitude, but I wondered if this would make her feel lonely, watching the two of us together, seeing that I had some- one who was eager for my company. James asked for a copy of my course schedule so that he would know when I was free. Sometimes the tele- phone in my suite would ring just minutes after I'd returned from class. "Setsu, can I see you? Will you come over? I miss your face."

Then Opal would roll her eyes as I put down the phone. "Didn't you see him about five minutes ago?"

"Jesus, Setsu, aren't you in charge of your own life?" Francesca would look up from her Baudelaire reading or from *Paris Match*. "James isn't *God*, you know. His requests are not holy commandments!"

Until this point, I had always shared in their jokes, never before been the object of them. But I only laughed, too happy to care. My heart rac- ing, I would throw my books on my bed, tear off my bulky sweater and jeans, and stand before my closet, searching for the clothes I thought James would find prettiest. Now and then, Opal would peek in, hesitat- ing in my doorway, then giving some excuse about missing her hair clip or wondering if a piece of her mail had been mixed in with mine. But I knew why she'd really come. "You know, if you do this for yourself, it's one thing." She would gesture toward the spread of clothes on my bed.

"But if you're doing all this——" And her chin would stiffen as if there was something unpleasant she did not wish to say.

"You all worry about me too much. It's like living with three mother hens!" I teased, but I was beginning to feel annoyed by my suitemates' preaching. I had seen the time Opal had taken before our evenings with Clay and Andy, as much as we had dismissed them. So if she'd had a boyfriend, certainly she would go to all the same measures.

I knew my roommates thought me silly, but it was *they* I felt sorry for, in their T-shirts and woolly socks, with no plans for the afternoon aside from watching Oprah Winfrey on our common room TV. I particularly pitied Ruth with the stack of molasses cookies she had taken from the Ratty, pushing them away as if she'd thought better of it, then breaking off new chunks. When she was partway through the stack, she would bring the remaining cookies into her lap, as if she thought none of us would notice that she gobbled down what would only make her larger. She seemed always to convince herself that an exercise walk down to the water with Opal later in the day would undo the damage. For some reason, her wordless watching, as I dashed from my room to the bathroom and back, was far worse than the others' nagging.

I would brighten my lips with pink gloss and brush my hair facing the tabletop mirror I had placed on my desk, thirty strokes on either side of my part to bring out the silkiness, as Opal had taught me. Then I would stare into my black-brown eyes and whisper, "When did you become such a lucky girl, Setsu?"

As I was growing up, my father and Toru had paid little attention to the way I dressed. But James seemed to notice every detail of the clothes women wore. He critiqued the costumes of the actresses in old movies we rented and on mannequins in store windows when, on occasion, we drove to Boston. And he liked to give me gifts—diaphanous scarves, an angora sweater, a pair of ivory-colored hair combs, stockings embroidered with a pattern of rosebuds. "You are so feminine, so dainty, Setsu. You *deserve* to be adorned in lovely things," James insisted whenever I hesitated to accept one of these extravagances. He bought a silver bangle bracelet with a small turquoise stone and clasped it around my wrist. "Now you have something to remind you of how much I care," he murmured in my ear. "Promise to wear it always."

"Yes. Oh, thank you, yes." And I did as he asked, never removing the bracelet, not even when I washed or slept. At unexpected moments, it would catch at me from the corner of my eye or its clasp would rub my skin, and I would shiver with happiness.

To increase our time together, as James suggested, I began to skip the stop at my suite before heading to his apartment after my last afternoon class. We met on his front porch, bundled in our barn jackets and scarves, and drank the flavored coffees he had picked up at Peaberry's on Thayer Street. Seated on his wooden porch swing, we watched people hurrying along the sidewalk. Dog walkers, RISD undergrads in drab black and gray, their bulky canvases balanced awkwardly under their arms. Brown students, many of whom I recognized by face if not by name, some with their feet bare-toed in clunky, buckled sandals even in the late-fall weather—shoes we wouldn't choose in any season, we agreed. Sometimes James would point out the girls whose hair hung half-tangled, who had allowed a coating of dark stubble to cover their legs. What exactly were they proving? Who would be impressed by their deliberate unattractiveness? His mouth curved as he slurped his Madagascar roast. Was it any surprise they walked alone? How fortunate we were, we felt, to have each other.

When we grew chilly, we moved inside for warm soup and baguettes. On several occasions, I offered to reciprocate, volunteering to serve a meal at my place instead. If my suitemates only had the chance to spend time with James beyond the quick interchanges when they ran into the two of us on campus, then certainly they would realize their concerns had been misplaced. But always James refused, smiling as if my invitations amused him. "Wouldn't you rather be here, where we can have privacy?" he would ask, leaning down to kiss the top of my head. "Here we can enjoy each other without interruption."

So the regular meals I had shared with Fran and Ruth and Opal grew less frequent. And sometimes days would go by without my seeing any of them. It seemed strange at first, a little like my first nights at sleepaway camp, when I would wake feeling there was someplace I had forgotten I was meant to be. But this would not last. I would hear my roommates rustling sleepily in their sheets as I slipped out for my first early class or find notes they left on our memo board—*Setsu, your lab partner, Jillian, called. She has a question for you. Setsu, this is your week to clean the common room*—this followed by a lopsided smiley face. But after a time, their messages grew shorter and sloppier, as if they had tired of writing so many reminders in my absence.

One morning before I left, I found Opal waiting for me on the common room sofa. She sometimes woke before breakfast to do stretches at the athletic center, but even for her this was an unusually early hour. Moments before I had heard her speaking in a hush to Ruth, who must have risen to use the hall bathroom. I had waited until their voices ceased before emerging from my room, hoping to avoid being seen leaving, to avoid, especially, Ruth's longing stare.

"Do you have a minute?" Opal placed a hand on the empty seat cushion beside her.

"Okay." I wondered what the two of them could possibly have been discussing. If they missed me.

"When I was fourteen," she said, "just after we moved to Puerto Rico, Mother left me for three weeks with her boyfriend Paulo's aunt, whom I'd met only once before at some birthday party. Mother and Paulo had tickets for a cruise down the Windward Islands. An adults-only cruise, so I could not be taken. She joked with me that she would come back if I was lucky. Twenty-one days I stayed in this woman's house. She spoke almost no English, and I sat on her rocking chair on her front veranda in the choking heat and wondered if Mother would ever return." Opal pressed her thumbnail into the groove between her two front teeth. Her face was pale. I could see the rivulet of a vein below the white of her cheek.

"That must have been awful. I can't begin to imagine how you felt."

Opal nodded. It was long minutes before she was able to speak again. "When a woman gives up everything she is for a man, she's playing with fire." Opal leaned her left arm against her chest, her fingers curled as if she were digging up the right words to make me understand. "You know, when you allow your own life to be swallowed up——" She stopped, her eyes looking into mine. "You're very sweet, Setsu, but you have to protect yourself. You have to protect who *you* are. No one else in this world will."

When she had finished, I placed a hand on hers. "Thank you for sharing this," I said. I smiled to let her know I understood what she implied. Still, my throat tightened with irritation. There was no reason to tell her she had wasted her time. But the comparison was preposterous. I was *not* Opal's mother. And James certainly was not one of her mother's sleazy boyfriends. Did the fact that I *loved* a man mean I was snuffing out some truer, stronger self? My situation was different in *every* way.

In the first months of that year, I had saved the colorful party flyers that arrived in my campus mailbox, sticking them with thumbtacks to the corkboard over my desk. But now, it seemed, James and I always had our own plans, and invitations became crumpled balls in my wastebasket. Two Wednesday afternoons, I even failed to show for my scheduled monthly meeting with Professor Yolen, my academic adviser, remembering only hours later, long after he'd left his office. James had surprised me on those occasions, finding me on my way out of Chaucer class. "Let's take a drive." He'd rattled his car keys. "The day is too nice to waste."

"You are turning me into a delinquent!" I said. But the missed parties, the stammered apologies to Professor Yolen, seemed a small price to pay for my blissful time with James. How good he was to me, always showering me with compliments, even claiming to adore what he referred to as my delicate appetite. Fondling my nape, more than once he confided that the way I had eaten during our first dinner together had endeared me to him. "Just like a tiny fawn or a gentle dove," he said, licking the tips of my fingers. "Sweet, sweet Setsu, you are perfection embodied."

So when we shared lunches or dinners, I tried to measure the portions I placed on my plate—a single thin strip of filleted fish, two spoonfuls of rice, three small chunks of squash.

James sometimes joked that the full glass of wine he poured for me each meal seemed out of proportion to my modest helpings. "I'm going to get fat spending time with you," he would tease, gesturing to the mounds of food remaining on the table, filling his dish with seconds, even thirds, as if the small quantities I took fueled his hunger.

And I was reminded then of how much older James seemed than most of the males in my classes or the nearby dorms. They were still boys in many ways, but James, at twenty-five, with his thick voice, his sure opinions, was unarguably a man, unafraid to ask for the things he liked. In one of his dresser drawers, he had placed a number of my belongings as well as several of the purchases he'd made for me. And as we grew to know each other better, he began to buy things exclusively meant for our time alone. A lace brassiere, a baby-blue garter belt. One night, after we had pushed aside our dinner dishes, our emptied glasses of wine, he took my hand, leading me down the hall to the cool of his darkened bedroom. "Would you?" He dangled the brassiere and a string of glass beads from his fingertips. "You're so beautiful. Too, too beautiful to remain hidden." He began to hum softly—Edith Piaf's "La Vie en Rose"—then lit my scented candle, which had made its way from the dining table to his bedroom windowsill. "Walk for me, Setsu," he whispered. "God, you're as lithe as a nymph. I love to watch you move."

The first few times he had requested this, I shook my head, shivering slightly in my state of half-undress. But James seemed impatient with my reticence. "Don't be so modest, kitten." The flame from the candle made elongated shadows of my limbs on the walls as I paced James's floor. "Dance, will you?" James would lower himself into a corner armchair, then lean forward on his elbows. And I would hesitate, trembling now from nerves as well as cold. But even in the near darkness I could see such desire in James's parted lips, could hear it in the quiet grinding of his teeth, and slowly, slowly I began to sway my hips, wanting, willing to do things for him I had never done before. This was part of what it meant to have a man, I told myself.

Still, there were times when we lay together, bodies entwined in that most intimate way James had shown me, I felt I was no more than a child beside him. Pulling the sheets to my shoulders in sudden bashfulness, I would whisper these fears into the faint patchouli scent of his chest.

"Oh, no, no, Setsu." The things I complained of, he said, were the very things he most loved about me—the girlish dimple in my left cheek, the hips I managed to keep so slender, my tiny waist and thighs and breasts. And he would slide the sheet down, down, little by little revealing what I had shyly covered, then embrace the narrowest part of me where my stomach caved.

One evening after James had held me in this way, he jumped from bed suddenly and pulled a pad and pencil from the canvas knapsack on his floor. "Oh, that's so perfect. Don't stir. Don't move an inch." And with a towel loosely wrapping his middle, he began to sketch me. My whole body flushed, and instinctively I drew my arms across my chest.

"Please, please, Setsu. You trust me, don't you? I haven't done this in years," he said, lifting his pencil slightly from the page. "But, God, you are so gorgeous. Like a rare and fragile flower." And as he gazed at me, I saw, to my surprise, that his eyes were shiny with tears. So I agreed: for him, I would swallow my discomfort. I would even tie the band of lace around my neck that he had brought to me. He worked almost without ceasing for what must have been close to an hour, pausing only once to find the classical music station he liked on the radio. "Jesu, Joy of Man's Desiring" was playing, and James inhaled slowly, eyelids fluttering as if breathing in the splendor of the music. "Do you know this piece?"

I nodded wordlessly. Yes, I knew it, so well I could sing every note, so well my left hand recalled every fingering. I almost spoke this aloud, but for some reason it felt the wrong time, the wrong thing to say.

When James was finished, he drew me close to him. And I stroked his back and shoulders, the tops of his thighs in the manner he liked best, wishing to make him happy.

"Never before," I murmured, "has anyone made me feel so beautiful or so loved."

James had several friends who lived in Boston—teachers, artists, writers—acquaintances he'd made during the two years between college and graduate school, when he lived in Cambridge, working on the campaign of a Democratic state congressman and waiting tables. Coincidentally, two of them—Dominic and his girlfriend, Fiona—had known Francesca some years before in the New York art scene. And Fran had met Nicholas one summer at a resort in Saint-Tropez. One of them had suggested a collective evening out. "I can't wait for my friends to meet you," James announced one February afternoon as he reached for my face with his palms. "I keep telling them how wonderful you are. So they think you sound too good to be true. I can hardly wait to prove them wrong."

"I will be on my best behavior!" I had laughed at his compliment, but in truth, the thought of being introduced to James's friends made my stomach jumpy. I had heard Francesca's stories about her old crowd in New York, and I was sure I could never fit in. I wished, too, James had not praised me so highly, worried I would be a disappointment.

"So what are Dominic and Fiona like?" I asked Francesca some days before we were to meet them. Francesca was sprawled on our couch, thumbing through some French magazine. We had just returned from the Brown bookstore together, Fran in need of a text for her philosophy class, I to replace two notebooks I had somehow mislaid in my trips between James's place and mine.

"Oh, I don't know. It's been a while since I caught up with them." She tossed the magazine on the floor, but she hadn't looked at me, and I knew she sensed my nervousness and was annoyed.

Francesca made arrangements for dinner at a small Chinese restaurant in downtown Boston—Hunan Palace, a place James knew as well. "It's a little clichéd, I guess," she laughed from the backseat of the car on the way there, the three of us having agreed to make the trip together in James's Volkswagen.

"Yes, clichéd, but the food's not bad." James glanced at me in the seat beside him.

I smiled with a carelessness I did not feel and smoothed my skirt across my knees. I tried not to think about the evening section meeting for my biology class I was missing because James had wanted to leave early, taking the most scenic route into the city.

"You are stunning," he whispered, tracing a finger across my cheek. I was wearing an outfit he had helped me select, a white cardigan sweater with small heart-shaped buttons, a short flannel skirt, matching gray stockings. Beside me, folded, lay my ivory winter coat and a wool scarf threaded with the same color of turquoise as the bracelet he had bought me.

We joined James's friends in the back room of the darkened restaurant, beyond a screen of wooden beads that swayed and clicked as we parted them. They were quibbling over an exhibit at the Museum of Fine Arts of a contemporary French painter whom Nicholas, Dominic, and Fiona admired but whom Greta, Nicholas's date, deplored. "Have you seen it?" they asked Francesca and me as we took our seats.

Francesca hadn't but was familiar with the artist's work. "His early pieces do little for me." She combed a strand of hair away from her forehead. "But his recent work is really original."

Since they seemed to be waiting for my response, too, I said only, "I guess I don't have the chance to come into Boston as much as I'd like."

Like James and Francesca, the others at the table had traveled much of Europe, even Africa and Asia. They read books in German and Italian, attended gallery openings.

"*My São Luis* is playing in Providence now." Francesca leaned across the round table, addressing all of us. "You know, the Brazilian film? Setsu"—she turned to me—"make James take you if you haven't seen it yet. It's sublime."

"Oh"—Greta nodded—"and the cinematography is reminiscent of *Sonia's Song.*" She squinted slightly as she peered at me, as if concentrating to be certain I understood.

I nodded in a manner I hoped was vague enough to cover my ignorance as I crossed and recrossed my legs beneath the table. As I listened to them argue about political refugee poets, emerging fiction writers, a controversial sculpture of Christ, I marveled that Francesca, only a month older than I, was so informed, so sure of her opinions. Like Fiona, in her long-fringed tapestry shawl, and Greta, in a suede vest, Francesca had dressed boldly, wearing high-heeled leather boots, enormous hoop earrings, and a red wraparound dress with a plunging neckline. When she leaned forward, her deep cleft of cleavage showed, yet she seemed to feel no more exposed than the rest of us, only, somehow, more assured, more substantial.

Our waiter set down the many platters we had ordered, and I watched Francesca pile her plate with crispy wontons, a heap of stir-fried rice, a bulging pancake of mu shu pork. And before I had finished the few items on my plate, she was spooning seconds. As we emptied our glasses of plum wine, the conversation grew louder, the voices more rapid. I tried to think of intelligent comments to add, but always the subject seemed to switch before I could contribute. Conscious of my silence, the blandness of my wit, my careful clothes, my meager appetite, I stared at the napkin folded in my lap and picked at its frayed edge, knowing I had added about as much interest to the evening as the wooden coatrack wedged in the corner beside our table.

At the end of the evening, Francesca chose to remain behind rather than riding back to Brown with James and me. She had made plans to meet another friend at Emmaline's, a club in the neighborhood, and would take a late bus home. I half wished James had agreed to stay when she'd invited us along. I turned to watch her dash around the corner, the cape she'd slipped over her dress sailing behind her like some great wing.

During the return drive, with words sloppy from wine, I spilled out my insecurities to James. "Do you think I could ever be more like them? I wish I were. More like Francesca."

"What do you mean?" James wanted to know.

"She is so self-assured, so strong. Greta and Fiona, too. The way they talk and laugh, even the way they eat—"

"Hah!" James swatted the side of the steering wheel, in surprise or amusement, I could not tell which. Lines creased either side of his down-turned lips in an expression I had never before seen him wear. I was being foolish, he said, far too easily impressed. Why would I want to be like Fran or his friends' girlfriends? They were as obstinate as I was sweet, as contrary as I was agreeable. Had I *any* idea what most men thought of women like Francesca? And had he told me how many crazy demands Fiona placed on Dominic? James's bottom lip disappeared behind his front teeth, and I heard a quiet sucking noise, a sound I had come to associate with his attempt to predict my reaction to something he was about to disclose. "Even Nicholas agrees. He said your lines were poetry."

"What do you mean?" But before he even answered, before James parted his lips to speak, I knew Nicholas had seen the sketch.

"Are you feeling modest, kitten?" he said, shaking his head. "It's not a photograph, just a drawing, an impression. Besides, Nicholas is a painter. It's his work. When he looks at a human body, he sees art. Anyway, you should be flattered by his praise. So how can you even compare yourself to these women? No, you could *never* be them. They are nothing next to you." And he pressed my fingers to his mouth. "Promise you won't ever change, sweet Setsu," he whispered.

So I nodded my assent. "Never, never——" But I turned toward the window to hide my eyes, which, for the first time in James's presence, burned with something like anger.

For days after our dinner at Hunan Palace, knowing how James disapproved of Francesca's conduct, her style, I was careful not to mention her name to him, or Fiona's or Greta's, for that matter. But on occasion and at unexpected times, flashes from our meal together returned to me, a clever phrase one of them had uttered, a wry smile, an ironic hand gesture. Every now and then as I rooted through my closet for a scarf or earrings or a pair of shoes, I could not help posing in the mirror, the scarf tossed over my shoulder, my hair pinned up to reveal my earrings, as I thought Fran might. And now when James was teaching or studying, I could not so easily ignore a panging—for a cheese omelet, batter-dipped shrimp, a piece of cake. Some women ate such foods without a second thought. Couldn't I, too, afford a small indulgence here or there? So with an egg sandwich, a bag of fried onions, or a slice of rhubarb pie from the cafeteria, I would fill my mouth until the aching in my stomach ceased. Perhaps a part of me had hungered for these things always, and I enjoyed, for a few moments, the warmth and heaviness below my ribs, the satisfaction of having dared something so bold, even defiant. Only later, dressing to meet James for supper or standing before him in candlelight as he unfastened the buttons of my blouse, would I regret my weakness. And for the next few days, I would nibble only fruits for breakfast, vegetables for lunch, working to undo the fat I was afraid would appear on my hips and bottom, a change I worried James would notice.

.   .   .

For the four-day Presidents' Weekend in mid-February, Francesca was returning to New York and had invited me along. James would be gone anyway, needing to attend a conference in New Hampshire. Ruth, too, would be home with her family in Riverdale; Opal was choosing to remain on campus to complete an art history paper.

As a child, I had spent two short vacations in New York with my family. I still remembered the bracing winds aboard the Circle Line tour boat, Toru leaning against the railing with crackers in his outstretched hand, daring two gulls to pluck them, I with my windbreaker zippered to my chin, standing a safe distance from the screeching birds. More recent New York visits had been to accompany my parents for a stay in the Parker Meridien and the chance to see Toru perform with other Juilliard students at Lincoln Center.

I would not be seeing Toru this weekend, though. He was swamped with work, he had explained when I called. Francesca's family would be away, too, touring prospective colleges for her brother, Christopher, but I had always been curious about Francesca's home, having heard from Ruth, who'd visited Fran during the summer break, that the Covingtons' apartment made even the Taj Mahal look a little shabby. As soon as we stepped from the elevator vestibule and through the front door, I understood what Ruth had meant. The soaring ceilings, the framed paintings illuminated by brass-shaded lights, the grand staircase to a second floor!—things Francesca seemed to take for granted, dropping her bag to the marble floor, tossing her coat over the banister as casually as if we were back in the cramped suite on campus with its university-issued furniture.

"This is so beautiful, Fran!" I said, but she only laughed, kicking off her shoes, allowing them to remain overturned in the middle of the foyer.

"Thanks. Well, it's home anyway!" she said, as if it had its draw-backs, though I couldn't imagine what.

As I soon learned, we did not have the apartment completely to our-selves. Carmen, the Covingtons' housekeeper, lived in the residence full-time. I rarely saw her except passing her as she ironed linens in the breakfast room or delivered upstairs, to the round table in Francesca's bedroom, the meals Fran requested. Now and then, Carmen would call to Francesca, though—a question about an appointment with the win-dow washer, then about the placement of two newly arrived topiaries for the dining room. In Maryland, different cleaning ladies had worked for my mother one afternoon a week; but not one of them had ever deferred to me on a single matter, seeming to find my presence an intrusion, in fact, if I did not vacate any room when they vacuumed or dusted.

"We could do the Guggenheim after breakfast," Fran said on our first morning, propping herself up on her elbow, pushing back her bedspread. "And then why don't we head to the Village. There's a vintage clothing shop I want to show you and the *best* place for chocolates just down the block."

"Sounds fun," I said from my bed across the room from hers. I had been awake for some time, but my thoughts hadn't moved beyond the liquid silk of my sheets and the way I had seemed to drop into the thick of my mattress as I'd slept.

Over the weekend, we watched *Roman Holiday* two times through on cable; we swam in the pool at Francesca's mother's health club. In the evening, we skated on the ice rink in Central Park, Francesca insisting we stay in the loop of fastest skaters near the center of the rink, though we tumbled several times onto the cold ice.

"You're a terrible influence!" I told her at the end of the night, hold-ing the ice cream she'd bought, rubbing two bruises along the side of my leg as we walked down the lantern-lit path out of the park. But with the mint of the ice cream filling my nose, cooling my tongue, and with the waltzing music of the skating rink sounding through the dark trees as tinklingly clear as the pendants of fine icicles suspended from the boughs above us, I felt I was suddenly wide awake in a moment so alive I wanted to breathe it deep, deep into my lungs.

Some days after our visit to New York and two weeks after our dinner together in Boston, Francesca invited Dominic and Fiona, James and me to join her for Sunday brunch at The Hill Club near Bristol, where her grandparents, who lived part of the year in Rhode Island, had a membership.

"You're here! The directions must have been okay," she said when we arrived. She looked more glamorous than usual, in a faintly sheer sweater, gold bracelets jingling at her wrists, her hair swept from her face in a broad cotton headband. She ushered us to a table covered with peach linens, beside a great bay window overlooking a terrace and a sloping, snow-blanketed lawn, at the center of which was an enormous scallop-shell fountain, now filled with a glistening mound of snow. Dominic and Fiona had already arrived and rose to kiss us on both cheeks in the European fashion. I knew to turn my head slightly as they did so that our cheekbones would lightly press.

Once we had been seated, Francesca moved to the window, lowering the shades several inches. "There was a glare, wasn't there?" She dropped into the cushioned chair beside mine, shaking her napkin into her lap.

"So, I hope everyone likes grits and scrambled eggs with salmon." She pulled her box of cigarettes from her handbag. "I took the liberty of ordering for the table." She winked at me, and I could not help smiling, liking to be singled out by her.

James, seated to my right, uncrossed his legs. He tapped his knee with his fingertips, an obvious sign to me of his displeasure. But Francesca took no notice. And watching her lean back comfortably, planting an el-bow on the padded leather back of her chair, I knew she would not have relinquished her role even if James had voiced his dissatisfaction.

James and Dominic began to talk of the apartment Dominic was renovating, one he and Fiona had just moved into. Francesca lit her ciga-rette with a new marbled green lighter and turned to Fiona. "So how was the show the other night?"

Fiona worked days teaching English as a second language to native Spanish speakers, she explained to me, but evenings, when she could, she sang at clubs or hotels or restaurants in the area—any place that would hire her. Her hope, she admitted, was to someday make a career as a jazz singer. "Music is my obsession," she laughed, but beneath her lightheart-edness, I could hear a tension, a longing I thought I recognized. "I guess it's hard for other people to understand." She shrugged.

But I understood. Yes. And in a rushing murmur, I told Francesca and Fiona of my years playing the violin. Of how music had seemed to live in me, how it had seemed impossible to imagine a time when it would not.

"Why didn't I know this about you, Setsu?" Francesca squeezed my arm. "All this time you never said a word about it! I knew you'd taken lessons, but I'd no idea this was your passion. And you gave it up! That's a crime!"

Fiona agreed. I must do something. Not just let part of my being die! It wasn't too late, she said. Didn't I know the reputation of Brown's or-chestra? What an opportunity I had here!

"No, no." I shook my head. I was just sharing the story, that was all. Too much time had passed, too many things forgotten. Anyway, my brother was the true talent in the family.

"Ridiculous. It will come back to you like *that*." Francesca snapped her fingers to indicate her point. "You have to take charge of your own life, Setsu. Claim it! Often I suspected there was more to you than it seemed, a side you've kept hidden. And it's true—" She rapped her box of

Parliaments excitedly against her palm. "Doesn't James beg you to play? He must." Leaning forward, reaching for a pitcher of pineapple juice at the center of the table, she interrupted James's conversation with Dominic. "Why did you let your girlfriend keep such a secret from us?" she said with a ringing of her bracelets. "I had no idea she was a *real* musician. You must encourage her. Tell her she mustn't waste her gift."

From the stiffening of James's jaw, I knew I had made a mistake by confessing things to Francesca I had never shared with him. "I know. She's wonderful, isn't she?" He reached for my hand, clasping it in his, but before he did so, I thought I saw a flickering as his eyes shifted from Francesca to me, a darkness, something unfamiliar.

Returning to Providence, James chose the most direct route, rather than the quieter one along the river we had followed on our way to The Hill Club. Few cars were on the road, and there was little sound but the whirring of his tires on the paved highway. Each time James adjusted his legs or cleared his throat, I prepared for him to mention the revelation Fran had made. But for many, many miles his only comments were about a crow we spotted perched atop a decaying tree and the gathering clouds overhead.

So I was left to my own thoughts, and my mind began to wander, to dream of unlikely things, of old abandoned hopes. And when I could no longer bear the suspense of trying to guess James's opinion, I blurted the question that had been aching in my throat since leaving the club. Some students from the music department were starting their own chamber ensemble, I explained. Last week I had seen their posters near the campus mailboxes. They needed a violinist and auditions would be in the spring. "I didn't really consider it until now, until Fran . . . Do you think it would be silly of me? You know, with just a few months to prepare . . ."

James's eyes narrowed without blinking, puckering the skin between his brows as if he were focusing hard on some object in the road. For a time he said nothing, and I felt the blood rush to my ears, certain that

James was about to point out the irrationality of my suggestion. But when he finally turned to me, it was with the half-smile he saved for our most private moments. No, no, of course he did not think me silly. It was only that he had some concerns, he said, petting my forehead, running his fingers through strands of my hair. Wasn't my schedule full enough already? Hadn't he heard me complain that I was beginning to fall behind in my Chaucer reading, that I had needed an extension for my most recent Dickens paper? "I just don't want you to feel overloaded," he said. And as I nodded, he peered at me intently, then lifted my wrist to his lips.

James was right, I was quite sure. It was probably unreasonable to think I could manage another demand on my time. For a day or two, I tried to forget my conversation with Francesca and Fiona and any foolish notions about joining the chamber ensemble. Francesca could talk of independence and daring, of living life with courage, but, of course, these things came easily to her, things one could not fake or pretend, and I did not know if they could be learned.

But then memories began to disturb my nights. I would wake in the dark to the sound of a Mozart symphony or a Beethoven sonata, only to realize the music was playing in my own head. Beautiful sections of pieces, the notes clear as crystals, as if I'd practiced them just the day before. One night I was startled from sleep by a dream I had not dreamed since early girlhood: I am in Japan, never having been taken to America. I am sitting on a stone bench in a small garden with my birth mother, who is alive and well. She is playing the solo part of Mendelssohn's "Violin Concerto in E" on an instrument with wood that shines gold-brown in the sunlight. When she finishes, she bends her head to kiss my cheek, then, smiling, passes the violin to me, waiting for me to play with notes as strong and clear as hers. Lying in James's bed, having woken from my dream, I stared at the ceiling, at the faint shadows of tapering tree branches, and brushed at the tears that slipped silently from the corners of my eyes.

So the following morning I unpacked, from beneath my dormitory bed, the violin and stack of sheet music I had decided at the last minute to bring back with me to Brown. For the first few days, unsure of how I would sound, not wanting to humiliate myself, I only risked practice in private, in the solitude of my room if my suitemates were out, or in one of the music department's soundproof cubicles. To my surprise, fingerings and bowings returned more quickly than I had anticipated. For my audition piece, I selected a section of Tartini's "Sonata in G Minor." I began to play every spare moment, and though uncertain if my sound had the precision, the style, the fire necessary to be chosen, I soon felt glimmers of hope.

For some reason, my time on the violin seemed to make my appetite grow. Often, after an hour or two of practicing, I discovered I was starved. From the snack bars on campus, I would buy cheese-filled calzones, plates of fried falafel, bowls of sesame noodles, savoring each bite, scraping every last crumb. And though I intended to repent later, to restrict my diet as I had done before, I found myself too ravenous at each meal for such discipline.

As I grew more careless in my eating, I became, also, less particular about where I practiced. After the hesitation of the first week or two had worn off, I dared to play in one of the larger common areas of the music department if the individual cubicles were taken or even, on occasion, at James's apartment before he returned home. So one early evening when I discovered him leaning in the doorway, his thumbs tucked into his belt loops, silently watching me, the bow faltered in my hand and I lost my place on my page of music.

"I've decided to try out after all," I laughed, feeling warmth rise to my face. My hands shook, but to my surprise, I heard a confidence in my voice. I believed I had sounded as definite as Francesca would have. For a moment James did not respond. He was chewing the inside of his cheek in concentration and seemed to be mulling over some private thought.

"Sorry. I didn't mean to disturb you." He nodded with unusual formality, then disappeared down the hall to the kitchen, leaving me gripping the violin neck, the bow dangling from my other hand. I could hear him loudly dropping cubes of ice into a glass.

That night throughout dinner and later, curled beside him in bed, I waited for James to mention my playing, to give some small hint of approval or dismay. But he made no allusion to it, as if he'd forgotten what he'd seen and heard.

The following day, he came down with a cold. His eyes swelled; the skin around his nostrils reddened. He was too ill to attend classes, and I should have offered soup or company, asked what he needed. But every time he blew into his plaid handkerchief, I felt only irritation. Of course he had his own concerns, but I could not help noticing that, as he recovered, the violin case, which I had stowed in the corner beside his bedroom chair, where I kept my coat and textbooks and a spare change of clothes, continued to go unmentioned. As I practiced, though, certainly strains of music must have reached where he lay in bed. So, once he was well enough to go out, I could not stop myself, as I played, from listening for James's returning footsteps on the veranda. Once or twice I thought I recognized the familiar thud of his feet then a long pause before his hand turned the doorknob, bringing in a rush of icy outdoor air. But still I waited, and still he said nothing.

"Men are so insensitive," my suitemates sometimes complained— especially after the parties Fran occasionally convinced Ruth and Opal to attend with her—and always I had contradicted with stories of James's thoughtfulness. But what would they say of this? And I supposed, if I chose, I had every right to tell them.

With just two months until the audition, I continued to practice the Tartini whenever I could find time. But now I began to fear that my optimism of the past weeks had been hasty. There were tricky spots where I thought I caught mistakes in my rhythm, notes that needed more vibrato, phrases that required faster bowings. And soon, though I knew

James was no musician, though I knew the impossibility of such a thing, I could not help feeling that somehow he, too, detected flaws in my playing—as Toru once had—that this, all along, had been the reason for his silence.

One afternoon, returning from a practice session, I found Francesca, Ruth, and Opal at home sprawled on the floor of the common room, sections of the *Brown Daily Herald* open before them. Their textbooks and class notes lay piled on the coffee table, the favored spot for any deferred work. And since they seemed to be reading only absentmindedly, I confided my worries.

Ruth put her section of the paper aside, reaching out her hand, placing it on mine. "I'm so glad you're using your talent again, Setsu. It's incredible! Really. I wish I had a gift like that."

"But it's been such a long time since I've played—"

Francesca stopped reading. For a moment, she gazed at me, the corners of her mouth curving almost indiscernibly, her brows lifted ever so slightly. It was an expression she wore when someone contradicted her with an argument she found persuasive. Perhaps she had not truly believed I would try out, but I could see she was pleased I had. "Just stay focused, Setsu. Don't get distracted. If you really want this—" Francesca stopped for a moment. "You do really want it, don't you, Setsu?"

"Yes, of course. Of course. It's only . . . Well, I don't think James—"

"James! *What* does this have to do with James?" The forcefulness of Francesca's tone startled me, and I caught Opal glancing at Fran.

But they were wrong. James would understand once he knew what it meant to me. Still, for the rest of the day, I thought of what Francesca had said. For some reason, it made me feel quarrelsome, though with whom I was not quite sure.

I began to wake early in the mornings to play before my first class. I practiced during the late afternoons while James was teaching. And with this more strenuous work, many nights I found too many thoughts sparked through my mind for sleep.

.   .   .

Auditions were on a Saturday. James had some research to do at the Science Library and had left early, before I had wakened. Other mornings when he'd done so, he had placed a romantic note or a blossom from his potted violets on the pillow where he'd slept. I had not mentioned the chamber ensemble tryouts since first telling him of them weeks before, but somehow I had expected him on this morning, especially, to leave reminders or written good-luck wishes. I tossed off my blankets, neglecting for once to smooth the sheets and coverlet, to arrange the pillows as James liked.

On James's kitchen counter, I found a thin paper bag filled with croissants and sugared doughnuts and on a shelf in the back of the refrigerator, three kinds of marmalade and a brick of butter wrapped in gold foil. I gobbled part of a doughnut, an entire croissant, then removed a second from the bag, slathering it with preserves and leaving it on a sheet of paper towel, knowing that thirty minutes into my practicing I would crave more.

I calculated that I had an hour and a half to warm up and run through the Tartini before heading to campus, to Grant Recital Hall, where auditions would be held. Perhaps it was my excitement; perhaps with the nervous thumping of my heart I could not hear the imperfections, but as I played the piece once and then twice, I could not help pressing my lips with expectation. But in my enthusiasm, I must have been deaf, too, to the tramp of James's steps on the front porch, to the heave of the door, and the clip of his heels against the floorboards on his way to the kitchen and then back to the living room where I was playing.

"Setsu—" I was startled not only by his presence but by the strangeness of his voice, tensed and hushed as though something had frightened him. Slowly he seated himself on the long living room sofa, then extended an arm, motioning for me to join him. It was only that he was worried for me, he said. He had seen, in the kitchen, the evidence of my breakfast. And though he hadn't mentioned it, two days ago, unable to find his apartment key and searching my trench coat for the spare, he had discovered a handful of egg roll wrappers and crumpled, emptied bags of fried noodles. "This is not you, Setsu, is it? I hardly recognize the way you are eating."

I bowed my head and stared at my stockinged knees and my violin, which I had laid across my lap. For days I had imagined how, if necessary, I would defend my decision to James, but now I could think only of how humiliated I was by his discovery, and by the disappointment I had heard in the way he spoke my name.

"You've just taken on more than you can handle, yes?" he said, pinching his chin between his forefinger and thumb. "It's nerves, don't you think?"

"No, I believe . . . I'm really fine—"

"But you were planning to audition after all? On top of everything else? Maybe you should take a break, hmm? Or—" He paused for some moments. "Maybe it's this that you don't want." To my horror, he made a small semicircle in the air with his hand, gesturing to himself and then to me. "Life doesn't allow us time for everything, does it? You have to prioritize. You must make choices. It is too painful for me to have you in fragments, Setsu." He straightened in his seat, slowly turning his head so that his profile was to me. From this angle I could see the nearly imperceptible shiftings of his rain-gray eyes, the slight narrowing of his lids, and I knew, as a coldness like frigid water passed through me, he was considering other choices.

"No, no. You won't have me in pieces! You will have all of me. It's what I want, too!" And it was. It was!

As I placed my violin down on the couch cushion, James beamed at me, then began tenderly to kiss my cheeks and chin and mouth. "All I wish for is your happiness," he said as he stroked my brow, wound a wisp of my hair around his finger. "I hope you know that. It hurts me to see you so burdened." He leaned over to caress my neck behind my ear.

How deeply James cared for me, how wisely. It seemed he knew me better than Ruth or Francesca or Opal, even better than I knew myself. How wrong Opal had been in her concerns. And Fran in her dismissiveness. I belonged to him, and he to me. It was what I needed, more than anything, more than claiming some part of myself, as Francesca had said. And because of their influence, I had nearly lost him by not accepting who I was, who I had to be! I was blessed, yes, truly blessed. Because James loved me in ways my suitemates could never understand. Only *he* had seen that, over the last several days, I had been different, not felt my old self at all. Glancing at my watch, I saw that the audition would begin without me in less than twenty minutes. But there was no reason for sadness, was there? No reason for these tears brimming at the corners of my eyes. For what was I sacrificing? It was not that I had ever been found to be a significant violinist. It was only for fun I had decided to try out. Only a few months of time I had dedicated to practicing. So it was a matter of small consequence. After all, I was not Toru.

James massaged my right shoulder. "Why don't we get away for the day? I know a beautiful drive along the shoreline. The weather should be mild enough for a picnic lunch." He had bought chicken salad the night before. With the leftovers he could make sandwiches, he said. "How does that sound?"

"Yes, lovely," I nodded.

"And, sweet girl, I nearly forgot. I bought you something when I was downtown yesterday. Something only you could do justice to." He kissed the tip of my nose then rose from the sofa. He returned with a red rectangular cardboard box tied with a gauzy white ribbon. "I'm going to the kitchen." He leaned close so that his mustache tickled my bare neck. "Maybe you could surprise me when I come back. Wear this," he whispered, "until we leave?"

I could hear James in the kitchen removing dishes and utensils from cupboards. I crossed the living room to gaze out the window. Outside on Benefit Street, clusters of students, their cheeks rosy from the still-cool spring air, were hurrying to one place or another—a Brown lacrosse game, friends' dorms, a late breakfast at the Ratty. After a time, a solitary girl with braided hair, in kneesocks, and carrying a pennant that I recognized from one of the neighborhood middle schools, was singing in a clear, pretty voice. The Danube Waltz. It was part of a collection of Strauss waltzes my parents had played again and again when I was young. How beautiful I had thought the piece. I could remember standing motionlessly before the record player, humming, trying to make my voice swell and recede to follow the cadence. I pressed my forehead to the glass, watching the girl as she moved down the sidewalk, straining, straining to hear the notes until they faded and then finally died.

My gift was a filmy pink negligee and matching robe. *Extra-Extra Small*, read its label, and I had to work some minutes to fit into it properly. Countless tiny silk ribbons wound the nightgown's bodice, wrapping me like a spool of thread. At the slightest inhalation my ribs ached. But James would think it perfect. I could see that in my reflection in the windowpane. When he saw me, he would say something generous, something admiring.

James had prepared sandwiches. He had crackers, a wedge of cheese, fruit salad. How much would I eat? he called from the kitchen. Exactly what should he pack for me?

"Oh. Just a half sandwich. Thank you." I breathed carefully, carefully, shallowly in my gown and robe. "A half sandwich and maybe a little fruit salad." Yes, yes, that would be plenty. That was all I needed.

BUILDING RESISTANCE

(Opal's Story)

• Junior Fall •

Mother's patience for the occasional reports I gave of my suite-mates' lives was limited. Ruth's pregnancy, Setsu's relationship that left no time for her music—these were simply part of the unpredictabilities of life, she said. Anyway, why was I fretting over someone else's journey? What I needed was to find my own. "Routine is death, Opal," Mother pronounced loudly into the receiver. She had a philosophy that the moment one's life began to follow any sort of pattern, it was time to make a fresh start. "Always over the next horizon are a thousand new experiences." It was for this reason that after three years in the Caribbean, we had moved to Sanibel Island, Florida, where Mother had painted pottery and small watercolors, selling them to several of the local shops. And the reason we had spent a year in Puerto Rico, another two in the blistering heat of Acapulco, and then, three months before my junior year of high school, returned to California. This time we had set-tled on the southern coast, an hour south of Los Angeles. Crossing the border to reenter the U.S., I had asked about our old neighborhood in San Francisco. But Mother only laughed. "Haven't we used up our adventures in that city? Won't it be more exciting to try someplace new?"

Wherever we went, Mother found boyfriends. In Florida, of course, there had been P.T., the sporting goods salesman who took us deep-sea fishing on his motorboat. In Mexico, a series of men she'd met in the nightclubs where she went dancing—the handsomest one had given her welts on her arms and black-and-blue marks on her legs, which she'd masked with the same creamy foundation she applied to her face. Not long after I returned to Brown for my second year, Mother had sent a letter: in California, she had found someone new—Antonio, a travel agent. "We fight like cats and dogs. But he's gorgeous and the most exciting man I've ever known."

Despite what she referred to as their fiery relationship, Mother had agreed to go into business with Antonio. Together they had opened their own restaurant on the cliffs overlooking the water. They called it Paradise Jungle. The menus, the chairs, the bar stools were covered in animal prints. Thick vines wrapped the railings of the outdoor terrace. The restaurant served every exotic dish Mother and Antonio could think of: venison, buffalo, sea turtle, shark. "World food," Antonio called it, the selections changing daily depending on what was available. And soon local papers and magazines began to hail Paradise Jungle as the newest hot spot.

Since I would be living at home during summer break, Mother expected me to work nights at the restaurant waiting tables. "I don't think I'm up for the hustle and bustle of a restaurant. Maybe I'll just volunteer at the women's shelter like I did last summer," I told Mother my first night in the new apartment she and Antonio now rented together.

But Mother would not hear it. "No, no. This will be a broadening experience," she'd insisted. "Mingling with our diverse clientele will be a *far* better use of your time." The summer before she had complained that my time at the shelter made me mopey. "You soak up the worries of those women. But it does no good for anyone! You're sponging up their unhappiness just as you did with that suitemate of yours who got herself into trouble." And she had tossed waves of hair over her shoulder as though shaking off the very thought, almost annoyed, it seemed to me, by Ruth's problems.

The apartment Mother and Antonio had found was a small two-bedroom just blocks from the ocean. Its kitchen walls were painted pink, the living-room-dining-room aqua-blue. Everywhere there were closets with mirrored sliding glass doors; I could not turn my head without glimpsing my reflection. How perfect for Mother, I'd thought, and for Antonio, too, who, with his shellacked black hair, designer, torso-hugging shirts, and perfumey aftershave, reminded me of some evening game show host.

At Paradise Jungle, the rest of the waitstaff were a few years older than I, transplants from as far as Vancouver and Tulsa, aspiring actresses and musicians in need of money. Despite the gap in our ages, they seemed to find me a worthy companion. They cooed over my clothes and the way I wore them: the bright, spangled skirt from Cabo San Lucas that fluttered against my thighs, my dangling coral earrings from Barbados, a white blouse with a plunging neckline I had borrowed from Mother's closet. Almost nightly they asked to hear stories of the places I had lived, the sights I had seen. Chewing candied mints from the straw basket near the entry, they bemoaned what they claimed was the comparative dullness of their own lives. "God, Opal, I would *die* to have done those things." For a time, I enjoyed their attentions, until I learned the reason for their interest.

Though I would stay only through mid-August, I dreaded the nightly shift at the restaurant and the way the men who came to dine winked at me across the room or tugged at the ties of my apron as I passed. What was it, I worried as I scrutinized my reflection in the mirrors over the bathroom sinks, that made them single me out, made them think I would like their overtures and that I might respond? I tried to walk quickly when I crossed the room, holding my hips straight and steady. I played a game with myself: if I could hold my breath from the moment a group of men entered until they were seated, they would be guided to another girl's table; if I couldn't, their table would be mine. Sometimes, however, they broke the rules of my game and made a special request. I could see them murmuring in Antonio's ear, glancing in my direction. Some asked me riddles, or complimented my eyes or the way I wore my hair— far more, it seemed to me, than they did with the other girls. Occasionally I felt, from beneath the table, a knuckle grazing my knee.

The other girls at Paradise had countless friends, social plans every night after work. They made regular trips to the restaurant's pay phone, arranging and rearranging their coming evening activities. So why did they pull me aside, seeking advice in rushed whispers? There were things they had done with the California men they dated, things their boy-friends wanted them to do. What did I suggest? Should they? What was it like? What did they see in me that made them disappointed and con-fused by my fumbling replies? And why did they stare at my high-heeled sandals and the chiffon of my shirt as if certain I was keeping secret knowledge?

It seemed they concluded I was experienced but aloof. I knew this from the snatches of conversation I overheard in the restroom stalls or from behind the kitchen's swinging doors. In spite of my attempts at friendly chitchat, my offers to cover their shifts when they were busy, there seemed nothing I could do to improve their opinion.

"Don't be sulky," Mother would chide if she caught me rushing through an order, hurrying from a table of men. "Do you want to chase away good customers?" She pressed fingers to the corners of her mouth, lifting her lips, her signal for me to smile.

So I tried to look pleasant as I served. "See, Mother, I will be the pic-ture of cheerfulness!" But I could not help my disgust with the way they tore meat from their chops and ribs, until nothing remained but tiny bloodied shreds. Drink glasses collected on their tables more quickly than

I could clear them away. Their lips and fingertips glistened with gravy, with marinades, with butter, with chocolate mousse, and dark fruit juices, their eyes seeking, every now and then, to meet mine. I glanced at the other members of the waitstaff, who formed giggling circles near the kitchen sinks. But they had no such complaints or revulsions. So during lulls in our work, while they joked and gabbed, I hunched on the corner kitchen stool over a magazine or a book I had brought from home.

One late afternoon, as we were getting ready to leave the apartment to open Paradise Jungle for the evening, I knocked on Mother's bedroom door. She was thickening her lashes with black mascara, massaging dabs of perfume behind her knees.

"What is it, dearheart?"

Feeling suddenly too uncomfortable to look in her eyes, I pulled at the ruffled edge of her bedspread. Did she ever tire, as I did, of the reactions of men? I asked. I never greeted the men at the restaurant or introduced myself. I said not a word until necessary. Maybe I gazed back too long. Or swayed my hips. Eduardo, a boy I had dated one summer in Acapulco, once told me my lips were like ripe berries and that my hips, when I moved, rocked like a boat on waves.

"Is *that* what's bothering you? I thought Brown was so progressive, but old conservative New England must be taking its toll!" Mother pinched my cheek as if to show how I charmed her. After all of the people we'd met, all of the places we'd been, had I learned nothing? "Men will be men," she laughed. "Most women would kill for a walk as sexy as yours, for pouting lips, for your figure." She tucked a strand of hair behind her ear, studying her reflection. She blinked slowly, pleased, I could tell, by what she saw. "Believe me, Opal, getting noticed more than other girls is something you will soon stop complaining about.

"Feel better?" She smiled as she clasped a silver choker, a carved tiger's head at its center, around her neck.

I nodded, but the loose, watery feeling in my stomach had only grown worse. The notion that I might somehow be contributing to the urges of "men being men" sickened me. "Don't you think there can be consequences to enticing a man?" I asked Mother. I thought of Ruth and Setsu and the notions they had picked up in school about how to dress, how to carry themselves—small sparks that had ignited roaring fires. But Mother was rummaging through her closet in search of shoes that matched her outfit and had not heard.

Before I returned to Rhode Island, Mother took me shopping for some early-fall items—a stylish trench coat, two silky, light wool skirts, and what Mother referred to as "a lady's bathrobe," a thin, satiny one to replace the frayed cotton one I wore around the apartment.

In the car on the way home, stopped at a red light, she squeezed her fingers to my wrist and whispered, "If you like, Opal, I can make an appointment for you with my doctor before you leave. You know, if there's *anything* you might need."

I knew what kind of doctor Mother meant and exactly what kind of things the doctor would give me. "There's nothing I need!" I shook my head vigorously as I gazed out the window at a group of schoolchildren walking in double file behind their teacher.

During the last few days of August, Mother had arranged for us to visit her East Coast friend, Marla, and her family before classes resumed. "Marla and I haven't caught up in years, and I know she's looking forward to seeing you. You were just a bit of a thing the last time we were together!" But at the last moment, Mother's plans changed: Antonio's brother, whom she'd never met, was flying in from Rome. She absolutely had to stay to meet him. "Marla's still expecting *you*, though."

The Dunhams lived in New Canaan, Connecticut, and Marla and her husband had three sons. The youngest, Daniel, was my age, and when I arrived, he was filling duffel bags in preparation for his own return to Amherst College in Massachusetts.

"Did you remember your windbreaker, Dan? And those all-weather boots we just bought?" Marla dashed in and out of his room a number of times, checking his progress.

"She still worries I can't organize my own belongings," he laughed after Marla's last trip upstairs to be sure I had everything I needed in my room across the hall from Daniel's, then bringing him a folded stack of laundry. "Mothers! They just can't help themselves, can they?"

"I guess it goes with the territory," I answered, laughing agreeably, though I could not remember the last time Mother had overseen *my* packing.

The Dunham home was rambling and old, with sloped floors and ceilings, and more corridors and staircases than I could follow. There were fireplaces everywhere, their mantels cluttered with family photographs and children's artwork. Three little-boy handprints in plaster casts hung on the wall near the door of my guest bedroom. Despite the late-summer heat, the Dunhams used no air conditioners, only a few dusty window fans.

Marla called us to the table at seven my first night, the regular dinnertime in the Dunham home, she mentioned. "It's such a treat to have you here, Opal. I wish your mother could have joined you. How is she? I haven't seen her in *eons*. I want to hear all about her restaurant. Oh, and I want to hear about Brown! My niece is applying for next year—such a great, great school." Marla smiled and set her fork down, tucking her thin, yellow, chin-length hair behind her ear. In her striped Izod shirt and her belted Bermuda shorts and her pea-shaped pearl earrings, it was hard for me to imagine she and Mother had once been close. She seemed like the women whom Mother rolled her eyes at in airports, toting their golf bags or tennis rackets in zippered cases, and their compact suitcases that matched their husbands'. "You look at them and you just *know* nothing in their lives ever distinguishes one day from the next. God, I think I'd shoot myself! If my husband didn't do it first!"

But I liked the way Marla talked to me, wanting to know about my suitemates, my decision to major in art history, the way she looked up from her plate as I answered, as if she wanted to be careful to catch my words. After we had sat for some time, she offered seconds, even thirds of pork tenderloin and rice pilaf. But Daniel, I noticed, turned these down, to my surprise, eating with none of the abandon of the men at Paradise Jungle. He refused the Bordeaux his father served the rest of us. "Daniel's in training for cross country," Marla said as explanation for his restraint. "He's very dedicated. Did he tell you he was the captain of his high school varsity team?"

"My mother likes to brag about me." A deep crease formed in Daniel's left cheek as he smiled.

After my second day in the house, Marla began to drop hints to Daniel. "Dan, why don't you take Opal for a drive around town today?" Or, "Honey, show Opal the stream out back. I'm sure she'd love to see it."

I denied the small pull of disappointment in my chest as I watched him push his tortoiseshell-rimmed glasses closer to his face and frown as if his head were too full of other thoughts to find room for her suggestions. At night, from my bedroom, I could hear soft strains of music as Daniel thrummed the strings of a guitar. While his brothers sped off in their shared convertible Saab, he played songs by Simon and Garfunkel and James Taylor and Crosby, Stills and Nash, now and then quietly humming snatches of the melodies. Once, waking from sleep to use the bathroom, I glimpsed him through the door, which he had left slightly ajar, seated on his braided rug, under the soft light of a single lamp, his head bent toward the guitar still cradled in his arms. The following evening, rather than playing music, hair falling in a dark fan of curls across his brow, he pored over the pages of a thick hardcover book resting on his knees and nodded to himself as if in agreement with the material in his lap, oblivious to my presence. He seemed different, more likable than most boys. Still, I was not interested. Unlike Setsu and Ruth, I would be in charge of my own life.

⁓

It seemed to me that friends washed in and out of one's life like pebbles tumbling in the surf. You were tossed together for a while and then circumstances swept you apart. This was what my suitemates and I had promised to avoid. But to succeed was another matter, wasn't it? So I was relieved Fran and Ruth and Setsu had wanted the same living arrangement for our junior year, in the dorm near Hope Street we'd had the year before. They had always assumed we would stay together, they said. Hadn't I? Didn't I wish it, too? "Yes, of course!" I told them. I could not say that perhaps I had even wished it more, that I had worried *they* might have a change of heart. Still, I sensed they were different from me, a part of something I was not. It seemed easy for them to join in what was popular or communal on campus. Last April, waving their Brown banners during a Spring Weekend concert on the Green—some band in black army boots and slashed camouflage shirts—they had tried to get me to dance with them. "Isn't this fun?" I had not told them how I could not take my mind off the stale smell of the crowd, how the pounding of the amplified music made my ears throb. I pretended to enjoy myself as much as they did at Acoustic Night, at the few campus parties I attended.

Always, growing up, in every school I had been the "interesting new girl," never sticking around long enough to fit in. College would be different though, I'd thought—all of us brand-new from the beginning, all of us staying four years in the same place. It was the *wanting* to be part of things that mattered, I was learning. An ease, a readiness to join what others did, breezily, cheerfully. This was how you were enfolded into the social swirl, into happiness. I understood these things, still there must have been something I was not doing. I had heard references to multiple phone calls between my suitemates over the summer, though I'd spoken to each of them only once. And when Fran and Setsu had spent the weekend at Fran's house the winter before, their assumption that I would not wish to go along had been obvious.

So I joined Fran and Ruth (and Setsu when she was not with James) for regular meals at the Ratty. I did not admit that the heavy smell that wafted over the steps leading to the dining hall still nauseated me. Or that I had never grown accustomed to the din of voices and clanking silverware inside, the mess of crowded tables, the oiliness of the food. *Cattle heading to the trough!* I would think as we stood on line with our scuffed trays on which we balanced scratched plates and glasses.

Each morning before we left for classes, Francesca would check the second page of the *Brown Daily Herald* and report to us the school's menu for the day: " 'Ham and Macaroni Casserole, Franks and Beans, Potato-Zucchini Hash.' Another gourmet dinner tonight, ladies!" But as much as they mocked the cafeteria's offerings, Francesca and Ruth seemed to polish them off without complaint, Francesca often returning for second helpings—"Amazing what we can adjust to when we're starved, right?" she would snort. And when Ruth abstained from large portions it was only because she had finished off two chocolate doughnuts or carrot muffins from one of the snack bars before we came and had more wrapped in a paper towel back at the suite. Was she hoping to fool us or herself that these would be saved for some other day?

"Aren't you hungry, Opal?" she and Fran would ask as I poked at my food.

"I had a late lunch," I would say, not wanting to admit I could swallow only small servings of what they gobbled down. So I would think of other things to talk of. Like pocketing shiny stones, I would collect amusing anecdotes throughout the day to share with Fran and Ruth later: I had caught Cleo Parker last night locked out of her room, in poodle pajamas and matching powder-puff slippers, of all things! (Her room-mate, Noelle, had tied a ribbon around the doorknob, and we all knew what that meant.) And in Ethics class I had accidentally referred to Professor Reinhart as "sir."

"You didn't, Opal!"

"If you saw her, you'd understand! She has hair cropped like an army sergeant's. I think she might even shave her upper lip!"

As we laughed over my stories or theirs, I would forget any sense of separateness. For that time, I was as much a part of the hum of the room as the girls from the social dorms at the table beside ours, discussing their plans for the weekend as they ate bowls of cold cereal and disemboweled bagels, the innards balled up in napkins. Or the European transfer students and their boyfriends on the other side of us with their matching loose hair and clingy dark shirts and scarves, telling jokes in French and Portuguese.

To belong, though, to really belong, always meant to talk of men. The way the girls from the social dorms watched *every* fraternity brother who passed as if they would bait them just by looking. The way Setsu gushed every time she mentioned James. Even Fran and Ruth bounced out stories of one boy after another—Kevin Starr, who Fran said kissed with the finesse of a bowling ball slamming pins. Malcolm Kingson from Ruth's political science seminar, who had a reputation as nothing more than a charmer—but was it true? Then sometimes they seemed to be waiting for something from me. "You could have *anyone* you want," Ruth had said to me once, intending it as a compliment.

A party in our suite had been Fran's idea. Or Fran's and Ruth's together. Fran wanted wine, and beer from bottles, not the gutter runoff they served from kegs at most parties, she said. Ruth was considering inviting Malcolm Kingson. And Setsu thought if James came he would invite some of his grad school friends—a more interesting crowd than most, according to her. I had not shared my suitemates' enthusiasm when the plan had first been made, disliking the idea of a swarm of guests I hardly knew stuffing themselves into our private space. But as we'd pushed our furniture to the edges of the common room, looped streamers from our ceiling, and set votives along the windowsills, singing with the U2 album sounding at top volume from Fran's CD player—"With or Without You" and "Red Hill Mining Town" and "In God's Country," until Kimberly from the adjoining suite pounded on the wall, making us curl over with laughter—I thought perhaps, *perhaps* I could enjoy myself, too.

Fran mixed fuzzy navels as we waited for our guests to arrive. When we'd lived in Mexico, they had been Mother's favorite. They were sweeter than I remembered and cool along my throat. Somehow I finished a second, started a third.

"Are you going to wear your red cocktail dress?" Setsu and Ruth had wanted to know.

"It's a little much for a dorm party, isn't it?" I thought I had protested. But with the fuzzy navels—had I finished a third?—and the music and the excitement of my suitemates, the fragments of our conversation would not stay threaded together in my mind.

The dress was too short, it seemed to me, and everywhere too tight. "No, it looks so great on you!" they had insisted. They would wear dresses, too.

"I'm glad we decided to do this," I thought I remembered saying to Fran as we sat on the couch with Kimberly and Christie, who'd come from next door. Others from our hall had come, too, and from upstairs. I had arranged the crackers and cheeses we'd bought earlier on our terracotta platter, passing it to each of the guests. But the door to our suite kept opening, more and more people squeezing in, until I couldn't stand without pressing against the bodies of strangers. Their sour beer breath in my nose, their smoke in my eyes, someone's fingers on my thigh, on the hem of the dress I should have known not to wear.

"I can't move three inches!" Ruth laughed. Malcolm Kingson hadn't come, but she was flirting with some other boy whose hands kept moving to her shoulders and down her arms.

"You should be careful," I said, but the words did not come out clearly or loudly enough for her to hear me. She seemed to be tilting, falling as I watched her. Or was I? "I think I need to lie down for a few minutes," I told her, though she would not hear that either.

I pushed through one group and then another. "Where are you going?" Two seniors grabbing my wrists. And then the boy who'd been with Ruth just a moment ago. How had he made it through the crowd to me? "Can I get you another drink, sweetheart?"

"No. No, nothing!"

And that was all that stayed with me of the night.

When I woke, it was not quite morning, only hints of cloud-gray light seeping through the cracks around my window shade. Something seemed to be smoldering in my head, behind my eyes, my stomach still sick from the drinks and the smoke. And from the egg and cheese sandwiches and pizzas someone had ordered at some point, congealing, I imagined, somewhere in the pit of me. But what made me sicker was the discovery of my red dress crumpled at the foot of my bed. It seemed to me it had been on when I first crawled in. Hadn't it? Now I wasn't sure. Was it possible I'd allowed someone in? One of the seniors or the boy who'd been talking to Ruth? No. *No.* But how was it I could not even remember? How unbelievably stupid! This had happened to several of Fran's friends. And to Cleo and to Noelle. But it was not the kind of thing that happened to *me.*

Wrapping myself in my robe, I walked into the common room with the thought that I would begin to clean the mess. It reeked of spilled alcohol. Cheese and cracker crumbs were smeared into our carpet and littered our couch cushions. Cigarette butts floated in half-empty drink glasses. Ruth had left the door to her room ajar and was snoring, her jaw hanging open, her hair matted to the side of her face. I thought I could hear James in Setsu's room—a sleepy male groan. Always she went to him; this was the first time he'd stayed here. I imagined the slabs of his limbs stretched out across her dainty white sheets, across her. She seemed so helpless with him sometimes, as if he had devoured every bit of her strength. How could she *stand* it? I needed to get out suddenly. To sort my thoughts. A clearer yellow-pink light was washing through the windows now. I grabbed a sweatshirt, leggings, and sneakers and slipped out as my suitemates slept.

This was mid-September and I could feel the clean tang of the morning air as it moved down into my chest. I walked north along Hope Street and then turned east toward Blackstone Boulevard, almost empty of cars at this early hour, its manicured houses placid behind their green shade of trees. Here my thoughts no longer seemed to ricochet like so many pellets inside my head. There were only the birds and the branches above me, the whir of the occasional biker passing, and the padding of my own sneakers along Blackstone's dirt walking path. The pounding behind my eyes had ceased, and I quickened my pace until I was running, any unpleasantness from the night before falling away like the shrinking memory of a dream.

I decided to run the next morning, too. And then the next and the next—three miles and four, then five—liking the clenched feeling in my hamstrings and calves and the way, as I ran, my mind seemed rinsed and cool as glass.

"Jesus, Opal, are you training for the Olympics? We all finished breakfast over an hour ago," my suitemates would say.

"Was it that long?" But I knew it had been, having wanted to stave off the less settled mood that I knew would creep through me once I stopped.

I still accompanied Fran and Ruth to the Ratty for meals, but I was more reluctant to share what they ate now, not wanting to lose the light, scrubbed feeling of exercise. "I think I might get a head start on my Ibsen paper," I told them after one dinner. I emptied my tray in the trash and headed down the steps, onto the grass and out a side gate. It was only six-thirty; the sky still held paling light and the street had not yet quieted.

Before beginning my work, I decided to stop into Eastern Garden, the health food store on one of the side streets south of campus, for a raspberry seltzer and maybe some fruit.

"Hello, Mr. Wu," I said to the owner, who was behind the counter every time I entered, his wife often out of sight downstairs, their cat—its tattered fur the same black-gray as the few strands of hair on Mr. Wu's head—curled always on a wooden stool near the register.

"My favorite university student. It's been awhile." Mr. Wu often helped as I sorted through the bin of kumquats or stack of yellow pears, picking out the choicest. "So, University Student, such a pretty girl. When you coming in with boyfriend, heh?" he would ask.

"Not yet. No time for boyfriends!" I would answer.

"You must work too hard. Or maybe you go to school with fools—boys who don't see a pretty girl right in front of them."

"Thank you, Mr. Wu."

And he would laugh, dropping a sample bottle of honey shampoo or a few lychee nuts into my bag, his round face, as he looked at me, wrinkling in the kindest smile that always, for some reason, made me sad.

That evening in Eastern Garden, I noticed a new rack, displaying books and magazines, near the shop's entry. Tracts on Eastern religions, travel guides—one with photos of an island I thought Mother and I had once, long ago, visited—and a number of health and fitness publications. I picked up a magazine with a cover of a woman swimming. The photo of the woman had been taken under the water, capturing the stream of bubbles from her nose, from the churned water behind her bare feet. "The Many Virtues of Exercise" was the title of the first article. *Body, mind, and spirit are subtly and delicately intertwined*, stated the opening paragraph. *That a regular fitness routine is beneficial to physical health is well proven, but according to many exercise devotees, its virtues go deeper.*

Standing near the entrance to Eastern Garden, I read the article from start to finish. Then after paying for the magazine and wishing Mr. Wu a good night, I read through it again. *Discover for yourself how the right exercise program combined with a healthy vegetarian approach to eating will keep your body cleansed of harmful impurities while bringing harmony and balance to your very core.* This seemed an exaggerated claim, but I knew the calm I felt when I ran, and I was fascinated by photographs accompanying the article of three vegetarian women—in one picture jogging, another biking, in a third, their legs crossed in the yoga lotus position, their faces serene as sleeping children's. *Be inspired. Take ownership of you!* read the caption below the final picture. It made sense to me as I studied the article once again the following morning. Yes! And I wanted what it promised.

I increased my running route to six miles, some days seven or eight, despite the skin rubbed raw in spots below my anklebones. And I began to miss some meals with Ruth and Fran at the Ratty, electing instead to visit the Ivy Room—the only vegetarian snack bar on campus—though this meant dining alone. ("The Ivy Room? The food looks like plant fertilizer!" Fran and Ruth refused to join me.) I made trips to Eastern Garden and Green Tree Market for fruits and vegetables fresher than what I could find on campus, and for rice cakes and soy crackers and tofu for cutting into cubes and storing in Tupperware on the shelf of our common room refrigerator.

"Opal! You won't touch the food at the Ratty, but you're going to eat *that?*" Fran and Ruth laughed and pinched their noses when I unloaded packages of dried mushrooms or bean paste from my paper bags, arranging them in neat piles around my room or in my corner of the fridge.

"It tastes much better than it looks," I defended, trying not to care because what I was seeking, I told myself, mattered far more than belonging.

And it was working. After a time, I believed I could feel it—just what the article had predicted—a new calmness, a quiet, as if a constant buzzing in my brain, a jingling of nerves had suddenly been hushed. I wanted, as the article encouraged, to *own* myself. Because everything was a choice, after all, wasn't it? What we ate, who we gave time to, even how we dressed. I saw how James fondled Setsu in her tights and small skirts, remembered how Ruth had worked to allure Gavin. For everything there were repercussions. I thought of the red dress my suitemates had convinced me to wear the night of our party. Of the wardrobe of clothes I'd displayed at Paradise Jungle. But plenty of girls dressed far more conservatively. Kimberly and Christie, who lived next door, wore crewneck sweaters and turtlenecks everywhere. In the cold, they wore hooded parkas and knitted scarves.

"Can I ask where you bought that?" I asked Kimberly one afternoon, indicating her pink button-down as I passed her in the hall. So with money I had saved from waiting tables at Paradise Jungle, I bought two collared shirts from B. Clark's, the women's shop downtown Kimberly had mentioned. *Where Practicality and Style Meet*, promised the words printed across its front window as well as on its Christmasy plaid shopping bags. Some weeks later I ordered canvas slip-on shoes and pleated khakis and two cotton cardigans—not shapeless, fogy sweaters but ones with ruffles at the sleeves and collar—from the catalogs featuring laughing, outdoorsy-looking families I received in my mailbox.

"That's a different look for you. Is that yours?" Setsu asked the first time I slipped into one of my new sweaters. She and I were in the laundry room waiting for our wash loads to finish. Setsu smiled, lifting her brows, as though she meant only to be friendly, but she fingered her own gauzy blouse in a way I knew meant she disliked it.

"Oh, I needed a few new fall things," was all I told her. It seemed pointless to explain what Setsu could not understand.

It was true, of course. The new clothes were less feminine. There were times my reflection would surprise me—as I caught it in a glass door or a mirrored window—the very crispness of it. But in these clothes I felt smart and freshly sealed—a girl who kept her life ordered, who knew how to move unscathed through the world in which she lived.

"What are you doing?" Ruth and Francesca and Setsu returned from a piano concert in Alumnae Hall one night and found me piling some of my older garments in a small white plastic trash bag I had found in a box in the basement laundry room. "You're not throwing those out, are you? They're beautiful."

"They aren't really my style anymore," I said, pleased with the stack of clothes. I pushed up the sleeves of my J.Crew oxford. "You're welcome to whatever you like." I stepped away from the bag at the center of the floor, inviting them to search through it.

"Are you sure you want to give these up?" Setsu took my seashell-print miniskirt and my orange strapless sundress. She held the dress against her, checking to see how it would lie across her small breasts and waist, wanting the lines of her body to show, I guessed, as they did now in the clingy black leotard top she wore beneath her jean jacket. "Will you tell me if you change your mind? You can have them back anytime."

"Sure, Setsu." But she did not need to sound so apologetic or blink in that way as if she pitied me. What reason would I have to reconsider? I was learning things I imagined Setsu never would.

Ruth would not fit into my clothes, but she liked my white patent leather pumps, my starfish sandals, my gold lamé purse. "What's wrong with these, anyway?"

"There's nothing *wrong* with them. It's just . . . it seems so easy to give men ideas . . ."

Ruth paused for a moment, the gold purse's strap in her fingers, but Fran squinted at me as if observing something she had never before noticed. "Good for you, Opal! This campus is so full of sheep. Despite what everyone says. Full of conformists and man-pleasers. Good for you for choosing what makes *you* happy."

Setsu pushed back her thin shoulders and drew her lower lip behind her front teeth until the skin whitened. We had offended her, I knew. Still, I liked being complimented by Fran. Fran was not blown around by circumstances, by winds of fortune; she determined her own life.

. . .

Setsu's twentieth birthday fell at the end of the month. Fran and Ruth and I would take her to Maria Mexicana off Brook Street to celebrate. James had arranged a dinner for just the two of them the weekend before, but when he heard of our plans, he said he wanted to join us later in the evening after a meeting with his study group. He recommended the bar at the Biltmore Hotel and mentioned he might bring a friend. For that reason—I could imagine no other—Ruth spent a good part of the afternoon peeling outfits on and off, experimenting with various hairstyles, trotting between her room and the hall bath to check herself in two different mirrors. During the course of this activity she stopped to weigh herself, and then once again an hour later, as if hoping the scale might have changed its mind upon further consideration.

"Are you going to be ready in time?" Ruth looked slightly alarmed as she noticed I had not yet changed after the run I had taken later than usual, my shirt and leggings wet with perspiration.

"I'll be fine! I don't need a whole *day* to get ready," I laughed. Though as soon as I said it, I wished I hadn't. I caught Ruth's eyes drop to the floor, her arms fold across her middle in her black sweater dress—the chubbiness she could not hide no matter what she wore.

After showering I combed straight my hair, working through any tangles. I lathered my face with Noxzema lotion until it tingled. In the flickering fluorescent bathroom light, as I rinsed the lotion away, it struck me that my complexion appeared cleaner without blush or lipstick. Missy from across the hall was using the sink beside mine, running pencil across her hooded eyelids, sponging foundation onto her rough skin, concealer on the crop of small pimples dotting her forehead. And it irritated me somehow, her eagerness for what she hoped would make her more appealing. That evening, rather than styling my hair with a blow-dryer and curling iron as Mother had taught me, I pulled it into a ponytail at the base of my neck.

Ruth could have saved herself the afternoon's effort: just before we left James called to say his study group was meeting later than anticipated; he and his friend would not be joining us after all.

At Maria Mexicana our waitress brought us rounds of margaritas, but I abstained. "Not even a sip?" my roommates asked.

"Did you know your body actually responds to alcohol like a toxin?" I told them, quoting the magazine article I'd saved from Eastern Garden.

"And what does your body do when it's fed nothing but gerbil food?" Fran cackled, and pointed to the vegetables I'd separated from the meat of my taco.

I smiled and stabbed a small chunk of tomato with my fork but didn't answer. Fran could tease all she wanted. Maybe certain things had to be endured to be true to what I needed.

Alternate Sundays I phoned Mother. During one call I described to her the changes I had begun to make. But she just laughed at my "puritanical ways."

"Everyone else goes to college to do the forbidden. You leave home to become more prudish!" Sometimes she would tell of a beach bash or restaurant opening she and Antonio had attended earlier in the week, then joke that she lived a life more corrupt than her undergrad daughter's.

My suitemates were still intrigued by the snatches they caught of my conversations with Mother, as they had been since our first year together. On the nights we stayed up talking for long hours, putting off studies, neglecting sleep, always the topic arose: "She sounds so fascinating," they would say. "God, she enjoys the most interesting life."

"If you grew up as I did, you might have had your fill of fascinating."

"Oh, Opal! How bad could it have been?" Setsu thought I did not recognize the benefits of my unusual upbringing. "Traveling to exotic cities with your ultra-chic mother!"

"Don't you miss any of it?" Ruth tried to be sympathetic whenever I spoke of my past, but I could see how her eyes glowed like little moons when I told of the many places I'd called home, the number of men who had come and gone from Mother's world, the drama of her relationships.

"No, not the slightest bit."

"Really? Not at *all*?" I heard their disappointment, or perhaps it was disbelief. And I began to see that because they had not lived what I'd lived, they could never understand my relief at finally having found some serenity, as if I had reached shelter from a long-raging storm.

I n November, Setsu invited me to a party at the Liberty Gallery, an art gallery just blocks from the RISD campus, overlooking the river. James knew the owner, and for the next two weeks, several of his drawings, along with the works of some other unknown artists, would be on display. "You're an art history major. Will you come, for a little while at least?" she said. "I know you don't love big parties, but this will be a subdued group. And it should be interesting."

The gallery was an L-shaped room with white walls and bleached-wood floors and two enormous skylights, through which I could make out a few faint stars between filmy clouds. Setsu stood with James among a circle of guests. She delicately balanced a glass of white wine between two fingers. She was in a sleeveless black cocktail dress that showed every willowy curve, a sheer, silvery-black scarf with tiny scattered spangles, which had once been mine, winding her neck. She had pulled her hair into a tight twist, pinning it in place with two long gold crossed sticks. Her back was to me as I approached. Otherwise, perhaps, she would have stopped James's hand, which slid down the center of her back along the zipper of her dress, until it rested on the soft of her backside. She did not flinch, so accustomed was she to his touch, I imagined. I thought of the party we'd thrown in our suite and then, for a moment, of the men at

Paradise Jungle, at how their nearness had made me jumpy. Setsu's only movement was a slight shift toward James so that the bare skin of her shoulder brushed his arm.

"Hi, hi!" she called, leaving James's side when she spotted me. "I'm so glad you're here! You won't want wine. Can I get you a Perrier? I'll show you around."

We began with the long wall to the left of the entry, a series of acrylics by an artist named Carlotta Saunders, patterns of geometric shapes, the color of each square or triangle bleeding into the edges of its surrounding shapes. The first half of the adjoining wall displayed several large collages of street scenes, clipped from magazines and overlapping at unexpected angles. Then, beyond these—Setsu squeezed my elbow—a number of sketches, all pencil on paper, James's works. She pointed to a drawing of a mirror reflecting two French doors, and to one of gnarled driftwood beside a clump of sea grasses. Then she stopped before a figure of a woman. A nude, reclining on a bed, dark hair spreading over the pillow like great bird's wings. Setsu sipped her wine. She glanced at me quickly, then took a second sip. Oh! The facial features were blurred, too vague to discern, but I knew.

"You let him? And display it for all these people!" An old familiar sickness coiled at the pit of my stomach.

But Setsu just shrugged, her cheeks two red-pink blossoms as she pushed back her shoulders. "It was just a fear. Fears can be overcome, I suppose." She tilted her head slightly and lowered her voice. "It's like sex, I guess. You know, scary in the beginning, but after the first time, easier. Until everything is wonderful." She glanced over at James, still engrossed in conversation with the group he had been standing with when I entered. She lowered her eyes, smiling down at her hands cupping her glass, as if she were too modest to boast of her happiness with James, too considerate to prattle on since she had *him*, and I was alone. How could she think I envied her? She had contorted everything she was to please James. I saw this more clearly now than ever, just as everything had seemed clearer over the last weeks. Even more than I, Setsu needed to understand. But she couldn't, loving the water she was drowning in.

That same week, I was surprised to find, in my thin pile of mail, a postcard from Daniel. His message was brief, merely wishing me luck with my junior year, but he had signed it *Fondly* above his name, written in a beautiful script full of flourishes. For several days, I kept the card on the covered crate I had converted into a bedside table, examining and reexamining it, as if expecting the sentences to re-form themselves into some clue as to Daniel's reasons for writing. Some days after, I received a second postcard and then a longer letter. In its four pages, Daniel described the foliage of the Amherst campus in autumn, the surrounding college town, a Victorian literature class he was taking that had become his favorite. On the envelope he had carefully printed his return address, and I spent hours considering my response.

Perhaps he sought nothing more than friendship. But if he intended the letter as some romantic overture, he might be hoping for a signal, some words of encouragement. At his house, I had noticed, among the framed photos on the living room mantel, what must have been a fairly recent snapshot of Daniel and a girl about his age, sitting on the grass before a small white cottage, Daniel's arm draped around the girl's shoulders, pulling her close. But from his mother's attempts to find us time alone together, I had wondered if Daniel and the girl were no longer attached. And now I was sure. But it might be easier—yes—to ignore Daniel's letters altogether rather than to suggest I was interested in some relationship I wasn't. This way there would be no complications, no misunderstandings.

So I tucked Daniel's letters away in a drawer and returned to my usual routine: morning and afternoon classes; evenings at the Rockefeller or Science Library; my daily run along Blackstone, its trees with leaves now thinning, softening from the vibrancy of weeks earlier. But as I jogged, I found my mind wandering now and then to my visit to the Dunhams, remembering Daniel after returning from his own long run. "The best way to spend a morning!" he had said.

I turned down more of Fran and Ruth's invitations to dinners and Setsu's occasional invitations to lunch. "Opal, are you trying to make us feel guilty? There's more to life than work, you know! Don't you want to relax for a few minutes before you get back to it?" But I did not waver.

After they had gone, often I remained alone in the suite, behind my closed door. The phone rang on occasion, but never for me. The electric clock click-clicked unceasingly on the common room wall above the sofa. Aside from this, silence. Sometimes, after preparing a tabbouleh or eggplant salad, I would wrap it in spinach leaves and eat en route to the library's seventh floor, needing, at least for a time, some escape from my solitude.

After many days, I began to notice a reserve in Ruth and Fran. Their smiles, their passing comments to me were suddenly overly courteous. But they had misinterpreted my choices. "It's nothing personal. Believe me. It's just there's a diet I'm following—"

"It's okay, Opal. Sure, we understand."

But it was what I said of James—stupidly, stupidly—that made things far worse. Only rarely did he come to our suite to pick up Setsu. But one Wednesday evening the spicy sweetness of his patchouli cologne filled our rooms, filled my nose, even my mouth. Setsu had called to me to get the door since she was still dressing. I offered James a seat on the couch or on one of our two chairs. "I'm okay," he said. "We'll be sitting all evening. Ballet tickets." He grinned, revealing only his bottom teeth, even but faintly yellow. "*Coppélia*." He pulled at the curls behind his ear. "Bores me, honestly, but Setsu likes it." He stepped slightly nearer. "How about you? How do you feel about the ballet?" He tapped my wrist with his hand, making me start.

"Yes. Yes, I like it." What could possibly be taking Setsu so long?

"I get discounted season tickets through a friend, so we go regularly. You could be a dancer yourself, actually." His eyes were on my knees, my thighs, my hips in my leggings. "Do you know that? Anyway, if Setsu can't make it sometime—" I heard the opening and closing of Setsu's closet door, knew he could, too. Still he didn't turn but watched my face, waiting. His tongue darted out from between his teeth and touched his upper lip.

"No!" I mouthed. "No, no." And then Setsu emerged.

Setsu did not come home that night, so I found her in the morning, after Fran and Ruth had left for classes. She was seated at the foot of her bed near her window. I saw that she had moved to her windowsill a framed photo of her brother, Toru, though I remembered she'd once kept it in a less visible spot, on her dresser behind a snapshot of the four of us taken freshman year. She was now holding a compact and dabbing her cheekbones with peachy brown rouge. In the clear sunlight, I could see what I had never before noticed, gray shadows of fatigue beneath her eyes. She looked irritated before I began, almost as if she expected bad news. "I just thought you had the right to know. If I were you . . . I guess I would want to."

But her face twisted with a bitterness of which I did not think she was capable. "James would never—" Setsu stood to make herself taller, but she gripped the windowsill for support. "You see faults in everyone, don't you? You think you're superior to me, to James, to *all* of us. You think you are strong for the things you abstain from—even men! But it is not your strength. It's your weakness." Her voice came from deep in her throat. Each word a small scrape. "You even try to make yourself unattractive. What normal woman does that? Punish yourself if you want, Opal, but don't punish me!" She threw the compact on the bed and rushed past me out the door, leaving me alone in her bedroom.

God! How dare she! How dare Setsu turn this around as if *I* were the one with the problem, as if *I* were making self-destructive choices? Damn her! Damn her for stalking out when I had only wanted to help her see she'd get hurt! I should track her down and tell her so. But I was so dizzy with fury, I knew tears might come instead of words, and I would *not* break down in front of her. I moved to the bed where she had been. I should have known better! I should have known how, with me, these things always seemed to get distorted. I pressed my head to the cool of the window.

Was there something wrong in me? Some reason I always, *always* drove people away? In Acapulco, I had found Mother one morning after a date with Gerard, this time with a bloodied lip, and cheekbones black and swollen behind her sunglasses. "It's nothing you need worry yourself over, Opal." She had begun to bustle around our apartment, watering the potted hibiscus, fluffing the red throw pillows on our sofa. But I could see she moved stiffly and paused now and then to press fingers to the side of her face. So when Gerard phoned later in the afternoon, I lied. "No, no. She's not here. She's left town unexpectedly. I'll be staying with my uncle, and I can't tell you when she'll return." Days later, Mother learned of my deceit. For two days and two nights, she spoke not a word to me, would not even look at me. "Mother! MOTHER!" But she went about her business as though she'd heard nothing. A punishment far worse than any scolding or accusation I could have imagined.

Setsu should have come to me. She should have apologized for the things she'd said. *I* certainly should not have to be the first to offer peace. But would that be a worse torment than enduring the tension now between us? Could I ever make her see how wrong she was about me, how absurd the things she'd said about weakness and self-punishment? And what about the pact we'd made as suitemates the year before? *She* brought it up more often than I. In the end, I left a brief note for her under her door apologizing, telling her my intention had never been to offend, that I hoped we could let it go. But she never responded.

"If I were you, I wouldn't waste a *minute* feeling sorry. Sometimes there are consequences when you stand up for your convictions." Francesca had poked her head into my room on her way to a feminist rally on the Green. Clearly Setsu had told her of our argument. "You did the right thing. James is a creep. I always knew Setsu was better off without him. I know *I'm* usually happier without a man," she laughed. But somehow I did not quite believe she meant it.

I vowed to give no further thought to Setsu's insults, but they were not so easy to expunge. It had been two weeks since Daniel's last letter, and small doubts began to scratch at me. I began to wonder if my decision not to respond was genuine or weakness, as Setsu had said. I decided to write him a note. Coolly, cautiously, impersonally, referencing little more than the courses in which I was enrolled and an article I'd recently read about the history of the town of Amherst. Then, a week later, he wrote again, and then again, until after a brief time we began to correspond regularly, and I began to anticipate the arrival of his notes in my mail. I developed a ritual: rather than immediately unsealing the envelope and pulling out the pages inside, I forced myself to wait until I had returned to the quiet of my room. There I would heat a cup of ginger tea and, after a few sips, carefully study every line of his letter to be sure no implications of his words escaped me.

Though we exchanged no phone calls, over time I began to feel comfortable with Daniel, as if we had spent months, even years, as friends. He asked about my professors, a sketch I mentioned I'd been working on, the route where I took morning jogs. He included in his letters titles of books, names of songs he had recently discovered, details of his own favorite running routes around Amherst. We seemed to share a curiosity and certain appreciations, sympathies of mind. In the library I made a copy of "The Many Virtues of Exercise," the article from Eastern Garden I still reread from time to time. I sent it to Daniel folded neatly with a note attached: *Dear Daniel, I thought you might like to read this. Please let me know what you think. Yours, O.*

Opal, thanks for the article, he replied. *Yes, very interesting and I'm glad to have a copy. Fondly, D.* As I read his now familiar, precise hand, I reached for my cup of warm tea and imagined that Daniel could be sipping his own in his dorm room at the same moment I sipped mine. A clean, mild soap scent emanated from the notepaper—Daniel's scent, I believed—and I breathed it deeply.

As I walked the Brown halls, crossed the Brown quads, I thought how different Daniel was from the male students here. During an early December warm spell that drew students to the quads in herds, I passed a group of boys sprawled on the Main Green in their sweatshirts and sneakers; I watched as they devoured sub sandwiches as thick as their forearms, their chins shiny with oil, and I shivered at their animal appetites, content that Daniel would never be so coarse. Nor would he waste himself in drunkenness like the partiers I passed on my way back from the library each night or the men at the Mexican discotheques Mother had frequented.

Not long before the winter break, Daniel wrote to say he would be home the following weekend for his cousin's wedding; if I was free, he could stop through Providence on the way. So I penned a few short lines accepting his invitation, careful not to ramble on in eagerness.

For the next several days, I could think of nothing but our meeting. In the mornings, I allowed myself extra minutes in bed, turning onto my side, my bare legs hugged to me, my eyes still closed in half sleep, imagining how we would spend our time. So ridiculous, wasn't it? Still my chest rose and fell with unexpected anticipation. In the library at night, bent over my usual heap of books and papers, the black and white of the printed texts blurred like swirled snow as I made mental lists of what Daniel and I might do—a lecture by a new novelist named Edward Yan, a tour of a nearby historical home, an evening walk under the still canopy of winter branches.

In preparation for his arrival, I scoured my room, dusting the shelves, scrubbing smudges from the windowpanes. From the school bookstore,

I bought two volumes of poetry—one of Shakespearean sonnets, the other, Blake's *Songs of Innocence and of Experience*. I set them prominently at the center of my desk with the thought that Daniel would see them and perhaps want to browse through them.

We made arrangements to meet at Brown's Van Wickle Gates at half past three on Friday afternoon, but several hours earlier I selected my outfit. Then I changed my mind, replacing it with another. God, I was no better than Ruth! I recalled the clothes I had worn during my stay at the Dunhams'—a flimsy tank top, a low-necked blouse, skirts cutting mid-thigh like some show dancer's—ensembles Daniel must have found distasteful. I was anxious to show him the more restrained style I had adopted over the past months. I selected an ivory turtleneck, a heather-blue Fair Isle sweater with a band of snowflakes, and a pair of beige corduroys—not baggy, mannish ones like those I had seen on the girls on campus who left their hair hanging in uncombed strings and preferred their legs unshaven, but a flattering tailored pair I had found at B. Clark's. I tied an off-white silk scarf around the elastic holding my hair, removed it, then tied it again.

For two days before our date, I had added to my running route—hoping to soothe the jumpiness in my stomach—finding new side streets to proceed along until every muscle stiffened and solidified, until my thoughts seemed to calm. By midday Friday, some of my nervousness had subsided, and so I assured myself that once Daniel and I were in each other's presence, any anxiety would fall away.

Browning seed pods crunching beneath my flats as I rocked on my heels, waiting for Daniel at the university's main entrance, seemed the only sound aside from tires singing along the road down the hill. When a red Saab drove up College Street, I recognized the car belonging to Daniel's brothers; but in picturing his arrival, I had imagined an entirely different kind of vehicle, though what, I wasn't sure. He hopped out and simultaneously, awkwardly shook my hands and pecked my cheek. We grinned at each other silently for what seemed long minutes, then made stuttering, blushing attempts at conversation, both of us kicking at dried leaves scattering the side of the road. He was taller than I remembered or more muscular or older-looking, and, watching him out of the corner of my eye, I had the sense I had never seen him by true light of day. He had cut his hair so that the longish curls were now short waves, drawing attention to the angles of his cheeks and chin. He was more handsome, I supposed, than before, and it would take me some time to feel that he was familiar.

As we climbed into his car, I told him I thought he had changed, but he rubbed the stubble of hair at his nape and laughed. "Not as much as you, though, Miss Collegiate!" He smiled broadly, but from the glance he gave my hair and face and clothes, I could not tell if he was pleased.

As I was about to pull from my pocket a leaflet announcing Edward Yan's lecture in Sayles Hall and a brochure for the historical museum down the street, Daniel slapped the sides of the steering wheel with a sudden thought.

"Have you seen *The Poet*? That new movie? It's supposed to be great. There's a matinee in a theater over the border in Massachusetts, not too far from here. Do you want to go?"

"Sure, good idea." I nodded in a manner I hoped seemed enthusiastic. I considered asking about the film, but it sounded intellectual (perhaps it had even been adapted from a book), and I was reluctant to reveal my ignorance.

For the first thirty minutes of the movie, I stole glances at Daniel in the dark for some indication that either we were in the wrong theater or that the film was not what he had expected. *The Poet* was a gory thriller about a writer plagued by violent visions. Soon fact and fiction became confused for him and he began to act out his madness in a string of brutal murders. But Daniel appeared completely unperturbed; in fact, he seemed to enjoy each bloody scene, sucking vigorously on his iced tea straw, his dark eyes shining in the gloom.

"What did you think?" he asked as we zipped our winter coats, filed out of the theater and down the block toward his parked car.

I cleared my throat to give my opinion, but just as I did so, Daniel opened the car door for me, watching to be sure I was comfortably settled before gently closing it. So, instead, I laughed away the question for fear of spoiling the remainder of our evening.

Dusk had fallen. The temperature had dropped, and black tree branches, their few remaining shrunken leaves curled inward, bounced in the wind. Daniel suggested dinner at Pilgrim's Hearth, a few miles away, which he promised had good food.

The restaurant was a popular one, and by the time we arrived, most of the tables had already been filled, the chatter of overlapping conversations echoing off the walls and high ceiling. At Daniel's request, we were seated near a back corner that afforded semi-privacy. Our waiter offered us two giant leather menus, and, looking around, I noticed that everything—the chairs, the hurricane candles on the tables, the platters of food—seemed to be of enormous proportions. I ordered pumpkin soup and a garden salad—the only vegetarian options I could find on the menu. But Daniel ordered sirloin steak with gravy, deep-fried onion rings, a bottle of Chianti for us to share.

"I hope you don't mind my making the selection," he said, pouring two tall glasses, "but I'm sure you'll like it. I tried it at a friend's wine tasting and everyone there loved it. Cheers!" He tapped his glass to mine, though I hadn't lifted it, then tipped back his goblet as if it were ice water. "I know you won't be disappointed," he said, plucking two plump rolls from our wire bread basket, smothering them with butter.

I had seen what the bottle cost and saw now how he watched me as though he'd chosen a present he worried I would not appreciate. So I sipped it, nodding, allowing myself this exception.

Daniel emptied his glass, and when our dinners were eventually served, he bolted his food in chunks, seeming to consume each mouthful almost without chewing. He refilled his glass. And before I could stop him, he'd topped off my own glass, though I'd finished only enough to be polite. But my expression must have conveyed the queasiness beginning to spread below my ribs because, yanking his fork suddenly from between his teeth, Daniel asked, "What's wrong?"

"Oh, oh—nothing. It's only . . ." I paused, wanting to find the right words. "I guess your habits seemed different when I stayed with your family, that's all. And I thought you said you liked the article I mailed you—"

"Is that what's bothering you?" He let out a guffaw and swallowed a hunk of meat so large I thought I could see the bulge of it slide along his throat. "I did like the article. It intrigued me, actually. But I'm no longer in training for cross country and, God, there are some things I would miss too much. I'm no masochist, you know what I mean?" He laughed and held up another forkful of steak as indication.

"But it's not about giving things up," I said. "It's about what you *gain*." It was the way it affected your sense of well-being, I explained, that made it worthwhile. I babbled on and on and could not stop. If I only talked long enough, about the things we had communicated in letters and the topics of my imagined tête-à-têtes with him, the first half of our date would sink into distant memory, and the rest of the night would unfold as I had pictured. I described the tranquillity of College Hill in early morning, the quiet, staid symmetry of its brick buildings, the New England maples and oaks whose stout, toughened trunks seemed impervious to the fluctuations of time and weather. The way, on clear nights, pale stars sparkled through the maze of overhead boughs. I chattered about Coleridge's poetry, having read through much of a collection the night before, and about a chamber music concert I had attended on campus the previous week.

After a time, I noticed that Daniel had set down his fork and, having pulled his chair closer to mine, was leaning forward, concentrating. "Maybe we could do these things together sometime," he said, smiling, his voice suddenly hushed, as though moved by the subjects of my conversation.

A happy relief washed over me. *This* was what I had envisioned; *this* was right. Releasing a small, contented sigh, I reached for the glass of lemon water beyond my goblet of wine, my fingers almost brushing Daniel's. But before I had grasped it, Daniel's hand stopped mine. And without warning, his lips pressed against me and, for a moment, a thrill fired through me as everything around us dropped away. I felt my fingers folding into his, felt my throat melting. But then with his free hand, he began to caress my knee and then the inside of my thigh. And as his mouth opened, I could feel the slipperiness of his tongue, like a panting dog's, along my teeth, and his hand shifting higher.

"What are you doing?" I hissed loudly enough to draw the stares of diners at the neighboring table. They looked at me, at Daniel, at the overturned glass I had knocked with my wrist and the ice cubes littering our tablecloth.

"I . . . I thought . . ." Daniel's face broke into a rash of crimson splotches. His lips hardened into a thin line and he began to carve furiously at a gristly bit of meat still left on his plate.

During the remainder of the meal, we exchanged not a single word. Daniel paid our bill without raising his eyes to look at me. In the car speeding back to Brown, we sat in silence, heavy and thick as a raincloud, both of us squinting through the windshield at the yellow shafts of light from the headlamps. Now and then Daniel lifted a finger to his mouth, chewing at the nail and skin. For an instant, I longed to comfort him, to apologize, to start over. But that was all it would take, wasn't it? Just one instant of weakness to send splintering cracks through everything. With a man like Daniel, I could never maintain the serenity I had recently worked so hard to achieve. Why had I even gotten involved with him? Wasn't it just to prove something to myself? Or to Setsu? Or Ruth? There was no use indulging the idea for another minute.

Our goodbye was mumbled and hasty. Daniel pointed to the door handle, which I had been fumbling for in the dark, not bothering to open it for me as he had before. It had grown colder and drizzled steadily during our drive, leaving the roads slick, so we had agreed that Daniel would let me off where we had met earlier that afternoon rather than risk the narrow side streets near my dorm. I set off along Prospect, dimly lit by the glow of the campus, but turned when I was sure Daniel could no longer see me in his rearview mirror. I watched the red of his taillights dipping, blinking, curving, until they disappeared in the distance. Then I listened for some moments after, distinguishing the faint whine of his engine, until that, too, had faded. It struck me, though I wasn't sure why, as a lonely, lonely sound. And the absolute silence that ensued as even lonelier.

The sky had cleared and a silver half-moon had risen, softly illumining the arcing trees above me, their branches silhouetted against the star-dusted sky. As I gazed upward, a saying printed on my box of ginger tea rose to my consciousness: *It is better to be alone and have harmony than to have companionship in disharmony.* With this in mind, I drew my coat closer for warmth and began trudging the path toward my dormitory, accompanied by the bobbing of my own shadow.

AFTERNOON AT MOON BEACH

(Francesca's Story)

· *Junior Spring* ·

Before Ruth's debacle during our first year, my complaints about Brown had been mere grievances, a topic for conversations during late-night phone calls to my high school friend Sharon. The university had a reputation for being a socially and politically enlightened institution. College guidebooks boasted of it to prospective applicants. It had been reiterated ad nauseam by my high school adviser. Besides its academics and its supposedly active social scene, this was the reason I had chosen it. There was plenty to do, of course—symposiums, theatrical and musical performances, nightly parties on and off campus. For the first few months, I'd gone out several evenings a week. But gradually I had begun to open my eyes. I was surrounded by a sea of single-minded hypocrites. "The men are hopelessly shallow," I'd informed Sharon. "And half the women are like plastic mannequins. You know the kind I mean—skinny everywhere except for their high-perched breasts."

"Hell hath no fury like a woman scorned!" Sharon had laughed.

I'd considered hanging up. Sharon had the infuriating habit, when I was upset, of making a comment she knew would increase my irritation.

"No, that has absolutely *nothing* to do with it!" How did she know about the countless fraternity parties I had attended without being approached once, not once! Brown was just as bad as New York—maybe worse. Here the only girls visible to men were those who lived on diet shakes and salad greens to maintain their board-flat stomachs, their fleshless thighs, the ones who exercised more religiously than they attended classes, trotting to the athletic center in their shorts clingy as Saran, and who had memorized Cindy Crawford's *Shape Your Body Workout* but could not name a single poem by Ezra Pound or T. S. Eliot. The closest I'd come to dating here had been the few desperate nights, post frat parties, when Dillon Mahoney had stumbled back to my room, or I to his on the third floor of the Delta Tau House, where the football players lived. His walls, I'd seen, when he turned on the lights, were plastered with posters of swimsuit models thrusting their balloon breasts. One night, he'd put his arm around me, his breath reeking of beer and garlic. "Now why can't you look like that?" he'd whispered in my ear.

"You can get off on your damn posters!" I'd yelled, slamming his door with all the strength I could muster. That had been early January, the last ridiculous party I had attended, the last time I'd wasted myself on fools.

"What you don't know," I'd lectured Sharon, "is that the women are as guilty as the men. They encourage this, each one more obsessed with her appearance than the next. God, they remind me of Mother!"

From Sharon I had heard a halfhearted "hmm." She believed my stories about Mother to be exaggerations. But Sharon had never been the victim of Mother's superficiality. And Mother was relentless. Before my departure for school, she had collected, from various department stores, an assortment of slacks in blacks and charcoals, dark-hued cashmere V-necks and turtlenecks. "These are very figure-flattering," she had whispered, though there had been no one else around, draping them across my bed for me to see. From the way she'd sniffed as she smoothed the garments, I could picture her humiliation when she'd had to ask for a size twelve. She never once mentioned my weight, the twenty or so pounds I had gained in junior high and never shed. But previously, on a handful of special occasions—a Christmas Eve dinner at the Essex House, my sweet sixteen party at The Water Club, watching me dress for my senior prom—she had sighed and stroked my cheek with her fingertip. "What a pretty, pretty face you have, Franny." This was her subtle hint she wished I had the body to match.

"It's just as bad at Vassar. I guess there's no escape." Sharon had decided to sound more agreeable now.

"Even my own suite has not been spared." I opened my door and peeked out to be sure no one could hear. "Setsu's as bony as a stray cat. She never eats more than a few bites at a sitting. The longer she stays with her boyfriend, James, the more emaciated she looks. And he likes it! And Opal with her obsessive running. She'd probably major in aerobics if the school would let her. And she eats the most disgusting health food crap! She might as well eat the grass on the quad! It would be cheaper!" And then Ruth—still trying to make herself attractive to snakes like Gavin. You'd think she'd have learned her lesson. Gavin's life had hummed along without one skipped beat. He knew *nothing* of what Ruth had endured. For him, their encounter had been only a fleeting indulgence. Days later, he'd started dating Gina Whitaker, chipper and chesty, with legs skinny as candy sticks. And *this* was more his style. Opal had heard him with a friend. *The heavier girls are easier because they're lonely but just a little too much woman for me. Know what I mean?* He'd grabbed his haunches, laughing.

I told Opal, "If I come across him, I'll flay him alive!"

Even recently—during the last winter break when the four of us had spent a few days at the cabin in Stowe my parents had rented for the ski season—Ruth had confessed to Opal she thought maybe if she were prettier, at least if she were slimmer, things would go differently for her with men, might have gone differently with Gavin. Lowlife that he was and she still continued to question herself! While the rest of us skied, she'd stayed in the lodge, cocooned in her large brown duffel coat reading some corny novel. But we knew it wasn't just inexperience with skiing that kept her indoors. We all saw how she scrutinized Opal and Setsu in their snow pants, sleek as winter ermines. She ate grapefruit breakfasts and lunches, but later would tear open bags of chips or packages of cream-filled cakes she bought at the lodge, cursing herself and her lack of self-discipline. "You don't need to change a thing," we told her. But she must have known if we were not trying to protect her, we would have admitted the truth: she *was* being passed over. Males had minds as closed as mollusk shells! And until women stopped torturing themselves to appeal to *men's* preferences, nothing would ever change!

At Vassar, Sharon said, several women shared my views and were banding together to educate their community. "Maybe you should consider something similar."

Yes! Sharon was right. There was influence in numbers, and women at Brown needed to be encouraged, to be empowered, to no longer be conformers. They needed to claim their strength.

Not long after the new semester, and with the thawing of the cold, I learned of a march being organized through the streets of Providence. Thousands of women, it was hoped, would take over the city, moving as one like a river—forceful and uncontainable as surging water. We walked at night, not for the cover of darkness, but because these were the hours when some of us had been heinously assaulted, targets simply because of our sex. Our voices rose in great waves of sound—*Take Back the Night!*—reverberating, it seemed, through the whole of the city, each chant pulsing through me like an electric charge. We, as women, needed always to be this bold.

. . .

In March, I procured a campus post office box and a weekly meeting space in the basement of Barbour Hall for the organization I had decided to call BREMUSA, for the Amazon warrior whose name meant "raging female." I regretted that my suitemates had not shown up for the first meeting. I thought I would at least have persuaded Opal. She understood the lustful biases of men and had even changed her appearance to avoid unwanted attentions. "You'll be interested in this," I'd told her. But she claimed she was trying to simplify her schedule rather than make it busier. It was Ruth, though, I was most disappointed not to see; more than anyone, she needed to hear our discussion. But ten students attended the first meeting on a Thursday evening, and the following week, thirteen. Three of them women I recognized from my Women in Fiction course— friends who sat together in the front row in patched jeans. I'd appreciated them, how quickly they raised their hands to refute the comments of bubblehead Loni Greves with her mascara and hair combs and sleeveless pastel sweaters, they seeing as I did that she spoke only to be noticed by the few men in the class rather than because she *cared* about the circumscription of women's roles in literature or the marginalization of the female voice. On that first night, we pushed the furniture to the far wall, enlarging the space where we would sit, speaking over the radio sounding from some room above us—Van Morrison at a volume that made the floor beneath us vibrate. But we would be louder. And we shared stories of our frustrations, the ways in which the media celebrated only one female form, a form we deemed unrealistic, even unhealthy, the ways our friends, our families ignorantly perpetuated these so-called ideals.

We began during the morning and afternoon rush between classes to stake out posts where we could not be missed. We handed out flyers with sketches of skeletons in skirts, *Is This Where We Are Headed?* printed across the top. We held rallies on the Main Green; standing on desk chairs we had dragged from our dorm rooms, we shouted statistics of girls who had starved themselves in pursuit of impossible dreams, of large women who swallowed pills to relieve their feelings of worthlessness. "Men don't suffer for their appearance. Why should women?" we asked when onlookers paused to listen.

In the Brown dining hall, the members of BREMUSA ate collectively. Our plastic trays in hand, we jostled past soccer, lacrosse, rugby players with their muscles flexed in their varsity jackets, their faces still flushed from afternoon practices. Just as they did, we lined up for hot food, avoiding the salad-and-fruit bar most other female students on campus favored. We paraded to our seats, our plates piled high with spaghetti marinara, turkey tetrazzini, chicken pot pie. On Sundae Night, while other girls warily tiptoed around the tables spread with cartons of ice cream and bowls of sweet toppings, dropping tentative teaspoons of caramel or mere dribbles of hot fudge onto saucers, giggling guiltily, we scooped three flavors into bowls, smothering them with whipped cream, almonds, two kinds of sprinkles. What did we care that the only boys who approached asked for our unused chairs, preferring to join the "lettuce-eaters"—as we had dubbed them—at neighboring tables? We ignored their laughter. We ignored the way they gazed at their girlfriends, patted their feeble thighs, their buttocks compact as coconuts—pint-sized as mine had been in elementary school, I guessed, but not for a single day since. If these men were too narrow-minded to see that beauty should be measured by character, not by the circumference of chest, waist, and hips, then we had no time for them anyway.

When I was not busy with BREMUSA, I sprawled on the couch in my suite, with my Ancient Civilizations and Intro to Chemistry assignments, my pages of econ problems. I sped through the majority of my work, eager to dive into the reading for my women's studies course: pieces by Mary Wollstonecraft, the Brontë sisters, Simone de Beauvoir, Gertrude Stein. I was fascinated by their daring—Charlotte Brontë using a male pseudonym to publish her novels, the provocative subject matter of Simone de Beauvoir's *The Second Sex*, Stein's naked professions of love for another woman. What pioneers they had been, and I read long sections of their writing aloud to my roommates.

"Are we getting credit for this course, too?" Opal teased. "I think we've learned all of the material."

Bored by the subdued outfits Mother had bought me, I took trips to Boston and purchased a hip-length brown leather jacket, brown boots with buckles, suede pants, a red suede skirt with a fringed hem, a series of hats—a maroon beret, a checkered cap, a coffee-colored brimmed hat with a thin ribbon, which I was quite sure made me look like a female Indiana Jones from *Raiders of the Lost Ark*.

I wore my new red-fringed skirt everywhere and ordered others in olive green, deep purple, and gold. I wore them with my buckled boots, loving the way my heels pounded against the cement campus walkways, ignoring Mother's old warnings that mid-length skirts with tall boots accentuate the fleshiness above one's knees. I ignored, too, my suitemates' surprised expressions as I emerged from my room each morning with my leather jacket on my shoulders, stiff as any military aviator's. "Where are you jetting to today, Captain?" Setsu joked once when I'd added mirrored shades to my ensemble. This sent Ruth into an epileptic fit of giggles before she apologized: "Sorry, Fran. Sorry! But do you think this is your most becoming look? It's just quite a *statement*," as if she were only being helpful, as if this made up for her laughing—an annoying reflex Ruth had developed since the pact we'd all made early sophomore year, the little "truths" she now felt safe, even obligated, to share in the name of lasting friendship.

"Did I *ask* your opinion, Ruth?" It didn't take much to shut her up. Anyway, what difference did it make if the jacket added bulk? What did it matter if the hat dulled the blue of my eyes, cast shadows on my nose and mouth, the features everyone agreed were my finest? I had priorities of greater consequence.

By later in the spring, Setsu and Opal seemed even more preoccupied with maintaining their baby appetites, dominated by self-denial. Or maybe it was just that I observed them through a sharper lens. And Ruth, who, I knew, enjoyed food as much as I, still only envied them. I had given up on any of them joining BREMUSA until the morning Ruth and I crossed the campus together en route to early classes. As we entered Metcalf, a junior from my chemistry course held a door for a stalk-limbed, strawberry blonde but allowed it to close on Ruth. "You're a pig! A damn PIG!" I yelled after him. But Ruth flushed fire-red as if she, *she* were to blame. I stopped her, my hand on her arm. "Don't you feel embarrassed! Not for one minute! He's the one who should be ashamed, don't you know that?"

The skin around Ruth's eyes broke out in pink blotches as if she might cry. She glanced over my shoulder; it was clear I was adding to her discomfort. But if I could just make her see that she was suffering unnecessarily, that if she could only have my vision, BREMUSA's vision, she could be free from self-reproach. "Your size has nothing to do with your worth. Nothing whatsoever!" I said. "Come with me to my BREMUSA meeting tonight, will you?" I did not notice my fingers gripping her arm, sinking into the pillow of her flesh until she flinched. "Will you?"

She dabbed her eyes with the cuff of her sweater sleeve and smiled. "Yes. Okay, okay," she said. But when I came to her room that night, she began to make excuses: a long essay for her Irish authors course, a persistent throbbing headache. She would not join out of conviction, but reluctantly, and perhaps only because she'd grown tired of my arguments. But the reasons were inconsequential. Once she was a part of BREMUSA, she would gain confidence and strength; she would be released from the bondage of self-criticism and loathing. *This* was what mattered.

Gradually BREMUSA began to make its presence felt on campus; its reputation grew. One of our members, an art student, sculpted a nude, life-sized woman of plaster, with legs generously proportioned, stomach protuberant, arms rounded. *Barbie Is a Lie. This Is Reality* we etched into the statue's pedestal. In the hours just before morning, we hoisted her on our shoulders and set her before the entry to the Sharpe Refectory. Two days later, a short article on our prank appeared in the *Brown Daily Herald.* A series of response letters ensued, some supportive but most critical.

Though we were not identifiable as individuals to most students on campus, BREMUSA's mere name made an impression. Sometimes a boy would whisper a "hello," jostling past me in a crowded corridor, or wink, handing me a brightly colored folded invitation to some weekend party. If he presumed to graze my hand or leaned too close, I would flick the invitation with a fingernail. "I might have a BREMUSA meeting that night," I would say, watching as his face fell, knowing he'd addressed me only because no dainty, miniskirted girl was nearby.

After such encounters, I would track down Ruth. We would stand on the steps of Faunce House, overlooking the Green, and, leaning against the railing, watch the women and men watching each other. We saw how even the girls in torn tights and baggy skirts—to prove their impatience with the conventionalities of fashion—still tossed their loose hair over their shoulders when males turned. Recently, Benny Alpert, from down the hall—whose room we called whenever my Apple Macintosh jammed up—had begun to leave regular phone messages for Ruth, wanting to chat or stop in for a visit. "Have you noticed," I asked, "you and I are the only BREMUSA members to receive even minor attentions from men? And do you know why?"

"Yes." She nodded and crossed her arms, tucking her hands into the crooks of her elbows. She knew. Though we were not thin, we were not as large as several girls on campus, not as obviously heavy as most other BREMUSA supporters.

So BREMUSA was making an impression on Ruth. She was beginning to understand. "It's offensive, isn't it? So shallow. How many pounds do we have to gain before we are *completely* shunned as well?" And when

I asked if she saw that the problem was ubiquitous, that everywhere—I gestured with my lighter toward the swarm of activity below—women were straightening, tightening, thrusting for men—men who measured them only by their physical proportions, Ruth agreed.

I began to notice other small changes in Ruth, but ones I believed were significant. She was more vocal now during BREMUSA meetings, clapping with the rest of us when an insightful point was made, offering anecdotes of the ways she, too, had been slighted or judged for her plumpness, not only by males but by members of her own sex. And it had been days, as far as I could tell, since she had attempted to skip a meal. But then, one evening she didn't appear, and I returned to our suite to discover Setsu in Ruth's room, both of them stretched on Ruth's floor, humming to some sappy song playing on Ruth's daffodil-yellow radio, a yearbook and a few photos of Setsu's friends spread on the carpet before them.

"We've been making some plans." Ruth glanced at Setsu, sucking her cheeks, unable to stop from smiling. They both smelled of minty gum. Ruth held one of the photos in her hand. I made out the blond-brown curls of a young man standing near a large sports arena. "Setsu's introduced me to someone." Ruth gave the photo a small wave.

God! Didn't she have any convictions! Any perseverance! "What about our priorities, Ruth? You missed our meeting just to talk about men!"

The tip of Ruth's tongue shot from between her teeth like a nervous turtle poking out from its shell. She licked her lips, made a small popping sound with her gum, then turned the photo so that only its back was to me.

Setsu flicked a strand of hair over her shoulder. "Must *everything* be an argument with you, Francesca? I'm trying to do Ruth a favor." Some weeks before, at the Science Library, Setsu had met Brian Nicholls, a senior from Ontario, Canada. "Very polite. A little shy. He works most evenings scanning books in and out of the system to supplement his tuition. He just seemed so sweet," she said, smiling at Ruth. "I thought Brian might help her get her mind off past disappointments. You know, wipe away the bad with good."

I propped a booted foot on the rung of Ruth's desk chair. Was *this* her excuse? I asked. Had she even thought about the example she was setting for other BREMUSA supporters? "Besides"—I kicked the metal tip of my boot against the chair's silver rung then turned to Setsu—"you think a *man* can wipe away the bad with good? That's the last thing Ruth needs."

"Maybe you should let *her* decide." Setsu, on her hands and knees, her tiny underfed kitten bottom in the air, began to gather the scattered photos and fit them into a neat stack.

But Ruth was not listening, her jaws working more vigorously on her gum. "Oh, Fran, I almost forgot to tell you! Brian has a roommate— Sanjeev. His father is from India, so he has this beautiful complexion, beautiful dark, dark hair. His family spent some time in London, and he has this faint British accent."

"Very sexy," Setsu added. She and Ruth laughed.

"So, anyway, I showed him a picture of you, and he said you were lovely. He said you had warm eyes, and—what was it?—fetching lips."

Something snagged in my throat, but I coughed it away. I could tell from the pleased expression on Ruth's face, from the way she watched me expectantly, that she believed this—my inclusion in the matchmaking— would dissolve our tension.

"What's *that* supposed to mean? And 'fetching'? Who even uses that word?" I plucked a cigarette from a pack in my jeans pocket and lit it, exhaling in a stream between my teeth. In recent weeks, Ruth had begun to try a drag or two when I'd offered, but the smoke seemed to irritate her now, and she rubbed her eyes with the back of her hand. But I made no offer to move to the window or extinguish the remaining stub. "Besides, Ruth, why are you showing my picture to strange men?"

"He's not strange. Setsu knows him, and I've met him twice." She shook her head and twisted the small silver ball earring in her left ear, a habit she had when she was feeling defensive. She went on to say that

Brian and Sanjeev had suggested a double date. An afternoon at Moon Beach, since we were enjoying unusually warm weather for spring.

"Ha! You're kidding." I snapped my tongue to the roof of my mouth.

Ruth only stared blankly, her eyes round and bovine. "What do you mean?"

"How perfect. God, how typical. What better way to see girls half-naked—"

"I'm sure they didn't intend . . . I don't think—"

"No, Ruth, you didn't think at all, did you? Haven't you been treated badly enough by men lately? You want more?" I gave Ruth's chair a second kick, and as I did so, I heard a soft snuffling. Ruth was blowing her nose into a tissue.

"What's wrong with you?" Setsu was sitting up now, straight as a pillar. "How could you possibly be so insensitive?"

After her procedure, those first days back at Brown, Ruth's face had been puffed and swollen from tears, and those early nights I'd heard her, crying in bed, almost without ceasing, like some small, abandoned animal. But even now there were times I woke before morning to coughing from her room and knew she was not sick but covering sadder sounds. Maybe Setsu was right: I had gone too far. And so I found myself apologizing, pulling more tissues from the package on her desk, stroking her hand, and somehow, somehow, agreeing to spend the second Saturday of May at the beach with Brian and his roommate, Sanjeev.

A week before our date, I found Ruth in her room holding a floral-printed bikini with hot pink straps. "My cousin gave this to me last year," she said. "She bought it on sale from some fancy swimwear catalog, but it was the wrong size. I don't even know if it fits me. I've never had the nerve to wear it."

"I'm sure it's fine." I tossed a red sweatshirt aside to stretch on Ruth's bed as she, stepping behind her opened closet door for privacy, wriggled out of her clothes and into the suit, arranging her breasts until they rested like plump cupcakes in their wrappers. She winced, her scrunched-up nose against her round cheeks reminding me of a rabbit as she studied her reflection in the mirror adhered to the closet door. In the overhead light, her skin shone almost blue-white. It dimpled at her stomach and below her bottom. But the pattern of the suit drew attention to the even proportion of her chest and hips. Perhaps this was what she wanted to hear, but I refused to flatter her.

Ruth chewed her bottom lip and wrapped an arm around her middle, where her flesh was softest. "Maybe I should stick with a one-piece."

I rolled onto my elbow, loudly, impatiently clearing my throat. "I hope you're not doing this for Brian."

Ruth shrugged and examined the tag still attached to the back of the suit.

"If he's going to judge you for the way you look in a bathing suit, I don't know what you're doing with him in the first place."

"Are you getting a new suit?"

"Heh! What do you think?"

Ruth nodded, giving a rueful downward glance at her waist.

"Have enough confidence not to change yourself for a man. Right, Ruth?" I said, reciting one of BREMUSA's mantras.

"Right." Ruth made another blushing nod of agreement, then reached for the sweatpants and striped T-shirt she'd been wearing when I entered. "You always think sensibly, Fran."

True to my word, I did not buy a new swimsuit for our beach date. Each morning, along my bleary-eyed stroll to the coffee shop in town for my cup of dark roast with cream, I passed University Sports, a store that sold athletic gear and swimwear. In the window, a maple-colored mannequin (chicer than any they had displayed before), her arms akimbo, posed in a sleek black bathing suit with a plunging neckline. At the base of the vee, a small gold buckle sparkled under the store's track lighting. I could almost feel the slipperiness of the material, could almost see in the store's front glass how the suit might flatter me. One morning, as Setsu and I walked together, she must have seen me turning to glance at the suit.

"That would look *great* on you," she said, reaching to press my arm. She meant this as a compliment, I knew, but I felt annoyed at having been caught, annoyed at her pausing on the sidewalk at the shop's entrance, as if expecting me to follow her inside.

The second Saturday of May was, according to the morning announcer on my bedside radio clock, perfect weather—a cloudless eighty-one degrees with the softest possible breeze. I had overslept, having stayed up late the night before on a two-hour call with Sharon, gossiping about our old New York schoolmates. With no time to shower, I quickly combed fingers through my hair, fastening it with the rubber band I'd tossed on my night table before bed, then rummaged through my closet shelves until I found my tangled pile of old bathing suits. I plucked a smoke-gray one with a broad stripe of red across the middle. When I had bought it two summers before, in a pricey boutique on Ninetieth and Madison Avenue where Mother sometimes shopped, the saleslady had complimented me, claiming it enhanced my figure. At the time I had agreed with her. Something about the cut and pattern seemed to narrow my waist, diminish the bulging around my hips. But now I was not so sure. The area below my navel protruded more than I had remembered, my thighs appeared thicker. But I shook off the thought, fishing in my straw beach bag for my dark sunglasses, which Jessica Adler, who'd had the locker next to mine in high school, once said lent me a mysterious, sophisticated air.

Ruth had left a note to say she was taking an early walk but would meet me in the parking lot behind Brian and Sanjeev's dorm, where Brian kept his car. I spotted her from a distance, standing beside a slightly battered Jeep Cherokee, bouncing her canvas bag against her knees. "Hi!" she yelled when she saw me, her voice ringing across the quiet lot. Her hair was swept up and pinned into a careful twist, a style she reserved for special occasions. As I drew close, I saw she had dusted her cheeks with an iridescent blush. Her lips sparkled with the same silver-pink gloss that Setsu sometimes wore. Her face looked more defined, an effect of the makeup. She wore a white cotton sundress, but through the dress's straps, I could make out the hot-pink ties of the bikini she had modeled for me and, obviously, despite her initial reservations, decided to keep. I adjusted my shades on my nose, irritated by the thought that she had risen hours earlier to primp and preen.

"Great day, huh?" Ruth arched her neck and gazed at the sky. She set her bag on her left shoulder, then readjusted it to her right. "Doesn't it feel like summer?"

My mouth was full with the warm coffee and buttered bagel I'd stopped to buy at Peaberry's, so I didn't answer. But she seemed not to notice, too absorbed with checking her reflection in the car's windows and watching the door of Brian and Sanjeev's dormitory, waiting for them to emerge.

Brian was tall with thin, slightly knobby-kneed legs, like the men who played tennis at Father's club but paler. He had full blondish brows and rimless glasses. His wavy hair was parted neatly to one side. He kissed Ruth politely on both cheeks, making her blush, and opened the front passenger door for her. He then shook my hand and leaned to open the rear door, but I reached the handle first.

"It's okay. I've got it." I stepped up onto the seat, heaving my straw bag before me and somehow colliding with Sanjeev, who was sliding in through the opposite door. He laughed loudly, but I only cursed under my breath, dabbing with my beach towel at my cut-off jean shorts, which had been splattered with coffee. So I didn't lift my head to really glance at Sanjeev until we had been several minutes on the road, by which point Ruth and Brian were deep in discussion about some Bergman film that had been shown in one of the auditoriums on campus and that they had both seen. Ruth and Setsu had mentioned that Sanjeev was dark-haired and tall but had said little more about his appearance, and for some reason, I had assumed he was only mildly attractive. But with his tan skin, his sculpted nose and cheeks, his large, even teeth, he resembled a television actor or someone whose picture you might find in a magazine for men's apparel. I yanked at my suit, which had twisted beneath my T-shirt. I could feel the nubby material, worn in spots from the previous summer, and could not help thinking for a moment of the black suit in the window of University Sports. From behind my tinted glasses, I peered sideways at Sanjeev once more, wondering what photo of me Ruth had shown him. I guessed it was the one I had used for the Brown student directory, a small square I'd cut from a picture taken during a family vacation to Bermuda, my skin browned, my hair slightly lightened from the sun, a shot revealing nothing below my shoulders. Yes, I was quite sure that was it, quite sure he would not have expressed interest otherwise. I needed no more than a fleeting look to determine his type: he liked his girls toy-sized. Certainly *I* was not what he had bargained for. Ha! I hoped he was miserably disappointed. I tore off a large chunk of bagel and silently congratulated myself for not having bought the new suit.

The beach was fairly empty, still too early in the season for large crowds. A gray-haired couple in Docksides and matching red hooded windbreakers walked with a yellow Labrador near the surf. Two children in madras shorts raked the sand with plastic shovels, standing on hopping feet now and then to observe their work. We spread our towels side by side on a flat area free of stones and seaweed and plopped onto our stomachs. To my aggravation, Sanjeev insisted on placing his towel beside mine, so close that the edges overlapped. From some sense of obligation, he seemed to feel it necessary to feign attraction. For this same reason, I imagined, he had attempted several conversations with me during our car ride, leaning close now and then as if to make himself better heard.

But I was not fooled and began methodically applying sun lotion to my face and arms, careful to stay centered on my own towel.

Ruth lay on the other side of me. The floral bikini fit her more becomingly than I remembered, and she seemed to feel less self-conscious in it now. She and Brian sprawled on their bellies, facing each other. The fingers of her left hand and his right nearly touched as they brushed the sand with their toes and spoke in low tones of things I could not hear, Ruth's voice softening now and then to a whispery purr that would have made other BREMUSA members gag.

As the sun climbed in the sky, the light breeze that had cooled our necks and backs and faces lessened and then quit. We fanned ourselves with our hats and magazines. Eventually Ruth and Brian announced that, despite the chilly temperatures of the Atlantic this time of year, they were going to brave the ocean. Giggling, they ran to the water's edge, pushing each other, squealing like children as they plunged into the waves. I could hear Ruth's laughter above the surf, throaty, free of strain for the first time in a long while. I should have been happy for her, but for some reason, this only added to my annoyance. I lit a cigarette, then opened a book I had packed—*Nineteenth-Century Women Writers*, a text I planned to reference for my final comparative literature term essay. As I turned the pages, Sanjeev began to whistle, off-tune snatches of Beatles songs from the radio station we had listened to in the car. He lifted a pure white clamshell from the sand and ran his forefinger along its smooth edge. He was not used to being ignored, I guessed, especially by members of the opposite sex. But this was no concern of mine. He could squirm until he went mad, for all I cared. Yet after several minutes, he inched closer, grinning and giving my arm a poke with his elbow. His skin was warm, already darkening, and he smelled of the Bain de Soleil lotion we had all shared.

"Please don't tell me you're studying! Are you going to waste this entire beautiful day with your nose buried in a book?" A hint of his

British accent emerged as he spoke, a trait I imagined made other girls woozy. He kicked off his black beach sandals, squinting directly into my sunglasses, trying to gaze through them. But over me his charms were powerless. I responded with nothing but the tiniest nod.

"How about a quick dip in the water? You can't tell me you're not hot, especially in all that." He gestured toward my outfit, the T-shirt and denim shorts I had not removed. I felt his gaze drift below my face to my shoulders, backside, legs.

"I'm fine," I said.

"You're not one of those girls who doesn't like to get wet, are you?" Sanjeev laughed and winked, flicking a small spray of sand onto my wrist.

"Please," I snorted, crushing the remains of my cigarette into the sand.

But Sanjeev shrugged his shoulders, his lips curled as if he weren't sure he believed me. And soon thin trickles of perspiration began to drip from my hairline, along my brow, into my eyes, blurring my vision so that it became impossible to read. So out of vexation and despite my better judgment, I stood up, sweeping sand from my clothes, and agreed to walk down to the water. Without glancing at Sanjeev, I pulled off my shorts and top and tossed them onto my towel. I resisted the impulse to fold my arms over my midriff, a silly habit from girlhood. Anyway, why should I care what Sanjeev thought? He could sneer; he could laugh until his guts split. His opinion had no effect on me. But when I removed my shades and threw them into my beach bag, I saw that Sanjeev's expression remained unchanged. "Shall we?" He smiled, motioning that he would follow me, and for the first time that day, I wondered if, perhaps, I had criticized him too quickly.

As we made our way over the hot sand, Ruth and Brian came dashing from the water, shivering and shrieking, their lips purple as plums. "It's *freezing!*" they shouted. And when the first wave lapped at my toes, the cold stopped my breath, stinging to the bone. After mere seconds, my feet and legs went numb. But this seemed to make it easier to wade out until we were waist-deep.

"What do you think?" Sanjeev called over the pounding of the surf.

I turned to answer him, but as I did, the rush of a retreating wave caught at my ankles, dragging me down until my knees scraped sand and sharp pebbles. Before I could regain my footing, a second icy wave cascaded over me, submerging me in the chill so that, for some moments, I lost all sense of direction. Above the roaring in my ears, I could hear Sanjeev's voice. Then I felt his fingers grasping my wrist, pulling me to the surface. Even once I was standing again, he refused to loosen his grip. So I began to pry myself free, to tell him I needed no help; but I coughed on a mouthful of water I had swallowed, and when I stopped, something about the way he looked at me, with worried, penetrating eyes, made me relax my wrist in his hand.

As we flopped back onto our towels, Brian was returning from the snack bar down the beach with two bulging plastic bags. He laughed at our chattering teeth. "This should heat you up," he said, settling into a cross-legged position on the edge of his towel, pulling from the bags hot dogs with onions in cardboard sleeves, foil-wrapped cheeseburgers, fries, hot pretzels in sheer paper. Ruth took only a diet ginger ale and a hamburger, which she removed from its bun and sampled with small bites. But at the smell of the food, my stomach began to churn with sudden hunger, and I reached for a soda, a hot dog, tore off half a pretzel, slathering it with mustard from plastic pouches. I swallowed the food in great bites, feeling the warmth of it slipping down. When Brian offered chocolate-dipped cookies as big as saucers, I quickly accepted one, but as I held it in my open hands, I realized that of our group, I had polished off the most food. I picked off an edge of the cookie, not wanting to finish too long before the others.

Rattling the ice in his soda cup, Sanjeev laughed and indicated my empty hot dog wrapper, the crumpled packets of mustard. "I like a girl with an appetite," he said. He glanced at the remains of hamburger and bun on Ruth's plate, then, turning back to me, he nodded as if agreeing with his own words. I didn't answer but couldn't help smiling into my lap. I allowed myself a larger chunk of cookie. By the time we finished our lunch, the sun had dried us, leaving our hair stiff, our bodies filmy with patches of salt. Like four cats, we stretched facedown on our towels once more. Ruth and Brian lay with foreheads almost touching. Sanjeev rested his chin on his fist and gazed out at the ocean, his brown eyes reflecting almost gold in the light. I saw that he had taken the white clamshell from beside his belongings and placed it on the sand in front of me.

"For me?"

"To keep forever and ever," he laughed.

Somehow my towel or his must have shifted, for each time one of us moved, our knees would lightly brush. I marked my page in *Nineteenth-Century Women Writers*, shut it, and replaced it in my bag. Every now and then, I could hear from Ruth or Brian a murmured intimacy and couldn't help wondering if Sanjeev had ever been in love.

Since our arrival, the only newcomers to the beach had been a few middle-aged fishermen in rubber waders and two young families holding babies, bundles of pink-white half-hidden by floppy sunhats, so when a mud-splattered Subaru wheeled into the narrow, sandy parking lot abutting the beach, we all turned to look. Music blared from its radio, temporarily breaking the relative silence. Peering over my arm, I could see, through the windshield, long tresses of hair. Four girls—college-aged, I guessed, as they hopped out—who, like us, had decided to take advantage of the day. After crossing the wooden-planked walkway that led from the pavement to the beach and stepping onto the sand, they removed their shoes, slinging them over their shoulders with the coolers and blankets they already carried. As they headed toward us, I was conscious of Sanjeev's nearness, conscious that, surely, we appeared to be a couple, conscious of the pride rising in my chest. As they drew closer, I could more distinctly make out their features, the slender curves of their waists, their slim hips twitching side to side in their cotton shorts. One girl walked slightly ahead of the others, every so often tossing her head to flick a strand of blond hair from her face. And a familiar heaviness settled at the pit of my stomach. The blond girl coiled a lock of hair around her fingers with the deliberateness of someone who is used to commanding attention. When she was just steps from us, her eyes swept in a cursory glance over Ruth and Brian and me, then, almost seeming not to notice us, she slid her lower lip behind her front teeth and lifted her hand to Sanjeev, waggling her fingers in a wave as she passed. Sanjeev's hands remained curled beneath his chin, but I saw him give a nod of acknowledgment before the girl turned away.

"Whew, Sanjeev, you lady killer! Did you see that?" Brian propped himself on his elbow and inhaled with a slow whistle, laughing at Ruth's mocking smack to his shoulder.

Sanjeev shrugged, but he could not hide the blushing splotches darkening his cheeks. And though he rolled onto his side and began inquiring about my friends in Manhattan, my summer plans, I was sure he was fighting, fighting not to turn and stare after the long-legged blonde. So I gave curt, one-word answers to his questions, then rummaged through my straw bag—annoyed at the mess of old receipts and empty cigarette boxes I'd neglected for months—and plucked out my book, opening it once more with a loud snap.

For some time, while Brian and Ruth strolled along the shore, Sanjeev attempted conversation after conversation. But I was immovable. He could chatter until his eyes crossed, until his throat ached; his sugary talk had no effect on me. "Is something the matter? Have I offended you in some way?" he finally wanted to know. But I was deaf to his words and only swatted noisily at the pages of my book.

By the time Brian and Ruth returned from their walk, the sun had weakened, obscured by streaky clouds. We tossed away the wrappings from our lunch, slapped sand from our limbs and shorts and shoes. Something seemed to have changed during Brian and Ruth's walk. They moved more in unison now, shaking out each other's towels, checking to be sure the other had gathered every belonging. They were too busy to notice

Sanjeev's and my silence, the way we stepped around each other, refusing to make eye contact, the downturned corners of Sanjeev's lips, as if *he* were the one who had been wronged.

During the ride back to campus, I pretended to sleep, clutching my bag in my lap, my head pressed against the side window. Ruth and Brian chatted incessantly, Ruth's voice an excited burble that made my jaw stiffen. Occasionally Sanjeev added an opinion, a joking comment, but I heard the effort in his voice, the strain each time he laughed. Good! Ha! I thought, for he was nothing to me now, nothing more than fodder for gossip, another ironic anecdote for the members of BREMUSA.

Ruth missed the next BREMUSA meeting and the next and the next. "I'm absolutely swamped with work," she complained to me. But time and again I caught her lolling with Brian on the grass of the Main Green, perched beside him on the stone wall outside our dorm, swinging her hand in his, as if they had all the time in the world to squander. I knew from Setsu that Brian would be moving back to Canada just after his graduation to attend medical school in Ontario, closer to his home. "There's nothing serious between Ruth and Brian," she said. "But he's a good distraction, don't you think? Considering all she's been through?"

"A good distraction would be finding something to believe in, something to work for. Something to make her *strong*."

"I don't know. Maybe her idea of strength is different from yours."

"What does that mean?"

"Maybe for you finding some cause . . ." Setsu stopped, biting lightly on her lower lip. "We *all* have our ways of tricking ourselves, don't we? Of denying ourselves in the name of other things?"

"What exactly are you implying, Setsu?" She had a nerve trying to make this about *me*! She must have heard about Sanjeev. God, Ruth and her blabbing mouth! And of course Setsu disapproved of BREMUSA. We were *everything* that terrified her. But I wanted to hear her say it, wanted her to have spine enough to tell me to my face!

But she shrugged like a coward, refusing to add another word. And I would not waste my breath on contradictions.

My stops at Ruth's room for chitchat grew less frequent, my invitations to join the other BREMUSA members and me for meals more sporadic. Ruth made continual, feeble attempts to maintain our connection. "What are you doing tonight?" "It's been *so* long since we talked." But if I opened a real discussion, about BREMUSA's goals for the remaining few days of the year, or a recent news article about women's health concerns, she listened for no more than a minute before apologizing and excusing herself to run off to some commitment.

One evening, as I sorted papers for that night's BREMUSA gathering, I heard Ruth on the phone with Brian, making plans to meet for a screening of *Gone With the Wind* in Salomon Hall. Then came the sound of her humming as she opened and closed dresser drawers, the brief whir of her blow-dryer, the unzipping of her cosmetics bag. The day before I had reminded her that this evening's meeting would be a crucial one: Lucille Portman, author of *Equity of the Sexes*, had agreed to come speak to us. "Oh, great! Thanks for letting me know," she had said, but it was now obvious she had no intention of going. Later she emerged from her room, releasing a small cloud of cheap perfume—the imitation Chanel she had been wearing for weeks, obviously believing it passed for quality, her hair full from brushing, her keys to our dorm jingling in her hand.

"Did you forget about tonight, Ruth, or is it just not of interest to you?" I knew I had startled her with the flames of anger in my voice, but I didn't care.

"Oh, sorry. I'm sure it will be wonderful, but Brian and I—"

"You know, Ruth, I started BREMUSA for you. For girls like you. Girls without confidence. Girls who'd been wronged—"

A small shudder moved through Ruth's body. "Who asked you,

Francesca? I never asked you!" She pressed her balled fist gripping the keys to her chest and dashed to the door.

I might have told Ruth I had a few regrets over the things I'd said, that I had not been *entirely* fair. But the right opportunity never seemed to arise. Some days later I returned to my room to find that Ruth had dropped off a handful of belongings that I had lent her or forgotten in her room over the course of the year. She had stacked them neatly on my bed: a hooded Brown University sweatshirt, a slightly faded denim skirt, my battered copy of *The Catcher in the Rye*, a plaid headband, and a photograph taken of all four suitemates on the first day of our freshman year. In the picture, we are smiling and standing before Brown's Van Wickle Gates, the university's scrolling, wrought-iron crest visible behind us. The day had been mild for late summer in New England. We are wearing thin sleeveless shirts and sandals. And as I studied the snapshot, I realized this was the picture Ruth must have shown Sanjeev—not merely of my neck and face but every bit of me visible from head to toe. The suite seemed suddenly, strangely quiet, the others all having disappeared to various destinations. Even my own breathing was noiseless as for some motionless minutes I stared at the photo, my mind beginning to wander with doubts that were probably useless. So I tucked the snapshot carefully between the first two pages of *The Catcher in the Rye* and slid the book to the back of my desk drawer.

Days before final exams and the end of the school year, the members of BREMUSA reached a consensus about our culminating statement for the term. In the news there had been much talk of late about the age at which girls were beginning to diet. Interviews with children as young as eight and nine had recently been aired on a regional public television station. Many of them had already begun to turn down certain foods, explaining that they wanted to look skinny in their gymnastics leotards and ballet tights. So we devised a plan to bombard the campus with our message. We had convinced our local station to send us a cassette tape of the documentary. One of our supporters, Skylar, a guitarist, owned a sound system with speakers and amplifiers. During the Friday of exam week, while students dashed madly from classes to mailboxes to rushed lunches, we would position the speakers in Skylar's window overlooking Wriston Quad. At top volume, we would play the taped interviews. We would make a banner to be unfurled from her windowsill. *We Fear for Our Youth*, it would say. *You Should Too.*

Friday morning, we had agreed, we would assemble in Skylar's room. I had volunteered to transport the banner, which I had been storing beneath my bed, tightly rolled and encased in a plastic tarpaulin. I headed to Skylar's just before ten, the wrapped banner balanced on my shoulder. The sky was overcast with yellow-gray clouds, and a light drizzle had begun to fall, dotting the windowpanes of the buildings along the quad and the winding paved path to the dorm. I adjusted the leather hat I was wearing, nudging the brim forward to protect my eyes from the wet. Just as I did so, I saw a familiar figure striding toward me. Sanjeev was holding a folded newspaper over his head, squinting at the now thickening rain, and appeared not to recognize me until we were almost face-to-face. When I waved he seemed startled, his neck jerking inadvertently as he checked to make sure my gesture was not intended for someone else. Then after a moment of hesitation, he lifted his hand in response. "How have you been?" he asked, and seemed to be gathering his thoughts, fumbling for a way to engage in conversation.

"Fine. Busy, I guess." I rocked nonchalantly on my heels, but my voice sounded wispier, shakier than I had intended.

Sanjeev smiled and nodded. "It's a busy time of year." Then his eyes flickered as if with a sudden question. And my heart rushed, a drumming

I could feel in my ears. But before he could continue, a girl's voice sang his name from across the quad. A petite brunette in a rosebud-pink rain jacket bounced on her toes under Wayland Arch.

"Hi." Sanjeev twisted toward her then back to me. He seemed suddenly befuddled, as if he'd lost the words on the tip of his tongue. He cleared his throat, searching for what he had wanted to say. The girl in pink remained under the dry of the arch for some moments, then eventually, seemingly impatient, opened a fuchsia-handled umbrella and headed toward us. Beneath her coat she wore navy leggings. Through the clingy material, I could make out slender thighs, narrow knees, ankles I nearly could have encircled with my forefinger and thumb. In just a few seconds, she would be standing beside us, fluttering her eyes, rubbing Sanjeev's arm in greeting with her doll hand. So without waiting for Sanjeev to regain his composure, I muttered something about my morning schedule. Then I hurried off, my boots striking the ground with purposeful claps that would have made my fellow BREMUSA members proud.

When there had been trouble between Mother and Father, long ago, I sometimes caught her watching him from across a room. Adjusting the clips in her hair, or the neckline of her blouse so that it dipped more becomingly across her chest, waiting for something from him—something she believed would make everything good again. But couldn't she see that Father's mind was far away, that he was not even *noticing* her?

"What are you *doing*, Mother?"

"Oh, Franny. Things you'll understand when you're all grown up!" she'd laughed, surprised by my question, I could tell, but without turning to me.

But I *was* older now. And I had no interest in the lessons Mother had expected me to learn. I continued on to Skylar's, at every step refraining from glancing back.

Part

THREE

UNNECESSARY BURDENS

(Opal's Story)

· *1992* ·

I n the fall of my senior year, Mother uprooted again. This time to
Tempe, Arizona, with Sebastian, the new man in her life. Her life was
a whirlwind, she said, between the demands of her latest work design-
ing jewelry and the renovations to their new home. For two months, I'd
heard nothing from her. When she finally called, I kept my voice blasé,
cool as ocean water. If she thought I would bubble with excitement or
tremble with emotion, she was in for a sorry surprise.

By this time, my suitemates were beginning to settle their future
plans: Setsu taking a position as a research analyst at a bank in Boston;
Francesca would be off to Europe. Ruth, among other options, was considering a connection through a family friend to some prominent international organization. Other classmates, I knew, had applied to medical
schools or for internships at law firms in cities where they had friends or
family. Kimberly Anderson, who'd lived next door to us both junior and
senior year, was hoping to be accepted into Emory's business program,

closer to her parents in Coral Gables, Florida. I watched as they breezed through the halls in suits or skirts, heels and stockings, their faces set as they rushed to various meetings with recruiters from prestigious corporations. But none of the printed cards that arrived almost daily in my campus mail or banners that stretched like oversized bedding across the entry to Faunce House announced opportunities I could begin to imagine for myself, few of them applicable to art history majors anyway.

In Brown's career services office, I flipped through binders thick with applications for positions in research, in sales, in communications. Boring, boring. Blah, blah, blah.

Then one afternoon, Kimberly mentioned a friend of her mother's in Naples, Florida, who was in need of an assistant for her art gallery. "I can put you in touch with her if you like. I think you would be just right for this," Kimberly said, showing me a clipping from a Florida paper: *Seeking Responsible Employee with Art Background to Assist in Managing Gallery and Health Bar.* In smaller print below was added: *Enjoy a peaceful work atmosphere. Bask in the southern sunshine.*

Yes, the position seemed *designed* for me, and so I accepted Kimberly's offer to pass along my résumé.

F lorida? All by yourself? I know Kimberly will be nearby part of the year, but it's home for her." Ruth and I were seated on the new spring grass of the Green, putting off our Ancient Greek Poets reading.

"I suppose it's no different from anywhere else," I laughed. "Actually, I spent a few months there with Mother just after I turned fourteen." And I had done my research on the owner of the gallery and learned she was beginning to establish a bit of a national profile for some of her recent exhibitions. "Choices are limited with a degree in art history," I told Ruth, "but I think this could be a good opportunity. . . ." Anyway, what did I have that was holding me here? Why suffer through another New England winter, months of cold that left my skin dry as parched earth, made my hands and ankles swell?

"No, it makes sense. I guess it's just hard to believe we'll all be scattered next year," Ruth said. "But traveling has always been part of your life. I wish I had half your spontaneity." Ruth dropped her neck back, gazing up at the daytime moon, so lacy thin it seemed almost translucent. And she sighed in a way I knew she was wishing for what, after four years together, she still imagined my life to be. "I know you won't lose touch, though. You've promised . . ."

But I wondered if Ruth was naïve to think the pact we made years before would last beyond our time at college.

"Of course not," I said.

And then, near the close of our final term at Brown, I sent my signed employment contract to Ms. Amara Silver.

When I first opened the door to Art of Life Café and Gallery, a bell tinkled softly. Amara emerged from a back room in a filmy white blouse and pants that rippled as she walked. Through the thin material, the lean curves of her silhouette were visible. I guessed she was no younger than Mother, but her figure seemed firmer, more perfectly proportioned than what I had ever been able to achieve, despite my years of dieting and daily jogs.

"Oh, come on in, Opal," she said as she approached. In one hand she held a glass of some pale iced liquid, in the other a stack of papers. She lifted these up, a silent gesture of apology for not greeting me with a handshake. "So," she laughed, "I guess you're undaunted by a tropical summer or you wouldn't have accepted the job."

I nodded.

"Me neither. The heat cleanses the system, don't you think?" When she laughed again, white flashed against her olive skin. Her square teeth were large, as were all of her features—her mouth broad, her nose prominent, her cheeks wide, her gray-streaked hair swept into a thick twist, a solid mass at the back of her head. Nothing about her face was classically pretty, but the angles were so unusual, so bold, that I imagined people stared at her as they might gaze at someone beautiful.

When she had found a place for her drink and her papers, Amara showed me around. The gallery and health bar shared the single front room, its walls pale, pale blue—the color of sky through a fine mist of cloud. Two of the walls displayed evenly spaced, framed watercolors— all of the same oval pond, at its center a tiny rock island dotted with grass and wildflowers—the hues varying slightly from one to the next. "Faye Hallowell's work, a resident here in Naples," Amara said. "She's begin- ning to gain some recognition. I just love her style, don't you? It's so subtle."

Amara showed the work of artists from all around the southern U.S. and had recently begun to feature some South American works as well, but she was particularly drawn to local artists and, whenever possible, gave them opportunities. She had shared this during the course of our correspondence the previous spring, explaining her process of selecting art that she deemed not only of high quality but which complemented her space. And, yes, I admired the paintings, too, I told her. I loved the sym- metry of their composition and the way each differed just a shade from the one before so that the overall effect was of completeness, the fullness of a day. I stopped before the final representation in the series: dusk—the island and its grasses mere silhouettes, reminding me of the Asian draw- ings with their delicate, evocative lines I had found myself attracted to in art history courses, their negative spaces leaving room for reflection. A year ago Mother and Antonio had taken a weekend in New York, and I made the three-hour train ride south to meet them. Visiting the Metro- politan Museum, we had strolled through the Asian wing. "It's so peaceful in here, isn't it?" I said to Mother. When we reached the Chinese scroll paintings, I told her I could spend all day studying them. But Mother found them excruciatingly dull: "We might as well return to the hotel and stare at the toile wallpaper, for God's sake!" She and Antonio wanted to make their way to the modern wing. Mother loved the Expressionist paintings with their tornadoes of color. I knew their mad-dream visions were artistically important, but I found them disturbing. And it bothered me that they inspired Mother, her eyes shining as she drank in a darkness I imagined might manifest itself not only in her painting—which had suddenly begun to take over hours of her day—but in her very being.

But now Mother was immersed in her jewelry making, in her new life in Arizona with Sebastian—whoever he was. And I assumed she had not touched a paintbrush or pottery wheel in months, though at one time she'd claimed each to be her passion, her raison d'être. She had always been that way—plunging into something and swimming through it, then emerging onto dry land in search of some other pool.

"I love what you've done here," I told Amara. There was an easy lightness to the gallery, a cleanness like the cherry blossom scrolls of Chinese art. It seemed the space of someone who understood calm, understood contentment, making me hopeful that coming here had been a right choice.

The café—or health bar, as Amara referred to it—took the center of the gallery, creating three sides of a rectangle, or a "U" with corners. The counters were of beveled glass topping the pale-wood structure, ten bamboo stools placed around them. Inside the "U" of the bar stood a lemon-yellow board listing a range of fresh vegetable and juice drinks, salads, fruits in season. Behind the counter, I could see that the drink-ware and plates had been arranged neatly along one shelf, equally ordered stacks of plastic to-go containers filling the shelf opposite.

At the back of the room, a pair of louvered doors led to a small workspace. A young woman in a cotton skirt, several wire-thin silver hoops piercing her right ear, sat at a low table studying art catalogs, one of them from a Florida auction house whose name I recognized.

"Calliope's with me just two mornings a week, when she's not in classes," Amara explained, introducing us. "But she's been immensely helpful. Faye Hallowell, whose work we're now displaying, was Calliope's find."

Calliope tugged at the bottom hoop in her ear and smiled, her eyes wide with pleasure from Amara's praise.

During the remainder of the morning, Amara introduced me to my various responsibilities. The health bar was a snap, really self-explanatory. In terms of the gallery, I would be expected to be well versed in the work of whatever artists we were showing, of course. Most customers came in for the café and to browse, she supposed, but some clients were serious buyers, a few were dealers. What she hoped most from me was that I had a good eye. She expected I would, given my background. She was pleased with my response to Faye Hallowell's work. As I would soon learn, she said, many artists would approach us directly with their work. Others she and Calliope had discovered at festivals or street fairs, even at work with their easels by the beaches. "So keep your eyes wide open for talent!"

"I will!" In fact, I was eager to get started, I told her.

But just before noon, Amara excused herself. She had some figures to go over with Calliope. "Last month's business," she explained. "There's no need for you to waste your time." So, though it was only my first day, I was given permission to leave early.

"Are you sure? I'm happy to stay."

But Amara swatted the air with a folder she held in her hand. "Go enjoy yourself."

So I stepped out into the small, only half-filled lot that provided parking for Art of Life as well as for Lily's Shoes, Sunshine Stationers, and Petra's Hair Salon. And, retracing my route of that morning, I made the ten-minute walk along Hibiscus Drive to Everglade Avenue until I reached the painted sign that marked the entry to Emerald Cove, where I had found a modest one-bedroom rental. If I'd been honest with Amara, I'd have told her I didn't mind the extra hours in the gallery. Save for the whir of the AC, my apartment was almost noiseless, especially in the late afternoon. The wind hardly stirred the palm fronds of the tree outside my kitchen window, and there was little in the way of distraction—an occasional car on the complex's sleek winding road, a tomato-faced cyclist swabbing perspiration with the back of his wrist. But perhaps Amara would have thought it odd, a request for added work. And the last thing I wanted was to start off on the wrong foot.

I changed into running shorts and sneakers with the thought that I would head toward the beach, a chance to combine a jog with my first bit of research for the gallery, scanning the area for any interesting artists at work. As it turned out, though, the path near the beach was empty aside from a few other runners and walkers. None of them seemed to be melting quite so much in the weather as I was, still not yet adjusted to the southern heat. But making my way down to the shore, I ran what I judged was another mile and then another, listening to the rapid, steady rhythm of my feet on the packed sand interspersed with the slower rhythm of the sweeping waves.

Aside from jangling earrings and a chunk of purplish stone that hung from a cord around her neck, Amara dressed with none of the ornamentation most women her age—Mother's age—favored: her face was absent of added color, her nails unpolished and trimmed close. The preening other women undertook in order to catch the eyes of men held no interest for her; the attentions she gave to her appearance seemed solely for her own gratification. When I worked up the courage to question her on the subject, she rolled her eyes, clearly humored.

"Oh, Opal, men can make life so much more complicated than it needs to be, don't you think?" She tossed the fringed end of her gauzy scarf over her shoulder. She had once been married, but it was long ago. "In another lifetime," she sighed, as though the very memory bored her, "when I was young and thoughtless, before I knew what was good for me." She dropped trimmed strawberries and cubes of pineapple into the blender. "I live a life unfettered now," she laughed, and loosed a few strands of hair from the clip holding it in place. "A simpler life."

And after I had been with her for a few weeks, I began to learn the ways Amara kept herself free. Not infrequently, men who entered the Art of Life made requests for her phone number, for her work hours, murmuring to her across the counter of the health bar—as they often did with me—only pretending to take an interest in the art on display as they ordered fruit shakes or vegetable drinks for youthful energy. Some were Amara's contemporaries, others mine, more than one with a strip of un-tanned skin around his finger where a ring, quite obviously, was normally worn. A few were artists themselves, toting portfolios of their work, but even this seemed sometimes an excuse to own Amara's attention or mine, to stand beside us, heads bent together. As each of these men exercised his particular charms, evenings spent awkwardly at Mother's elbow re-turned to me. But while Mother had fluttered her eyes invitingly, Amara offered smiling excuses, and the men would shrug their shoulders or twist their lips sourly, as if to say they had meant no harm. Once their backs were turned in retreat, she would wink at me, and I would flush at having been included in her amusement.

So Amara would never sob over a man until her face was puffed and mottled as I had seen Mother do more times than I could count. Never would she attempt to swallow sorrow, calm her nerves with rounds of tall rum drinks that left her moaning with sickness. No, she was too indepen-dent to let someone else turn her life upside down. And the more I watched her, the more I felt I could learn her strength. If I wanted to believe in fate or destiny, maybe it was for *this* reason I had come to Flor-ida, more than for any career opportunity.

. . .

In the summertime, the off-season for tourists, Amara explained, patronage of the gallery as well as of the health bar was lighter than during the remainder of the year. So she and I often had hours of unoccupied time, and we sat at two of the bamboo stools, sipping blended shakes of celery, carrots, parsley, wheatgrass, or whatever concoction Amara had most recently discovered, as she described for me the vitamins and nutrients of each ingredient. Just as I did, Amara adhered to a vegetarian diet, but she had stuck with it for years and was a font of knowledge. She understood how to balance a meal precisely, how to complement proteins or roots or berries for maximum nourishment, how to stop eating before fullness set in to prevent the storage of excess fat. "I believe in conditioning the interior as well as the exterior of my body, don't you?" Amara asked. She agreed to come running with me along my route by the water one afternoon. "I don't know how people can *stand* to live in cold climates," she said once we'd found a matching stride. "This is heavenly, isn't it?" And she held out her arms as if she were drawing the beauty of our surroundings into herself.

My breath was too heavy in the sticky air to speak much as we ran, but Amara talked of the gallery, of the artists whose work she'd been lucky enough to show. It was really a matter of being discerning, she thought. There was so much done in the name of art these days that was crass, sloppy, wasn't there? "But art is like anything else in life, isn't it? There is a purity, a harmony in that of highest quality." Did I agree?

Yes. Yes! Amara was saying all of the things I already believed but had never quite put into words. If my legs had more strength in them, I could have run and talked with her like this forever. I thought of the drawings I'd been working on intermittently over the past months, from photos I had taken of children playing on a playground near Brown. More than once I had thought I'd finished them, but always, later, something would seem off. Maybe I had emphasized too many elements, trying to make too many aspects come to life. Maybe what it lacked was just what Amara spoke of—a purity of vision. When I returned to it, I would keep this in mind.

"I enjoyed our run, Opal," Amara mentioned the next morning. Later, if I liked, she would show me her own exercise regimen, one she followed on a daily basis. So I mirrored her as she worked through a series of elongating bends and muscle-toning poses that she held for impossibly long stretches. One after another after another, until by the time she had finished, I could not remember how she had begun. In a single day with Amara, I could gain more than I had gleaned from any health magazine, any philosophy or self-help book I'd ever read. And with each secret she shared, I became hungrier for more.

For eight hours of each Tuesday through Saturday, Amara and I were together, and I noticed that I was beginning to develop the almost reflexive habit of asking myself how *she* would handle certain choices, various situations, sensing that her decisions would be the braver ones, the stronger ones. She had begun to compliment my instinct for finding art that worked in the gallery's space, that was of the style she wished to promote. I had discovered Lia Chelsea's work at an outdoor art festival in Bonita Springs and Joy Ling's beautiful landscape photos at the Sun Gallery. At the evening parties Amara had held at the gallery to honor the debut of each of these artists, she interrupted the passing of champagne and hors d'oeuvres to toast me in front of the crowd. But in other ways I was frustrated by my many mistakes. Whenever male customers talked of my smile, my eye color, drew me into lengthy conversations, I stiffened with self-consciousness, aware that Amara observed me, certain that she would have dismissed these unwanted attentions more quickly and with a flair I did not possess.

. . .

We were just days from transitioning from Faye Hallowell's work to the watercolors of a friend of Amara's, a popular local artist whom she had showcased some years before, selling all but one of her paintings. This was late August, the air, even at night, thick and hot as breath, the temperateness of my apartment and of the gallery always a happy relief. The young man who entered Art of Life I hadn't seen before, but from the way he stepped in so purposefully, confidently, I assumed he was a friend of Amara's or Calliope's, that he'd spent time in the gallery previously and knew his way around. But he didn't inquire after either of them, and I saw that he held the handles of an artist's black portfolio case in his left hand. He stepped close enough for me to smell the salt air on him, and he was smiling widely, almost grinning, as if he expected some effusive or enthusiastic greeting from me. I returned a more lingering smile than I'd intended, my voice too high, too soft in answering. So stupid. He irritated me, even before he said another word, the way he seemed so sure of his likability, his masculinity, with his shoulders pushed back in his U Penn T-shirt, smiling his too-radiant smile, which I supposed he knew made up for his deep-set eyes, his slightly crooked jaw. I was not interested. And the Art of Life, unfortunately, I told him—though I would check with the owner—would probably not be a fitting venue for his work, primarily sculptures, of which he'd brought photos. "We're not set up to display them," I said. "Ms. Silver's focus is solely on two-dimensional art."

"Oh, but wait." He'd done a few watercolors, as well, he said. Still these, too, I was sure, were all wrong for the gallery. I could see that he had proficiency as a painter, but I found his work distasteful: bare-armed carpenters sawing lumber, their hunched backs bulky; a dock full of thick-legged fishermen gutting their catch.

Amara's response was what mine had been: the paintings—she was sorry—were unsuitable for the gallery. If she decided at some future point to consider sculpture, she would be in touch with him—Marco Everly—taking his card. And so, just like that, she turned him away, civilly and without ado.

For the next day or two, the stifling temperatures kept the café and gallery nearly empty. We counted six hours one Friday without a single customer until two men entered, allowing in a cloud of hot, heavy air. They were friends, or father and son, perhaps—the slightly taller one seeming to be a younger version of the other—their hair identically styled, slicked off their foreheads with some sort of shiny gel. They wore similarly patterned flowered swim trunks and cotton shirts, each with the top few buttons unfastened to reveal a wide vee of tanned chest.

"Like twin Hawaiian Elvises!" I whispered to Amara.

"Or Elvis impersonators," she laughed.

"Do you ladies mind some company? It's so nice and cool in here we just might stay all day." The older man grinned, leaned his brown-speckled arms on the counter, and propped a thick, sandaled foot on one of the bamboo stools. He and his companion ordered Caribbean smoothies— coconut milk, papaya, mango, pineapple, honey—then straddled their stools and began to chatter, making repeated attempts at small talk as if they really did intend to settle in for a long while. The older one directed his conversation toward Amara; the younger one had a stream of questions for me. I occupied myself behind the bar, rinsing berries, stacking glasses, so that I could keep my answers to his inquiries brief. Perhaps I was finally learning Amara's techniques. So when he asked if I planned to take a break soon, this time words came quickly. No, I was sorry, I said. I would be very busy all day checking inventory. But as I spoke, my voice echoed Amara's, or was hers trailing mine? We glanced at each other, biting our cheeks to suppress our mirth, realizing we had simultaneously conjured up the same excuse. With tight lips, the younger man dropped crumpled bills on the counter for their drinks; then the two turned, hustling out, their elbows stiff at their sides, their chests puffed like waterfowl, with no more than a mumbled "goodbye" over their shoulders. As soon as the chimes above the door jingled behind them, Amara and I exploded.

"Quite taken with themselves, weren't they? They really believed they were doing us the biggest favor of our summer!"

"God, how ever did we resist?" We laughed until tears welled in our eyes, until our ribs ached. And I sensed, with a shiver of happiness, that this was the beginning of a change, of a new closeness.

It was not long before Amara began to divulge details from her past, plans for her future. "I'll tell you because I trust you, Opal," she would sometimes whisper before she began. So I would savor each tidbit, nodding silently as she spoke, still not quite believing she had chosen me for her confidante, feeling a sudden rush of pride when she glanced over her shoulder to make certain Calliope, whom she had known far longer, could not hear. And in these intimate moods came a sudden urge to share my own secrets. My voice quaking, I told things no one else knew: of how I'd panicked at my first school dance when my date walked me down to the sports fields, then pinned me against the equipment shed. Of how I'd begun to wheeze and shake—knowing, *knowing* what he would make me do for my release—though he'd only laughed at me and then stalked off, calling over his shoulder that I could not take a joke. I told of my own pencil sketches I'd been collecting for the last few years—I would show her someday when they were more finished. I told, too, of my hope that I might eventually try color. Each revelation made my heart pound from nerves but also with the thrill of having disclosed a truth to Amara, and Amara alone.

Soon I began to dread Sundays and Mondays, when the Art of Life was closed. On these days the hours ticked by sluggishly. In the glaring sun of late summer, it was too hot to lie on the baked sand of the beach, too sticky even to last long in the tepid water of Emerald Cove's unshaded pool, where, within minutes, I was swallowed into a circle of lumpy-legged older women in their confetti-bright bathing suits who liked to tell me what a beauty I was and that they remembered a time when they'd had pretty, pretty figures like mine. I read books that I borrowed from the neighborhood library—an anthology of Native American lore, a biography of Jackson Pollock, two novels by Isabel Allende—as I soaked in cool baths—far more refreshing than the pool water—until my fingertips shriveled. From the photos I'd taken of children at play, I attempted other drawings, this time using, instead, a very soft pencil. I thought of Amara's suggestion that the best art creates a sense of balance. And so I darkened certain lines and shaded areas so that your eye moved around the drawings but then found rest. Still, I wasn't sure this worked. I contemplated bringing the new sketches to the gallery at some point for Amara's opinion.

I ran after sundown, or early in the morning when the sun was not bright white and overhead but low and yellow and blurry-edged near the horizon. Lacking the structure of a workday schedule, I ran often without a planned route, sometimes looping the sand-dusted asphalt paths of Emerald Cove then through the more sprawling complexes south of it, sometimes following the never-ending stretch of coastline. One morning I thought I recognized Marco Everly—the artist Amara had turned away just days before. He was in a black short-sleeved wetsuit, a paddleboard under his arm, his hair dark with water, his face crinkled from squinting into the sun. As he turned, I tucked my chin, dropped my eyes to the ground, though I thought as I picked up speed, I could see his hand lifting in a wave. "Hi! *Hi* . . ." His call shredded by wind. Or had it been merely one of the raucous gulls circling above the waves? Perhaps I'd only imagined he'd seen me. Maybe I should have stopped and offered at least a polite greeting. But for some reason, I could think only of creating more distance, and I ran without looking back.

Not until Tuesday morning, when the café and gallery reopened, did life seem to settle once again into a purposeful rhythm. I looked forward to the routine Amara and I had begun to establish: our shared breakfasts of soy milk and cereal, eaten while seated on the low stuccoed wall of Art of Life's small patio, watching the geckos that darted to and fro and the ibises strolling about the plantings of the gravel lot. And later, our cups of caffeine-free tea, our lunches of chopped salad—that day's special from the health bar. If the gallery was empty of customers, I would follow Amara in her daily sequence of stretches. Her back solid and reaching, like the trunks of the palms beyond the windows, her arms, in her breezy tunic, easy at her side, she showed me how proper breathing through each movement united body and mind, how the right cadence of inhaling and exhaling gave one focus. "Like this," she said, nodding, her eyes sliding closed as her diaphragm swelled and then drew in. And soon I had proof that the things she told me were true. Always I had feared there was something wrong in me, something that kept me from being whole. More than once, while we worked together, in the comfortable silence that seemed usually to belong to families, I almost told her so. But accompanying Amara in these rituals, I felt myself shifting to a higher level of well-being; it seemed I was beginning to absorb her energy, her confidence, her completeness—suddenly sure of my thoughts, sure of making right choices. When the two of us were together, I could be like her, soaring with a sense of invincibility I had never before known.

But later, in the solitude of my apartment, the strength, the discipline that came so easily in Amara's presence turned elusive. So, hoping for inspiration, I studied the pamphlets that Amara kept on one of the tables in the gallery's back room, stacked beside brochures from other galleries and auction houses. Pamphlets on yoga and meditation, on diuretics, on herbs and vitamin-rich fruits known for promoting equilibrium. I pored over a book she had lent me called *Living in Health*, memorizing the pages she had dog-eared, the paragraphs she had underlined on exercise, on diet, on eliminating stress and the importance of meaningful work. For suppers, I attempted recipes listed in the book's appendix, favoring the ones Amara had marked with asterisks.

Aside from the nights Ruth or Setsu or Fran phoned, I could lose myself in these pursuits for hours. Always their calls caught me off guard, as each one of them checked in with me at the beginning of the month. But this was what we had agreed, to stay connected, to keep the bond of friendship that would not be cracked by distance. The easier thing would be to drift apart, but after all we'd survived at one another's sides during our four years of college, hadn't we become part of each other? Hadn't we made ties that should not be frayed, or carelessly allowed to unravel? These were the things we'd said to each other. But I knew people found it hard to make promises last. So I suppose I hadn't believed as much as they that closeness would continue. "I miss you," Ruth told me in the first days of September—her voice familiar enough to be part of my own thoughts, leaving me, after she'd hung up, with a twinge like homesickness, but for where I wasn't sure.

I decided what was best for me was to avoid outside distractions, to keep myself busy—with running, with work on my sketches, with Amara's books. So when Bethany, my neighbor across the hall—a premed student and summertime fitness instructor at Gulf Coast Sports Club—slipped a folded card under my door, inviting me to a party, I returned a scribbled note of apology. For over a week, I ignored the recorded messages on my phone from Kimberly, who had returned from a family vacation along the Outer Banks and was now back in her parents' Coral Gables home until her courses at Emory began. And I waited some days before responding to new messages from Setsu. In a couple of months, she would be in Fort Myers for a four-day work seminar: "I could easily drive to Naples. Can we get together?" But despite our pledges of friendship, over the past year and a half the rift caused by my accusation about James had never entirely closed. Repeatedly Setsu had insisted we no longer need let petty arguments come between us. Still I'd sensed her covered resentment. I had seen it in her eyes, the set of her face when I bumped into her with James at the student post office, the library. I had heard her stiffness with me when talk in our suite turned to men. I imagined a visit from Setsu now would be vaguely uncomfortable. And I had new priorities.

. . .

In mid-September, three months after I had begun working at Art of Life, was my twenty-second birthday. That morning Amara surprised me with a small potted fern, its container wrapped in gold foil. "So, what are you doing tonight?" she asked, the thought seeming to occur to her at that moment. "I have a million leftovers from a gathering last evening. Any interest in dinner?"

"Yes. Sure, that sounds great!" I hoped my lack of plans was not quite as obvious, the words sounding not quite as eager to Amara as they did to my own ears.

She had invited me for seven o'clock. Her house was within walking distance of my apartment, so at six-thirty, after finding the perfect spot on my windowsill for my birthday fern, showering and changing, I exited the gates of Emerald Cove. With a half hour, I would have enough time to stop at the gift shop on Morning Drive. But to my disappointment, nothing in the store seemed quite right. The shop's scented soaps were full of chemicals I knew Amara would dislike. The printed hand towels looked cheap. In the display window was a pretty sapphire-blue crystal vase, but I worried it would appear an overly expensive present. Finally I chose a set of cork-bottomed coasters painted with tropical fish but fretted during the remainder of my walk that they were not her taste.

Amara's home was a white-shingled ranch bordered by palmettos. A path of smooth round stones led to the front door. Two mobiles of iridescent seashells hung from either end of her small porch. "Come in, come in," she called from the other side of her screen door. "Make yourself comfortable. I'm in the kitchen. I'll be right out."

Inside, I recognized the sweet, slightly musky fragrance that sometimes emanated from Amara's clothes, but here it was stronger; I could taste it on my tongue. Her hall opened into a wide living-dining area, where I imagined she wished me to wait. The walls, as I had expected, were white with only a few sparse hangings, but the furnishings were surprisingly cozy—a deep-cushioned sofa and matching chairs, two cur-tained window seats. In one corner of the room, thick maroon pillows, intended for reclining, formed an intimate circle around a low table.

Amara, in a flowing turquoise shirt and pants, her feet bare, greeted me with a kiss on either cheek, and I was aware that I had dressed too stiffly in my pressed slacks and collared linen blouse. Her hair smelled of the perfume that was everywhere in the house but also of cooking scents, spices I couldn't quite place. "Ohh, is that for me?" she asked, glancing at the wrapped package in my hands. "You really shouldn't have, and on *your* birthday."

"It's only something small." I shrugged, wishing she would wait until after I left to open it. But to my relief, she seemed to like the coasters. She had seen them at a friend's house before, she said, and thought they were lovely.

"Thank you. Thank you, Opal." She gave my hand a tiny squeeze, and a tightness below my ribs, which I had not noticed until that mo-ment, began to ease.

"So how about some wine?" She had a bottle of merlot that had been made without pesticides or sulfites. "A healthy bottle!" she laughed. "What do you think?"

"Believe it or not, I actually gave up drinking in my junior year of college," I told her. "My suitemates thought I was crazy! But now doesn't research say there are actual *benefits* to wine in moderation? So how can I argue with a healthy bottle?" I laughed as she brought out two full goblets, placed them, with the tropical fish coasters, on the low corner table, then curled onto one of the dark red pillows, motioning for me to do the same.

The wine tasted of fruits and warm cinnamon. And after a time, ev-erything seemed to slow—Amara's voice and mine, the movement of our hands and limbs. Her pillows were more comfortable than any chair, and I felt I could sink into them until I became permanently attached.

Before serving our dinner, Amara lit candles, clusters of votives lin-ing the bookshelves, windowsills, dotting the floor near the room's entry. She arranged two in frosted glass holders on the table between us, then disappeared to the kitchen and returned bearing a large tray holding several bowls.

"Have you tried Vietnamese food?" She shook a wisp of hair from her eyes, her silver earrings vibrating. "I have a *ton*." She set the tray at the center of the table, then identified each dish: curried tofu, vegetable stir-fry, glass noodles, steamed rice rolls.

"It looks delicious," I said, and watched as Amara's chopsticks lifted a few small pieces of tofu, two rice rolls, some thin strands of translucent noodles and placed them on her plate. I was careful to take a portion no larger than hers, to chew unhurriedly as she did. As we nibbled, Amara added to our glasses, and it was not long before our talk turned to dreamier things—what it would be like to own a gallery on the Mediterranean instead of here, the vine-covered villas we could rent in Italy, the weekends we would spend in Morocco, the boats we would charter to southern France.

As the sky through the open windows melted from pink to orange to navy-black, the candles projected flickering shadows on the darkened walls, making the garnet liquid in our glasses glow. The flame closest to Amara pulsed across her cheeks and illumined her gray eyes, and as I gazed into them, I had the sense that I could see past them, through them, into something I had once belonged to.

When the last traces of blue faded from the night sky, scattered crystalline stars emerged, below them a sliver of moon. Leaning back into her pillow, Amara began to recite verses from a few of her favorite poems—Coleridge's "Kubla Khan," two sonnets by Shakespeare, Auden's "Stop All the Clocks." And a long-ago memory resurfaced of Mother and me sitting after dusk on a deserted beach, a blanket wrapped around us both for warmth as the water grazed our bare toes. "What do I need in this world but you, Opal?" Mother had whispered in my ear, hugging me close as she began to hum a lullaby. And I had breathed with such a deep contentment (a rare, almost foreign sensation for me during my childhood) and rested my head on her shoulder and closed my eyes, believing, for the moment, that only the two of us existed.

" 'Two roads diverged in a yellow wood/ And sorry I could not travel both/ And be one traveler, long I stood . . .' " Amara nodded, her hand drumming her knee in rhythm with the words. And with these few lines I knew, I joined my voice to hers. How I wished for a thousand more nights just like this.

"You're lovely, Opal," Amara said suddenly, her broad lips curving slightly. She tilted her glass for a slow sip, exposing the length of her neck, and closed her eyes. "Really lovely."

"Oh—thank you. You too," I murmured, my tongue swollen and dry in my mouth. What was she saying? When she opened her eyes again, she leaned forward, her elbows pressing the table. There was little distance between us now, so little I thought I could feel her breath on me. Why wasn't she speaking? What was she waiting for? Would she . . . ? Did she think that I . . . ? Something in me was trembling, crackling. Never had I touched my lips to a woman's. Perhaps if I didn't look, if I didn't think— If I could only swallow away the nervous, sick clog in my throat, I could make myself want what she wanted— It would be, I imagined, like kissing a man, only softer, warmer. But now the room was shifting, shifting, and Amara seemed to be listing to one side.

"You look pale, Opal." She was patting my hand between hers.

No, no. It was my fault—I was just— It was just my low tolerance for wine and it was late and I was overheated. I stammered in the dimness as I fumbled about for my purse. Our cheeks pressed in a clumsy, hurried embrace before I dashed down Amara's porch steps and into the humid night.

When I rose the following morning, I could see, through my bedroom window, that the sky was cloudless, almost lavender, weather that normally filled me with optimism, but on this morning made my chest ache. Overnight, a handful of the fern's leaves had shriveled. Had I given it too much sun or too little? Unsure, I watered it, plucked the dried sections, and after some consideration, found a new spot for it on my coffee table. I gulped a glass of vegetable juice, gobbled a small handful of berries, then rummaged through the embroidered cloth box where I stored baubles I had collected over the years until I found a pair of tiger-eye earrings Amara had complimented a few days before. When she mentioned them today, I would pull them from my ears and fold them into her palm, proof that there need be no awkwardness between us. "I do love you," I would whisper. Then she would know that, though my feelings for her were different from what she had hoped, they ran just as deep.

Along my route to the gallery, I fiddled with the dangling earrings, my stomach beginning to churn. I tried to imagine how we would greet each other. The gift of the earrings would help heal any hurt pride, any discomfort, wouldn't it? Still, until then, what would we speak of?

But I could have spared myself these worries because Amara, for the first morning in the three months I'd known her, was late for work. In fact, she did not appear until close to noon, and when she finally arrived, gave a hurried apology but no explanation for her absence. For once there seemed little time for chitchat; the gallery was busier than usual, the seats around the health bar filled, and Amara had to use the slower moments for the paperwork and phone calls she had missed that morning.

"Thank you, again, for dinner," I said during a brief spell of quiet, offering a section of the apple I had just sliced, hoping to find some way to ease into a discussion of what I was certain had almost occurred between us.

But Amara only smiled and blew a stream of air between her teeth as if to say my expression of gratitude was an unnecessary formality, as though nothing whatsoever had happened. "Oh, you don't have to *thank* me, Opal." Then "Pretty earrings," she added, as if she had never seen them before, and returned to her work too quickly for any further interchange.

At the end of the afternoon, Marco Everly came back in. Calliope had left hours earlier and Amara had disappeared again, too, driving to

Cape Coral to meet with a photographer friend whose work we would be exhibiting in late fall. I wished Marco hadn't reappeared, showing up now when I was alone, interrupting time I needed to think.

"I've done a few new paintings. I thought it couldn't hurt to ask if they might be of interest." His smile was all sunshine.

But I disliked his new paintings more than those he'd shown me the first time. These were of carnival performers—jugglers, clowns, a tattooed man—all posturing in a Toulouse-Lautrec sort of style. The reds and yellows in the nighttime scenes jarred, and the exaggerated angles of the figures felt garish.

"You're not a fan," he said, smiling but with something sober in his cheeks now, amused and disappointed at the same time.

"To be honest, I find them a bit dislocating but not in a way that's understandable."

"Dislocating but not understandable? Wow! You're a tough critic." He tugged at his earlobe as if forming a thought, as if I had all the time in the world to muse over his artistic style.

"I'm sorry, but I'm just getting ready to close up," I began to say. But he was talking again—

"I'm at a loss, I suppose, to prove my meaning. But are you going to tell me you understand *these*?" He gestured to Lee Claybourne's watercolors currently on display, depictions of placid pine groves, of window-boxed cottages nestled behind sand dunes. "Do *they* mean something?"

"They don't have to mean something for me to admire them." I admired them for the mood they created, I was about to say. Instead I turned to the register, intending for him to leave.

"Okay. I can take a hint!" he laughed, and closed his portfolio case. "Are you always so serious, Opal?" He turned as he reached the door. "You are, aren't you, but I'm fond of you anyway." He grinned almost too brightly as he had the first time we'd met.

What nerve he had! Returning to the gallery, suggesting his work had value beyond what we were showing, attempting to endear himself to me.

When I saw Amara the next day, I would tell her every maddening detail. And we would criticize the whole interchange and the presumptuousness of men.

Over the next days and weeks, Amara missed another three mornings. More than once, she disappeared for an hour or two at midday. And now, rather than lingering after five to share an additional cup of tea, as had been our habit, she appeared in a hurry to rinse the last of the glasses, plates, and spoons, to empty the register, and close the store. So I had wounded her more than I'd known. I needed to make her understand that the mere thought of this made my head throb with surging tears. I ached as much as she! Maybe more. But each time I attempted a conversation, she winked at me or smiled broadly, often giving mere half-answers to my questions, sometimes tapping a finger to her temple as if simultaneously trying to remember some other thought. How masterfully she masked her feelings. How unusually cheerful she seemed, humming to herself as she readjusted any of the framed pieces that had been nudged out of place during the day or tossed strawberries and sections of orange and honeydew into the blender.

Soon Amara made our shared exercise routine an impossibility as well. With her depleted hours at the gallery, there was no longer a free half hour for calisthenics. Perhaps I only needed to be patient, I told myself; perhaps, after a time, everything would return to normal.

It had been a week or more since I'd last worked on my drawings, and it occurred to me that showing them to Amara might be a good way to break the ice. I slid them into a plastic sleeve to bring with me to the gallery. But each day, Amara seemed more preoccupied, and a right moment to approach her with my work never seemed to arise. When we ran out of wheatgrass, of filters for the water purifier, of the soft cloths we used for dusting the frames of the artwork, she neglected to reorder; and when I pointed out these oversights, she only shrugged her shoulders and laughed. And now, to my irritation, when male customers fed her flirtatious lines, she no longer turned to me with a commiserating smirk, rather smiled to herself, as if she harbored some happy, private thought. So she was taunting me, punishing me. And though I tried to steel myself against her torments, I began to feel that if something did not change soon, I would fly into a hundred pieces. So one Friday, just before closing, I determined to confront her. She was spraying the spider plant in the front window.

"Oh, Opal!" She looked startled, jogged out of some reverie or surprised at my presence, as if she'd forgotten I had not yet left. "It's late, isn't it?" She glanced at her wrist, though she wore no watch, then slid one of the spider plant's spindly leaves between her forefinger and thumb. "Such pretty little things, aren't they? Simple but so lively. So what is it, Opal? What's on your mind? You look absolutely *tragic*."

I crossed my arms over my waist to hide their fidgeting. My lips went numb. But I had to speak. Yes, there were things that needed to be said. "We used to talk, Amara. You used to tell me things."

"Have I been distant lately? I'm sure you're right." She held her lower lip between her teeth, and I watched her work to suppress a smile. She gazed at me but with eyes unfocused. And as I studied her face, I knew—I had misunderstood—she faked nothing. She *was* happy. *I* alone suffered. And a familiar queasiness oozed through me, the same unease that had seized my stomach for days prior to each of Mother's announcements that we would, once again, be moving, a sinking feeling of what I had intuited was coming before she'd even said a word.

"Well, since you ask . . ." Amara was beaming now. The truth was she had met someone. A woman. Was I surprised? "I was slow to tell you only out of apprehension," she said. "It's not everyone who feels comfortable with such things. But you, of all people, Opal. I should have known better." She gave my elbow a squeeze.

Amara had met her at the small party she hosted the night before my birthday. Fosca had been her neighbor's houseguest for some weeks. She was from Florence originally but now lived in Nevada. "Las Vegas, of all places! Can you believe it?" She tossed her head nonchalantly, but crimson flowered across her cheeks as she spoke. And I noticed, as she lowered her eyelids, a pale dusting of sea green beneath her brow bones and faint yet unmistakable pencil lines darkening the rim above her lashes. Amara paused, her hands clasped behind her neck. I was aware that she awaited my reaction. But long seconds passed before I found the self-possession to mutter a choked "Congratulations."

"Thank you, Opal, thank you. So, listen! Fosca wants me to go away with her." Amara's voice grew louder, her words rushed. She clutched my fingers as if believing I shared her enthusiasm. "She needs to be in Rome for four weeks on business. At first I declined. You know, with all of the work we have here." She swept her hand through the air. But she knew how reliable I was, she said, and that with Calliope's help, I could handle things on my own for a while. Of course, she would pay me extra for my added responsibilities. Besides, it had been ages since she had taken a vacation, and didn't Italy sound too, too tempting?

I said almost nothing, only returned to some receipts I had been sorting, flicking each one to the counter with an audible snap of paper. What a fool she had made of me! Even if my wants had not been what she must have assumed. What right had she to say things, to make me believe things! A receipt fell from my hands to the floor beside my feet. I made no move toward it. Let Amara crouch to retrieve it! At the very least, she owed me this, this tiny gesture. Silently I took the slip from her, my face burning.

"We leave a week from tomorrow. For exactly a month," she promised. But I knew well how these things went: four weeks stretched into five, five into six, and so on.

"I'm so glad we had the chance to chat," Amara said as we stepped into the damp air of early evening. She locked the door behind us, oblivious that for the last thirty minutes I had spoken not a word. Then before parting, she kissed the top of my forehead, an old habit of Mother's when the thrill of a new man in her life filled her with uncontainable feelings of affection and largesse. I closed my fists, my nails biting into the flesh of my palms.

A mara had vowed to send postcards, snapshots, the predicted itinerary for her travels, but I counted on none and none arrived. The only contact information she had left me was a phone number for the pensione where she and Fosca planned to stay. "It's not necessary. I won't need it," I had told her, dropping the bit of paper dismissively onto one of the bamboo stools. But when I dialed it in a panic one afternoon, unable to find the shut-off valve for the back bathroom toilet, which had a tendency to overflow, the woman who answered explained in broken English—and shouldn't I have expected this?—that Miss Silver and her companion had vacated their room two days before.

On the morning before Amara's departure, she had handed me a page of notes, including numbers for the cleaning service and trash collector, directions to the bank where our weekly deposit was made, the hiding place beneath the bar where two spare keys and some "emergency" petty cash were kept. But nowhere did she list how to reset the alarm when it was triggered accidentally, how to compensate Calliope when she worked overtime, the proper procedure for returning incorrect orders to distributors. By the middle of each afternoon, my head ached from fury. I fantasized about the look on Amara's face when she returned after long months to find her store flooded with water from the broken sprinkler system, the gallery walls naked of art with no arrangements for future exhibits, imagined how she would gasp with horror and beg me to help her. I struggled to calm my nerves the only way I knew how: I ran both mornings and evenings now, worked through Amara's calisthenics routine in solitude in the quiet of my living room, afterward sipping tea with royal jelly. But even this seemed to do little good. Unopened mail began to pile on my kitchen table: bills, advertisements, letters from Mother and Kimberly that I could not find the will to open. I ignored the flashing red button on my answering machine, messages from Ruth and Fran and Setsu, I guessed, because I had neglected to contact them this month, had not responded to their attempts to contact me. On days when business in the gallery was slow, I spent hours perched on one of the stools of the health bar with a stack of magazines and books and newspaper cross-words. On the days Calliope came, she would join me for a time, then disappear to the back room to make murmured phone calls to her boyfriend.

During the first week or two after Amara was gone, I had kept care-ful track of the days, but after a while, time began to blur. I would wake without knowing if it was Thursday or Monday or Saturday, needing to switch on the local news to check whether or not I needed to dress for work. I rotated the same few outfits, having no desire to search my clos-ets for the skirts or tops I thought most became me. And I must have managed to brush my teeth, scrub my face, to pin up my hair with no more than a glance in the mirror, because what stared back at me one Sunday afternoon, from the glass walls of the yoga center that Amara had recommended, stopped my breath. My complexion under the fluorescent lights was white and flat as paper. The knot into which I had pulled my hair accented the shadows below my eyes and new faint lines etched on either side of my mouth. And there, in Studio Three of the yoga center, as I studied my reflection, without warning, a sob swelled from the very depths of me.

That night I sat at my kitchen table and sorted through the stack of neglected cards and letters. I listened to my string of outdated phone messages. Why hadn't I called them back? Setsu and Fran and Ruth wanted to know. Should they be worried? So many calls they'd filled my answering machine. I had considered giving up on them, but I under-stood now they were not giving up on me. The final recording on the machine, now a week old, was from Setsu. She would be arriving in Fort

Myers the following Thursday and could use company while she was in town, she said. Was I around? She still hadn't heard back from me. It would be good to talk to a friend. "James and I have been having some trouble lately. Maybe it doesn't surprise you. I know you never liked him. And maybe years ago I should have listened. Anyway, I can never, *ever* get you at home. But please let me know if you have time next week. Call me, okay?"

I played her message a second time and then again. Yes, I thought I could discern it, could hear it in the softening of her voice, her genuine wish to make things right between us.

O pal, I'm so glad you called back. Where did you disappear to? Anyway, it's so great to see you!" she said when we met for coffee near her hotel her first afternoon in Florida. She asked about the artist we were showing now at the gallery, about how I was getting along without Amara. She quizzed me about my drawings, the books I had been reading. She talked about a recent trip to Los Angeles she had taken for her job, her coworkers at the investment bank where she had been employed since June, and then of James. For some time she'd had suspicions, sickening doubts. But James denied every insinuation, accused *her* of degrading their relationship, of wearing away at it with every question, every evidence of mistrust. But this last time, she'd seen it with her own eyes.

"I'm sorry for what you've been through, Setsu," I said.

"You probably think I'm ridiculous. You've always been so smart about men."

My voice cracked with the start of a laugh, a sound I had not intended to make. So smart for years I'd hardly moved, hardly taken a breath. "No, I don't think you are ridiculous, not at all." And then I told her. The secret from childhood I'd never before had the courage to speak aloud. Yes, I knew, too, terrible, terrible dangers that could come from seeking affection in the wrong places. But I was beginning to see that at some point, yes, we had to cut loose old hurts, or they would swell and swell until they infected the parts of our true selves that remained.

W̲e made plans to meet again on Setsu's final day in Fort Myers. That morning she called me at home. By the way, she said, she had just discovered that one of the analysts at her firm who'd also come for the seminar, Charlie Blithe, was a fellow Brown alum, graduating only a year ahead of us. "And he remembers you, Opal. Do you know him?"

I had a vague memory of having met Charlie at some International Awareness Fair in the gymnasium at the end of my junior year. He had managed the Latin American table, crammed with plates of fried plantains and mangoes, stacks of books by Gabriel García Márquez, postcards of Rio de Janeiro and the rain forests of Costa Rica. During the hour or so I had spent at the fair, I passed his table twice. The first time, he shyly offered a plantain, the second, attempted a conversation about literature, accidentally tearing the cover of one of Márquez's books as he spoke and neglecting to attend to two other customers. I remembered whispering to Fran as we walked away that if his responsibility was to sell food and books, he was doing a rotten job. "Do you ever give *anybody* a chance?" Fran had laughed, nudging my shoulder with hers. "No!" I'd answered, coming to a full halt in the middle of the crowded floor, shrugging without turning to her, which had made us collapse into giggles.

How long, long ago this seemed, but I could still smell the tangy, thick scent of the gym, still hear the reverberations of our laughter in the high-ceilinged hall. And I felt, once again, what I had tried to hide from Fran at the time—the straining in my cheeks as I fought to keep my hilarity from disintegrating into tears. Tears at the recognition of a truth that had been closing me in like a fortress.

"Charlie said he would be meeting some friends later today. Do you want me to ask them to join us?" Setsu asked.

But I told her, if she did not mind, there was someone else I might like to invite—an artist who'd twice brought his work to the gallery and who, just the other day, had stopped in to see me, asking me to lunch, though at the time I'd refused.

Marco's friend owned a restaurant downtown, he told me after he got over the surprise of my phone call. "Carmine's. It's pub fare mostly—burgers and melted cheese sandwiches, chicken fingers, though I think they have some salads. Of course, we can always go somewhere else. You'll probably want to run a full marathon to work off his meal!" Marco laughed. "It won't be the health stuff you sell at the gallery!"

"Thanks for the warning, but it's okay!" I told him, something in me, as I laughed, breaking free, sailing upward. "Yes, Carmine's will be fine."

At long last, I discovered what had been missing from the sketches I'd worked on these many months. What had kept the parts disjointed was not some inadequacy of technique. Rather, in trying to make everything perfect, I had been afraid to risk and so had created nothing that satisfied. So I returned to the drawings, this time using bolder lines, freer strokes. And with these changes, the sketches came to life, becoming what I must have always, somehow, known they should be but had to dare to make true.

THE BRIDE

(Francesca's Story)

· 1994 ·

A month before my twenty-fourth birthday, I returned to New York, to a one-bedroom off Central Park West. What I had been offered, through a friend of my parents, was an editorial position at *Real*, a new magazine that encouraged a realistic portrayal of women. The models, though attractive, were average-sized, many of them big-boned, even plump. The focus was on healthy attitudes, self-acceptance. Articles included autobiographical pieces by prominent female figures—politicians, social activists, artists—as well as by recovering anorexics and bulimics. Each issue featured suggestions for preparing foods you loved. The words "skinny" and "diet" were strictly taboo. "Our goal is to empower women," Myra Jones, the editor in chief, reminded the staff during our frequent meetings. And when she smacked her palms on the arms of her chair for emphasis, a shiver shot through me as I thought of the important work we were doing, this strong, new voice of which I was a part.

After graduation I had spent two years in Europe teaching English to Parisian schoolchildren. For a time, this had felt like an adventure. I lived in Paris's fourth arrondissement in a flat with two Florentine women. But I had sensed the criticisms of the mothers and nannies who retrieved my students at the end of each afternoon, always smiling, greeting me politely, but taking in every inch from my neck to my ankles behind their lightly shaded glasses. And, eventually, I'd had my fill of their silent judgments, the narrow-mindedness of a people in a country of scrawny-assed women.

I believed with Myra that, at *Real*, external appearances mattered little, were, in fact, practically insignificant. No one on the staff took notice of colleagues' lunches, the number of sugar cookies or glazed doughnuts snatched from the afternoon snack tray. Each morning when I dressed, I chose whatever struck my fancy, confident that if the cut of my pants, the lines of my skirt accentuated my widest parts, I would receive no disapproving stares. If I gained a pound or two, it would go unnoticed. Even the few men on the staff had refreshing attitudes. Here we were all professionals: we were independent and equal, appreciative of one another for our talents, our beliefs. In any other setting, I would have bristled when Carlos, a member of *Real*'s creative team as well as one of its photographers, bent close, studying my features, the dark curls of his hair almost falling over mine. I would have told him just exactly what he could do with his *goddamned* camera when he asked in his lilting, slightly Spanish accent whether I would agree to a shoot, whether I knew what a very photogenic face I had. But this place was different. So when he invited me to pull at my blouse, revealing my shoulders, to "be sexy, Francesca. Don't be afraid to be sexy," I saw there was nothing lewd in his smile, no lascivious expression in his eyes. For him, I knew, this was serious work; it was art.

I had a photographer's eye, good instincts, Carlos said, and he began to ask me to critique the shots he planned to submit for each upcoming issue. He brought his lunch to my desk, double portions so that I could share. When we had finished, he would disappear to the bakery on the first floor of our building and return with a slice of fruit pie or a square of frosted cake and two forks. I ate un-self-consciously in his presence; I was comfortable with him. So when he confessed he needed a roommate to split the cost of his Greenwich Village apartment, that he hoped I would give this some consideration, I could see no reason not to. Adamant that I would no longer rely on my parents' supplements, my own rent payments had been a stretch of late. And the thought that they would cringe at this living arrangement only made it more appealing.

Carlos's apartment was a loft with windows that reached nearly from floor to ceiling. The kitchen, dining, and living areas were spacious, all flowing into one another. The walls were hung with large-scale black-and-white photos of women, many of which I recognized from old copies of *Real*. In one corner, beside two sofas, stood an easel displaying an unfinished canvas of bold, abstract shapes. Down a narrow hall were two bedrooms—a smaller one, which Carlos had taken, and a larger one, which he had generously cleared for me.

As I soon learned, Carlos loved to cook. The lunches we'd been splitting over the past several weeks, he admitted, had been his own creations. And now that he would no longer be eating the majority of his dinners alone, he said, he was inspired to prepare his favorite dishes. So as soon as we returned home from work, he would turn on a recording of some famous Spanish vocalist or guitarist and begin a slow-cooking stew or casserole—paella or poached fish and potatoes, scallops in tomato sauce. As in Spain, where Carlos had spent the first sixteen years of his life, we ate late and emptied glasses of sherry or sangria while pots bubbled on the stove, roasting pans simmered in the oven. We talked for hours, amazed by our common frustrations with society, our shared understanding of the traps people fell into, the things they did out of weakness. How many couples we could both name—we counted them on our fingers—who had married in blind imitation of their parents. How many women, upon reaching a certain age, attached themselves to the nearest man who offered stability. It was pitiful—these decisions that came from fear, from insecurity, the very things we at *Real* were hoping to counter.

"There should be more women like you," Carlos would say as he spooned potatoes with paprika sauce onto my plate.

I would laugh dismissively, fanning my hand before my face, shooing away his comments.

"No, no, Francesca, I am serious. You are strong. You don't care about the meaningless opinions of others. Such an admirable quality, for a woman especially, I think."

He admired, too, my sense of adventure, as I did his. Life was not meant to be met on one's ass, hands cupped passively in one's lap awaiting whatever dropped into them. No! One was meant to march purposefully into life, we agreed, shaping it as one went. We were drawn to what energized us. We both loved the crackling charge of New York, and I loved Carlos's descriptions of it: its currents pulsed deep into the ground, skyward through its towers, he said, and outward in all possible directions from its broadest avenues to its remotest alleys. He guessed that I, as he, pulled energy from nature, too. Was he right? Because he needed it, craved it from time to time. He'd welcome my company if I ever wished to hike with him. He went many Saturdays and Sundays. And he could see I might like it.

"Sure, why not," I told him. "Sounds like fun." I'd bought hiking boots two years earlier in France, planning to spend some of my holidays trekking the countryside of Provence. But these had turned, instead, into driving tours through Burgundy and seaside visits to Nice and Saint-Tropez—Natalia and Mona, who'd shared my flat, averse to any exercise more strenuous than strolls through dress shops or food markets.

The first morning I joined him Carlos smiled as I pulled my hair into an elastic, looping my ponytail through the opening at the back of my Brown University baseball cap. "Easy as the breeze," he'd winked. "Why must some women torture themselves before the mirror for hours, fussing over every lash, every pore? It can be maddening!" And I'd wondered for a moment about the women Carlos had dated, women, I imagined, who reapplied lipstick before gym workouts, who, before evenings out, kept Carlos waiting as they considered the complete contents of their wardrobes.

"Are you sure you haven't done this before? You're a natural," he told me an hour or so into our hike. We were a morning's drive northwest of the city, navigating a section of the Appalachian Trail Carlos had tackled a few years before. I'd surprised him, he admitted, how well I'd negotiated the steep paths, slick in spots from thawing ice, crossed by streambeds of wet, loosened rocks.

"Guess I'm just a sucker for a challenge," I laughed, adjusting the brim of my cap.

As we continued our climb, I could feel Carlos watching from his position two steps behind me, so I did not admit to the contracting in my legs or that this gradually turned to a smoldering. But I was able to tolerate it and even manage a smile when we returned to our starting point, where Carlos squeezed my shoulders with enthusiasm and approval.

On another trip, I impressed him further, hardly groaning when I lost my footing on a skin of decaying leaves, landing on a stone sharp enough to slice my jeans and leave a small gash across my kneecap. "I'm really sorry, Francesca." Carlos swabbed the cut with peroxide, patched it with a bandage from the first aid kit in his backpack. "Should we head back? I should have warned you this trail can be treacherous in places."

But when I insisted on forging ahead, he smiled as if he'd suspected I would choose to continue.

"How are you feeling?" he asked some time later.

"Great!" I called over my shoulder, though my knee still throbbed like a bitch in heat.

. . .

Carlos had no shortage of compliments. He respected so many things about me, he said, not the least of which was my appetite, my clear love of food. God, if he counted the girlfriends who'd refused to admit hunger, who were afraid to finish a meal! . . . And I imagined a whole parade of them, skinny as paper dolls in dresses small as swatches. I wondered if one of them had been Petra, who'd left two messages on our phone since I'd moved in. "But *you* don't worry about conforming; *you* do what you enjoy," Carlos said. "There's something so sensuous about a woman who admits her pleasures, don't you agree?" We ate gazpacho and garlic soup, prawns and empanadas, fried custard squares and flan until even my roomier clothes grew too tight and I needed to make after-work visits to the retail shops in the neighborhood for looser dresses and blouses and skirts.

People who ate daintily, dabbing at every trickle of juice or crumb, were not truly experiencing their food, Carlos insisted. When my lips turned dark from gravy or glistened with basil oil, he was happy, he said, because he knew I was eating with passion. Then, sometimes, he would startle me by rising suddenly to his feet. "Beauty! Beauty!" He would dive for his camera and snap photos as I licked a drip of red wine from the edge of my glass or sucked the pulp from a crab leg.

It was one such evening that, after pushing his camera aside, he pulled me to him, his hands unfastening the hair clip at the base of my neck, the ties of my dress. In the dark of his room, stretched out on his duvet, he propped himself up on one elbow before drawing me close and whispered, "This is okay, isn't it, Francesca? We are both adults, yes?" And from this I understood that he sought pleasure, not obligation.

"Yes, yes, of course." I tilted my head back and laughed, showing him that I, too, was independent, free from the need for emotional attachments.

Later, on nights like this, Carlos would close his eyes, arms thrown back over his head as we lay side by side, and hum snatches of melodies from the Francisco Tárrega or Andrés Segovia CDs we had listened to earlier in the evening. Afterward, when I stood to return to my own room, he would grab strands of my hair and murmur, "Francesca, you're amazing." And I knew it was my ability to enjoy him as he had me, without further entanglements, that he was praising.

Other nights, when Carlos filled our bathroom with the scent of cologne and dressed in his most tailored pants and the silky shirts that rippled over his arms and chest as he moved, the ones he saved for evenings out, I asked no questions. I merely waved a hand, hoping to seem casual as he walked to the door. This was our unspoken arrangement. If I had been the one leaving, I knew he would do the same.

After he had gone, I would search the fridge for leftovers or turn to the stack of takeout menus we left at the center of our coffee table, then press the Play button on the living room stereo and listen to whatever recording Carlos had left in from the night before. Sometimes I flipped through the pages of my address book and directories from high school and from Brown, marking the names of women I knew who might take an interest in *Real*. I sent the most recent issue to all former BREMUSA members. For Opal and Setsu and Ruth, I included the gift of a year's subscription, though I was not sure what they would think of the publication. I hadn't mentioned it when we'd spoken just a week before, as we always did at the beginning of each month. And I'd hesitated before sending Ruth's, not sure how she'd interpret it. *Let's get together soon*, I wrote on a note taped to her magazine's front cover. *Let me know if this is of any interest.* After our junior year, Ruth and I had rarely spoken of BREMUSA, and never of our day on Moon Beach, my accusations. "I'm not one to make formal apologies," I told her during the week we had packed our belongings for the last time, our final week at college and as suitemates. "It's okay. That was long ago," she had said, her arms full of packing tape, folded lavender sheets and pillowcases. She had understood my meaning. At the end of the previous spring, after Brian had left for Ontario, Ruth hadn't cried as I'd thought she would. But for some time she'd spent most of her waking hours behind her closed door, suddenly interested only in her studies. This was temporary, though, I'd thought then, nothing she couldn't get over, with a little determination, in a matter of days. But as I sealed her copy of *Real* in its padded envelope, I wondered if her struggle had lasted longer than I had at first assumed.

I n February, overnight, snow blanketed the city, a deep layer like some giant feather mattress. Cushions of snow capped street lamps, filled the square beds along the sidewalks where trees were planted, lined fences and windowsills, drifted up along the brick walls of buildings, the doors of half-buried cars, stuck in small clots to tree trunks. Carlos was out of town in the Carolinas until Monday. "Just a weekend with a couple of old college friends," he'd explained as he filled his leather travel bag with slacks and shirts, his shaving kit, a change of shoes. Petra had left a message again, but I'd heard Carlos delete it before bothering to listen to it in its entirety. It meant nothing, silly to think she had anything to do with his weekend away.

The whiteness of outside must have made my room brighter than usual, and I woke early. I dug out my snow boots and hat from one of the boxes at the back of my closet I'd never unpacked, zipped my parka over my sweater and long johns, and strapped Carlos's camera around my neck. Still shaking off sleep, I tripped down the three flights of stairs and out into the transformed street—glittering and softened. I photographed as much as I could capture—a few snapshots to keep but most to show Carlos. "Should I tell you to take care of yourself? Not to miss me too desperately?" he had joked just before leaving. "No, not you, Francesca, who is always, always just fine on her own!" At one point I had made plans for Opal to stay with me while Carlos was gone. She would be traveling north to the Boston area for two job interviews, she'd told me. She could stop through New York on her way so that we could spend a couple of days together. But at the last minute, because of the winter storm, she'd needed to make rearrangements—flying directly to Logan, avoiding the snow.

A blond couple I recognized from one of the buildings across the street was completing a life-sized snowman, smoothing out a lumpy section near its middle, adding a turnip nose, sprigs of parsley for hair. When they'd finished, the woman lifted her face to the man's and he bent down and kissed the tip of her nose. "Magical out here, isn't it?" They turned to me before climbing the steps to their building.

"Yes!" I waved. I hoped I hadn't been too obviously watching them. I had a sudden urge to call Carlos, to try to explain what he was missing. But it wasn't even eight yet; he was surely still asleep.

I was on my own on the sidewalk now in a stillness that did not belong to the city. Nothing stirred but a few falling flakes. The only sounds were small and far away: the scrape of a snow shovel on some other block; children laughing, their voices seeming to echo from some distance. But this part I would not share with Carlos: how I began to feel a bit lonely after a while, gazing in solitude at the snowdrifts. I ran back inside for more layers, determined to trek through what would keep most others indoors or at least close to home. Maybe I would trudge as far north as Central Park. Then I would tell Carlos about my venture after he returned.

⟡

On the six-month anniversary of our moving in together, Carlos bought a bottle of champagne. He lifted his glass in a toast: "To the many ways you have enriched my life. You never cease to astound me, Francesca bonita. You are the most secure woman I know." He leaned forward somewhat awkwardly, shifting his champagne from one hand to the other as he kissed me, making me suddenly self-conscious and shy. Never having become an official couple, refusing to fall into dependent roles, we usually saved such gestures of affection for the bedroom. In public we eschewed such displays so that none of our colleagues ever guessed our relationship was anything but the most platonic of friendships.

Carlos and I did not speak of a shared future. I had gathered from a comment he'd once made that he felt this would shatter the spell, mar the beauty of all that was spontaneous and unrestrained between us. So it took me some time to truly understand what I discovered in his room the Saturday following our six-month celebration. I had woken late that morning to find him gone. The previous night, as we had stood undressing beside his bed, Carlos, kicking at the discarded pool of our clothes, had removed my earrings and a silver cuff bracelet from my wrist. "I want nothing but you," he'd said, and dropped them with a tinkling of metal on the surface of his bureau. Rarely did I enter his room when he was away, and I could not help feeling this was some sort of violation, but after a glance at the dresser's top, I saw that only one of my earrings remained beside my bracelet. So I began opening various drawers, rummaging through rolled socks and jockey shorts and stacks of magazines, thinking perhaps it had accidentally been swept in.

The small box was midnight blue leather and nestled between two folded T-shirts, a secret place not meant for my eyes. But my whole body seemed to pulse from the pounding of my heart, and the thought of not knowing made me shakier than the possibility of what might be inside. Oh! Oh, it was perfection! Carlos's sophisticated, elegant taste. A single round diamond, not ostentatious in size but shimmering and brilliant. I dared not touch the stone itself but ran my finger across the crushed velvet of the box's interior. How sweet Carlos's words had been to me the night before, but this, *this* I never could have dreamed. And I sank to his bed, unaware I had been crying until I saw the spots of wet on my lap. Always I had claimed this was something I was not sure I would want. But now that it was real, now that *he* was real . . . I closed my eyes and sighed with a happiness fuller than I had ever known.

Over the following days and weeks, Carlos seemed perplexed by my good humor. I caught him frowning when I sang along with the Spanish ballads I was beginning to learn or gave him unexpected squeezes from behind as he chopped onions and cilantro, rinsed mussels for our supper. To ensure that he would not guess the reason for my exuberance, I should have worked harder to maintain my usual habits, my former disposition. But what a struggle that would have been! I was far too joyful! Even the things that had once made me grind my jaw in anger or frustration seemed less irksome. When Mother called, wanting to send a few slimming items she'd picked up during her latest midtown shopping spree, I did not object. I refrained from argumentative retorts, disparaging comments when she bemoaned the most recent coif given her by her new hairdresser, the wine stains that had ruined a silk dress she'd planned to wear that weekend to a wedding for one of Father's business associates. Her concern over her appearance seemed suddenly less ridiculous.

In early April, a card arrived in my mail with a return address I did not recognize. Inside was a folded news clipping, a page of wedding announcements from a month earlier. At the top right of the page was a photograph of a buxom bride, ringlet curls too tightly coiled around her hairline and at her temples, her hand hooked through the arm of her groom, who grinned down at her proudly. Jesus! My high school friend Sharon. It had obviously been weeks since her ceremony, and she hadn't even called. Before my return from Paris, she had disappeared to graduate school on the West Coast. Over the past year or two, we'd talked only a handful of times. But she had phoned some months before to say she was engaged and that she and her fiancé, Claude, were planning a very small ceremony—just family—at Claude's parents' home in La Jolla. *Hi, Fran! Claude and I tied the knot in March!* she had written in the note attached to the announcement. *We are now living outside of San Diego. Just a plane ride away, so I hope you will come visit soon. I want you and Claude to meet.*

I studied every detail of her picture—the tilt of her head, her bouquet of pastel peonies, the delicate string of pearls about her neck, the sprinkling of beads at her waist. How boringly conventional, how un-enlightened, my coworkers and I had deemed posed images like this. But, gazing at Sharon, I saw something different now—a hopefulness in her diffident smile, the knowledge of reciprocated love in her shining eyes— things I now believed I understood. That night, as I leaned into the warmth of Carlos beside me, I thought of Sharon—of the boys we'd known in ju-nior high who'd teased her for her ears and for her constant rash of pim-ples, and of the many she'd been sick over in the years afterward, telling me not so long ago she'd just about given up on ever finding anyone. And now *this*. One decision, one moment could transform everything.

The next morning, stepping from the shower, I glimpsed my reflec-tion in the wall mirror and loosened the towel wrapping my hair, drap-ing it like a veil. How the staff at *Real*, if they'd known, would have ridiculed me, but I was too elated to care.

I made no conscious decision to restrict my diet, to hold back from in-dulging. But the muffins and brownies passed each afternoon at work from desk to desk tempted me less. How bland food suddenly seemed, how mundane compared to the things that now preoccupied me.

At first Carlos did not seem to notice my decreased appetite, but af-ter some days, I saw that during dinners, glancing at the fork and knife at rest on my plate beside my unfinished food, he shifted in his chair as if he could not make his legs comfortable. "Is it overly salted? Too many spices for your taste?" he wanted to know when I shook my head at sec-onds. For a night or two, I imagined, he assumed I was simply not feeling myself, but after several evenings of this, he drew another conclusion.

"Ai, yi, what is this sudden self-denial? Since when did you want to be so skinny? Skinny like the runway models? This is not the Francesca I know." The music from the stereo, though soft and melodic, seemed suddenly to irritate him, and pushing his plate aside with a clattering of silverware, he rose to mute it.

Someday, I thought, with a secretive smile he could not yet understand, I would be able to tease him about his pouting, his sudden flashes of temper. For now I would simply try coaxing him into a better mood. Laughing, I stood and joined him where he leaned, his back to me, his palms flattened against the living room window. I wrapped my arms around his waist and pressed my cheek to the hollow between his shoulder blades. "What if I told you, you make me too happy to eat," I whispered, feeling him flinch.

For much of the next week, I saw little of Carlos. He had no obligation to tell me where he disappeared to, but after my discovery of the box . . . I suppose I had begun to make presumptions. For four straight days, I met him only passing in the hallway as he rushed to the door. He seemed fretful, only half aware of my presence. He took no notice of the reddish-gold highlights I'd threaded through my hair or of the new jojoba oil perfume I had begun to spray on my throat and wrists. Many men, I'd heard, grew skittish and withdrawn before mustering the courage to ask the most significant of questions. So I wouldn't push. I would remain patient and approachable.

One evening Carlos arrived home early, having been out for little over an hour. Not expecting him back for some time, I had lathered my forehead and nose with a cleansing scrub, combed a hot oil treatment into my damp hair. I flushed at the thought of my appearance when he called my name, but after a moment, realized that Carlos hardly saw me. He sank into a couch and began scratching at a clump of hair near his temple. He wished to apologize, he said. He had been snappish lately, short with me. He was sorry I had borne the brunt of troubles that did not involve me in the slightest. He hesitated, rapping his knuckles against the tops of his thighs. There was someone—a woman. "I can tell you, yes? Always our relationship has been an honest and open one. For you, too, Francesca, so attractive, so capable, I can only guess there have been others as well."

For an instant, he paused as if awaiting some confirmation. But I said nothing, only wiped from my face as much of the cleanser as I could with the sleeve of my robe. Even had I wanted to reply, the words would have stuck to the roof of my mouth. My chest, my ribs, my lungs felt suddenly compressed as they had in childhood when, learning to skate, I had fallen forward, smacking the hard ice.

"She's not like you. She's so . . . *so* erratic. One day she wants one thing, the next day . . . God! All women should be as rational as you, Francesca. Isn't that what I have always said?"

From the periphery of my down-turned eyes, I could see that he was attempting to flash me a smile. But I did not raise my head, pretending to be busy with a loose bit of skin along the side of my thumbnail, wishing he would look away from my baggy robe, my hair hanging in limp strings, my face caked with white.

"So if I have been edgy lately . . . It's just, you know, sometimes she makes me *crazy*." Carlos stretched out this last word, rolling the *r*, his accent thickening. Then, letting out a soft yet audible stream of air through his teeth, he pressed his fingers between his knees until I could see streaks of white between the veins of his hands. And as he did, I understood what I should have always suspected, that what lay protected in velvet in his bureau drawer had never been meant for me.

I t took me no more than two weeks to sign a lease for a one-bedroom sublet in a brownstone on the Upper East Side and, through the same friend of my parents who had found me my position at *Real*, to make contact with the editors of another fledgling magazine. The focus of this publication was outdoor recreation, a subject about which I was far less passionate; but, I told myself, I was in no position to be choosy.

Carlos was distraught. As I packed my belongings in cardboard boxes, he pestered me with questions. He hovered at the edge of my desk at work while I organized papers, emptied folders. "What is it, Francesca? Is it something I've done? Is it the things I confessed the other night? Because I thought you and I had agreed. I thought we understood each other."

I said nothing, wanting him to beg, to sicken and choke on his own regrets. But I knew he was right. *He* had betrayed nothing. *I* had been the fool. *I* was the one who had filled my head with silly notions, sugary delusions.

In the past, when faced with a setback, a bit of hard luck, quickly I had dusted off disappointment, the grit of humiliation. More than once friends had marveled at my capacity for nearly instant recoveries. This was my trademark. "You're a rock, Francesca," they'd said. "If only we could be more like you!" So I refused to be shaken by this nonsense with Carlos, to be haunted by a few sentimental and short-lived daydreams. Evening after evening, I stayed awake for hours watching late-night talk shows so that I would stumble into bed exhausted—no time for remembering or wondering, for running a hand in the dark over the cool of the empty sheet beside me. Each morning I made long lists of daily errands—notes to write, calls to return, chores to be completed in my new apartment—revising them regularly, filling my mind with practical matters, filling my schedule, stopping up the spaces where loneliness tried repeatedly to seep in.

As the newest member of *Outdoor Playground* (or *OP*, as I learned to call it), I would exude the same professionalism and confidence I had been known for at *Real*. But small things, I found to my disgust, began to unhinge me. Criticisms for an editorial mistake that had not been mine stunned me. An exasperated glance from Jo Redding, one of the ad executives, whom I'd accidentally jostled at the ladies' room sinks, made my eyes smart. And then this: twice within the same week a fitful dream about Sanjeev, the friend of Setsu and Ruth with whom I'd spent a spring afternoon at the beach years before. In both dreams, I lost him in a crowded market square. I had an important message to give him, but in the chaos of vendors hawking wares and throngs of shoppers and pedestrians, he is impossible to find. I had woken cold with sweat, un-nerved by the strangeness of the dream and my mind's unearthing of bur-ied memories.

Soon my appetite seemed as unpredictable as my moods. For days on end, I would desire little, feeling sated, even bloated, after a mere but-tered roll, a modest bowl of soup. But after these periods of abstinence came roaring, ravenous hunger, the amount I could consume sometimes frightening me. And the fullness that followed was not accompanied by the thrill of protest or the satisfaction of having scoffed at societal pres-sures, but rather by nausea, stomach cramps, a lethargy resulting from my own insufficient will.

So this was no time to be embarking on a new relationship. This was a time, I told myself, for self-fortification, for weeding out the thoughts, the habits that were softening me, weakening me. What did I care that Jonathan, one of *OP*'s staff writers, flashed me dimpled grins across the table during meetings? That he left gifts on my desk of boxed pencils, notepads, and paperclips from the supply room, and, one day, even a small grass nest with two bluish eggs inside, which he had found beneath an oak in Central Park? He'd mistaken me for the sort of woman who'd be charmed by this kind of attention. But he was knocking at the wrong door. This was the *last* thing I needed.

"You are wasting your energy," I told him when he asked me for the third time in as many weeks to join him for dinner. But he was undaunted by my rebuffs and only shook his head, smiling as if still unconvinced by my refusals.

The stronger Francesca, the Francesca I had been just months before, would have stood her ground. With each of Jonathan's advances, she would have toughened further until he had thrown up his hands in defeat. But in my current uncertain, distracted state, I could not master the will for prolonged opposition, and on what must have been his fifth or sixth attempt to date me, I gave in.

What I swore to myself would last only one evening turned into two, then three, then Saturday afternoon strolls around the park's boating lake and picnic sandwiches under the trees along the edge of the Great Lawn. Despite myself, I found I thought often of Sharon, wondering what it was about Claude that had made her fall in love. Something about the way Jonathan pulled absentmindedly at the back of his hair when concentrating or cocked his head to one side when listening for birdcalls or to far-off music or to me as I spoke, reminded me of how my brother, Christopher, had looked when we were young, drawing close to me, losing himself in the stories he liked for me to read him from our *Treasury of Children's Tales.* Time and again I stopped the instinct to ruffle Jonathan's hair, to fold my hand in his.

Just after the Memorial Day holiday, Mother called to say she had run into the Frasiers having lunch at Olivia's. Sharon and her new husband had been with them, having flown east for the long weekend. "She asked for your number. She said she would give you a call soon."

"Oh, that's nice." But it irritated me the way Mother said it as if she thought I'd been anxious for such news. And I felt suddenly irritated with myself, too, remembering my sappy reaction to Sharon's wedding announcement. Years ago, when Sharon and I were girls, our families had both frequented Olivia's for Sunday brunches, often sitting just tables apart. Sharon always coloring contentedly in her yellow Disney coloring book or—when we were older—looking up at her parents every now and then, between small, polite bites of her French toast, to add chirping comments to their anecdotes or observations. How was it she remained oblivious to Father's smiling winks at her mother over the heads of the other diners (gestures I knew my own mother pretended not to see, stiffening in her chair, her cheeks pink)! Sharon was blind as a mole rat! But I knew what Mother and Father were thinking: that it was too bad *I* couldn't uncross my arms and be as pleasant as Sharon was. I'd known it by the way Mother invited me into contrived, cheerful conversations. But this had only made arguments swirl up in me like hot, twisting air before I stuffed down my cheese omelet. And later, I would congratulate myself for my fortitude, for refusing to imitate goody-two-shoes Sharon.

Why, exactly, was Mother phoning now anyway? It was the third time since last Monday. Was she checking up on me? Because of my silly sniffling during one or two of my calls after I'd moved out of Carlos's? Would she hint around again about Jonathan as she had the last time we spoke, annoyingly remarking on how thoughtful he sounded? Did she think talk of Sharon's happiness would fill me with sentiment, inspire me to find this for myself? She spoke of Sharon's new haircut—short, but according to her, surprisingly flattering. The sweet cape near Coronado Beach she and Claude were hoping to buy—they'd shown Mother and Father a picture. The job Claude would eventually be taking in the West Coast branch of Mr. Frasier's firm. I imagined Mother cooing over Sharon and her husband and the Frasiers as they nibbled their chicken crêpes and watercress salads. I had not yet told Mother what I had discovered after rereading Sharon's announcement: Claude was a graduate of Oceanside High School, no mention of a college. And Sharon with her bachelor's and her master's. There would be worlds of things they could never *begin* to discuss. Great dull spots in their shiny future. But something about the way Mother's breath dropped into a slow hum made me stop myself.

"She just seemed *happy*," Mother said, and then, for a time, she was quiet—while the faint treble of Judy Garland's voice sounded from her stereo—as if she were remembering something she'd once wished for, something she thought Sharon had found.

S pring unwound into summer and then early fall. Despite my better judgment, Jonathan and I began to spend longer days together—all-day Sunday excursions to Cold Spring Harbor or up the Palisades Parkway to Bear Mountain. On one drive to Boscobel, a historic home and museum along the Hudson, Jonathan pulled the car over to watch a red-tailed hawk perched on a high, thin limb. He leaned forward to give me a better view. "They look so stoic, but did you know red-tails mate for life? It makes you wonder if their feelings run deeper than we know." Jonathan squinted, gazing through the windshield, then turned to me with the same look of appreciation and intensity. And I felt he was seeing through me to things that had never been uttered aloud, but things he somehow understood.

I had quarreled with myself over the best time to bring things to a close. The following Saturday, during a weekend in New Hampshire, I told him point-blank. It was what I had been meaning to say for weeks, even months: "I'm sorry. Very sorry. You and I want different things. I'm just not looking for anything long-term." But when I spoke them, the words sounded all wrong. I had practiced them at home so that I would not falter, but each time, a conversation I'd once overheard between Ruth and Setsu our first year together returned to me:

"I could never be like Fran, could you?"

"No, it's funny, isn't it—the way she just needs no one at all."

Afterward—silently, behind my closed door, into a balled-up woolen scarf—ridiculously I had sobbed. Now, in Jonathan's presence, what I meant to be resistance began to unravel. And he had arguments: "Are you sure about this, Francesca? Please, I want to be with you. No, it's more than that. I feel—no, I *know*—I love you." He took one of my hands into both of his. "Do you think you might love me?" So I hesitated. For too long I wavered. Until it was too late. Until something broke and I succumbed, until all willpower faded.

⁓

Some lessons take longer to learn than others. If I had obeyed my own stubbornness, I could have gone a lifetime without ever learning mine. But as I gazed into Jonathan's eyes on the morning we were married, I understood with a certainty that steadied even my bridal jitters that I had been waging futile battles, seeking strength in empty places.

On the evening of our first wedding anniversary—before Jonathan's transition into finance, before my graduation from law school, before a house, before children—we left our rented apartment on East Eighty-first Street and took the Number Six train to Canal Street. From there we meandered to Mulberry in search of the most affordable yet romantic Italian restaurant we could find. To our delight, our host seated us at a small linen-covered table in the back corner of a lantern-lit patio. A breeze stirred the leaves of potted plants crowding the patio's high brick walls and swayed the strands of lanterns strung overhead. "Let's order whatever our waiter recommends," Jonathan suggested. So we were brought heirloom tomatoes and buffalo mozzarella, homemade linguini, paper-thin cutlets of veal with capers. A slow forkful and then another: the mozzarella sliding to the back of my mouth like milk, the veal melting on my tongue. And I realized as Jonathan paused to beam at me that I was not gobbling my food in defiance. My stomach did not churn from an emptiness I had never been able to fill. This was only pleasure. And for what seemed the first time in more years than I remembered, I could truly taste every flavor. Then when I'd savored enough mouthfuls, how surprisingly easy it seemed to push my plate aside. Too long it had taken. But now I knew. I felt what it meant to be satisfied.

THE GOOD SISTER

(Setsu's Story)

For two weeks, I learned when I arrived, Toru had left his bed only to bathe and to empty his bladder and bowels. "Such injustice!" Shiro mashed the flats of his palms together as we stood in the hall outside Toru's bedroom door. "I would take his place in this if I could." He reached for my hand as if to say, "Only you and I understand. We endure this together."

The three of us would now share Toru's apartment off Broadway on Manhattan's Upper West Side. Having both of us here, Shiro believed, might lift Toru's spirits. It was Shiro who had ushered me into the apartment as if he were the brother I had seen only occasionally over the past five years. "Please come in, little sister. Toru is sleeping. He needs his rest, so if you don't mind . . ." He had gestured toward my shoes, indicating that I should remove them and place them in the foyer on a small rack beside two pairs of men's loafers, one pair shiny and uncreased, a pricey brand I recognized as Toru's, the other misshapen and scuffed.

"Even the slightest noises disturb him these days. You can appreciate this, I'm sure."

Shiro had been one of a handful of Japanese music students whom Toru had taught until the illness, as he claimed, made teaching an impossibility. I remembered first meeting Shiro at Toru's concert in Franklin Center. He had sat in the front row, not far from my family, and for an hour and a half dabbed repeatedly at his nose with a handkerchief he kept wadded in the sleeve of his wool sweater. But not once did his eyes stray from the stage, from Toru's fixed jaw, his lightning fingers. After Toru's final encore, he had slipped eel-like through the crowd so that he could introduce himself to my parents and me, accompanying us to Toru's dressing room. As we walked, Shiro had trailed me so closely his shoes caught on the straps of my slingback heels. He had curled his fingers around the knob of my shoulder. "Tell me—what was it like?" he had said, leaning so close that I could see the flecks of yellow-brown in his black eyes. And so I had understood that he envied me, for *I* was the sister of Toru.

Shiro led me down a dimly lit corridor to the apartment's third and smallest bedroom, a room, I gathered, Toru had once used as an office. "Too much light is a source of irritation." Shiro pointed to the half-lowered shade. Then, for some seconds, he paused in my doorway. "Well, let me leave you to your unpacking," he said, still without shifting. He pulled a rumpled tissue from his breast pocket and blotted his nostrils. "It's really so good to have you." Here his voice cracked with sentiment. And though we had met only twice before, I sensed that if I had not stooped to unzip my bags, he would have approached to embrace me.

It was during my second month of unemployment that my mother had suggested I make the call to Toru. I was, once again, short on the payment for my studio rental in Cambridge. "You're twenty-five, Setsu. He's your brother. How many years will you let pass?" She had sniffled with relief when I eventually acquiesced. "Life is too fragile to harbor grudges, don't you think?" By this she meant that now, with Toru's condition, it was petty to withhold forgiveness. Unreturned holiday calls, the mailed birthday gifts that went unrecognized, Toru's absence from my high school and college graduations, from the party my roommates had thrown the year I turned twenty-one (though he had been in Providence that weekend visiting friends)—these, in the scheme of things, were small matters.

But I knew the unspoken reason for my mother's request. I knew the guilt that plagued her now that she could only make occasional visits to Toru. In the winter she had required surgery to replace her hip. Trips to New York had become difficult for her, and she could make them only with my father's assistance, leaving her far less time for Toru. So I was the perfect solution, wasn't I? I who was always expected to sacrifice myself for Toru. Mother's conscience would be clear as sky after rain if I would only yoke myself to Toru in her stead. But it was unfair to blame her, self-ish, I knew, to expect her to give more consideration to my feelings with all that now weighed on her. Still, the truth of it was I would call because I feared if I didn't, I would make the same stupid, stupid mistake I had made too many times to count—give in to James, returning, despite what I knew. That there would always be others. Younger ones, doting ones, ones whose telltale scents lingered on James's hand towels, in the upholstery of his couch, and whose proclivities, whose most intimate pleasures would reveal themselves in the things he later asked of me.

I called Ruth first, then Francesca, who was living in Manhattan. "I think I may be moving to New York. We'll be able to see each other regu-larly now," I said. I told Opal during my stay at the small ranch house she and her fiancé, Campbell, had been renting in northern Massachusetts since their engagement the previous spring and Opal's return to New England for her work at a graphic design firm. We were sitting on the screened porch, listening to the twitter of warblers and finches on the square of fenced lawn and the tap of insects against the windows. But when she heard my plans, Opal said little. "But the things you told me of Toru . . . Are you sure this is what you want?"

"Beggars can't be choosers, right? I guess my choices are limited." I laughed to show she needn't worry, that I was making the best of the situation.

Opal replenished my half-emptied glass of iced tea with the pitcher on the low table between us then resettled in her armchair, the wicker creaking gently as she folded her bare feet under her. The skirts of her yellow sundress fanned around her on the cushion of her chair. How much prettier she looked now than in the drab clothes she'd worn over the last few years. She traced her thumb and forefinger down the narrow line of her nose, her old reflex when pinching back what she felt she should not speak aloud. "You know the small bedroom here is yours as long as you like."

And I knew she meant it. But I couldn't. Every time Campbell reached for her hand, even when he smiled at her without speaking, even when he called her name from another room, I felt the loss that seemed to live just below the surface of every, every breath.

Then, three days into my visit, through my parents, James tracked me down. I should have guessed he would. He had never given up anything without a fight. It was why, this time, I had uttered no warning, not so much as a whisper, quietly terminating my lease, packing my studio, and procuring a storage locker for the furniture I could not use for the foreseeable future. And then one evening, while James attended a faculty meeting, collecting those belongings of mine that had been kept in his apartment and slipping away at dusk. How long would it take him to realize that his hall closet and bedroom dresser drawers were cleared of my coats and clothes and shoes? His bathroom cabinet emptied of my moisturizers and soaps? I had known to fill my mind with other things as the train rattled along the tracks in the dark to Opal's, where she had agreed I should come.

But when James called, he made no accusations. This time he spoke only regrets, even apologies. "Setsu— Oh, God, Setsu . . . These few days have made me see that *nothing* matters but you." His voice was different, quavering, almost like a young boy's. "Tell me, Setsu, are you really going to walk away from all we've had? Do you even care what this does to me?"

"Please don't say that. I can't. No, I can't do this anymore. I won't!" I felt each word as it ripped from my throat.

Then only long silence. James had begged me. A thing I had thought he would never do, and I knew he never would again. And then his voice was his own once more. "I have made a mistake. A very bad one." And I knew it was not only the phone call he meant. But me.

I found Opal in her garden pulling small clumps of crabgrass from between the paved stones of the short path between her driveway and front porch. "So does he know it's really over?"

I nodded. "It was strange, though. At first he sounded so changed, almost broken." It was some time before I could speak again. "Do you know, for the first time he admitted—"

"Setsu! You aren't reconsidering, are you? After what he's done? After all the chances he's been given?"

"No. No! Of course not. That's really not what I meant—"

"Oh, good. That's good." With her gloved hand, Opal shook soil from the roots of the crabgrass, then brushed the clods of dirt back between the stones, patting them into the earth. "Because it's so easy to toss our lives away, isn't it?" She smiled. "So easy to believe our own deceptions."

Yes, and maybe for some of us it was easier than for others. Among the blades of crabgrass in a section of the path Opal had not yet reached, grew a single narrow weed with a violet flower. It was moments from being plucked, but kneeling, I touched it. It nodded then straightened, unaware of its fate. Its delicate petals were double hearts, each petal etched with veins of white. It was so perfect, I almost had the silly urge to ask Opal to spare it—a common weed! Yes, moving in with Toru was the right thing. I was glad his apartment was waiting. Glad to have no opportunity to contemplate returning to what would undo me.

It was through Shiro that I had made the arrangements in the end. "I take care of Toru's correspondences now," he'd said. "One less thing for him to concern himself with, you see." Toru would continue to cover the rent. The modest income I would be making through the position I'd been offered at Isaac's Music House selling instrument replacement parts and sheet music—a far cry from my previous employment as an analyst for Ridley Lauer (but a temporary solution until I could find something more lucrative)—would go toward my portion of the utilities, grocery bills, and the cost of the apartment's upkeep.

Shiro's contribution was similar. "It's the very least we can do considering his generosity. I'm sure you will agree," he had said in a hush, as if we were speaking of something sacred. So I had nodded my head, though *generosity* was not the first word that had come to *my* mind—the percentage of earnings I would part with being considerably larger than what would come from Toru's savings. And how much could Shiro possibly make from the articles he wrote for classical music magazines?—work he was grateful to be doing from home so that he could be of regular assistance to Toru.

Toru's disappointments had begun a year earlier, the first incidents occurring while on tour in Japan. Twice he had fumbled the final movement of Barber's "Adagio for Strings." Then, the following month, a disastrous performance at Ballantine Hall. Uncomplimentary reviews had followed. So he'd booked appointments with doctors. His body was uncooperative, he'd insisted. He had complained of muscle pains, restless sleep, monstrous headaches. The first five doctors had found nothing; still

Toru had canceled two concerts with the Santa Fe orchestra, claiming, my mother had told me later, that his head was as heavy as rocks, that he could not possibly budge from his hotel room.

I assumed Toru's symptoms were temporary, nothing more than anxiety. When my mother called again, I suggested this: "Perhaps the strain of these letdowns . . ."

"Oh, no! Please don't repeat such a thing to Toru!" I heard the clinking of her glass-beaded necklace as she wound and unwound the strands of it, a habit of hers in nervousness. "He says he feels it in his bones, the curse of disease. This has all been such a blow to him, you know, your brother the perfectionist."

It was not long before Toru found another physician, one who gave a diagnosis for what the others had not—a chronic lack of energy, a syndrome with a name my mother could not remember. He had given Toru capsules, informational pamphlets on his condition, advice for treating it. I had called Toru that first night to offer my sympathies, and in his voice I heard a stirring, a forcefulness that I had remembered but had not expected. "So you can see, this was *not* my imagination," he had said. I thought I could hear the rattling of pills in a jar, the click-click of a bottle cap turning.

"Yes, Toru, yes. So very sorry."

I organized my belongings on the shelves of my room's shallow closet and in a single emptied drawer of a small maple chest in the corner (the other drawers stuffed with music scores, spare cakes of rosin, G, D, A, and E strings still coiled in their paper envelopes). I placed my violin in its case against a corner wall. Now, I hoped, with a predictable and less demanding schedule, I might finally find time for more than the sporadic practicing I had done my last couple of years at Brown and while at Ridley. I heard Shiro pacing the corridor. At times there were long pauses between steps, as if his foot hovered before finding a spot on the floor-boards least likely to groan, least likely to rouse Toru. For an hour or more, the apartment was otherwise noiseless until several coughing grunts sounded from the direction of Toru's room. When I emerged into the hall, Shiro's pacing had ceased. For some moments, he said nothing, seemingly contemplating whether or not this would be an acceptable time to escort me to Toru.

Toru reclined on a large bed, his shoulders disappearing into a stack of wide pillows. Despite his recent illness, he had retained some of the bulk that he'd carried throughout adulthood. A small fold of fat showed above the neckline of his silk robe, his face rested like a boiled dumpling above his blankets, and his arms, which stretched before him, seemed to sink heavily into the depths of his duvet. A dimpled wrist slid out from his glossy sleeve to remove a set of black plastic headphones from his ears, and as I watched him, a familiar sensation returned to me, a sudden awareness of the smallness of my body compared to his. My weight had hardly fluctuated since high school. "A mere puff of air could blow you away!" Toru had sometimes mocked when we were children. Even then, his legs, his chest, his hands had made two of mine. Toru blinked at me placidly, as if my presence in his apartment were an everyday occurrence. "*You* haven't changed."

I shrugged, uncertain how to respond to his observation. Aside from my size, it seemed to me I looked quite different from the last time I had seen him. My hair, once straight and hanging past my shoulders, was now styled in a series of layers that fell no lower than the base of my neck. And my girlish frocks and pleated skirts had been replaced by tailored pants, collared shirts.

"It's been too many years, yes, Toru?" I took a few steps forward so that I stood at the center of his carpeted floor, wondering if I should continue toward him. That would be the sisterly thing to do, wouldn't it? To perch at the foot of his bed, where we could chat more intimately? But before I could make a choice, Toru squeezed his knuckles to his temples.

Shiro rushed past me, bumping me slightly. "What is it? Is it a headache, T?"

T? Nobody in our home had ever shortened Toru's name in this way, and I tried to interpret Toru's reaction, but his eyes were pinched shut, two tight, wrinkled knots. Shiro snatched a small white plastic bottle from Toru's bedside table, tapping its side until two red-orange capsules dropped into his palm. "Open, open," Shiro murmured, and Toru's lips parted, his pale pink tongue protruding just beyond his teeth.

"Could you?" Toru's voice was a whisper now, too, as he turned to Shiro, motioning toward the overhead light. Only once it had been extinguished did Toru's eyes reopen. "You can't possibly understand how fortunate you are to have your health, Setsu." He spoke with an uncharacteristic evenness, a softness; but I noticed, despite the gloom, a contracting in his cheeks and around his mouth, an expression I knew well. It was the way he had watched me in childhood during our shared lessons with Mrs. Dubois.

At Ridley Lauer, I had given thought to nothing beyond the next report, the next project, though even this, according to management, had not been enough. When Tilly Spaulding had terminated my employment, she had smiled and folded one thick hand over the other, baring her white teeth. "You're a pussycat, and we need a tiger," she'd said, her attempt to turn my rejection into some sort of compliment. For days I had fumed over her comment, fantasized about things I could have said in retaliation, revelations of what the whole office knew: that she could smile all she wanted, but it would do *nothing* to soften her—she had all the feminine wiles of a hyena dismembering its prey. That the fires of hell would form icebergs before a man ever looked at *her* with desire. But though these imagined retorts amused me, they did little to lift my mood. And later I had worried it was Tilly who had seen some truth in me: a passivity, a compliance. Wasn't this, years before, what Ruth and I had found we had in common? And what Francesca had often criticized me for? Maybe this was part of the appeal of Isaac's Music House—here my responsibilities were nearly error-proof and never required confrontation.

It was late October, the weather fluctuating from mild, almost spring-like, to blustery and raw. On warmer days, I often walked the twenty-eight blocks from Toru's to Isaac's. In rain or chill, I waited on the west side of Broadway to catch the downtown bus. Each time I entered the shop, I was struck by its particular, pungent scent; but it was one I did not dislike, a mix of rosin and newly printed books, which clung to my clothes after I'd left. As I worked, I studied the musicians who entered, especially the young ones with their encased instruments nestled under their arms, their brows deeply creased above their glasses as they scoured bins of Mendelssohn concertos, Tchaikovsky symphonies. In their stooped shoulders, their slow-blinking eyes, the traveling of their fingers over the sheets of music, I saw their focus, their purpose. And as I watched, something ached in me, an almost imperceptible tugging, a sensation I would never have had time to distinguish from any other during my frenzied days at Ridley Lauer. From fragments of their conversations, their postures, the tones of their voices, I found hints of their successes—a lucky audition, a well-received performance. But even when their tensed jaws, their bowed heads gave evidence of failures, I envied them, for they seemed to follow an inner voice calling them to strive, to struggle toward *something*.

It was Shiro's belief that no part of Toru's body escaped the ravages of his condition. "Even his intestines give him trouble," he confided to me one morning as I stood beside him at the kitchen counter, watching him stir a small pot of thin oatmeal and spoon applesauce into a bowl, one of two breakfasts alternately served to Toru on a gray plastic tray with blue handles. I was breaking off bite-sized pieces from a low-fat berry scone, which I had picked up, along with a hot tea, from the corner bakery.

"Certain foods can be irritating, even painful for him to digest," Shiro explained. He glanced at a smudge of blueberry on my thumb, and I sensed he felt this was somehow disrespectful, my consuming of foods Toru could no longer eat. So I could not refrain from sucking noisily the bit of scone on my finger. It was not that I believed Toru's illness was an invention. Purplish shadows ringed his eyes, and to his every movement there was a sluggishness. But what had become of Toru the feisty one? Toru the fighter? Only now and then did he rise to circle the apartment, pausing to gaze out a window, squinting into the light. Sometimes, after such excursions, he would call for Shiro to give him his arm as he made his way back to his room. As they passed, Toru would turn toward me with lips curled ever so faintly, as if savoring some victory. And I could not help wondering if some hidden part of him found pleasure in this, the pampered easiness of his current life.

The majority of his waking hours Toru spent propped up in bed, browsing through magazines and paperback mysteries or, more often, with pencil in hand, examining lined pads of paper crammed with notes, which he turned facedown into his sheets whenever Shiro or I drew close. Other times, he would remove one of a collection of cassette tapes from his night table drawer and insert it into the portable Walkman he'd bought in high school. He seemed rarely to tire of these, often rewinding a single tape again, again, again until I thought his ears would grow sore from so many hours in tight-fitting headphones.

"The life of Riley, wouldn't you say?" A small huff escaped me, sounding more like a snicker than I had intended. Toru had fallen asleep openmouthed, his cassette player in one hand, the silver television remote in his other. Shiro was unfolding the powder-blue cashmere blanket that lay at the foot of Toru's bed, smoothing it so that it draped Toru's arms and shoulders, and he blinked at me with wide, humorless eyes in that infuriating way he had of making my words sound more callous than I had meant them.

One morning, as I helped Shiro scrape our breakfast plates at the kitchen sink, he shook his head, pointing a potato-white finger toward the half-swallowed boiled egg and untouched dry toast on Toru's tray.

"He will never mend, you know, if he eats like this." Then, though there was no one else around, no one to overhear us, he took a step closer, until I could feel the hot moisture from his nostrils. "I hope you don't mind my saying so, Setsu—I hope you don't think I'm crossing a line—but *this* only makes things more difficult." He indicated the remnants of my spinach omelet, my partially finished buttered roll. His lips flattened against his gums in a half-smile, revealing a morsel of the dry toast he had shared with Toru caught in his teeth.

"Shiro, there is a limit to what I will sacrifice—" I began to say. Did he really expect me to eat the mush he cooked for Toru!

But Shiro peered at the kitchen door as if concerned we would be disturbed. "I suppose it would not matter if Toru were not so attached to you. You must realize how he *relies* on you."

For a moment I forgot the sour smell of Shiro's breath and the stub of his knee bumping mine. What was he saying? Was this a joke, his idea of a tease? A repeated disappointment from my childhood surfaced, having been long submerged: *I am nine or ten or twelve; Toru, eleven, twelve, fourteen. He is on his bedroom floor arranging pictures of his life in Japan in a three-ring leather album given him by our parents; he is constructing a fort with logs from our backyard woodpile; he is at the kitchen table, scanning the* Encyclopedia Britannica *for his report on Louisiana. And I am watching at a distance I have carefully gauged is close enough to observe but far enough not to irritate. "Why are you just standing there, Setsu? You want to help?" "Yes! Yes, please," I say, never, never learning. "Well, then, this is what will help me: if you GO AWAY!" So I bow my head, jabbing my fingertips into the corners of my eyes to plug up the tears.*

"You must have misunderstood," I said to Shiro.

But he shrugged his shoulders and splayed his hands, palms outward, as if to say, "I know what I hear. I know what I see." And he seemed so sure that I could not ignore the temptation to believe him.

In the days following, I woke early in the morning or lay late at night in my fold-out bed studying the slivers of light slicing between the slats of my room's Venetian blinds, wondering if there were really things Toru had said of me to Shiro, kind or complimentary things. Certainly the Toru I knew would never talk this way, but maybe in his current condition . . . Perhaps I had been too preoccupied with my own frustrations to notice something in him had changed.

So, "I'll have what Toru is having," I said to Shiro one evening as he prepared unsalted noodles, boiled vegetables, clear soup. As we ate, I searched for topics of conversation I thought might distract Toru from his troubles. I described the musicians I had met at Isaac's the previous day, the well-known cellist who had stopped in briefly to purchase a new D-string, the beautiful recordings I had heard on the shop's sound system. But when I spoke of these things, Toru massaged his temples as if trying to stave off another headache. So I learned the subjects that most pleased him—recountings of his many adventures, his past successes. "Do you remember your debut performance at Merrick Hall?" I would ask, or, "What about your concert with the Lansing Symphony Orchestra? Mother wrote me letters describing how masterfully you played each piece." Then Toru would direct Shiro to a drawer in his bedside table that stored photographs documenting these events, and I would point out details in the images—the expansiveness of the crowd, the grandeur of the hall, Toru's own confident, determined expression. From the same stuffed drawer, Shiro dug out various programs saved from Toru's appearances, and I would remark on the difficulty of the pieces he had tackled, compliment him on his notable career until the darkness in his eyes began to fade. Then a tiny shudder would move through my chest at the thought that *I* had been the one to cheer him. And how he needed it. Why had I not seen before the depths of his torment?

It was not long before I began to notice, as I stepped out of Toru's building on my way to work, a fluttering of the fifth-floor curtains: he was watching me—he the prisoner, I the escapee. And when I returned later in the day, I saw how he manically busied himself with his tapes or notepads, sometimes refusing to acknowledge my arrival. So I smiled, with an expression I hoped spoke kindness and sympathy, the only offering I could think to give in recognition of his suffering. And because Toru's hardships were greater than my own, I would endure the repeated grazing of Shiro's fleshy hand or thigh or chest as he reached across me to adjust Toru's tray, pass him a napkin, whisper some small reminder in his ear. I would not overly dwell on what I put aside for our time together: the missed invitations to join Rachel from Isaac's at Mallory's Pub; the repeated canceled dinner plans with Francesca, and once with Ruth when she was home with her family in Riverdale—"Just a subway ride north of you," she'd said; the various master classes and music recitals announced in the several newspaper clippings I kept tucked inside my straw handbag, not one of which I had yet to attend. I would not even brood over the practicing I had hoped to do at home (this now an impossibility as our suppers extended later and later into the night, Toru often nodding off as we talked, lulled into slumber by pleasing recollections, not to be roused, the cautious padding of Shiro's feet would remind me, by the living room television or my portable radio, and *surely* not by the unmuffled strains of a bow on strings). These were things I could place on hold for a time. The same way I turned my face from my reflection, stepping out of Toru's shower at the close of the day—no need to stare at what I knew was true, that there was less of me now since following Toru's diet, that the skin drew tighter across my pelvis, my ribs, the bones of my shoulders.

But then a new thought came to me, a possible solution, dancing before me like sunlight on water. It was early evening when I rapped on the shut door to Shiro's room.

"What a surprise, little sister!" Shiro leaned in the doorway as an interior mildewy smell, as of damp papers or wet wool, wafted into the hall. Though it was not yet evening, he had unfurled his shades, the only light in his room emanating from the small, single-bulbed lamp on his night table.

"I miss music, Shiro," I said. "I see that you have found a way, some-how, to put it aside, but I feel—I don't know—a void, I guess." Shiro said nothing, only studied me in silence. So I continued. My expectations were modest, I explained, yet if I were ever to take lessons again, I would need space to practice. "This room is the farthest from Toru's. With the door closed, with Toru's door closed, how much would he really hear?" An hour a day is all I would ask, if Shiro would be generous enough to spare me these small intervals.

For a moment Shiro's lips parted as if he had the inclination to smile. "If circumstances were different, Setsu. But I have a duty to Toru, you understand, to limit all *unnecessary* disturbances." He shrugged his shoul-ders as if to say, *I hope you wouldn't ask me to compromise that.* "Surely, you of all people . . ." Shiro's trace of a smile stretched into a long, thin-lipped grin, and he shifted his feet until he was just inches from me in his room's entry.

So I nodded, not out of agreement, but because, in that instant, I could conceive of nothing to add to my argument.

"You're a good person, you know," Shiro said, squeezing one of my hands with fingertips that seemed too softly moisturized to be a man's.

"Thank you," I answered. And then my fingers were tightening around his as well, a fleeting grasp at the subject that would drop once Shiro drew back into his room.

But perhaps Shiro took my pleading for enjoyment or as some sort of invitation. His slippery smooth palms traveled upward until they rested just below my shoulders. He leaned forward, nearly brushing my cheek with his. "I feel very comfortable with you, Setsu. As a brother with a sister." And this seemed an apology, as if he were sorry he could not offer more. His voice was powder in my ear, his nose in my hair, poking my neck. I could hear him inhaling, sucking at the scent of me as if he would like to convince himself but couldn't.

I pulled my hand from his. "Shiro, I am not asking for— And I *wouldn't*—" I straightened, smoothing stray hairs back from my forehead.

"Even if you thought of me that way! Even if you thought of me as you do—"

"Who?" Shiro emitted a small bark of a laugh. In an instant, his face had hardened, his cheeks stone-still, his eyes narrowed slits of black ice.

"What are you implying, little sister?"

"What I'm implying, Shiro, is that you have made a whole life out of protecting Toru! In ways beyond what he even requests. Don't you think that's *peculiar*?"

Shiro tapped his chin, as if my accusation amused him, but his hand was rigid. "So I suppose you think you are very smart. Let's hope your cleverness does not go the way of your looks, Setsu." His voice was spiny, cutting with a sarcasm I had never before heard. "Besides, you have flattered yourself too much, little sister. If it *were* you I wanted, you think you could do so much better? All the time your beauty is slipping away like sand through parted fingers. You're not really foolish enough to believe you can turn back to what was?"

Miserable, spiteful Shiro. I should have let his petty insults roll off me like rain. Still I could not stop myself: that night after bathing, I wiped the steam from the brightly lit mirror over the sink and studied every hard angle—prominent ribs, the shrunken cushions of my breasts, the deepened hollows of my cheeks. More months on Toru's diet and I would waste away to nothing. Some weeks before, Francesca had come to Isaac's Music House just before closing. "So good to see you, Fran. You look wonderful!" I'd said, kissing her cheek.

"Thank you. So this is what I have to do to meet up with you? I can't seem to pin you down for dinner, but you can't make any excuses now. I'm taking you for a drink," she had laughed.

Sitting at a wine bar a few blocks from Isaac's, we had talked about Jonathan, whom she was still seeing, about her plans for law school, and about her work at *Outdoor Playground*, the job I knew she found far more rewarding than she had anticipated. I could not believe it. Francesca the critic, the agitator. She had never looked prettier and, for the first time, seemed actually content.

"It's really good to see you, too." Francesca asked about my work, when I had last spoken with Opal and Ruth, if I planned to continue my living arrangement with Toru. "Do you love being in New York? It's the greatest city, isn't it?" She tucked a strand of hair behind her ear, her hair longer and a shade lighter than I remembered. She nodded as I answered, but before we'd ordered our drinks, I noticed her smile begin to stiffen. She cleared her throat as if about to speak but then only adjusted the bud vase on the table between us. For a moment she looked away to the window behind me. When had Francesca ever been at a loss for words? It wasn't until later in the evening when we stood to leave that I comprehended her awkwardness. "We should have done this much sooner. Take care of yourself, Setsu," she said, frowning into my eyes, as if to make the words mean something more. And it was then I understood. I caught her staring at the places where my silk tank top gapped—places the curves of other women's arms and shoulders and chests would have filled but where there was little more to me than thin tissue and bone.

God! God, what was I doing! How long did I think I could continue this without damaging myself in ways that could not be undone? I remembered something Rachel had mentioned to me during one of our shared shifts. She needed a new roommate, she'd admitted, to cover costs. At the time, I had ignored her offer. But I began to think I had been too hasty. I had only planned to stay at Isaac's until I could find a better opportunity with higher compensation, but even if I picked up a few more hours at the Music House, I could manage half her rent, couldn't I? And was this wishful thinking, that perhaps I would even find enough remaining for a weekly music lesson? The mirror clouded over once more, and I slipped my robe over my shoulders, pulling it tightly across my chest. No. No! I could not be expected to neglect my own needs forever. So this is what, clearly, calmly, head held high with self-assurance, I would explain to Toru.

But when I returned Thursday afternoon from the music shop, I discovered Toru swaddled in blankets, huddled in his corner rocking chair, a large embroidered handkerchief dangling from one hand. He turned to me with swollen eyes.

"Shiro left. He packed his things this morning. What kind of warning is *that*?" The words shot from Toru's mouth like little pellets. "He said the arrangement we had in this house did not suit him. The three of us together here. What am I supposed to glean from this?" Toru swiped, with his hankie, a trail of wetness trickling from his left nostril. "Is *that* an explanation? Always there was a friction between the two of you. I sensed it. Did you know about this, Setsu?"

"No, Toru, no." What good could come of repeating what had occurred? "I'm sorry you are so upset," I said, my voice thin, shaky as my limbs, which were now shivering from the realization of what I had caused and from the slowly emerging thought that Toru was now my responsibility and mine alone.

So my plans would wait. What choice was there? Until I was able to find someone to replace Shiro, someone Toru found agreeable, I was accountable for his meals, the laundering of his sheets and pajamas, the sorting through bills, catalogs, the slow dribble of fan letters. I even drew Toru's bath for him each evening, and now and then, to my deep embarrassment, he requested I hand him his towel as he emerged from the dripping water, buttocks sagging, penis hanging like a limp white worm. I learned to take phone messages for him on the small tabs of memo paper he had given me for that purpose. What little time I had left I spent in the kitchen, craning over slow-stewing meats and vegetables, stirring pots of unadorned noodles, soft rice. "To your health. For energy, brother," I would say as I placed his tray of food on the bed beside him.

After some weeks we fell into a rhythm. As Shiro had done, I found I was able to anticipate most of Toru's needs before he asked. And then— this was not pride, a figment of my imagination, was it?—I began to notice small improvements in his appearance. Minor changes since I had begun to care for him—a ruddy hue in his cheeks, a fullness in his face, a straightening of his shoulders. Even his appetite had increased. The food I set before him began to disappear more quickly, and often, after finishing most of his own serving, he would let out a small grunt, pointing with his fork toward whatever remained on my own plate. "Were you going to eat that, Setsu?" So always I handed over whatever I had left, reasoning that he needed it more than I.

At Isaac's, I now found myself often too weary to engage in conversations with the other employees. I listened quietly as they joked or compared stories of disappointing dates, overcrowded parties. But one late Tuesday afternoon, Rachel pulled me aside. Her violin coach, the well-regarded Gregory Palevitz (whose name I had now heard repeatedly from coworkers and patrons), had a single opening on Thursday evenings. She remembered that I had mentioned wishing to resume my studies. Was I interested in auditioning for him? She would put in a good word but needed an immediate answer. Gregory's sessions filled quickly. Days before I would have dismissed this as an impossibility, but twice in the past week, on returning home from work or errands, I had glimpsed Toru (unaware of my presence) making his way from the kitchen back to his bedroom with energetic, almost clipped steps, humming, a glass of juice in hand. So early Wednesday, as I arranged a plate of coddled eggs and wheat toast before him, I introduced the topic. "I've been considering something, Toru. I believe . . . I think I might like to try taking lessons again."

Toru moved aside the notepad he had been inspecting to make more room for the tray. He arched his brows. "This is your business. Why should I wish to stop you?" But he quickly lowered his head over his food so that I could not ascertain whether or not my announcement had surprised him.

"My audition for the teacher would be tomorrow evening at six, so I would not be here for your supper. But most of it I could prepare ahead of time," I said. "You would need only to boil your rice, reheat your chicken and vegetables. It's really very simple. I could leave directions by the stove. I would not suggest this, Toru, but you have looked so much healthier of late. Perhaps you, yourself, have noticed in the mirror?"

Pink flashed across Toru's cheeks for the briefest of instants, then he shrugged his shoulders. "Well, let's see how I am faring," he said, massaging his throat with his fingertips. "You know I can't possibly predict how I will feel from one day to the next." Leaning on an elbow, he rummaged through the top drawer of his bedside table until he found a tape he wanted to place in his Walkman, then plunged a spoon into the center of one of his eggs.

During the remainder of that day and night, I could not take my mind off the appointment with Gregory Palevitz, nor could I stop myself from regularly scrutinizing Toru's appearance or listening to the muted noises that sounded from behind his door for signs of recuperation or decline. It was shameful to dread his deterioration because it would interfere with *my* plans. Still, I could not suppress the knot of irritation that rose in my chest the following morning as Toru began to moan of burning in his joints, of a leaden heaviness in his head.

"I guess your lesson this evening is out of the question, Setsu," he said, blowing a thin hiss of air at the very impossibility of the thought. "Too bad I can't control my ups and downs, eh?" He turned to me with a half-grin, half-grimace, which vanished before I could begin to read it. Then pointing to the cluster of bottles on his dresser, he asked if I would mind handing him the two farthest to the left. I watched as he gingerly unscrewed their caps and shook two pills from each into his palm. I should have offered words of comfort but could think of nothing but my own disappointment, the ill timing of Toru's relapse.

"You know, big brother, I have faced some discouragements, too. And I think, well, sometimes I think moving on is only a matter of making a decision. Perhaps you just need to press—"

Toru snorted and swatted at a strand of hair drooping onto his brow.

"And what have *you* suffered, Setsu? Are you comparing your losses with mine? How could you have the *slightest* inkling, the faintest notion of what I am enduring?" His mouth pinched into a thin crease, as if challenging me to answer. But I could find no words. What came to me instead was a memory of sitting beside my parents in a large and darkened auditorium, watching as Toru's violin glimmered under the stage lights, as his fingers galloped up and down the fingerboard playing the pieces of which I had memorized every note. Of crossing my ankles in the ladylike manner my mother had taught me, of holding my folded hands tightly on my knees because my heart was aching for reasons I did not understand. Yes, Toru was right. From the beginning, he had attained far larger successes, climbed to far greater heights. How much longer a distance, then, when he fell. So how could I begin to judge his struggles? What advice had I to offer?

"I am sorry, Toru. I did not mean to distress you," was all I could think to say.

But Toru only squeezed his lips, turning them a mottled white, then closed his eyes. Within moments, I could hear the raspy exhalation of his breath in slumber.

How I hated for Toru to be angry with me. The few times I had made him cross in childhood the whole house had seemed blanketed in the same awful loneliness that clung to my insides. And despite the passage of years, little felt different now. So with silent hands, I slid open the drawers of Toru's nightstand and began sifting through newspaper clippings, yellowed programs—the many proofs of his past accomplishments—hoping to find those that would best placate him when he awoke. Toward the back of his middle drawer lay stacked pads of paper covered with the notes I found him so frequently reading, beside them his tape player and a pile of cassettes. Lifting the top few tapes and pads from the drawer, I could see that he had marked them with various labels and dates and that each tape seemed to have a corresponding set of notes. Several were from recitals and conferences, but others appeared to be simply recordings of old lessons and practice sessions. In the far corner of the drawer, a cassette in a scratched case caught my eye. It was more battered than the rest and was dated only a short time after Toru had come to live with us. As I held it to the light, I could see that its label was smudged and browned with age and that the blocky numbers and letters of the date were in Toru's boyhood penmanship. So, curious, and judging that Toru would not wake for some hours, I inserted the cassette into his Walkman and, settling into the rocker across the room from Toru's bed, fitted the headphones over my ears.

For some moments nothing was audible but the whir of the plastic ribbon around its spools. And then notes—so familiar, though at first I could not place them. Oh! Was it? Yes! The Corelli—the piece Toru and I were to have played as a duet. Two different violins were distinguishable. Somehow, without my knowledge, he must have taped one of our shared practices, borrowing, I assumed, the old, large-buttoned recorder that my parents had kept in the living room armoire. How very strange all these years later to hear preserved our childhood sounds, and I could not help feeling, with a stinging in my breast, that I was rousing sleeping ghosts, that these were fragments from a dream, from a life I'd long forgotten. But I could not bring myself to stop the music, and as I listened, I could not deny that one instrument stood out—its notes sweeter, more melodic, as if singing its very sorrows and joys. So it was just as well, perhaps, that Toru had performed the piece alone.

A series of slow, fluid notes concluded. A far livelier section commenced. But moments into this new rhythm, my breath froze in my lungs. Despite the warmth of Toru's room, I was too rigid with cold even to shudder as I heard a sound I recognized, a sound as familiar as my own heartbeat. How was it that I had confused the two? How could I have missed my own playing? To be certain I was not mistaken, I consulted the notes Toru had taken on that day. And there it was—in Toru's own scrawled hand—an accounting of his progress and below that, an accounting of mine. Here was proof of the things he had hidden. Here were all of the truths he had denied. For Toru had known then what I had been unable to see. And he had made me believe what I had been too ready to accept.

The bitterness that had contorted Toru's face as he drifted off had not lessened; even in sleep, angry lines cut along the sides of his mouth. On shoeless feet, I replaced the tapes and pads in the drawer where I had found them, then crossed Toru's room and slipped through the open door. Against a wall in the guest bedroom lay my violin, the top-facing side of its case flecked with dust from lack of use. Gently I took the instrument into my lap. I brushed my palm over its blond-brown wood, ran my finger over its bridge and around the scroll at the tip of its neck. Then, for a moment, I clutched it to me, as if somehow by gripping to stop the flood of regrets—the stretch of years I had lost, the wasted possibilities, the many things that might have been. But when I lifted my violin to my shoulder, fitted my chin into the smoothly cupped rest, a melody seemed to rise up from the center of me—Pachelbel's Canon in D, a piece I had adored as a child. "To be the daughter of two musical parents! So lucky! Surely you were born with a gift, Setsu," my adoptive parents had told me long ago when I was very young. Then I had nodded shyly, tentatively, only beginning to believe. But now I would say it aloud. I would whisper it to the empty room. "Yes, Setsu, yes. This, *this* is the truth of you. *This* is who you are."

My breakfast that morning had been a mere handful of crackers, a weak cup of tea, not nearly enough to fill me. And suddenly I was aware of a great gnawing, as if my stomach panged from years of portions that hadn't satisfied, from every missed meal. So making my way to the kitchen, I fished through the refrigerator for a package of maple ham, a wedge of cheddar; I plucked a bag of sesame rolls, hazelnut cookies, and a container of cocoa from the cabinet shelves. Not Toru's favorite things, but mine. As I layered a roll with slices of sweet ham and cheese, poured milk into a small pot for hot chocolate, I hummed the notes of the Canon in D. Then of a Strauss waltz, a Vivaldi concerto, a Tartini sonata. The pieces bubbled up in me like the steam rising from my saucepan. I returned my violin to its case then set it near the front door in preparation for my lesson that evening, and as I did, the aromas from the foods caused a small pool of water to form beneath my tongue. In just moments all would be ready. And this time I would eat and eat. And I would not cease until I had swallowed away the very last throb of hunger, until I'd had all that my body could hold. Until the music in me came out in sound that could be heard.

TAKING WING

(My Story)

For some time, I tried. To be agreeable. To be acquiescent. But an eddy of agitation had stirred in me, and it was growing. Until, one evening: "For God's sake, Ma! I'm almost a college graduate! Twenty-one years old! *Wake Up!* I'm no longer a baby!"

Since the close of my freshman year, a time Mama and I never referred to, I had watched with envy as my friends tasted new freedoms—semesters spent overseas in cities I'd seen only on maps, unsupervised vacations on islands off the New England coast. Setsu disappeared for a summer to Rome, Francesca to Madrid. My suitemates knew never to ask my plans. Knew, of course, none would be made. All of them seeing—since what had occurred—how my reins had only shortened. During my remaining years at Brown, Mama and Poppy had begun to make more regular visits to campus and to find reasons, every two to three weekends, for me to return home—a wedding for my second cousin Miranda, a bar mitzvah for Aaron, the Schafers' middle son. "How are you feeling?"

Mama now had the habit of asking offhandedly, attempting nonchalance when we were together. But I caught her running her tongue along her teeth and peering into my eyes for signs of fatigue, or frowning at my breasts or abdomen for evidence of sudden swelling. Always Mama had kept careful track of the foods I consumed, but now, when in her presence, I felt her eyes on me with every forkful I lifted to my lips, with every bite I swallowed. All this, for a time, I had endured in silence. What choice did I have? "You reap what you sow," people say, and I had sown seeds of foolishness, carelessness.

My outburst that evening had broken from my mouth unplanned, unchecked, but I'd felt a certain rush, a bristling of pride mingled with nerves, at my own defiance.

Now Mama's face was red as ripe currants. "After *all* Poppy and I have done for you? That's what you have to say! Tell me, Ruth, exactly when did it become a crime for a mother to look after her own?" She let her knife and fork drop from her quaking hands and clatter against her plate. "If you're so ready to take on the world, why don't you act like it?"

In her opinion, my last four years had been a series of fits and starts, with no sensible plan emerging. "It's just a matter of finding what's most worthwhile and then persevering," Mama had said when I'd called home with news of my classmates' decisions to be premed, to practice law, to follow the trails their fathers had forged into the world of finance. I had heard the knot in her voice, her ears closed to my hints at what I loved most of all—the writing classes I'd enrolled in, despite her reminders they held no relevance to my major.

Sarah and Valerie raised their napkins to shroud their smiles, their eyes darting, skittish as minnows, from Mama to me. This, from them, I would have expected. But even Poppy said nothing, scraping hurriedly at the remains of his supper. Mama pulled a balled tissue from the sleeve of her blouse. She sniffed nasally, and as she pressed her fingertips to her pinkish eyes, I sensed it. The turning in the rest of them, a flowing of sympathy from each of them to her. It occurred to none of them that there might be truth to what I'd said.

This moment of brazenness only made my family scrutinize me more suspiciously. "Who was that?" Mama asked after I'd received two phone calls in a single weekend from Brad Lewitt, the class above mine in high school, who, to the Lewitts' dismay, now managed the Red Moon Diner in midtown.

"*The Red Moon Diner? That grease-spattered eyesore on Tibbett Avenue,*" neighbors wondered.

"*No. No, some place in Manhattan.*"

"*I bet his parents wish they could get a refund on all that private-school tuition!*"

So went the gossip in town. And Mama had known it was Brad who had called, only she wished it wasn't and awaited some confirmation that Brad and I would not be *dating*.

During our teen years, my friends from Temple Beth Immanuel had complained about the ways their mothers were already probing for husbands, like gulls eyeing every silver ripple of water for fish. "You're lucky, Ruth. Your mother leaves you alone," they'd said, not realizing that it was only a trade-off, other things—my standardized test scores, my grades in trigonometry—occupying her thoughts instead. But now, suddenly, she seemed intent on finding some suitable relationship for me—someone with ambition, someone who shared our values, as if this would not only prevent me from veering wildly off track, but inspire me to pursue some worthy goal of my own. As if, then, my future would extend before me, a clear path solidly paved. So whenever I was home and accompanied her to services, she would point out someone new. Did I know Robbie Melzer had returned to Riverdale? Had she mentioned Lizzy Samuels's oldest son—the one who'd just renovated a beautiful apartment in Park Slope—always asked about me? According to Lizzy, he'd been a political science major, too.

"Oh, I don't know, Ma."

"Really?" She was surprised. She happened to know that Alice Berger was interested in *both* of them. And Robbie Melzer had just started working in his father's insurance brokerage firm, taking over the entire personal lines department. "He's always been so refined. Besides, how many Jews are there to choose from in this world, Ruthie? A piddling fraction. That's it!"

A circle of pink shone at the back of Robbie Melzer's head. By thirty he'd be as hairless as a newborn mouse. And there seemed something grim about David Samuels, dressed always in black suits, his cheeks long, as if he were perpetually sitting shiva. But when I wrinkled my nose at one after another, Mama cleared her throat, and I knew what she was swallowing down.

I shrugged my shoulders. "Don't bring me to temple if you find it an exercise in frustration. I can find someone for myself."

Mama snapped her tongue in a way that implied, *A fine job you've done so far.*

But I held my silence, despite the drumming of my heart, the hot, pulsing anger.

I n the fall of my final year at Brown, I won repeated high praise for my work in Advanced Fiction Writing—special attentions I had seen lavished on other students in other courses, but never expected to receive myself. Professor Wainwright, the author of *Blue Hill Sundown* and *The Pulling Horses*, read aloud in class my piece "Aside from Loss." He complimented the discussion I'd led on Hemingway's style as one of the most insightful he'd heard. And so I quickly forgot how, throughout the entire presentation, my words had echoed in my ears, trembling and thick, as if forming somewhere other than my throat.

During one weekend at home, I left "Aside from Loss" faceup on my bedroom desk, its black-markered *Outstanding!* unmissable, even from some distance. Mama had come in and out more times than I could count, to return folded laundry, check the heat from the radiator, retrieve my emptied hot chocolate mugs. But even though I had caught her skimming the first page of my story, she made no mention of it. As if this were as common as pennies in a wishing fountain, as if I'd been bringing home victories like this every day for years. Nor did she betray any hint of having noticed, during one of my subsequent visits home, a handful of brochures given me by Professor Wainwright (duplicates of those I kept with me at school) for graduate writing programs around the country, though I'd fanned them out in the same prominent spot. So! I knew what she thought—that she could discourage me through indifference. But she'd underestimated me. I was no longer the self-doubting, malleable girl I'd been as a child!

No classes were held during the latter half of Thanksgiving week. I was home for five full days. So I interrupted Poppy and Mama late one evening as they took to their usual after-dinner armchairs. I had a question for them, I explained. Still in the pleated drop-waist dress I'd worn to dinner at Aunt Helena's—the one I'd bought the previous spring on a shopping outing with Setsu because it slimmed my hips—I recited the proposal I had rehearsed repeatedly, animatedly, convincingly (I believed) in my room. But it was clear Mama had anticipated this, had already made her case. And this time Poppy was as unyielding as she. He worked his section of newspaper into a tight scroll. They were both impassive, their faces flat as earth.

Look how much had been handed to me, and I wanted to gamble it all on some remote seed of a notion a professor had planted in my head! It was the most unreliable of choices! Didn't I want to have something to *show* for what I'd been working toward? "No." Their answer was as simple as that. It was *their* hard-earned money. If I had the means to send myself, well, then, they supposed they could not stop me. But a single decision could change the course of everything. Surely *I* should understand this, Mama said as Poppy turned his eyes from me, rapping his fingers against his rolled paper. And so I knew. Mama had broken her promise. Fired her surest weapon. Revealed to Poppy what she'd sworn long ago she never would.

For days, I fixed her with long stares, chilly as frozen snow, intended to fill her with guilt. But she only blinked at me placidly, unrepentantly, holding my gaze in a way that meant, *I do what I have to.*

Shortly after I returned to school, Mama phoned with "great news!" She had made a call to Julie Guggenheim, the old friend of Nana Leah's who ran the entire Manhattan division of the Northeastern Jewish Federation but who was now planning a run for state legislature. "She said she can offer you a paid position working on her campaign. She's very connected. This could lead to all *kinds* of possibilities."

Mama knew I had no further arguments, had come up with no better alternative. I had sat numbly when Dean Salkin had outlined for me the popular and logical choices for graduates with political science degrees: law school, business school, careers in policy analysis. How decisively my classmates seemed to claim what they were moving toward, easily and without looking back. But as Dean Salkin talked, I had wanted only to stop the days from tumbling forward, had wished the campus walls could rise up and enclose us, granting more time.

Mama began, when we spoke, to refer cheerfully to the many things I would have to look forward to once I began work for Julie Guggenheim and returned to the apartment on West 256th Street, where it was assumed I would be resettling until I'd saved some income. "Over the summer, Ruthie, we'll re-carpet your room and update the wallpaper. Maybe a stripe? Would you like that?" As if this bit of redecorating could make up for any disappointment. And, oh, as long as I was home, I wouldn't have to worry about meals. It was fortunate, too, our apartment's proximity to the bus and the subway. Made for a cinch of a commute. She would chatter on in this manner until I lied, suddenly remembering I had a class to attend, allowing the phone to drop back on the receiver.

So the leaflets I'd placed on my desk at home remained in the exact array in which I'd left them, Mama and Poppy's mute declaration that this conversation was closed. It mattered nothing to them that these were some of the country's finest programs, the ones Professor Wainwright had specifically recommended and that Francesca (who had taken writing courses with me—"Whose life is it *anyway*, Ruth?") had rattled off when I questioned her once earlier in the year. They did not know, did not care to know, that this was the thought my mind returned to obsessively, as if having discovered some new chink of light in a solid wall. But I could be as stubborn as they. Without a word, using a portion of money I had made from babysitting to pay for processing fees, I mailed seven applications— one to California, one to Michigan, the others scattered along the East Coast.

The letters arrived in early spring. But what was I to make of this? Was fortune playing games with me, or was this a blessing in disguise? A congratulatory letter from Georgetown University, Professor Wainwright's first choice for me and the school where he had taught some years ago. But not only that—an attached page offering a generous scholarship. Georgetown—the one program I had applied to that did not provide a master's in writing but in English literature. "This will give you broader options," Professor Wainwright had explained. Georgetown's program included courses on teaching writing, and he was certain he could arrange for me to study fiction independently with his former colleague Professor Brennan—"Worth the whole lot of writing instructors you might be assigned elsewhere." With this degree I would be qualified to teach either writing *or* literature afterward. So wouldn't Mama and Poppy find this choice more acceptable? And perhaps overlook what blinked up at me from the bottom of my letter: a reference to the school's Jesuit tradition, its foundation in beliefs we did not share. But Georgetown's students came from a diversity of backgrounds. I'd definitely read that somewhere in one of its brochures. So it mattered less than other things, I could argue, couldn't I? Though the very thought of what Mama and Poppy might say to this made me flush with cold then heat. Still, this time I would not buckle. No, I refused to fold! Not now. Now I had a new resolve.

We sat robed and hatted and tasseled in long rows, in folding chairs perfectly spaced across the Main Green, on the day of our commencement. "You are new promises, your young lights beginning to flicker here," declared to us the Nobel Prize winner who had been invited to speak. "So, now, fling yourselves out, as if into the heavens. And set the world ablaze." The faces all around me tilted back, listening, shining, believing. I smiled to be as eager as the rest, to forget how Mama had looked when I'd turned—still and blank as glass in her section behind me. "I can only hope you'll find some sense and rethink this," she had said when I announced my decision to Poppy and to her two months before, explaining the package Georgetown had offered and my plan to use my savings (the remainder of my babysitting money and my modest inheritance from Great-Uncle Eli)—to find a work-study job, too, if necessary—to pay room and board. She had kept her voice even as sanded wood, but I had seen how she struggled to control the wobbling of her mouth. Despite what I said about *options*, she suspected it was still my writing I planned to pursue above all else. If I wanted to teach literature at the college level, I'd have applied to doctoral programs. She didn't know everything, but *that* she knew. "It's not enough to be able to turn a pretty phrase and put imaginings to paper, Ruthie. You could fill oceans with the littered dreams of men and women who've learned to do just that. And, you know, it's still a *Catholic* university. It doesn't matter all their claims about varied backgrounds. You want to abandon everything to chase some glittery dust your professor scattered in the air! How can you? Are you punishing me, Ruth, or punishing yourself!"

"No! That's not it at all!" I'd said. But she seemed not to hear.

Mama stood, her hand clamped to the edge of the living room piano as she watched me gather my bags near our apartment's entry. In an hour, my train would depart from Penn Station and whisk me away, more than two hundred miles south to the campus on the hill overlooking the Potomac River. This would be the first time Mama would let me cross the threshold of our front door without embracing me, without pressing her mouth to my brow. But I would not crack. I would keep my shoulders even, my chin steady. Even when Poppy did not lift his eyes to mine, only fumbled to pat my hand with his. Even then.

"You should pray you never have a daughter who treats *you* this way!" Mama called after the door had shuddered closed behind me. But then she could not see how my eyes burned, how my limbs shook like leaves in wind.

In photos, Georgetown's campus looked something like Brown's, with its neat quadrangles, its majestic trees. But the simpler features of Brown's buildings made them seem knowable even from a distance; while Georgetown's Romanesque and Gothic structures, with their arches and towers, formed hidden corners and shadowy curves, resembling, more than anything, illustrations from the fairy-tale book Sarah, Valerie, and I had pored over together as girls, drawn to the mysteries that the vine-draped turrets, thick woods, and garden mazes surely promised. And had I found Brown's layout this elusive when I first arrived? I took several incorrect turns before locating the Office of Student Affairs and then the most direct path to Thirty-ninth Street, where, with the help of the university, I had found an apartment just blocks from campus, which I would be renting along with another woman from my program. Angela McDermott had called me once over the summer. Two weeks later she sent a note on monogrammed, sherbet-orange stationery. *Can't wait to meet!!* she'd written. She had included a snapshot of herself standing on a wide, pebbled beach, her straight yellow hair blowing off her shoulders in wisps, a pair of black sunglasses crowning her head. Some distance behind her, a retriever dug in the sand, and a small group—her family, I gathered—sat on beach towels that matched the one Angela had wrapped around her waist like a sarong.

Angela, or Angie, as she insisted I call her, was even prettier in person, delicately featured and tanned. She embraced me as soon as she breezed into the apartment, smelling faintly of chrysanthemums, like those planted among the shrubbery of the homes along the block. We would be sharing the second floor of a two-story wood-shingled house with teal shutters. The owners of the home, Mr. and Mrs. Philips, occupied the first floor but only during certain seasons, spending the remainder of the year in California with their grown children.

Angela's mother and father had come along to help her get settled. From the McDermotts' efficiency, their perfect coordination, it was obvious this was, for them, a familiar routine. Around Angela's half of our large shared bedroom, in her closet, and on the bookshelves of the adjacent sitting room, they effortlessly found places for Angie's shoeboxes and cardigan sweaters, shampoo bottles, for her poster of Degas' ballerinas, her silver clock radio, her collection of photos in paisley fabric frames. In the narrow cupboards of our modest kitchen, they stacked her cans of sugar-free lemonade, her unsalted pretzels.

After a lengthy exchange of endearments, an elaborate series of farewell kisses, Angie watched her parents disappear down the steps of our front porch, across the square patch of trimmed lawn, to their red Volvo parked down the street. Then she returned to the bedroom and plopped onto her white eyelet coverlet, propping her slender bare feet on the foot of her bed. "So, we're *here*. I can't believe it's already September, can you? I was *this* close"—she made a pinching motion with her thumb and forefinger—"to forgetting the whole thing and moving to Illinois to be close to my boyfriend." She rolled onto her side, then reached for an oval-framed picture that she had set on her small lamp table. It was of a young man with strawberry hair and full shoulders, in a racing scull, oars in hand. She brought her fingertip to her lips then touched it to the photo. "Evan's at University of Chicago Law School," she said. "We met four years ago on vacation with our church youth group. But my parents talked me out of it: *You have too much talent to miss this! And if Evan's the right one, he won't be going anywhere until you finish*." She pronounced this in a falsetto then laughed, closing her eyes with a small shake of her head as if to say, "You know how parents are."

We talked about her younger brother, Allen—"Brilliant! An even better student than I"—the boarding school she had attended, her summer job at a girls' day camp, her friends from home. "Sorry! I've been blathering on and on." She blinked at me, smiling, waiting. So I offered small tidbits: Brown—where I'd met Fran and Setsu and Opal, my professors there, New York City, of which technically, I explained, Riverdale was a part. But other things went unmentioned. I could think of nothing that wouldn't widen the chasm separating Angie's life from mine.

"I think we have a lot in common." Angie said my description of Fran reminded her of her friend Libby at Williams, and she'd always adored New York, though she'd only been a handful of times. She gave my elbow a gentle squeeze before changing into tennis sneakers and cotton shorts, which just covered the perfect grapefruit roundness of her buttocks, and heading for the door.

So I nodded my agreement, though I imagined Angie would have offered this extension of friendship to anyone.

After she'd gone, I studied her belongings: a small glass canister of beach glass on her desk, another of smooth, oval white stones, an amber, cube-shaped bottle of perfume with a gold ball of a top. Beside these, *The Stories of F. Scott Fitzgerald*. "My favorite short story writer"—she had smoothed her hand across the cover of the book when, earlier in the afternoon, I had commented on it. "Do you know 'The Ice Palace'?" I had frowned at the book as if trying to recall the piece, though I was certain I had not read it, only the Fitzgerald novels assigned in high school.

At the center of her desk lay the salmon-pink telephone Angie and I had agreed she would bring from home for us to share. As I unpacked the last of my items, I was sure I caught, with each creak or rustle, the beginning of a ring: Mama calling with a storm of accusations. But my ears were playing tricks. No call came, and I spent the remainder of the afternoon arranging and rearranging my things in a vain attempt to make my half of the room as orderly and inviting as Angie's.

My first Monday at Georgetown, I climbed a wide, spiraling staircase, with a wrought-iron balustrade, to the third floor of a small-windowed building, which, for the life of me, seemed to have no etching or plaque identifying it. I slipped into a front-row desk of an empty classroom, white and clean, unadorned save for a bronze crucifix on one wall, and arranged before me my notebook, pens, my newly purchased copy of *David Copperfield*, and my syllabus for Victorian Novels, only to be informed by a teaching assistant that a mathematics class would be assembling in the room shortly. And though Professor Brennan had agreed to meet with me weekly so that I could pursue my writing in addition to my literature courses, it took me some time to track him down, his office having been temporarily relocated due to construction. In my scramble to find the places I was meant to be, I began to wonder if I was the only one having difficulty. No one else seemed distracted by the crosses or the occasional Jesuit brothers in their black shirts and Roman collars.

Angie's parents called her at seven-thirty on the nose every evening. "Hello, sweetheart. How's the future Edith Wharton?" Mrs. McDermott would ask if I was the one to answer. Sometimes it was Katherine Mansfield or Dorothy Parker. The same joke every time, and I could hear from Angie's response, when I passed the phone, that the joke was repeated for her. But I didn't mind, liking to be included and the way Mrs. McDermott always sounded so cheerful, and liking the background home noises—a television on some sports channel, the soft spray sound of what I imagined was Angie's mother cleaning her kitchen counters or dining table.

During this time, Mama made no attempt to fix all that was wrong between us. Three weeks passed with no contact, an occurrence that had once seemed as impossible to me as the ceasing of sunrise and set. Not that I was waiting. No. Just . . . just that I noticed. That was all. But then the letters began to trickle in: courteous notes, each no more than a handful of sentences. Far from the gushing declarations of affection Mama had sent me at college, these were simply terse updates: *Valerie ran into her old piano teacher, Manny Onassis. Poppy's arthritic knee flared up—doctor's appointment tomorrow.* She signed them simply, *Mama.* No *Love and kisses.* No *Shower of hugs.* Missives no warmer than those she might exchange with a business associate of Poppy's or some newly made acquaintance. How transparent her plan was! Injure me deeply enough, she thought, and I would cave, come rushing home admitting foolish misjudgment and that I should have listened.

But two could play Mama's game. For every note she sent, I penned one equally concise, equally matter-of-fact. For emphasis, I used

Georgetown postcards, which were sold at the student bookshop. I dropped them coolly, nonchalantly in the nearest campus mailbox, striding off before the thwack of the card reaching the bottom, listening, instead, to the bold hammering of my heels along the pavement. But always, later, despite the distractions of campus life and the busyness of my course work, it came: the familiar void I knew only one way to fill. The 7-Eleven on Wisconsin Avenue was a ten-minute walk from campus. Once inside, squinting under the fluorescent tubes of light, I headed for the stack of orange baskets beside the register. Ducking through the aisles to avoid the undergrad revelers, with their cheeks red as torches, their shirts clingy and thin despite the late-night air, I loaded my basket with sour-cream chips, fruit turnovers, handfuls of peanut chews—all the things required to sate the clawing emptiness. These I toted home in a bulging bag, turning from my distorted reflection in the windows of cars parked under the street lamps along my route. I needed no reminders; I knew well how I looked—fleshy arms wrapping piggish bundles, a chubby girl with no self-control. Then in the dark of the apartment— Angie having already turned in for the night—I flopped onto the sitting room couch. There, I pulled apart every plastic wrapper, eating my way through the mound of food, my breath dying each time Angie stirred, lest she awake—she of yogurt-and-diced-fruit breakfasts, of wheat-bread sandwiches and vegetable soups—panicked she would reach for her bedside lamp and throw open the door, flooding the room with light, exposing all.

Then, in mid-October, something happened. A stroke of luck, a turn of events that would bring Mama and Poppy to their knees with repentance. I met someone. A grad student from Georgetown's business program. For fun, he was auditing my Victorian literature course. Joshua Weiss. Even before I glimpsed his name printed across the spiral notebook that lay on his desk, I discerned something familiar in the curve of his lips, the flaring lines of his nostrils. His mouth had the fullness of my uncle Leonid's; his eyes, behind wire-rimmed glasses, shone the same brown-black as countless boys from my childhood Hebrew school classes. When they learned that, *here*, I had found one of my own—and not just anyone, but a man who was considerate and kind and full of humor, and a business major to top it off—God, it was almost a cliché!

I memorized all the romantic details, planning how I would recount them later to my sisters. How our first date was magical, far better even than the ones we used to imagine with Neil Keller from the top floor of our building, whom for years we'd spied on from our secret spot on the back stairs. I would tell them how I'd borrowed a tennis racket from Angie and how Joshua and I had played until sundown on one of the campus's outdoor courts, our long shadows bobbing. How Joshua had swung his arm with mine to show me a proper forehand stroke then backhand, how he'd complimented me for picking these up naturally. How we'd almost collapsed with laughter over his imitation of the Austrian instructor who had given lessons to his brother and him until they were thirteen and fifteen. And later, how we'd walked to Lucky's Café in town and found a private corner table upstairs beside framed drawings of horses. "We talked until a waitress began to sweep the floor and dim the lights," I would tell them.

That night, Joshua had spoken to me of things other people hadn't— the trip his family took to India five years before that changed him, the figures from history he most admired. And he'd had as many questions for me as he'd made revelations about himself. "You're very easy to talk to, Ruth," he had said, his lips moving to my cheek, full and warm, as we stood on the steps to my porch under the milky glow of the overhead lantern. Later, after we parted, I had lain awake almost until morning, listening to the sigh of the dogwood branches outside my window, the baying of some faraway hound, smiling and smiling to myself in the hush.

It was not until after three more evenings together and two leisurely afternoons strolling the cobblestone streets of town, pointing out the homes we liked best, that I discovered my mistake. We were on the path south of campus overlooking the choppy gray Potomac, our ears and noses chapped from wind. Joshua had tucked the icy fingers of my right hand into the crook of his elbow. Deep in the crease of his oilskin jacket, my skin began to tingle with returning warmth. Our feet found a rhythm that lulled me. But Joshua laughed suddenly when I asked if he was spending the High Holidays at home. "Did you assume? Because of my name?" An understandable conclusion. He supposed there was Jewish blood in his family somewhere, but watered down to a thin trickle, forgotten. Actually, the truth was he had been baptized and confirmed, a Methodist. Was this a problem? Did it make a difference? He stopped and turned to me, his dark earth-brown eyes large with amusement, or was it concern? I swatted the air with my free, numbed hand, as if to say this was nothing, an incidental matter—just as were the doubts he'd shared days before about going into business for the long term, because he sometimes thought he might prefer teaching history, as his father had. But I did not speak, afraid some splintering in my voice would betray my disappointment.

As the wind increased, strands of hair whipped my cheeks; my eyes watered. Then, as we turned back toward campus, I felt some inner part of me slipping, out, out, until it parted from the Ruth who continued to trudge along with Joshua. This, the same unnerving sensation I'd had just days before when Angie had stared quizzically at the gold six-pointed star on a hair-thin chain, which had dropped from my small papier-mâché jewelry box to the floor. "Oh? That? Yes, it's mine." Having scooped it into my hand, I had stood again quickly, knowing how my backside looked in the leggings I had not had a chance to change out of since waking. I had thought of Christine Millgrim from our program, Angie's constant companion, whose girlhood churches and schools and clubs seemed to differ from Angie's only in name. Christine had lived a life like hers, understood things I had only begun to glimpse. "It's the

Star of David. You know—a Jewish star. A gift from my aunt and uncle on my fourteenth birthday."

"Oh, yes, well, it's lovely," Angie had said, and seemed to mean it. But I had caught the merest widening of her eyes at having discovered this tangible evidence of what I had not bothered to disclose.

It had been over a week since Mama's last letter, and for the first time in four and a half years, she let two holidays pass without sending a white cardboard box of goodies—caraway crackers, gourmet chocolates, dried apricots from home. This was deliberate, of course, Mama knowing I would remember, and believing what? That this would undo me? Reduce me to a torrent of tears? Well, here was proof, wasn't it? She gave me far too little credit! I—*I* was an adult. I had concerns *far* greater than some silly care package. Things that she could never begin to guess, could not even begin to comprehend. Perhaps she'd suffered from certain missed chances, but what did she know of longing for something, for someone of which she was not already a part? So what say had she in the matters that troubled me now? *None*, I told myself late one night, as I wolfed down a plateful of lumpy cheese macaroni I'd cooked on our apartment's small stove. One more wedge and then another. Oh, and some of the sticky marshmallow cookies from the bag stashed under my bed. Until . . . until the quaking stopped. Yes, and the calm came.

Soon Joshua and I were together whenever we could find the time. Afternoons, we met in Lauinger Library at adjoining desks, beside an enormous window overlooking the river and Virginia on its opposite shore. As we worked side by side, I was aware of each sweeping of Joshua's textbook pages, every shifting of his arms or shoulders. Every now and then, he would turn from his work and, beaming, press my fingers with his, and then I felt a rush that made my chest fill. A rush that sent me flying, higher than my upstretched arms could reach, high as the changing streaks of cloud above the Virginia skyline. And at night, in private, we sighed and trembled in each other's arms, with a pleasure that my encounter with Gavin or with pock-faced Leonard Berkner, or the several tentative evenings with Brian (whom I'd met through Setsu junior year), never could have prepared me for.

"You won't believe it! I think I might be falling in love!" I laughed into the phone when I heard the familiar purr of Setsu's voice, after checking her work number in my rainbow-striped address book. Ever since our first year as roommates, she had tried repeatedly to find me dates. "When you find the right one, you'll know. I think there must be someone for each of us," she had reassured, raking her memory for possible new matches.

"Do you mean it?" she asked now. "That's so wonderful, Ruth! *Really!* You have to tell me all about him!"

This was what she had always wanted for me, but something about the way she emphasized every word sounded forced. I knew of her troubles with James, and I wondered if there was some part of her that envied me. I thought of Chester Benjamin from my Teaching of Writing workshop. He spoke with a softness like Setsu's, and I had recently learned he was a musician. Maybe if Setsu came for a visit, she would agree to meet him. Life was so funny, the way it could turn as quickly as a tossed coin. A year or two earlier I never would have believed that *I* would now be the one plotting to help Setsu with men.

Good fortune heaped upon good fortune. For the first time in my life, my course work seemed to come with little effort. Professor Brennan suggested that my "City Masquerade" was worthy of submission to literary magazines. And in early December, I was notified that I had qualified for a position as a teaching assistant for the following fall, the stipend from which would allow me to cover the tuition costs for my second year. What a strange thing to be, for once, the lucky one! Not long after, on a Monday evening, Joshua and I celebrated two months together at La Rive Gauche, a small French bistro downtown. Near the end of the evening, Joshua slid across the table a package wrapped in white paper and curled red ribbon I could tell he had tied himself. I teased him about the ribbon, its loops wrinkled and lopsided, one loop hanging over the edge of the package.

"Not my forte," he laughed. "Ignore the presentation." Inside was a fabric-bound journal—"For your writing," he said—and a tiny silk drawstring pouch holding a pair of jade and crystal bead earrings, the very set I had admired in a storefront window the weekend before.

"Oh! I never would have expected . . . When did you even get these? And I have nothing for you."

Joshua grinned at me as my legs turned shaky as water, my head fizzy as our dinner champagne.

Late that night, I returned to Thirty-ninth Street for a change of clothes before walking to Joshua's apartment. Despite the hour, I could see light glowing from beneath the bedroom door as I reached the top of the stairs. Angie sat cross-legged on her bed, her face mottled and pink, her eyelids bulgy. A dented box of tissues lay against her pillow sham, the contents littering her sheets.

For some minutes, she seemed hardly to notice my entrance. Then, almost absentmindedly, in a tired, nasal voice I had never heard from her, announced, "It's over with Evan. He said the distance makes things a torture. A *torture*. Can you believe that? *That's* the word he used to describe our relationship." She yanked another tissue from the box and snorted into it, her pink cotton nightgown falling forward, revealing the honey-gold of her breasts. But she didn't believe it. Not for one second. She'd heard from a mutual friend in Evan's law program that he'd been spotted on numerous occasions with Olivia Scully. Liv Scully! A total bore! Angie knew her from the Silver Lake Country Club. They'd skated together as girls. And now she remembered that Evan and Olivia had co-chaired the community service committee for their church youth group. God, it made her ill! she said, dabbing at her nose.

I'd had no practice offering consolation to someone like Angela Mc-Dermott, someone whose beauty and ease, I had assumed, somehow exempted her from trouble. So I groped for words of solace. "Maybe it's a misunderstanding. Or maybe with time—you know—after he's had a chance to think things through . . ."

But Angie only sniffled more miserably. She made a feeble attempt at a smile, feigning comfort in my suggestions. I wondered if I should sit beside her, drape my arm around the gentle slope of her shoulder as a token of solidarity. Here we were, two women bonded by the shared understanding of the trials of love. But what she really wanted, she said, nodding weakly toward the phone, was to call her parents.

"Yes, sure. Of course." I placed the phone beside her, knowing this would be the extent of what she would require of me.

"Oh, Mom . . ." And then she sobbed without words. And as she squeezed shut her eyes and rolled toward the wall, a loneliness I could not explain cried through me like cold air rushing through some spreading crack.

I eased open my bottom dresser drawer, noiselessly extracting a sweater, blue jeans, some balled-up panties. As I moved, my new earrings quivered, delicate as insect wings at my neck. Too fragile to fuss with, so I would keep my hands from my ears, lest with a tug or pinch I should snap the beaded strands. And I left with a silent wave Angie did not raise her head to see.

I t was sleeting and a low-hanging fog had rolled in from the river the mid-December morning that Mama and Poppy arrived. No warning. There they stood on the front porch, holding their collapsible travel umbrellas and two overstuffed canvas bags filled with groceries, Mama in her favorite wrap, a fur-trimmed cloak that had once belonged to Nana Esther. For some moments, I remained dumb in the doorway, fraying the hood strings of the track team sweatshirt Joshua had lent me, until Mama leaned in to kiss one cheek and Poppy the other.

"So? This is it?" I heard the effort Mama made to keep her voice cheery as she and Poppy followed me to the apartment on the second floor, though only the lower half of her face shifted into a smile. Her cheeks were ashy, her eyes flat, averted like Poppy's. They had walked through campus on their way here, they told me. I wondered if they had encountered robed Mother Mary on her pedestal near the university's entrance, her stone palms pressed together in prayer.

"Yes, home away from home!" I tried for a casual laugh, but little more than a croak emerged. As Mama's smile faded, her expression seemed to tighten and close as it had that morning not long before Valerie had first started school. We had taken the BX7 bus on our way to the doctor; and as Mama had rooted through her purse for some missing object, an elderly woman with a fringed shawl and bobby-pinned hair, seated across the aisle, had lifted from her pocket three plastic rosaries, which she had solemnly offered to each of my sisters and me. How delighted we were with what we assumed to be colorful necklaces. But later, steps from Dr. Rice's office, Mama spotted the foreign acquisitions. She snatched them suddenly from our necks, declaring them ritualistic nonsense belonging to a people who worshipped a condemning God. So jagged was her voice with indignation that Sarah and Valerie and I dared not argue, nor even glance back when she tossed our briefly loved jewels into a nearby trash bin.

But this time Mama only straightened her shoulders as if wishing to shrug off some distracting thought. So I knew there were other things she had traveled here to say.

"May I?" She gestured toward my bed.

"Yes, of course, Ma."

She and Poppy glanced around as if unsure where to set their bundles, then chose a spot on the carpeting just inside the bedroom door. I could see, peeking from the bags, tissues, jars of cherry preserves from Zimmerman's, mandelbrot, pumpernickel bread. Mama's breathing was labored, and I wondered if they had found parking nearby or carried these bundles some distance. She glanced at Angie's bed and then looked down at mine before lowering her bottom onto the edge of it as if she weren't quite sure she trusted the mattress. Then she smoothed wrinkles from a section of the bedspread, inviting me, I understood, to sit beside her.

"Last week Aunt Bernice had a lump removed." Mama ran her finger down one of the pleats in her dark tweed skirt. "I thought you would want to know. Her treatment begins Tuesday."

Bernice was Mama's favorite sister, but her voice held no hint of tears. Already, many times, I could see, she had told these things before repeating them now to me. "It's easy, I suppose, to forget how quickly life can crumble into pieces. Like a fragile dough." Mama tapped the tops of her knees, making an attempt at the beginning of a laugh.

I nodded silently, my throat sick.

For long minutes, Mama studied my room. I saw her gaze shift from the stacks of papers on my shelves—essays for my Shakespeare and Romantic Poetry courses, stories I'd written for Professor Brennan over the past months—to the letter I'd taped to my wall congratulating me on my position as teaching assistant the following autumn. And her eyes flickered. I caught some arching of her brow. Or I thought I had. No. No, merely my imagination. Of course, of course, she had other matters on her mind. She seemed not even to see the borrowed sweatshirt I wore, only swirled the fingers of her left hand over her right.

"What I came to tell you, Ruthie," she said, reaching for my hand to pat it between hers, "is that you are still my little girl, still my sweetest sweet. Life's too short, yes?" At this, she reached for a wadded hankie in her pocket. It smelled of Lady's Lace, the perfume she occasionally sprayed on the insides of her wrists. "We are woven together, threads from the same garment. When a strand is cut, the garment unravels. Nothing remains but shreds.

"Do you know what Bernice has been asking for these past days? Her family. Her dearest friends. Those who have loved her always, whose hearts, whose thoughts are one with hers. Without that . . ." Mama stopped and turned toward the room's single window, toward all that inhabited the world just beyond the glass. And I understood the things she implied.

"We *belong* to each other, Ruth. So, I forgive you," she whispered into my hair as she drew me close. "I forgive you, I forgive you."

If a sob had not clogged the back of my mouth, I would have said, "Oh, Mama. Mama, I forgive you, too." This was what I was thinking, but from the way she blew matter-of-factly into her handkerchief, I could tell she sought no forgiveness, that the idea, in fact, had never occurred to her. But as Mama's arms wrapped me in all the familiar places, I melted in her embrace. And at this moment, what else mattered?

In the afternoon, after Mama and Poppy left, I ate, in a single sitting, half the food they had brought me until each breath became a stab in the constricting denim of my jeans. I exchanged them for elastic-waisted sweatpants, my stomach engorged, tight as a stuffed apple, so full I dashed twice to the toilet, thinking all I had consumed would spew back out. Almost hoping, hesitating. God! What a wreck I had made of everything again!

That night I dreamed of Vanessa Randall's birthday party. The summer I was twelve, the Randalls had thrown Vanessa a gymnastics party. This, one of a handful of sports party invitations I had accepted over the year despite Mama's reminders that I did not need to attend *all* of them, that the frenzy of so many overexcited children at such events was a recipe for accidents. "Did Vanessa invite the whole class?" Mama wanted to know when I opened the envelope with the pink card featuring a drawing of a young gymnast in a purple leotard. "I don't know, Ma." I could tell she was surprised I had been included. Mama knew the Randalls only by sight—a family who lived in the estate section of Riverdale near the water and who took riding lessons and ski vacations and kept a hunter-green Jaguar with leather seats, which they packed each weekend to visit their house on the Connecticut shore. "Looks like they bought half the store," she'd whispered once when, on the way to a dentist's appointment in Manhattan, we had bumped into the whole Randall clan laden with bags, stepping out of Ralph Lauren on Madison Avenue.

"If they give you a choice, it makes sense to stick to the floor mats, don't you think?" Mama said the day before the party. "You spent all that time at Uncle Leonid and Aunt Nadia's practicing somersaults and cartwheels on their lawn last year. I remember you were quite good at those."

The party was held in the newly constructed gymnasium of a school near Vanessa's home. For days I had anticipated the celebration, having overheard Vanessa describe the delights that awaited us to a cluster of girls in our class. And when I first passed through the double swinging doors into the brilliantly lit room, which smelled excitingly of new vinyl padding, I could see that she had not exaggerated: gleaming silver rings hung from bars, lacquered balance beams stretched over thick plastic tumbling mats. There were climbing ropes and monkey bars and pastel hula hoops. The girls who had arrived before me were already swinging and dangling and swooping. These things, I could tell, were not new to them; in fact, they seemed near experts—calling to one another as they twirled, laughing openmouthed, loose hair fluttering. Three women in lollipop-red T-shirts supervised. "You've done this before?" the one with the gold-flecked ponytail had asked as I approached two long horizontal poles. "Oh, yes," I lied, allowing her to coat my palms with white powder and lift me up, up until I gripped the higher of the two bars. "Have fun," she said—this the extent of her directions. So I began to pump my legs as

I'd seen the others do, feeling suddenly clumsy and self-conscious. What I needed was enough momentum to plant my feet on the lower bar. Yes, was that it? Trickles of perspiration trailed from my brow, stinging my eyes. My arms ached. But I needed height, more height. I wanted to fly! So I did not feel the slipping of my fingers until . . . Despite the padding, the floor was shockingly hard. A great wind-knocking slap from skull to buttocks. A circle of sympathetic faces over me, a phone call from Mrs. Randall to Mama with apologies that I would have to miss the cake.

As Mama had helped me up the stairs and onto the sidewalk, wrinkles of worry creased the corners of her eyes. Her fingers squeezed deep into my left arm. "Sometimes, Ruthie, you lose sight of common sense, you know? You try for impossible things."

"Yes, Mama." I nodded, bruised and blurry-eyed with shame, leaning into her with each gingerly step.

Then Mama kissed me under the steamy July sun. "Think of this as a lesson, Sweet Pea. Then, perhaps, some good can come of it, hmm?" As she pushed my damp hair from my brow, I squinted in the brightness, knowing, even at that tender age, this day would sear into me like a brand or a scar—and, perhaps, yes, as Mama said, for my own good.

Professor Brennan had asked for a completed version of my story "Bird on the Tide" within the week; he wanted to enter it into a writing contest sponsored by a literary magazine that was gaining acclaim. But every breath of a new thought in me had turned to dead air. My character, Natasha, was at a crossroads, but each flickering idea for a conclusion sputtered out before I put it to paper. Over the next few days, I walked the paces of my usual routine, but my mind dragged. All this time, I guess I had known. It could not last: I, on my own, reaching for this life that defied Mama and Poppy and all I had ever been. Hadn't it all along been a fraud, a joke? Missteps down an unnavigable path. Ridiculous promises I had told myself of some splendid Ruth waiting to emerge. It had been a hope as distant and unlikely as the colliding of two stars. There was nothing left to do but drown my pride and disentangle myself from the mess I had created.

I would tell my professors first, they far less painful to face than Joshua. Five of them in all, so the announcements of my withdrawal should have grown progressively easier. But instead, with each, a greater burning flamed in my gut; I choked more over the explanation I had so carefully planned. And to Joshua, what could I possibly offer? He had met me near the university's observatory in a side passageway used by few students, a spot we had considered our own. In the damp chill, he stood hunched, his hands thrust into the pockets of his jeans, his face rigid from cold but also from the knowledge that I had something serious to discuss. "I'm sorry, I'm sorry! I've started something I can't finish!" My breath came in thick, frosty clouds. I paused to watch a couple in matching red hats sharing a cup of something frothy and steaming pass by. "The thing is, this, *this* is not who I really am. I don't know if you can understand."

"No. *No!*" Joshua either understood or heard nothing. His hands flew to my shoulders, pressing as though he would bore through the padding of my jacket, even through my flesh to bone, beginning to speak of attachments, of love, his voice engulfing us, until my own thoughts spun and spun, knotting, snagging. Until I could listen no more, until I wrapped my scarf around my neck to cover my ears and ran.

Near the end of the month, the semester would come to a close. Angie was now every waking moment in the library—disappearing before I tumbled from bed, returning after I was asleep. And so I had spent the past several days in near solitude, in kneesocks and the ruffled plaid pajamas I'd had since high school, holed up at my bedroom desk with notepads and the books necessary for my final papers. With pastries and bags of oily chips from the convenience store, I stuffed myself as I worked, hour following hour, until my stomach cramped, my eyes smarted, my fingers gripping my pencil throbbed. How else to fend off what kept prodding to sneak in? Doubts and second thoughts—the hundred plans that had erupted in me when my letter from Georgetown first arrived, the wave of hope that had come when I finished "Storm House," "The Last Diplomat," and "City Masquerade," and with each of Professor Brennan's notes of commendation attached to the returned stories. And Joshua—Joshua—when he caught my hand in his or brought his lips to mine—Oh!—how the very center of me had seemed to open.

Four days before my planned return to New York, a front of soft, mild air blew in. The campus seemed suddenly to teem with life, Healy Lawn dotted with students reclining on blankets, their notebooks spread before them, or kicking soccer balls, a few singing along with the FM station playing on their portable radios. In the early afternoon, I emerged from my seclusion and found a spot against the trunk of a towering oak. I had brought with me *The Collected Works of Charlotte Brontë*, assigned for Professor McGovern's class later that day. And I read until I found this: *The vehemence of emotion . . . within me was claiming mastery, and struggling for full sway; and asserting a right to predominate: to overcome, to live, to rise and reign at last . . .* Our first night at Brown, I had shyly recited this line from *Jane Eyre* to Setsu and Opal and Fran when the questionnaire we'd been given had asked our favorite passages from literature. I had chosen it then not because I considered it a favorite, but because strangely, for years, it had stuck with me. Still, for some moments after I'd spoken, there had been silence. And now I wondered if my suitemates had paused because something had caught at them, too. The something in each of us more expansive than what we'd known.

And so I cradled the pages in my lap. Again and again, I repeated the phrases, over and over, drinking them in until I owned them. I tilted my chin and gazed through the spreading limbs above me. And as the branches stirred, I almost heard a quiet whispering, a favorite saying of Rabbi Gerson's: *Rejoice! All creation is filled with greatness. Even ourselves.* Had I never truly listened, or had I not believed? In that instant, something strengthened inside me, like fingers tightening around a staff. And then I knew. I knew the choices I would make. I knew the things I would do to claim my happiness.

~

For the first five months of my engagement to Joshua, Mama made no acknowledgment of my decision. During our occasional calls, she chattered on about Sarah's premed courses at Cornell, the renovations to the buildings on either side of Broadway Paperie—improving the value of the block. And if I began to talk of Joshua, she skimmed along as if she hadn't heard. And so my status went unmentioned to the extended family, as if it were only the speaking it aloud that would make it come to pass. "I will tell them myself!" I informed Mama after the card arrived in my mail from Aunt Nadia announcing my cousin Gregory's engagement to Shari Fischer of Mamaroneck, his girlfriend of several years, but with no reference to my own plans. For a moment Mama was silent. "Well, I suppose it's your news to share."

I wondered if the things we had to say to each other were thinning, a binding tie wearing away. But then Mama began to call more regularly, pondering other matches for me, other futures. During my visits home her eyes, at all times, still avoided the small round diamond on my left ring finger. She asked if she had told me how her high school friend Rachel Cohen had suffered—the one who married a man she hardly knew, his background alien to her own. She seemed pleased when I joined her for Saturday services but then scanned the sanctuary for the tragic souls in the congregation. Did I remember Cheryl Mayer? After seven years and two children, she was divorcing. And, of course, poor Danny Horowitz. His wife had left him for a cardiologist from Brooklyn Heights. But as our wedding drew closer, her protests quieted. When I explained to Poppy and her that what Joshua and I wished was an interfaith ceremony—our families and friends with us, and the officiating to be shared equally by Reverend Harrington from Joshua's home church and Rabbi Gerson—to my surprise, they made no complaints. And on the morning Joshua and I exchanged our vows, on a small hill in the botanical gardens not far from Georgetown's campus, under a chuppah adorned with white gerbera daisies, I stole a look at Mama in time to catch her leaning into Poppy's shoulder, sweeping away a fallen tear.

J ust weeks after our ceremony, having begun to accept Joshua's permanence, Mama seemed preoccupied with a new concern. Since the previous winter, managing (for the most part) to give up snacks, to keep my meals moderate—no small struggle to attain what for so many years had seemed impossible—I had succeeded in shedding twenty-nine pounds! But in Mama's estimation, Joshua and I now both needed filling out. "How do you feel about latkes?" she would ask, rolling up the sleeves of her blouse so that Joshua knew to follow her to the kitchen. "I'll show you the way I like to make them. And after you try one, you can tell me what you think." She would position him beside her at the counter and show him how she grated the potatoes, combining them with the thinnest shreds of onion, how she beat the eggs lightly so as not to create excess air, how she lowered spoonfuls of the pancake mixture carefully, carefully into crackling oil. Then she would rummage through the kitchen drawer where she kept family photos until she unearthed some snapshot from my childhood or high school years that I had hoped would never resurface. "See how much healthier Ruth looked back then," she would say, pointing to the roundness of my cheeks. "Maybe it's the hours and hours of writing. You know, I think sometimes she just forgets to eat. . . . See if you can't get her to put a little meat back on her bones, hmm? Maybe she'll listen to you if not to her own mother." These were the things I could hear her murmuring to Joshua. And swinging my heels until they caught on the rung of the kitchen chair where I perched, I watched the two of them together, and I thought of the many things that changed and of those that never would.

ALOFT

· 2003 ·

Francesca presents me with a silver-ribboned box—a collective shower gift from Opal, Setsu, and herself, she says. Inside are three infant-sized knitted sweaters with matching hats: one in white, one in pink, one in pale green, with ribbon woven through their cuffs and collars. We pass the sweaters around the table. Setsu holds up one of the hats—the green one. It has a single tiny bow on its brim.

"Have you ever seen anything sweeter!" Most of Setsu's mannerisms are as I remembered, but her laugh is different now, bursting from her as if uncontainable.

Opal smiles. "Their colors are beautiful," she says, studying them. One of her new clients is Bridgeton, the hotel chain. The graphic design firm she owns with her husband, Campbell, is updating the chain's brochure and the green of this sweater might work perfectly.

"How is Campbell?" we want to know. "How is married life?"

"We're two peas in a pod!" she laughs. Children still seem a long time off, though, she says. "But if we ever have one of our own, and if it's a girl"—she reaches for the hat in Setsu's hand—"I want to find her an outfit just like this!"

Francesca disappears into her house then returns with a pastel pink cake molded in the shape of a bassinet. She smiles at us over the cake as if she knows what we are thinking—that this is a sentimentality in her we never could have imagined. But her steps are as clipped and purposeful as I remember them from before, when she marched in protest of everything that crossed her track. And when she talks of her work, her most recent cases at Bausch and Firth, where, since finishing law school, she has practiced as a women's rights advocate, the same flames ignite her words as they did long ago. Still, who could have expected this kind of celebration from the Francesca I lived with throughout our years at Brown? On the night the four of us first met, she had rolled her eyes when Setsu and I admitted that we hoped, before graduating, we might find true love, the men we would marry, even share children with. She reached into the back pocket of her jeans for a pack of matches and lit the cigarette she had long held in the fingers of her right hand. She blew a perfect "O" of smoke then broke it with her thumb. "You know, *this* is why we're suitemates. All colleges do this. It's policy. They match you with roommates as different from you as night from day." She shrugged. "I *guess* it's supposed to keep things interesting."

At the time, we'd believed she was right. But now I can see, though we walked different paths, we were more similar than we had thought: each one of us—whether or not she knew it—had been fighting her own bit of darkness. Each trudging, climbing toward what the best part of herself believed she could be. Toward the self that could soar.

"You didn't have to do all this!" I say to Francesca.

"I wanted to. Isn't that okay?" Having returned to her seat beside me, she gives my elbow a poke with hers.

Behind her on the lawn, which smells of newly mown grass and the sweet viburnum that borders her garden, her young son and daughter are toddling after each other. Every now and then, they tumble to the ground, soiling their party clothes. Then they turn toward Fran, their noses wrinkling in the sunlight, and explode into a fit of giggles. As I watch them, I feel a nudging against my ribs, the internal fluttering that still manages to surprise me though I am already in my eighth month of pregnancy. I look down at my hands folded across my swollen abdomen, then from Francesca to Setsu, from Setsu to Opal. Setsu, who had become reed-thin during our last years of school, her cheeks pale hollows so that people began to whisper, is still slender but full-faced, almost glowing now. She has joined an orchestra in New York, she tells us, a well-regarded one. She is modest as always, but the flaring of her delicate nostrils betrays her pride as she mentions an upcoming concert, one I promise to attend. "I've missed you, Setsu," I say. And she and I vow to see each other more regularly. We are lucky to be in the same city; we won't let so much time slip away from us again.

Opal is the only one of us to have returned to Rhode Island. She and Campbell have just finished building a house near the water in Bristol. She has begun a painting class, too, she says. Of course, work for her design company demands most of her time, but she could lose herself in her art for days if life allowed. "Well, you must know, Ruth!" She loved my last novel, *After the Clouds*, she says. She always checks the local bookstores to make sure they carry it. "You and Joshua should visit us sometime! Campbell and I would look forward to the company." "We will, we will," I agree, because her invitation, I can tell, is sincere and because the once plump, wide-eyed girl who had emerged from her parents' dented Chevrolet wagon at Brown will always hold that corner of New England in her heart.

And Francesca—I need only to look around—appears to have everything. She admits, when pressed by Opal, to having just made partner at Bausch and Firth. This will allow her to do more on behalf of her clients, she says. And she and Jonathan are about to celebrate their eighth wedding anniversary. Can we believe how the time has flown?

Suddenly the thought of the countless experiences my daughter has before her stops my breath. What a miracle it is—this life that awaits us with all its possibilities. But as she stirs once more, a sigh moves through me for the pains she will certainly endure, the aches of growing to womanhood no girl escapes. And for the battle she, too, must wage to triumph over herself.

Francesca's cake is spongy and light. Its soft frosting turns to liquid on my tongue. Somewhere I have read that, even from their first samplings of food, babies have definite likes and dislikes. I shift my hands, feeling for the firm roundness of my daughter's head and cup it lightly as if to speak through my fingers:

"May you honor your own inclinations. May you find the fullness of your strengths. And as bit by bit, year by year, Girl reaches out into Woman, may you take hold of the truth of yourself."

For this is my greatest hope for her. Even before she is born into this world.

Acknowledgments

I am forever grateful to my wonderful editor, Amy Einhorn, for taking a chance on this book, and for her vision and wisdom and guidance. To Liz Stein, for her calm and patient attention to every detail.

To my agent, Matt Bialer, for believing in this novel, for his instincts, and for his kindness and good humor. To Lindsay Ribar, for her suggestions and insights.

To the entire team at Amy Einhorn Books/Putnam, for their expertise and creativity, and for the great care they have devoted to this book.

To my mother, for her sound advice and for being, always, a most invaluable reader. To both of my parents, for teaching me to be true to myself, for encouraging my writing all of my life, and for giving me more than I can ever thank them for. To my husband, for his love and support, and the gift of time to write.

And to the family and friends who offered inspiration along the way.

About the Author

Pamela Moses grew up in New Jersey. She attended Brown University and received a master's in English from Georgetown. After graduating, she moved to Manhattan to teach English at a girls' school. She now lives outside of New York City with her husband and two children. *The Appetites of Girls* is her first novel.